LIKE *a*
HOLE
in the
WATER

LIKE *a*
HOLE
in the
WATER

J. NEIL SHEROUSE

also by J. Neil Sherouse
The Burden of Evil Times

"Your friend is your needs answered."
-Khalil Gibran, *The Prophet*

Like a Hole in the Water

Published in the United States
by Clearwater Publishing, LLC
1101 Waterfall Lane
Lakeland, Florida 33803

CLEARWATER
PUBLISHING, LLC

Cover design by Cathi Stevenson, *bookcoverexpress.com*
Book design by Gwen Gades, *www.beapurplepenguin.com*
Edited by G. Beth Sherouse, *www.gesherouse.com*
Cover image by VladGans under license with iStock by Getty Images
Bicycle image by Vladvm under license with Shutterstock.com

Library of Congress Control Number 2020918363

ISBN Paperback 978-0-9769465-1-9
eBook 987-0-9769465-2-6

www.JNSherouse.com

10 9 8 7 6 5 4 3 2 1

To my brother, Craig
—always present, always in my corner.

I SUPPOSE WE all deem our age as that most turbulent, that most fraught with danger and fertile with possibility. Surely, the 1960s in America were all of that. But they were also a time of failing innocence and soul-eating realities—a reckoning, of sorts, with our past. For me as a boy, the '60s were idyllic—brimming with excitement and personal freedom. At the same time, I, and millions of others, were beginning to open our eyes to the fact that our nation had yet to live up to the lofty aspirations enshrined in her founding documents. It was my purpose in writing this book to recover both that sense of wonder with which nearly every event was imbued, but also that disquieting awakening to the need for change.

I began this book in the fall of 2019—just months before the COVID-19 pandemic began to strangle the life out of our planet's people and the economic systems in which they strove to succeed. The superimposition of this crisis atop the political upheaval within the United States gave rise in me to the disappointing truth that we Americans are not who we have claimed to be—or even thought ourselves to be. As a result, writing this book, set in a period of frightening global tensions alongside unbridled confidence in the promise of the future, took on the feel of a mission—a mission to recover for myself the optimism of the 1960s in America. Whether I have done so in the pages that follow is not my claim to make. For me, however, writing this book, and my frequent visits with its central characters, have helped renew my fundamental belief that Americans are, at their core, good people who desire their fellow citizens to enjoy all the "blessings of liberty."

-Neil Sherouse, April, 2021

PART I

1.

MEMORIES ON THE WIND

MEMORY, I HAVE found, is a strange demon, and its most insidious manifestation is uncertainty. As I have aged, some memories seem to have disassembled themselves into a background clutter of jumbled parts, whereas others are preserved in sharp detail—the music that was playing, the singular blue of the sky, the taste of that morning's coffee, the texture of the silk tie that required three attempts to look as I wanted. I read somewhere that the olfactory sense—the sense of smell—is the one most closely associated with memory. Though I have no proof of that claim, I can nonetheless confirm that whenever I smell fresh-cut bahiagrass, I am taken back to that crisp spring day in 1965—the day I learned Sam Sanders was dead.

I was in eighth grade, and my junior high school was two blocks outside our back door. Consequently, I walked to and from school every day, rain or shine. Both my parents worked, so our grandmother was tasked with looking after us until my dad arrived home. My mother worked for the Clerk of Courts, so she didn't make it home until after 5:00. Now that I was thirteen, I had convinced myself that Grandma's supervisory responsibilities were limited to my younger brother. I was quite old enough to look after myself.

On this particular day—a balmy north Florida April afternoon—I was trudging home, carrying my books (this was an age when no self-respecting junior high schoolboy would be caught using a backpack), the smell of fresh-cut grass from the elementary playground carried by the warm breeze. The busses leaving my school drove past the elementary and down the packed-clay street I walked along, and I engaged in my favorite after-school activity—giving the middle finger to the kids riding inside. They, of course, returned the favor.

As I rounded the front corner of our house, I immediately realized something was out of place. My mother's car was in the driveway. That was never the case when I arrived home from school—she was never ill, and she never left work early. I entered the house to find both my mother and grandmother waiting for me. They looked anxious, distraught even.

"What's going on? Mom, why are you home now?" I could tell my mother had been crying, and this immediately heighted my own anxiety.

"Clint, son, have a seat. We have some sad news to tell you." My mind was racing—was Dad OK? Had something happened to my little brother? "Mrs. Sanders called me at work this morning to say that Sam had died." Three words: Sam. Had. Died. Three words that upended my young life.

"How? What happened?" By now tears were overflowing my own eyes. Sam was only nineteen. How could he be dead?

"There was an accident on the base. He was buffing the floor in the mess hall last night and somehow the buffing machine electrocuted him. They didn't find him until early this morning. They say he died instantly. I'm so sorry, Son."

The flood gates opened. My heart imploded. I ran into my room, flung myself on the bed and wept for what seemed like hours. Everyone left me alone—even my younger brother, Will. When dinner was ready, my father came for me. He knocked on the bedroom door—something he never did. "Dinner's ready,

Son. You need to come join us."

In my family, attendance at dinner was mandatory. There were only a few acceptable reasons for one's absence—a serious case of malaria or death. I knew there was no point in arguing, no possibility of a reprieve that would permit me to remain in my private misery. Sam Sanders was dead, but life, and dinner, went on. Grudgingly, but with resignation, I dragged myself to the dining room. I don't remember what we ate. I don't recall any conversation over dinner. In fact, the next couple of days remain a misty unknown and unknowable for me. I do remember phoning our mutual friend, Jake, that evening to break the news to him. I went through the motions of Sam's funeral on Saturday but otherwise kept mostly to myself through the remainder of that weekend. Monday came, and I returned to school feeling for several weeks like a shadow, like a dry empty shell of my former self. Gradually, the loss diminished, the searing pain retreated, and my life settled into an altered normal.

My hometown of Palatka, Florida, sits astride the St. Johns River about an hour's drive south of Jacksonville. Here, the river makes a tight horseshoe turn and suddenly broadens. It is said that the town's name was a corruption of a Timucuan word meaning "river ford" or "crossing," but, at the time of my youth it was best known for the large paper mill upriver that fouled the air on most mornings. Still, the broad St. Johns remains to me the best example of a southern river and is far more beautiful than any other large river I've seen. Its clear, tannin-stained waters run languidly across a sand bottom as they make their way north to empty into the Atlantic.

When I was a young child, our schools were still segregated, so both the white and African American communities each had a couple of elementary schools, a junior high, and a high school—separate, and decidedly unequal. My mother had grown up here, my father arrived soon after the end of World War II. They met somewhat by chance and married in 1948. I was born three years later. My younger brother, Will, followed in 1954. Ours was a very typical post-war, middle-class upbringing. My parents placed great value on education, hard work, and self-sufficiency. Our activities centered around family, church, Boy Scouts, school, and the river. Our weekends often included camping, a picnic, or a fishing trip. In short, it was idyllic. We never felt deprived or lacking for anything, though I know our parents were very frugal and seldom purchased anything—other than our tiny home and vehicles—on credit.

I had grown up with Sam Sanders, who lived three houses down the red clay street that led to the nearby elementary school. Sam was five years my senior—the big kid in our neighborhood teeming with post-war progeny. He lived with his mother, his father lost long before to the Korean conflict. To younger kids like me, Sam was an aspiration—tall, handsome, and remarkably friendly. His mother and my grandmother had become fast friends over the years, but I had very little contact with him. The age difference was a social barrier we younger kids dared not cross.

All that changed for me soon after Christmas, 1959. I had turned eight on December 27, and was determined to learn to ride my new bicycle—my first—without the use of training wheels. To be seen in my neighborhood using training wheels at my age would have meant immediate ostracism and ridicule from our gang of boys. After a few attempts by my father to teach me—each ending with me crying and him frustrated—he decreed that I was just going to have to learn on my own. Fortunately, my grandmother intervened and hoodwinked Sam Sanders, who was thirteen at the time, into teaching me. To this day I don't know what currency changed hands to convince him to do this for me—no thirteen-year-old would willingly be seen with an eight-year-old—but there must have been an exchange of something valuable. Thus it was that on a cold, blustery Saturday in late December, I pushed my bike down to Sam's house, gently laid it on the dead dry lawn, climbed the porch steps, nervously knocked on his front door, and met the person who would, in many ways—and forgive the cliché here—change my life.

At the time, I was a skinny, shy, bespectacled eight-year-old. The boy who opened the door that cold morning was a tall, athletic-looking, blond, teenaged god—everything I was not. I was immediately stricken speechless. But he smiled at me. "Hi, Clint, right?" I nodded in the affirmative. "You ready?" Nod. "Well, let's get goin'." He walked past me and down the front steps. I was fixed in place. "You comin'? Jesus, it's freezing out here! You got on enough clothes?" Nod. He picked up my bicycle and began to roll it toward the elementary school where, for some reason, there was a clay-surfaced track used by the high school two blocks away.

For the next two hours, Sam patiently taught me how to balance on the bicycle, how to work the pedals, how to steer, and how to control my speed. When I had mastered those skills, he suggested I ride home to impress my family with all I'd learned. So, off I rode—past the elementary school, past Sam's house, with him running behind me yelling encouragement. As I neared my house, I realized there was one critical skill that had been missing from Sam's curriculum—how to safely stop and dismount. Looking across the street from our house to where my grandmother lived, I saw my mother and grandmother standing in her yard watching me and applauding. I was instantly seized by the realization that this was not going to end well. Bouncing up Grandma's driveway, I chose the only option that presented itself—I bailed out. I landed hard and rolled on the dry grass. My bike traveled about ten feet further and then teetered over—no apparent damage to either of us. By then, Sam had caught up to me and was laughing hysterically. Once convinced I was OK, my mother and grandmother joined in, leaving me splashing around in my private pool of indignity.

Sam yelled toward me between gasps, "Oh, come on, Clint. You gotta admit that was pretty funny. But I guess I forgot to teach you how to stop. We'll cover that next time."

Next time? There was going to be a next time? This wasn't a one-time thing? This teenaged guy was going to spend more time with scrawny little me? A broad smile split my face from ear to ear. "Yeah. OK. You can teach me that next time!"

As it was mid-day, my mother insisted Sam join us for lunch. He readily agreed and I was thrilled. I could show off my new, much older friend to my family! As we gathered around the table, I could tell my little brother Will was in awe of our guest—so much so that I don't think he spoke a word throughout the meal. Sam, on the other hand, was very conversational with my parents in a self-assured, almost-adult way. Both my parents peppered him with questions—How was junior high? ("Pretty cool.") What subjects did he like best? ("English, history, PE, and science.") What sports did he play? ("Basketball and track.") Did he have a girlfriend? ("Not really.") Did he have any hobbies? ("Model building, reading, and stamp collecting.") Which kids in the neighborhood did he hang out with ("No one in particular.") I was thrilled to learn some of my fledgling interests aligned with his—I enjoyed reading, I liked science, I had a stamp album—but I especially focused on the fact that he didn't appear to have close friends in the neighborhood and spent most of his after-school hours at home alone. Maybe he'd hang out with me! Suffice to say that, by the time Sam left to walk home, I was under his spell.

During the coming week, I built upon my newly acquired skills at bike riding, though I intentionally avoided any attempt to figure out how to effectively stop without crashing. The following Saturday, Sam took me back to the track for an hour-long session in which I did, in fact, master the fine art of safely stopping and resting in a ready position on my bicycle. At the end of that session, I asked Sam if he wanted to have lunch with us again. "Naw, but my mom said you could eat with us and I could show you my room and stuff." I was so excited I became lightheaded. "You OK?" Nod. "You look kinda funny."

"No, I'm OK," I croaked. "I'll call my mama from your house to make sure it's OK for me to eat lunch with y'all." To this day, I remember that lunch—tuna salad sandwiches, potato chips, and cherry Kool-Aid.

Sam's room was tidy (more so than mine) and smelled like him. He showed me his stamp album (much more elaborate than mine) and some of the books he liked—*Treasure Island*, *Twenty Thousand Leagues Under the Sea*, and several *Hardy Boys* mysteries—and his model collection. His completed models—World War II airplanes, tanks, newer jet aircraft—were meticulously assembled and carefully painted. One model, a modern jet fighter, was displayed apart from the others. He picked it up carefully. "This is an F-86 Sabre, the kind of plane my dad flew in Korea. He got shot down. Bailed out over water and the Navy picked him up, but he was hurt pretty bad. He died from his wounds."

I was stunned, speechless. I knew that Sam's father had been killed in the Korean War, but I had never heard any details, and I had certainly never known any other kid whose father had been killed in war. I knew I needed to say something, but what can an eight-year-old say when faced with that sort of information?

"I'm sorry your dad died," was the best I could muster.

"It's OK. I was a little kid—younger than you. I really don't remember him much. I was about three or four when he went over there. It sounds kinda weird, but it's not like I miss him so much. I just miss not having a father. Does that make sense?"

"Yeah, kinda. I guess you really don't remember him much, so you don't know who you're missing. You just miss the idea of having a daddy, I guess."

"That's it. You're right. For a little kid, you're pretty smart."

The next several minutes were something of a blur after Sam called me "pretty smart." At some point, however, he suggested we go for a bike ride. Now this was a monumental suggestion. To that point, my bike riding, aside from my lessons with Sam, had been limited to trips up and down our driveway, around the house, and up and down the clay-surfaced street between our house and the elementary school.

"I'd need to ask my mama, but, yeah, that would be cool. Where are we goin'?"

"Let's ride over to the Ravine Gardens and mess around over there. There's lots of good places to ride, and if you're up for it, we could ride all the way around the ravines."

The Ravine Gardens were formed by both natural and human activity and over a period of thousands of years. Long before human habitation, the two deep steephead ravines formed through subsidence and the action of a spring-fed stream that still runs through the park. Then, during the 1930s, New Deal workers cut trails through the ravines, constructed pedestrian bridges, log and stone buildings, fountains and formal gardens, and planted thousands of azaleas throughout the park. In the spring, with nearly twenty varieties of azaleas in bloom, it was quite spectacular.

After securing the approval of my mother—with all the

attendant and requisite warnings and admonitions—we were off. The ravines were only two blocks from my house, and, I discovered, an easy bike ride away. Though there were imposing stone gates at the entrance, these were open, and we rode right in. In later years I discovered these gates—whether open or locked—never determined our ability to gain entry into the gardens. Once clear of the gates, we pedaled down the long entry boulevard. To the left was a long formal garden hedged on each side by wisteria-covered pergolas. At the end of the boulevard, we stopped in front of a cluster of rustic-looking buildings constructed of dark-stained wood and the local limestone chert. "These are really old," Sam explained. "They were built in the Depression by guys who needed work. They built all of this, the cabins, the trails, the bridges down in the ravines, and planted all the azaleas."

"My folks talk about the Depression, but I don't know what that is."

"Well, back in the 1930s lots of folks lost everything—their savings because the banks went under, their homes, farmers lost their land. Factories closed, people lost their jobs. There were millions of people out of work. It was really bad. So the government created these programs to give people jobs, and one of the things the government paid them to do was build stuff like this—not the ravines, but all the trails and buildings and stuff."

"I've kinda heard about some of that. My daddy worked for something called the WPA back then, before the war, but I don't know much about it."

"Yeah, the WPA was a part of all that. Anyway, let's mess around this old cabin some."

For the next half hour or so we tested and peered in the dingy windows, tried the doors, and climbed around on the cabin's porches. Needless to say, we failed to gain entry. The cabin seemed to be disused and in a state of slow decay. There were holes in the floor and shafts of light piercing the roof and the gloom inside. It was not a place I would have wanted to be in the gathering shadows of evening.

Our explorations of the old cabin complete, we remounted our bicycles. "Now this road is about two miles around. You up for that?"

"I guess. I never rode that far, but I'll try."

"Cool. If you get tired, we can always stop and walk our bikes."

The paved perimeter road began with a gradual decent and we coasted for what seemed like a half hour. To our right was a steep, heavily-wooded embankment topped by a chain-link fence. To our left, just off the road, the ground fell away immediately into the dark, verdant ravine. The effortless part of our ride ended suddenly as we entered a series of undulations that really taxed my new biking skills. At one point, Sam stopped abruptly, dismounted and walked over to the outer edge of the road and picked up something.

"Golf ball." He held up the white sphere. "The golf course is on the other side of that fence, and the golfers hit into the ravines all the time. They don't want to climb over the fence, so they just leave the balls here. My mom's boss pays me a dime for every one of them that's not messed up."

Over the next half hour or so, we stopped several times for Sam to pick up other abandoned golf balls. By the time we reached the large stone amphitheater at about the mid-point in our ride, he had collected over a dollar's worth. Toward the end of our ride, we came upon a series of ponds and the clear stream that fed them. We were tired from the ride—truth be told, I was exhausted and only pressing on to avoid embarrassing myself in front of Sam. Resting our bikes beside the stream, we used our cupped hands to drink the cold spring water. We then stretched out on the grass beside the stream under a dense canopy of trees and faced the cloudless sky.

"Sam, how come you're hanging out with me? Usually big kids don't play with little kids."

"Well, it's not like we're doing little kid stuff. I mean we're riding our bikes in the ravines. That's big kid stuff. If you asked me to play with Lincoln Logs or Tinker Toys I'd probably say 'Nah.'" He laughed and punched my shoulder. "Besides, you're pretty cool for a little kid. To tell the truth, I don't have a lot of friends."

"How come? You're a really nice guy."

"I don't know. It's kinda like the kid with no dad is some kind of freak or something. Plus, I don't really like jerks, and a lot of the kids at my school are jerks. You know I'm pretty good at sports, but a lot of kids aren't, and they get picked on a lot, and that really pisses me off. Plus, I study hard. I want to make good grades so I can maybe go to college someday, but I get hassled because I actually do my homework. It's like the stuff that adults think is important is not important at all to the kids at my school."

"That stinks. I try to make good grades, too, but nobody messes with me about it. Anyway, thanks for spending time with me."

"I enjoy it, really. I never had a little brother or sister, so I'm kinda thinking of you as a little brother. By the way, I kinda forgot something about this road. There's a long, steep hill coming up, then a long steep one going down. I don't think you can ride up that long hill, and I'm afraid you'll kill yourself going down the other side. I think we should walk our bikes the rest of the way."

"Can I try going up the hill? We can always walk if I can't make it."

"Yeah, OK. But you have to be honest when you just can't go any further."

Well, the hill Sam mentioned seemed like a small mountain to me. It was quite steep and seemed endless. I pedaled with all my remaining strength, standing up on the pedals as I saw him doing, but my legs were on fire and trembling.

"Sam, I'm done. I can't pedal any more. I'm gonna walk my bike to the top of this hill."

"OK, we'll both walk. I'm pretty worn out, too."

Panting, I pushed my bike up beside his and we set out. "I need bigger muscles to do this. I'm too skinny."

"It's not that. You just need to build up your endurance. Just keep going on longer and longer bike rides and you'll get stronger and your legs'll adapt to the harder work. Look at me. I'm pretty thin, too, but I run track and that helps my muscles do more."

"OK. I'm learning a lot of stuff from you. Thanks."

"You're welcome."

Within minutes we reached the top of the long hill, and I stared down the other side with growing trepidation. "You're right. This is really steep. I'm scared to ride down it. I don't know if I can keep from going too fast and crashing. Can we just keep walking?"

"Sure. If I let something happen to you, we'd both be in trouble. We'll walk."

The bottom of the long hill brought us back to our starting point and we then rode down the opposite side of the boulevard and out the other set of gates. I fell asleep that night with my legs still throbbing.

2.

SPIES, BOMBS, AND CRUSTACEANS WITH PINCERS

I WAS A child of the Cold War. The taut relationship between the US and the Soviet Union—each with the capacity to annihilate the other—influenced every debate and decision in Washington. On May 1, 1960, an American U-2 spy plane[1], piloted by Captain Francis Gary Powers, was shot down deep inside Soviet airspace.[2] Those who piloted these specially designed crafts

---

1 The U-2 is a high-altitude reconnaissance aircraft developed for the CIA by Lockheed. Equipped with a battery of high-resolution cameras and other data-gathering devices, the U-2 is unarmed and flies at such extreme altitudes—up to 70,000 feet—that it is difficult for ground radar to detect and nearly unassailable by enemy aircraft. The extreme altitude at which the plane is designed to operate requires the pilot to wear a pressurized space suit.

2 Capt. Francis Gary Powers left the Air Force in 1956 to join the CIA's U-2 program. On May 1, 1960, after his plane was struck and disabled by a Soviet Dvina surface-to-air missile, he was unable to activate the plane's self-destruct mechanism and ejected. The CIA's position at the time was that U-2 pilots, if shot down, should not allow themselves to be taken alive, so Powers wore a silver dollar around his neck fitted with a poison-laced injection device. While floating under his parachute, he was able to discard the silver dollar but kept the poison pin intending to use it if he was unable to avoid capture. However, when he reached the ground, he was immediately captured and taken to the notorious Lubyanka Prison in Moscow where he was interrogated for months by the KGB. During the course of his interrogation, Powers was able to convincingly provide false information to his interrogators about the capabilities of the U-2. On August 17, 1960, he was put on trial before the military division of the USSR's Supreme Court and, two days later, found guilty of espionage against the Soviet Union and sentenced to ten years' imprisonment. On February 10, 1962, Powers was released in a prisoner exchange on the Glienicke Bridge in Berlin. Upon his return to the US, he was at first criticized for failing to activate his plane's self-destruct mechanism and for failing to take his own life using the silver dollar device. Following his appearance before the Senate Armed Services Committee, and his commendation by members of the committee, he worked from 1962 to 1970 as a test pilot

---

were trained to avoid capture at all costs and provided with a means of taking their own lives should it occur; even so, Powers was taken alive and, several days later, displayed before the world. Needless to say, tensions with the Soviets ratcheted up significantly. Though I was only eight years old at the time, I was aware of the event and of the increase in national anxiety it generated.

About a week or so after the U-2 incident was first reported, Sam called and invited me to go crabbing with him down at the riverfront. Though I had no idea of what crabbing entailed—aside from proximity to crustaceans with pincers—I readily accepted. Keep in mind that this was a different era. Parenting was much more "free range," and my parents considered Sam a responsible young man who they could trust to look after me. The plan was to pack a lunch, ride our bikes to the grocery store for chicken necks—essential for crabbing—then go to the river.

Sam arrived at our back door with his lunch, a net, several stout sticks with string wound around them, and a burlap bag. I had no idea what most of this was for, but I was beside myself with excitement to be tagging along. After a stop at the Huntley Brothers Supermarket to purchase a dozen chicken necks, we rode to the city dock. The procedure for tidal river crabbing is quite simple—tie the chicken necks onto the ends of the strings, then toss them out into the water about twenty feet from shore. Then you anchor the sticks into the sandy bank, and the waiting begins. After allowing about fifteen minutes for blue crabs to begin feeding on the chicken neck, the crabber wades out along the shallow bottom, holding the string in one hand and the net in the other, then slowly lifts the chicken neck off the bottom. The crabs are so intent on feeding that they are reluctant to

for Lockheed. He was fired from Lockheed after publishing a book that was apparently not well received by the CIA. He then became a news helicopter pilot for KNBC in Los Angeles. On August 1, 1977, Powers was killed when the KNBC helicopter he was piloting crashed.

release their hold on the chicken neck, so they are easily netted and transferred to the burlap bag. All this is executed with a sincere effort to avoid their painful pincers. After about two hours, we had well over two dozen crabs, and it was time for a lunch break. Leaving our bag of crabs securely anchored in the shallow water, we chose a picnic table that afforded a clear view of our rigs.

"What'd you bring for lunch?" Sam asked me.

"Peanut butter and jelly and a thermos of milk. What about you?"

"Bologna and cheese."

That subject out of the way, I jumped right into what was troubling my young mind. "Do you think the Russians are gonna bomb us 'cause of that spy plane?"

"I doubt it. Eisenhower and Khrushchev are supposed to be meeting in Paris in a few days, so I think they'll smooth things over. Why are you so worried about this? You're just a kid."

"I don't know. I hear stuff on the news and it just makes me worry. I know we've got enough missiles and bombs to wipe them off the map, but they've got enough to do that to us, too. I just worry somebody'll push the wrong button and end up killing everybody in the world."

Sam looked away and toward the river, almost as though I were not there. Then, in a quiet voice he said, "There are worse things than being dead."

"What? What's worse than being dead?"

"Nothing. Just ignore me."

After we finished our lunches, we continued crabbing for another hour or so until Sam decided we had caught enough. Then we rolled up the crab lines, threw the chicken necks into the river, and rode directly to Sam's house. Once there, his mother said she would boil the crabs for dinner and that

I should join them. I rode home to clear it with my mother, who insisted that I immediately strip off at the back door and head directly to the bathtub. After a quick bath and a change of clothes, I walked back down to Sam's.

His mom announced that dinner would be on the backyard picnic table in about an hour. She assigned us a few chores after which we were to entertain ourselves until dinner was ready. First, Sam filled a huge pot with water from the sink and set it on the stove. We then watched as his mom placed different spices and lemon wedges into the pot. She had us spread a tablecloth on the picnic table and set out the flatware. Among the utensils we placed on the table were pairs of what looked like nut crackers. Sam explained that these were for cracking the crab claws to get to the meat. Once we had completed our chores, we went to Sam's room.

"What's the big pot for, anyway?"

"When the water's boiling, you drop the crabs in it to cook 'em. It doesn't take very long. They get done really fast."

"You mean you don't kill 'em before you cook 'em?" I was horrified.

"Nah. You drop 'em in alive."

"That must really hurt! Is that what you meant when you said there's worse things than being dead?"

"I really don't want to talk about that, OK?" That far-off look returned to his face.

"OK. I'm sorry."

After an awkward silence, he responded, "Look, it's just that there are some things that people sometimes have to go through that can be worse than being dead or being killed."

"You mean like being tortured or something like that?"

"Yeah. Stuff like that. And sometimes...I don't know... sometimes things just get to me and I wonder if being dead would be better." He then brightened. "But don't worry about it. It's just me talkin' crazy. Let's play checkers until dinner's ready, OK?"

A half hour later, and after Sam had beaten me in two quick games of checkers, Mrs. Sanders called us for dinner.

3.

A HOLE IN THE WATER

FRIDAY, JUNE 3 was the final day of school for our county. Knowing I was now a rising fourth grader gave me the sense that I was somehow much older. Having an older friend like Sam served to magnify that confidence. The next day—after watching "The Lone Ranger," of course—I walked down to Sam's house to celebrate the end of school with him. I rang the doorbell and Sam answered, looking uncharacteristically grumpy.

"What's the matter?"

"What makes you think somethin's the matter?"

"I don't know, you just look mad about something."

"Damn right, I'm mad." It was the first time I'd heard him swear, so I knew the issue was serious. "They've decided the high school is too crowded, so they're keeping the ninth grade at the junior high next year. They just told us yesterday."

"Man, that stinks. I'm sorry."

"Thanks. I was really looking forward to going to high school—football games, dances, you know, all that stuff. I don't know what they'll do about sports. Can we be on the high school track team? Are we even considered high school students if we're stuck at the junior high? They really didn't explain any of that stuff. Just announced 'Hey, by the way, you eighth graders are going to be spending another year here at good ole Palatka Junior High.' It stinks!"

Since Sam had opened the door to cussing, I walked right

in. "Yeah, it's a damn shame."

"Hey, don't pick up my bad habits, and don't let your mom hear you cuss, OK? She'll know where you learned it."

"Oh, OK. I really don't cuss. Just thought I'd try it since you did."

Sam broke out in uncontrollable laughter and pretty soon we were both gasping for breaths between the waves of hilarity. "You crack me up sometimes, Clint. You crack me up! Hey, let's go for a bike ride so I can take my mind off my misery."

Sam pushed his bike down to my house. My dad was working outside, so I told him our plans, and we were off. Our route took us up the hill to the National Guard Armory, then to the Ravine Gardens. Without preamble, Sam took us along the perimeter road with frequent stops to collect abandoned golf balls. Then, as before, we stopped at the stream toward the end of the ride for a break and a drink of the cold, clear spring water.

Were I to conjure a place resembling what I had learned in Sunday School about the Garden of Eden, it would have looked like this spot that Sam and I had claimed as our own. There was a lush, verdant tree canopy that shaded the area, birds chattering and flitting overhead, a carpet of deep green grass and the stream, clear, cold and singing to us. The air felt cooler than elsewhere in the Ravines, and held a distinct, clean fragrance. As we lay in the grass beside the stream, I began absent-mindedly poking my index finger into the water to watch the ripples spread before they were erased by the flow.

"You tryin' to poke a hole in water?" Sam chuckled.

"No. Besides, you can't do that."

"Do what?"

"Poke a hole in the water. You can't poke a hole in water. It just fills up. Watch." I then leaned over the edge of the stream and thrust my finger into the water again, removing it quickly. "See. You can't poke a hole in the water."

"Well, that's the way it looks, but for a tiny fraction of a second—faster than our eyes and our brains can realize—your finger left a hole in the water. There was a space there in the shape of your finger where the water was gone."

"Are you sure about that? How do you know that?"

"'We learned it in science this year. Two things can't occupy the same space at the same time. So, if your finger's in the water, then the water's gone in that place where you finger is, and when you pull your finger out, it takes just a tiny fraction of a second for the water to fill the hole your finger left. In that tiny fraction of a second, there's a hole in the water."

"Hmm. But when your finger's in the water, then the hole is full of your finger, so there's still not a hole."

"You're making this too complicated. See." Sam stuck his finger in the stream and quickly withdrew it. "There is a hole 'cause there's no water there. When I pulled my finger out, there was a split second where there was no finger and no water there, just a hole."

"OK, that kinda makes sense. Wish I could see the hole. That would be so cool."

"Yeah, but it happens too fast for our eyes to see it. To me, it's kinda like our lives. They seem really important to us and to the people who love us and know us, but in the giant span of time, we're not even noticed. We're here and gone so fast that there's no hole left."

"I don't think I understand what you mean."

"I know, I just get these weird thoughts sometimes. But, see, it's like my dad. Nobody but me and my mom and a few other people even know he lived. It's like to the entire world, except for us, he never existed. Unless you're somebody like Einstein, hardly anybody'll remember you after you're dead."

"Who is Einstein? People talk about him, but nobody ever

says who he is."

"He was this famous scientist. You'll learn about him in school in a few years. He helped figure out the atomic bomb and a bunch of other really complicated things about atoms and energy and stuff. My point is that people will study him and know about him forever. Everyone'll know he existed, he lived. Not like my dad, or most people, for that matter. So, if you want to poke a hole in the water, you'd better be famous." Sam laughed, punched my shoulder and stood up. "Let's get going."

I didn't quite understand all he said that day, but I never forgot his words and returned to them often—even to this day.

4.

DONNA WAS NOT MY GIRLFRIEND

ALL TOO QUICKLY, that summer moved toward fall and the start of a new school year. Our church held two fun-filled weeks of Vacation Bible School. Our family took a two-week camping trip to Manatee Springs northwest on the Suwannee River. I spent a week with my paternal grandmother in Campville—where, I should mention, there was no television—and the summer drew to a close.

Late summer in Florida often brings tropical weather, and the summer of 1960 was certainly no exception. On August 29, a tropical cyclone developed in the Cape Verde islands west of Dakar. Even before it was named Hurricane Donna[3] the system had amassed an impressive body count when it was considered the cause of the deaths of 63 in a plane crash in Senegal. Borne westward on the trade winds at 20 miles per hour, Donna reached the Lesser Antilles by September 4. As it sliced through the Caribbean, it left more death and suffering in its wake. By September 6, Donna had reached Category 4

---

[3] Hurricane Donna was the strongest storm of the 1960 hurricane season and is blamed for a total of 439 deaths along its track from West Africa, through the Caribbean, and up the eastern coast of the United States to Greenland. In Florida, Donna destroyed half of the buildings in the city of Everglades, damaged or destroyed 75% of the homes in Fort Myers Beach, and left half of that year's grapefruit crop rotting on the ground. Just in Florida, losses were estimated at $300 million and thirteen Floridians were killed. As is the case with other similarly destructive and deadly hurricanes, the name Donna was retired and will never again be used to name an Atlantic hurricane.

strength with peak winds of 145 miles per hour and with its sights set on Florida. On Saturday, September 10, Donna made landfall in the Florida Keys near Marathon with sustained winds of 145 miles per hour and gusts reaching 178 miles per hour before turning inland near Naples. By this time, the local and area radio and television stations were carrying round-the-clock updates on Donna's position and path of destruction. School districts across the state had announced closures for the coming week, and the controlled chaos that grips the state as a hurricane nears had taken hold.

My mother always purchased extra supplies for hurricane season—mostly canned soups, stews, and vegetables—and my father readied the emergency equipment, limited to flashlights, an ice chest, the trusty Coleman camp stove and our battery-powered radio. In the case of Donna, I noticed a sharp uptick in the scope and urgency of these preparations. By midweek the week before Donna arrived, my parents had topped up both of their vehicles with gas, stored additional cans of gasoline in the garage, filled several large camping water jugs and stored them in the laundry area, and my mother had made two additional trips to Winn Dixie for non-perishable foodstuffs.

On the Friday before the storm was to arrive on Saturday night, my father took a vacation day and stayed home from work—something he never did. When Will and I arrived home from school that afternoon, he busied us hauling things in from the yard and storing them in his workshop. By now, the wind was blustery and there was a steady, though light, rainfall. As the final outside task, my father had me help him hang a sheet of plywood over the living room picture window. All of this was unlike the routine annual preparation my family had made in previous years.

By Saturday morning, the winds were noticeably higher and

the rainfall heavier. I called Sam to see how he and his mom were doing—frankly, I was concerned that their preparations might have been lacking, given that there was no "man of the house." Sam, however, assured me they were fine and ready for what might come. He told me to stay safe and that he'd see me after the storm.

Hurricane Donna was the first of many such storms that would, in some way, affect my life. Despite the dire predictions and speculations we were hearing on the radio and television, I found the entire experience of preparing for Donna's arrival exciting, if not a bit anxiety-producing. As Saturday wore on, however, and Donna grew closer, the winds began to scream, and rain pelted the windows of our house. When my mother quietly asked my father if he felt the roof would hold, I became frightened. By nine o'clock that night, we had lost power and were huddled around the battery-powered radio listening to our local station. Somehow, they were still on the air and warning our community that the storm would pass to our south overnight.

Soon after the lights went out, my parents sent us to bed. Of course, it was impossible to sleep with the howling winds outside and the rain driving against the windows of our little bedroom. After about an hour of tossing and turning, I felt Will crawl into bed with me.

"You scared?"

"Yeah."

"Me too. Let's try to fall asleep."

"OK."

No further words passed between us, and, at some point in the early hours of Sunday, we drifted off into a troubled sleep. When I awoke in the early hours of morning, the outside world was bathed in a strange yellow-gray light that spilled through the windows into our room. Outside, the winds had subsided, and a gentle, steady rain was falling. Donna had moved on and left us unscathed. Will was still asleep, so I slipped out of bed and quietly went into the living room. My mother was on the couch, wrapped in an old quilt with her eyes closed. As I approached, she opened her eyes.

"Sorry I woke you up Mama."

"It's OK, sugar. I wasn't really asleep, just dozing. I couldn't go to sleep thinking the house might blow apart during the night."

"Where's Daddy?"

"He's actually outside checking everything out."

"Can I go outside with him?"

"No, not yet. There could be power lines down or other things blown around that could hurt you. We'll wait till your father gives the 'all clear' before we go out and look around."

Later that morning, after we had eaten a meagre breakfast of cold cereal and milk, we pulled on our raincoats and our father took us outside to look around. Will was still a bit overwhelmed and held tightly to my hand during the entire excursion. The wind remained blustery and punctuated by brief periods of light rainfall. Scattered across our yard, as well as the entire neighborhood as far as I could see, were small tree branches, roofing shingles, leaves, and clumps of Spanish moss. In the front yard of the house behind ours, a large tree had fallen and seemed to be draped over the front porch of the house. Part of the nextdoor neighbor's aluminum tool shed had blown against the fence between our back yards and taken down about twenty feet of fencing. Utility crews were already out by the street, working atop the utility pole at the corner of our yard. My father pointed out a couple of places on our roof where shingles had blown off.

"Is the roof gonna leak now, Daddy?"

"No, there's tar paper under the shingles, so it won't leak. As soon as the rain stops, I'm gonna get up there and make some temporary repairs until I can get some new shingles to put on. On the whole, we came out pretty good, but I don't ever want to get any closer to a hurricane than we did last night."

"Me neither!" Will chirped.

Our local schools remained closed through the following week, but my parents returned to work on Tuesday morning, so my grandmother was dispatched to our house to watch over us. Power to our neighborhood was restored by Wednesday and, to our delight, hot meals and television returned. Most of our hours that week were occupied with reading and playing games indoors. Other than a couple of brief phone calls to Sam, I hadn't heard from any other kids in the neighborhood all week, and no one was permitted to play outside while the utility crews were working and the debris was being collected. By Thursday, boredom had me in its powerful grip. In the afternoons, after our father came home, we collected the debris from the yard, piling it curbside for pickup. Surprisingly, that was the highlight of those long, drab days. Dad was able to repair the damaged fence, and, by Friday evening, had replaced the shingles blown off our roof. At dinner that evening, he announced a road trip.

"Tomorrow morning, we're gonna to drive over to Crescent Beach and take A1A south. The highway is completely washed out south of the Matanzas Inlet bridge, plus some of those houses along there completely washed away. I'd thought we'd go take a look."

The idea of seeing first-hand what was being reported on the local news was exciting to me, and I was both surprised and thrilled that my dad had proposed such a trip. "Can Sam go with us? Please!"

"Sure, if he'd like to."

"Just remember, Son," my mother cautioned, "he may have other plans."

As soon as dinner ended, I called Sam. He had no other plans and was excited to go with us to see the storm damage first-hand. The next morning, Sam arrived at our house a few minutes before nine o'clock, and we loaded into my mom's 1953 Chevrolet and headed east toward the coast. The drive from Palatka to A1A near Crescent Beach took only about a half hour and we three boys talked nonstop most of the way. As we crossed the Highway 206 bridge at Crescent Beach, however, we entered a different world—a landscape scoured and battered by Hurricane Donna. As we turned south onto A1A, there was storm debris piled along both sides of the highway—tree limbs, palm fronds, parts of roofs, sheds, decks, furniture, soaked carpet—the mounds were ten and twelve feet high. We stared out the car windows, agape and silent. Beyond the walls of debris, the homes and shops—particularly those on the beach side of the highway—were all damaged to varying degrees of severity. Further south, on the beach side, we passed a small motel that had lost its entire roof. Other than a few utility crews and law enforcement vehicles, there were few others on the road. Dad drove slowly, as one might drive in a funeral cortege. We rode in stunned silence, the excitement of the excursion tempered by the reality of the devastation to either side of us.

"I hope these people got out before the storm hit," Dad intoned.

"So do I," Mom replied. "Otherwise, I don't see how they could have survived this. This is a lot worse than it sounds on the news."

Within minutes, we crossed a second bridge—the one over the inlet—and came to a roadblock. There were barricades across the highway, and two sheriff's cars behind those, their emergency lights flashing. Other vehicles had pulled off the highway on either side, and we joined them.

"Guess we walk from here," said Dad.

As we climbed out of the car, my father walked over to speak with one of the deputies. "You folks can go have a look. The highway's washed out about a hundred yards up—completely gone. Right now, there's no way to go further south from here. Just be careful and keep an eye on those boys, OK?"

"Yes sir."

We walked down the center of the empty highway, our heads swiveling side to side taking in the scene before us. In the past, this narrow spit of sand had separated the Atlantic Ocean to the east from the Intercoastal Waterway to the west, the highway bisecting the hundred-foot-wide strand. It was apparent that the tidal surge had swept in from the ocean side and taken everything with it. The destruction along this short stretch of A1A was complete. All that remained were the concrete block walls of a few buildings—homes or shops, it was impossible to tell. The roofs were gone, the interior walls were missing, whatever furniture and personal effects might have been inside had been swept away into the ocean. It reminded me of the grainy black and white photos I had seen of villages in Europe after the war. We made our way in silence through this scene, arriving in a couple of minutes to what was, quite literally, the end of the road. It was abrupt and shocking—the road simply ended as though some otherworld behemoth had hacked it away with a massive broadax. Walking up to the barricades marking the end of the pavement, we stared down into a scene from a poorly made Japanese horror film—waves washing over chunks of pavement and other debris and a dozen or so cars piled helter-skelter on top of each other.

"Holy cow!" Sam muttered under his breath. "Were there

people in those cars when they got washed away?"

My father chuckled a bit, "No, Sam. Those are junk cars they dumped along the shoreline here to try to slow down the erosion from the nor'easter. The waves from Donna just piled them up with the other debris from the road when it washed out."

"I've never seen anything like this before."

"Me neither," I echoed.

"Either, it's either, not neither," Mom corrected.

"Me either," I responded.

"And me either," Will chimed in.

"You get that much water moving with the force of a hurricane, and there's not much that can stop it, but this is pretty amazing to see," Dad explained. "Well, I guess we've seen what we came to see. Let's head back home and maybe fire up the grill for some burgers. Sam, you're welcome to stay for lunch."

"Thank you, sir, I appreciate it."

Our drive back to Palatka was far more subdued than our drive over to the inlet. Our excited chatter was gone, and we spoke very little. My parents, as well, were quiet. As for me, I was lost in my own thoughts. Looking back, I suppose this was the first time I had been confronted first-hand with the destructive force of nature and its potential for harm. I had always viewed nature as a benevolent, creative, sustaining force—the sunlight and rain assuring growth, the lakes and rivers respecting their boundaries and providing food and recreation, the ocean timeless and constant but never rebelling against humankind nor attacking its achievements. The experience of that morning turned all those assumptions on end and left my young mind somewhat suspicious of the natural world and uncertain of my place in it.

5.

THE KENNEDY CONUNDRUM

1960 WAS A presidential election year pitting a handsome, dynamic young senator, John F. Kennedy, against the dour and rather dull Richard Nixon, who had served as Vice President under Eisenhower. My family was in a quandary. My parents and grandmother were Democrats[4]—always had been for all I knew—but they were struggling with the decision of whether to support Kennedy. First, he was a Roman Catholic, and the assertion by his southern opponents was that his allegiance would be to the Pope over his loyalty to America. Further complicating the decision was the fact that Kennedy was a New England liberal, which had our Deep South white culture shaking in its collective boots.

Since the 1954 decision by the Supreme Court in *Brown*

---

[4] The history of the Democratic Party in Florida mirrors that of Democrats in the South in general. Historically, Florida had been governed by Democrats. In fact, Florida did not see her first Republican governor until Claude Kirk was elected in 1967. Democrats began to lose ground in Florida as a result of Richard Nixon's and the GOP's "Southern Strategy," which capitalized on southern white objections to the advances made by Black people through the Civil Rights Movement, and with which Democrats like John and Robert Kennedy and Lyndon Johnson had become associated (particularly with the passage of the 1964 Civil Rights Act and the 1965 Voting Rights Act). With Nixon's victory in 1968, Florida swung decidedly Republican and, between 1968 and 2016, chose a Democrat in only four Presidential elections. In terms of state politics, Republicans gained a majority in the Florida Senate in 1992, and in the Florida House of Representatives in 1996. Since the 1990s, the numbers of Democrats in both state chambers continued to drop with the exception of the 2006 election when Democrats gained seats in the State House.

v. Board of Education, the white South—my little hometown included—had been fretful and fearful that, at some point, the federal government would arrive to impose desegregation on our school systems. That fear also played into the election that year. Kennedy had made clear his support of Dr. Martin Luther King, Jr. and his nonviolent approach to addressing matters of racial injustice. That position further exacerbated what would have normally been a relatively easy win in the South for the Democratic candidate.

One afternoon in mid-October, Sam and I rode our bikes to the bowling alley on the west end of downtown. As we rode along Lemon Street, many of the storefronts were displaying campaign signs for either Kennedy or Nixon. Knowing how conflicted my family appeared to be over the decision before them, I decided to ask Sam his views. "So, Sam, who would you vote for, Kennedy or Nixon?"

"Kennedy, no question about it."

"Why? You know he's a Catholic, right? He might obey the Pope if he had to make a choice."

"That's just bull-malarkey. Kennedy is a war hero, a US Senator. He's already taken an oath to defend the Constitution from all enemies. He'd never obey the Pope over the Constitution. Besides, he's young, has a beautiful wife. They're like American royalty. And he's in favor of civil rights. He agrees with Martin Luther King."

"I don't understand all this stuff about civil rights. What does it mean? Why are Negroes so mad about stuff?"

Sam braked his bike to a sudden stop, looked at me with a "you're an idiot" expression and proceeded to give me a lesson in racial justice. "Have you ever paid attention to how Black folks are treated around here, and all over the country, for that matter? Look in the Penny's store—separate water fountains for whites and coloreds. Look at Doctor Wexler's office—a separate door on the side and a separate waiting room for coloreds. Look at the Howell Theater—separate entrance on the side street for coloreds, and they have to sit in the balcony. Black boys my age can get lynched for just looking at a white girl. They have to go to separate schools that have old, outdated textbooks, no lab equipment, no books in the library. They call them separate but equal schools, but that's just bull crap. Blacks can't go to white colleges, they can't ride in the front of the bus, they can't eat in white restaurants. On and on. It's like that for them everywhere they go. It's not right. This is supposed to be one nation with liberty and justice for all, and it's not—not if you're colored." He paused for a breath, a bit red-faced and angry looking. I had never seen him like this. And I had never given any thought to the injustices he had just outlined. I had nothing to say in response, but plenty to think about in days to come.

A few days after my crash course in racial injustice, I was playing with a young neighbor girl named Christine Hawkins. Ordinarily, a boy of my age would not play with a girl of any age. However, Christine was an exception. She eschewed the sorts of interests that boys recoiled at playing—dolls, house, dress-up, and so forth. Instead, Christine was the archetypal tomboy. She loved rough and tumble play, war games, pick-up football, and any form of tag. The fact was that most of the neighborhood boys her age and younger were scared shitless of her and more than one had been ignominiously beaten up by her. In recognition of that fact, we called her Crazy Christine— but never to her face.

For some reason that day, Christine's father needed to run an errand and told us we could come along. So, Christine, her younger sister, Will, and I piled into the bed of her father's pickup and off we went. As we drove through town, Christine began yelling a pro-Nixon chant: "Nixon, Nixon, he's our man. Kennedy belongs in a garbage can." Within seconds, the rest of us had taken up the cause as we yelled at the good citizens of Palatka, wielding our significant political clout in an all-out effort to sway the election. All the while we were yelling along the brick streets of our little town, Sam was echoing in the back of my mind his opposition to our call, and this bothered me more than a little. In the few short days that had elapsed since Sam had lectured me on racial disparity in America, I had been weighing in my young mind the probability that such disparity was, at its core, wrong, and should not be allowed to persist. If such were indeed the case, then Kennedy, rather than Nixon, was the moral choice to lead the nation. Yet here I was, yelling at the top of my lungs that Kennedy should be relegated to the "garbage can" of American political life. Alas, what's a hypocritical eight-year-old to do? I chose the easy way out and continued to yell along with my cohorts in the back of Crazy Christine's father's truck.

Fortunately, the greater wisdom of the electorate prevailed against our passionate, if misguided, campaign efforts, and, on November 8, Kennedy became the youngest—and the first Roman Catholic—to be elected President. In looking back, I never thought to ask my parents how they voted and, to this day, I do not know.

6.

THE RACE TO SPACE

1961 DAWNED WITH a palpable excitement in the nation. We inaugurated a charismatic new president who, in his first days in office, began to steer the nation in new directions. The space race was well off the starting block and Florida was at the epicenter of America's urgent efforts to one-up the Soviets. On April 12, the Soviets strapped Yuri Gagarin into a rather primitive capsule mounted atop a massive rocket and beat us by a month in launching the first human into space. The result was a redoubled effort on the part of the US to be first to place a human on the moon.

One afternoon in late April I walked unannounced down to Sam's house. His mother welcomed me at the door and sent me back to his room where I found him attentively working on a huge model of the Mercury launch system that was designed to loft America's first cadre of astronauts into space. His back was to me, and he failed to notice my entry. "What ya workin' on Sam?"

"Jesus, Clint! You scared the crap outta me! Don't ever sneak up on me like that again, OK?"

"I'm sorry. I didn't mean to scare you. But what is that you're building? I mean, I know it's a rocket, but what kind?"

"Come over here and I'll show you. See, this is the rocket and the capsule we're gonna to use to put Americans into space." He held up the lower part of the model. "This is the

Atlas LV-3B[5] rocket. There's gonna to be a couple of rockets used in the Mercury Project. This one is the one they'll use to put a man into orbit." Next, he held up the crew capsule. "This is the Mercury capsule. The astronaut'll ride inside here."

"How many can fit inside?"

"One. The Mercury Project is a one-man project. Just one astronaut goes up on each launch."

I then pointed to what looked like a small oil derrick mounted atop the capsule. "What's this on top of the capsule?"

"That's part of the escape system. If something goes wrong at launch, this little rocket here on top of this little gantry will fire and pull the capsule off the main rocket and out over the ocean so the astronaut survives." Sam then assembled the various components of the launch system and demonstrated how it would all work. "See, the Atlas shoots the whole system off the launch pad. The first stage has two engines that burn liquid fuel. When it reaches a certain altitude, the first stage separates, and the second stage keeps burning and pushes the capsule up into earth's orbit. When it's time to come back to earth, this heat shield on the bottom of the capsule keeps the capsule from burning up on reentry."

---

[5] Like most of America's early manned launch vehicles, the Atlas LV-3B and its variants evolved from rockets originally designed to carry nuclear weapons. A massive rocket capable of placing a heavy payload into orbit, the Atlas also had a frightening history of launch pad failures. When NASA was faced with the choice of making safety improvements on the Atlas or spending years developing a new launch vehicle for manned space flight, it chose to retrofit the Atlas. In early 1959, after the Atlas had been selected for use in the Mercury program, the Mercury astronauts were taken to Cape Canaveral to observe a test flight of an Atlas D-series rocket. It exploded one minute after launch. This, in fact, was the fifth consecutive failure of an Atlas test launch. As the manufacturer, Conair, continued to modify the Atlas to improve its safety rating for human space flight, the Mercury Program moved forward with preparing the Mercury Seven astronauts. Once brought on-line in the Mercury Program in 1962, Atlas rockets were used in four of the seven missions, all launched from Launch Complex 14 at Cape Canaveral. Fortunately, the Atlas performed safely in all four of those crewed missions. Descendants of the original Atlas rockets were in development well into the new century by United Launch Alliance.

"How do you know all this stuff?"

"We're learning a lot about it in school now. I just got the model kit last Saturday and I've already just about finished it. I just have to paint some parts and put on the decals."

"It's really cool. How much did the model cost? It's huge. Musta cost a bunch."

"It was thirteen dollars and some change. I saved up for it for about two months."

"Wow! That's a lot!" When I visited Sam a few days later, the finished model was suspended from his bedroom ceiling with fishing line.

Although television was ubiquitous by 1961, not every American household had one. Sam and his mother were among that group. Thus is was, that, in the early morning of Friday, May 5, Sam knocked on our back door and joined my family in our living room in front of our black-and-white TV. This was to be an historic day for Americans. Alan Shepard, one of the original group of seven Mercury astronauts, would make the first American manned space flight, and the event was being televised live from Cape Canaveral. So momentous was this event that my parents had both taken the day off from work and had kept Will and me home from school to watch—a decision they had never before made for any reason, and would seldom repeat. As the five of us sat in hushed silence, the news team droned on about the anticipated flight. It seemed Sam knew every detail of the flight plan and added information even the news commentators failed to mention.

Several times over the ensuing hours the countdown was halted, pushing the launch time later into the morning. Finally, around 9:00 am, my dad determined that the launch might be scrubbed for that day and sent us all off to school with notes explaining our tardiness. When Will and I arrived at school, both our classrooms were empty. As it turned out, the entire school was wedged into the library watching the launch on the school's only television. Shortly after our arrival, at 9:34 am, Shepard was lofted into space atop the Redstone rocket, and, for a nail-biting fifteen minutes and twenty-eight seconds, flew 116 miles into space before safely splashing down in the Atlantic about 300 miles from the cape. America was now catching up to the Russians, and it was a proud moment for this nine-year-old. Sadly, the junior high school's leadership was not as forward-thinking, and Sam missed seeing the launch. I think it took him a good week to fully vent his anger.

7.

HIGHER GROUND

WITHIN ABOUT THREE weeks, school ended for the year and our summer break began. Summer for me was a joyous time. I had very few responsibilities and nearly unlimited time for play. As had become our pattern, my family spent two weeks on a camping vacation—typically at one of the state's freshwater springs. This summer, however, was to be different. We were going to the mountains! For a nine-year-old who had lived his entire life in the flatlands of Florida, this was the most exciting adventure imaginable. And if that weren't enough, Sam was going with us. Although Will and I were camping veterans, Sam had never spent a night outdoors, and, strangely to me, seemed a bit anxious about doing so. "What about bears? Do we sleep outside on the ground? What do we eat? Are there bathrooms?" He was full of questions, and, for once, I had all the answers.

My parents were remarkably organized as individuals, but as a couple, they were a force of nature. We had a brand new 1961 Chevrolet station wagon and my father had calculated to the cubic inch how much gear we could stash in the rear compartment. With my mother's input, he had designed and constructed a wooden cabinet that held our Coleman stove and all the pots, pans and kitchen gadgets Mom would need. It fit tightly in the rear of the station wagon leaving room for a large Coleman cooler and our five small suitcases. In addition, Dad had built a roof-top storage unit that would hold our large tent, kitchen tarp, cots, sleeping bags, folding chairs and more. Weeks before our departure, we had driven over to Campville—the wide spot along highway 301 where my paternal grandmother lived—and cut fat pine kindling from old stumps on land that had, years ago, been used for turpentine production. We had learned from past camping trips that firewood was readily available but kindling to make it burn would be in short supply.

By Friday evening, June 16, everything was prepared and loaded. To say I was excited could possibly be the understatement of the decade. I wanted Sam to spend the night with us before our early morning departure, but my father vetoed that idea under the correct assumption that neither Sam, Will, nor I would have gotten any sleep that night. So, promptly at 5:00 the next morning, we backed out of the driveway, turned the corner, picked up Sam, and headed north. We three boys were bleary-eyed and slept off and on until the sky began to lighten. Mom and Dad had planned our itinerary carefully, and Atlanta would be our first stop. At some point after daybreak, Dad announced that we were crossing the state line. I'm embarrassed to confess that I looked intently out the window but couldn't see it.

"Where is it? I can't see it."

"Where's what, Son?"

"The state line."

How he held it together, I don't know. "It's not a line on the ground, Son. It's just the border between Florida and Georgia. You can't see it."

"Oh." I thought Sam and Will would wet their pants laughing at me. I brooded in silent dishonor for at least the next ten minutes.

Up until that trip, Jacksonville was the largest city I had seen. As we neared the southern edge of Atlanta, I was awestruck by the looming skyline of that much larger metropolis. We were to spend the night at Kennesaw Mountain north of the city, so we passed directly through the city with plans to return the next day to visit Stone Mountain. We arrived at the National Park (it was on an actual mountain!) about mid-afternoon and immediately set about making camp. Though this was all new to Sam, he fell into the rhythm quickly. He was fifteen now and had gained in height and bulk over the past year. His extra muscle was a big help as we hefted the equipment from the roof of the station wagon. With Dad's direction, we unfolded and set up the tent, raised the kitchen tarp over the wooden picnic table, unloaded and placed Mom's kitchen cabinet on one end of the table, and set up our cots and sleeping bags. As Mom began preparing dinner, Sam, Will, and I began to scour the nearby woods for firewood.

At one point in our ramblings we came upon a low stone wall with a southern overlook and stared dumbfounded at the skyline of Atlanta backlit by the late afternoon sun. This vista was unlike anything any of the three of us had ever seen—a mountain-top view with what had to be the largest city anywhere in the distance. When we arrived back at our campsite with enough wood for several evening campfires, Dad dispatched us to the bathhouse for showers. There was no point in protesting as this was a routine part of daily camp life. The bathhouse had small concrete block cubicles, each with a showerhead, that afforded a modicum of privacy. Clean and refreshed, we returned to camp just in time for dinner.

My mother was a wonderful cook, and the limitations of a camp kitchen were no match for her creativity. I don't remember what we had for dinner that night, but I do recall that Sam stated—with the request that it not get back to his mother—it was the best meal he'd ever eaten. Is it any wonder my mom loved him?

My favorite time of the day while camping was evening, after dinner, when we would light a campfire. As Mom and Dad washed the dinner dishes, Sam, Will, and I stacked some of the pine kindling—we called it fat lighter—and then placed on top some of the dry deadfall we had gathered that afternoon. Within a short span, we had a roaring fire cracking in the fire ring. We then arranged the folding chairs around the fire and settled in for the evening. To this day I don't comprehend fully the mysteries of a campfire—the way its glow draws you in, the way its warmth melts the stresses of the day, the way the music of its crackle and pop summons Hypnos from his cave to bring drowsiness and sleep.

Music was always a part of our campfire ritual. Mom, with her clear, lovely soprano voice, would lead us in familiar songs, and, in later years, as Will learned to play guitar, we expanded our repertory to include the folk music so popular in those days. After we had sung ourselves out and were sitting quietly, mesmerized by the fire, I glanced over at Sam and saw the flames reflected in his wet cheeks.

"Sam, are you OK?" I asked gently.

"Yeah." By now, the rest of the family had glanced his way. "This is all just so nice, like a family should be. I don't know how to thank you all for bringing me. My mom and I don't get to do things like this. She works so hard, but we just don't have the money. This is the best thing I've ever done in my life." I looked toward my parents and noticed tears streaming down Mom's cheeks.

Dad came to the rescue. "Sam, we're just glad to have you. In case you hadn't noticed, the boys kinda like you." We all laughed—that sort of blessed laughter that instantly soothes the pain of moments like this.

"How about S'mores?" Mom sniffed.

53

The following day was spent in the city—first at the state capital building, then at a massive circular painting of the Battle of Atlanta called the Cyclorama, and ending at Stone Mountain Park. By the time we returned to camp, we were all exhausted. Since we would be breaking camp and leaving early the next morning, Mom prepared a simple dinner and we forewent an evening campfire. Instead, we made what preparations could be made ahead of time for departure and turned in early. The next morning, Dad had us up at first light to break camp, load the station wagon and depart. Our destination this day was a private campground in Cherokee, North Carolina—home of the Eastern Band of the Cherokee Nation. Our stay was to be only two nights, but my parents had planned a full itinerary.

We arrived in Cherokee mid-afternoon, found the campground and, within about forty-five minutes, had set up camp. The plan was to eat a quick dinner followed by attendance at the evening performance of an outdoor drama telling the story of the Cherokee people titled *Unto These Hills*. Somewhat sweaty from our work setting up camp, we three boys were dispatched to the bath house for showers while Mom prepared dinner. The bathhouse was a masonry block building with several separate shower stalls, each including a small changing area outside the shower. We each took a stall, undressed and took our showers. Sam took a bit longer than Will and me, so we finished up and left the bathhouse ahead of him. As we exited the bathhouse, we were confronted by three Cherokee boys—mid-teens—whose intent appeared to be to shake us down for money, rough us up, or worse.

The taller of the three spoke, "Well, looks like we have some white boy ass to play with." They moved toward us in an apparent attempt to force us back into the bathhouse. Just then, Sam exited.

"What's going on here?" Our assailants remained silent.

"They said they were going to play with our asses," I replied.

"There ain't gonna be any of that," Sam spoke, his voice infused with anger. "Will, go get your dad." Will ran off toward our campsite leaving Sam and me in a brief face-off with the other three boys.

"It's OK. We were just messing with the little guys. We didn't mean no harm." With that, the three of them ran back toward the campground entrance.

"Sam, what did they mean they were gonna play with our asses?"

"I'll explain it later. Let's just go get changed."

"I was pretty scared, and I was about ready to yell to you when you came out just in the nick of time."

"They were just bullies. They saw two young white boys and thought they'd have some fun."

"Thanks for rescuing us." About that time, my father appeared. Sam explained to him what had happened and the three of us walked back to our campsite together.

That night, as I watched the heartbreaking story of the Cherokee Nation play out under the stars, a conflict raged within me between sympathy for the Cherokee people and anger toward the three Cherokee boys who had threatened us that afternoon.

The next day was spent visiting the Museum of the Cherokee Indian and the Oconaluftee Indian Village. The following morning, we broke camp and drove toward Cosby Campground in the Great Smoky Mountains National Park. Along the way, I was lost in my memories of that visit to Cherokee—a confusing mixture of fascination, sorrow, fear, and anger. We arrived at Cosby that afternoon and established what would be our base camp for the coming week. Cosby lies at the northeastern corner of the park, set amongst dense old-growth forests. A beautiful freestone creek runs through the campground. Very quickly that creek became our favorite place to hang out and play. The water was numbingly cold, but ran gin-clear, tumbling over ancient boulders, plunging into waist-deep pools and running along shallow riffles. We swam, we climbed, we overturned rocks to find salamanders and other unknown creatures. But best of all, we managed to convince my parents that, after a day of playing in the stream, we really didn't need to visit the showers in the evening.

Our days in the mountains were idyllic. For three boys, there was an endless bounty of places to explore and things to do. As the days passed, it seemed that Sam grew younger and less withdrawn. He had always been rather reserved—particularly around my parents—but he gradually relaxed and became more childlike in his play, more open in his conversation. Nearly every day included a trip to some attraction in the area—Cades Cove, Clingman's Dome, Pidgeon Forge—but we always returned to camp in time for play in the creek, and each evening included time around the campfire.

One evening, as we were enjoying the crackle of the fire, my Mom asked Sam what he thought he wanted to do after high school. "I'd like to go to college, but we don't have the money for that. So, I'm thinking I might join the Navy for a few years. Then, when I get out, the GI Bill will help me with college. I'd like to be a teacher. I kinda like knot-headed kids." He looked at me when he said that, and all had a good laugh at my expense. "I'd also like to join the Peace Corps right after college, then come back and teach. It's all kind of a dream. I really don't know if I'll be able to pull it off."

"So, what's the Peace Corps?" Will asked.

"It's this program JFK started where you go for two years to a foreign country and help folks there with things like digging wells or farming or you teach school. Stuff like that."

"So, what would you do?"

"Well, I'd teach kids. It's for sure I don't know anything about farming." We all laughed with him at that.

"That's very noble of you, Sam," my mother interjected. "The Navy would probably give you an experience with other cultures but living and working with people in another country would be life-changing."

"You know what Fred Astaire sang, Sam?" my father asked. "'We joined the Navy to see the world, and what did we see? We saw the sea.'"

"Yes sir, I've heard that. Honestly, I've thought about the Navy because I think I might have less chance of being in combat. It looks like things are heating up in Vietnam and going to war is not my idea of a fun time. My father was in the Air Force, but the Navy rescued him after he was shot down, so I've always felt kinda partial to the Navy." At that, Sam grew quiet and an awkward silence followed.

"Boys, tomorrow we're taking a long trip to Asheville to visit the Biltmore mansion, so we need to turn in early 'cause we need to get going by six in the morning."

"Six o'clock! It'll still be dark!"

"That's right, but it's a long drive, and the tour lasts about two hours."

"What is the Bildmore mansion?"

"It's Biltmore, with a T," Dad replied. "It's a huge mansion built by a fellow named George Vanderbilt—that's the 'bilt' part of Biltmore. It's the largest private home in the country."

"So, do people still live there? Who was George Vanderbilt?" I asked.

"So many questions. Let's wait until tomorrow, and we'll

all learn together. But, no, nobody lives in the house anymore. Some of the family still owns it, but it's more like a museum. Anyway, you boys get ready for bed. Tomorrow will be a long day." After brushing our teeth, we turned in. Soon Mom and Dad joined us in the tent, and we all drifted off to sleep.

It was dark when Dad rousted us awake the next morning. Mom was already at work preparing a big breakfast. We ate in relative silence, still drowsy and trying to avoid waking other campers who were still asleep. The sky was just beginning to lighten as we drove out of the campground. The trip to Ashville and the Biltmore House took nearly two hours. Upon arriving, Dad purchased tickets for the ten o'clock tour and we spent the intervening time exploring the gardens. Our tour began in the cavernous atrium just inside the mansion's main entrance, then took us up and down numerous flights of stairs, through massive salons, work areas, servants' quarters, bedrooms, and dining areas. The scale of the place was astounding. After the tour, we drove into the nearby village, found a small restaurant for lunch, and began our drive home. As we drove, we chattered about all we had seen.

"Mister Cooper, how could anybody need a house that big?"

"Well, I think it was more about impressing his wealthy friends, Sam. Plus, Vanderbilt was filthy rich. His family made millions in transportation—railroads, steamships and such—so he would bring wealthy friends down to the mansion for these lavish parties, and they'd stay for days or weeks."

"Didn't they have jobs? How could they afford to stay away for weeks?"

"Sam, the kind of wealth folks like Vanderbilt had—and some folks still do—is huge inherited wealth. They work, but not jobs like Mrs. Cooper and I and your mother work. They work at making their money make more money, and they hire people to help them with that, too. It's hard for us to understand, but people with that kind of wealth make more money in a minute than we make in a year."

"I don't know. It just seems kinda unfair. My mom works so hard, and we pinch every penny, and people like that have so much and, I don't know, just don't seem to know how hard other people work just to make ends meet."

"I understand how you feel, but, you know, I don't think people with that kind of money have any more fun, or live lives that are any more enjoyable than we do, and I bet they've never sat around a campfire or taken a bath in a cold mountain creek."

"I guess you're right. I mean I wouldn't want to have missed those things. It's hard to imagine being so rich that you miss out on stuff that's really fun, really special. I really appreciate you all bringing me. This trip has been amazing."

"We're just glad you could come, Sam. You've been a big help in keeping these boys in line."

"Dad!"

All too soon, our adventure in the mountains drew to an end, and we made the drive home, arriving late in the evening on July 5. My parents had used all their vacation days and had to return to work the next morning. We unloaded only what was necessary that evening and finished after Dad returned from work the next afternoon. Until that trip, I had never considered there were those in my circle of friends for whom my typical American family—two parents and two kids—might seem altogether atypical, but such was the case for Sam. And for some time thereafter, I felt an uneasy guilt at having taken for granted what was, for him, so painfully lost and forever unattainable.

8.

LOOKIN' FOR LOVE

THE NEXT SEVERAL weeks were uneventful—a string of days riding bikes, playing tag football and just messing around. In August, my parents took me to my grandmother's home in Campville to spend a week with her.

As I have mentioned, my paternal grandmother did not own a television, so entertainment took other forms when I stayed with her. We played board games and read. The weekly visit by the book mobile was a highlight. In the evening, we sat in her small living room and talked. One might think that all of this would be rather uninteresting for an active nine-year-old boy, but my grandmother did not relate to me as a child. In our conversations and interactions, she never spoke down to me, but seemed to confer on me a status that I did not enjoy at home. In addition, I did not have to share her with anyone else. She was all mine for that week each summer, and I was the center of her attention. I'm confident my parents knew she spoiled me in this way, but also knew it was but for a brief period and would not ruin me for life.

Down the unpaved road from my grandmother's house lived a family with two children. They ran a small dairy farm, and the children spent several hours working there each morning during summer vacations. After their morning chores were completed, they were free to play the rest of the day. The boy, named Jesse, was a year older than me and the girl, Dianna, two years younger. Despite the fact that they called me a "city slicker," they were friendly, and I enjoyed playing with them. Adjacent to their home was that large tract of land where we had cut pine kindling before our camping trip. Not only had this land been used for turpentine production, but clay had been mined there in the past, leaving several large, deep pits filled with water. The only restriction Grandma placed on us for playing in this tract was that we never swim in the clay pits as, she told us, they were deep and dangerous.

One afternoon, Jesse and I were roaming there, and made our way toward the clay pits. As we drew nearer, we heard voices and laughter and realized other kids were swimming. Years before, when the Camp brothers had mined the area, a large volume of overburden had been removed to get to the underlying clay. This topsoil had been dumped in enormous piles on either side of the pits forming a high ridge with the water-filled pits about twenty yards below.

As we approached, Jesse whispered, "Quiet. Let's sneak up on them and see who's there."

Crouching now, we stole in silence up the tree-covered ridge and peered down toward the clay pit. There, at the shallow end of the pit was a group of about five or six Black teenage boys skinny-dipping in the blue-tinted water. They were tall, lanky, and several years older than either of us. Jesse and I stared in silence, transfixed. Though we had been stealthy and not spoken above a whisper, one of the boys looked up and saw us. Yelling to his friends, they began running toward us. Not waiting to learn their intentions, Jesse and I ran in the direction of his house, never stopping to look back. How far they followed us we never knew, but when we finally climbed over the fence that separated his family's land from the mined tract, we felt safe for the first time.

Panting, and with my heart racing, I asked Jesse, "What do you think they would have done to us if they'd caught us?"

"I don't know. Maybe beat us up for watching them. Maybe stripped us and thrown us in the pit. I don't know, but I wasn't about to wait around to find out."

"Man, that was scary. They were a lot bigger than us."

"Yeah, in a lot of ways," he laughed.

"Yeah. I know what you mean," I laughed with him.

In reflecting on this incident years later, I realized how mysterious and even exotic these boys had seemed to us. Growing up, as we did, in the segregated South, there was little to no opportunity to interact with Black persons or to play with Black children. As a result, we white kids knew nothing of Black culture and, in subtle and myriad ways, were taught to look with suspicion, even fear, on anyone not quite like ourselves.

School began the Tuesday after Labor Day. I was now in fourth grade and had a young, single, and very attractive teacher, Miss Bainbridge, on whom I developed a serious schoolboy crush. As a result—and in an effort to impress her—my studies improved rather dramatically. To that point, I had managed As and Bs with very little effort, but now I was determined to achieve that elusive goal of straight As. I also felt the need to confer with my older mentor, Sam, about the unrequited love I felt for Miss Bainbridge. So, one afternoon in late September, I broached the subject of true love with him.

"So, Sam, you know my teacher, Miss Bainbridge, she's really nice and really pretty. I'm kinda in love with her, but she's a whole lot older than me. So, what can I do to make her like me?"

"Clint, sometimes you're an idiot! She's an adult, you're a kid. She's your teacher. She's never going to fall for you. Besides, that would be kinda sick."

I was devastated. I knew he was right, but the absurdity of the situation had eluded me until that moment. I immediately burst into tears.

"Man, it's OK. You'll be alright. You just need to find a girlfriend your own age."

"I (sniff) know (sniff). I know you're right (snort). But the girls my age aren't nice to me like she is. And they don't talk to me like she does. (Sniff.)"

"I know. It's hard. Just back off a bit. You're awfully young to be looking for romance anyway."

"I know, but I don't much like girls."

"That will probably change."

"What about you? How come you don't have a girlfriend?"

Sam grew quiet for a minute. "I don't much like girls either."

"Yeah, I know, they're kinda gross."

"It's not like that, Clint. It's more complicated."

"What do you mean."

"Look, you can't tell this to anybody. Cross your heart?"

"Cross my heart and hope to die. Stick a needle in my eye."

"OK. It's like this. You know the way you feel about Miss Bainbridge?"

"Yeah. Kinda fluttery inside my stomach."

"Right. Well I don't feel that way about girls. Ever. I feel that way about some boys, though." His gaze dropped to the floor and stayed there.

"Oh." This was something I had never before considered. After it settled a bit, I asked him, "So, do you feel that way about me?"

"No, dummy."

I was hurt. "How come?"

He chuckled, "You're not my type."

"So, what's your type?"

"Guys my age. Not pip-squeaks like you!" He ruffled my hair

and we began to wrestle. In the tussle and the laughter, the awkwardness of the moment fell away.

In looking back, I realize we rarely discussed the matter after that. Though I could not have grasped the implications at the time, I understood that Sam was different in the way he viewed others. At the same time, I was secure in the knowledge that I was as special to him as he was to me. As I grew older, I understood more clearly that Sam was gay. I also understood that Sam was Sam—by which I mean I understood that he was not defined solely by his attraction to other guys, that he was still, in every way, my best friend, and that our friendship was unchanged by the fact of that attraction. From that day and until his death, I never shared this knowledge with anyone. Sam and I had an understanding, and, as I aged and that understanding matured, it was never once an obstacle to our brotherhood.

PART II

9.

YOU CAN'T GO HOME AGAIN ... BUT SOMETIMES, YOU MUST

IT WAS NEVER my intention to return to Palatka. When I left to begin my studies at the University of Florida in the fall of 1969, I assumed work would lead me to exotic and far-flung places—never back to Palatka. Yet life is riddled with ironies, is it not? After cramming a four-year degree into five years, I somehow managed to wrangle my acceptance into UF's law school and found myself in a serious sink-or-swim environment. Fortunately, I learned to swim rather quickly and left with a *cum laude* JD. I was recruited by and joined the firm of Williams and Blackwell in Jacksonville as an associate. The hours were long and grueling—mostly grunt work with little reward or recognition. Most of W & B's case load was in corporate law, which I found rather uninspiring. For the first year I did not even see the inside of a court room.

Early into my second year, I began a serious relationship with a bright new associate named Ellen, whom I too-late discovered was the niece of one of the partners. Needless to say, he did not deem me worthy of her, nor did he assess me as having the right pedigree for marriage into the family or the firm. Despite the long hours, Ellen and I tried to make it work. Though we struggled to carve out time for each other, we realized we might have a shot at something lasting. However, as the months progressed, our time together seemed to grow increasingly difficult to maintain. At the same time, I began to sense that my workload was growing beyond the excesses of even my first year. This trend accelerated into the fall and I began to draw the conclusion that it was intended to make me fail or to force me out. The end result was that it did just that.

I tendered my resignation at Williams and Blackwell on October 15th—strange that I can still recall the date—packed my 1965 Volkswagen Beetle the following day, met Ellen for a last drink that evening, and drove to Palatka the following morning. Returning to Palatka was enough of an indignity, and I had no intention of moving back in with my parents, so I had rented a small apartment in a massive Victorian house near the river and within walking distance of downtown. The apartment was furnished and included a small kitchen. Still, my finances were tight. I had spent very little of my salary from W & B— primarily because I had no time to do so—so I had managed to save enough to rent an office and furnish it modestly.

And so it was that, in November of 1978, I hung my shingle on the door of an office in the Kemper Building at 203 Lemon Street in Palatka—Clinton A. Cooper, Esq. Attorney at Law. I had no staff, no clients, and absolutely no reputation to draw business to my door. I had a desk, three chairs, two empty filing cabinets, a set of bookcases, a failing ficus tree, a telephone, and a small remnant of my dignity. But eighteen months of immersion in the Uniform Commercial Code had convinced me of two things: one, I was not cut out to be a corporate lawyer; and, two, I needed to find a way to enjoy the practice of law.

The day I moved into my office was gray and overcast. My parents came to help me with the furniture and the work went quickly. My mom was beside herself with pride—her son, the newest lawyer in Palatka. The fact that I lacked any activity even remotely resembling a thriving legal practice mattered not in the least to her. She insisted I come to dinner that evening. Will was now in medical school and she had yet to adjust to her empty nest, so I agreed. Around the dinner table that evening, I lamented the fact that I had no clients and wasn't really certain how to go about acquiring any. Mom was convinced that, as soon as the word got out that Clint Cooper, the brilliant corporate attorney from Jacksonville, had opened an office in Palatka, my phone would be ringing off the hook. I failed to be convinced by her enthusiasm.

At the time, my mother was still working as a Deputy Clerk for the Circuit Court of Putnam County. As such, she knew all the attorneys in the area who had business with the court. Among those was Kate Ingalls, whom my mother classified as "cracker jack"—meaning she was, in my mother's opinion, tops in her field. Mom suggested I visit Ms. Ingalls and seek her advice on how best to build my practice. Kate Ingalls was not unknown to me as I had met her on a number of occasions while I was still in high school. One of her nephews had taught me high school history, and regularly hosted informal gatherings of his more motivated students at his Aunt Kate's home on the river. She was an imposing figure—the only woman practicing law in Palatka—and had a reputation for being a brilliant barrister. So, not one to ignore my mother's advice, I telephoned Kate—as I soon came to call her—on that following Monday morning and asked to meet. When I explained my purpose for our meeting, she invited me to her home for dinner and drinks that evening.

I arrived a little after 6:00 pm, dressed in a sports coat and wool slacks. Kate met me at the door in a caftan and holding a tumbler of dark brown liquid. "Welcome, Clint. It's so good to see you again. Come in, come in. Let's sit in the den. I've got a fire going in there. We'll talk a bit, then have dinner. Can I fix you a drink?" I declined the drink; I wanted to be as clear-headed as possible to catch every morsel of wisdom she might dispense. She led me toward the back of the house into a room with a fireplace on the back wall and windows on either side looking out over the river. We settled into a pair of overstuffed leather chairs facing the fireplace.

"This is nice. I remember this room from when Bill would have some of us over here in the afternoons to tackle the problems of the world."

"Yes, I remember those gatherings. I always enjoyed having you young folks around. Bill just had no room for you kids at his little place, and I was happy for you all to meet here."

"Where is he now, by the way?"

"Well, you remember he walked out during that teachers' strike in '68, and the county fired them all."

"Oh, yeah. I had forgotten about that. I kinda lost touch with him after the teachers' strike. He was such a great teacher."

"Well, as soon as they fired him, he was immediately drafted and sent to Vietnam."

"Jesus! I didn't realize that! How did he come through that?"

"Well, he did OK, I guess. Believe it or not, he came back and went to law school at Florida State."

"Really? So where is he now?"

"He liked Tallahassee, so stayed and joined a firm there. Speaking of that, tell me about your time with Williams and Blackwell."

So, for the next twenty minutes I related to her the sad tale of my year and a half as a corporate lawyer, my sabotaged romance, and my decision to cut and run in a quest to find some fulfilment in the practice of law. She, in turn, quizzed me about the sorts of law I wanted to practice and what I wanted to gain from the work. After we had exhausted those topics, she announced dinner.

Kate's home was a large mid-1960s ranch-style brick house set high above the east shore of the St. Johns and paralleling the river. The formal dining room faced the back of the house and the river, but, as she led me through that part of the house, it was apparent that we were to dine elsewhere.

"Since it's just the two of us, I thought we'd eat in the kitchen. Nothing fancy. Hope you like chicken and dumplins."

"I love chicken and dumplins!"

"Good, 'cause that's what we're having." She showed me to the table where two places had been set, then went over to the other side of the kitchen and began to ladle the main course into a stoneware tureen. Opening the refrigerator, she extracted two salads, set everything on the table, and we began.

"Clint, I really empathize with where you find yourself now. For me, when I finished law school, the one thing I knew I didn't want to do was join some big, faceless firm—not that too many of them were recruiting women anyway. I knew I wanted to come back to this area and do what I could to help folks here. From what you've told me, I understand that your coming back to Palatka was something of a fall-back plan, but this is a good place. I've known you most of your life, and I've known your mother for twenty years or more. I've kept up with you through her. I know how you excelled in law school, so let me get to my point here. The fact is, I'm feeling tired—I'm sixty-one—and I'd like to begin to scale back my practice. I'm not looking for a partner to join me, but I'd be more than willing to throw some of my work to you, and to mentor you through some of my more complex cases—cases that won't resolve anytime soon—so you could take them over going forward."

"Wow! I don't know what to say. I certainly didn't come here this evening expecting this. I just wanted to get your advice as to how to jump-start my practice."

"Well, I was glad when you called and asked to meet, because I had already been mulling this decision for several weeks—really from as soon as I learned you were coming back to Palatka. So, unless you object, let's talk about how this could work."

Obviously, I had no objections. Kate's generous offer would advance my practice by months if not years. So, over the relaxed dinner and during drinks afterward, my career path gained significantly better definition. Within two months of our meeting, my place in the legal community of Putnam County was established, I had brought on a legal assistant that Kate recommended, and the phones were ringing consistently.

A few weeks after Christmas, I was at my desk when my assistant buzzed me. "Mr. Cooper, there's a Mrs. Sanders here to see you."

"Thanks, Paula, would you please send her in." Though I did not know who Mrs. Sanders might be, nor her purpose in coming to see me, I was certainly unprepared for the person who walked into my office—Sam's mother.

"Mrs. Sanders, so good to see you. Please, please come in." I quickly circled the desk and directed her to one of the two chairs in my office.

As she settled into the chair, she spoke, "Mr. Cooper, thanks for seeing me without an appointment."

"Mrs. Sanders, I've been Clint to you all my life. Let's not change that now."

"Thank you, Clint. How are you these days? I see your folks every now and then, but since Sam died…" and her voice trailed off.

"I'm doing well, thanks. Didn't enjoy the big corporate law world in Jacksonville, so I'm back here in Palatka, trying to make a go of it and feel like I'm making a difference at the same time."

"I'm glad to hear that, and glad you're back. I know your parents are proud of you. Sam would have been proud of you, too."

"I know he would have. I guess I've never really talked with you much since his death. I was too immature, and probably too devastated at the time to tell you what an influence he was in my life and how much his death affected me." As I spoke, I felt myself again slumped in the back seat of my father's station wagon after Sam's funeral, spent and broken. "I tried to put it into my eulogy at his service, but I was only thirteen. I was shaken to my core and could hardly function for days after his funeral. I've really missed him."

"I miss him, too. Every day. But your eulogy and your song were both just perfect. They meant so much to me at the time."

"Thank you. I hardly remember that day."

"I understand. For me, I remember every moment, every face, every hug. And that's why I'm here, really."

"How is that? How can I help you? Does this have something to do with Sam?"

Her next words landed like a punch to the gut. "Clint, I don't think Sam's death was an accident. I think he was killed, murdered, and I'm here to ask you to investigate the circumstances of his death."

"Mrs. Sanders, I'm absolutely stunned by what you just said. What makes you think Sam's death was anything other than an accident?"

"Well, and this is delicate, but you're my lawyer now, right."

"Yes ma'am, if that's what you want."

"I do."

"Alright then, I'm now your attorney, and everything we discuss from this point forward is protected by attorney-client privilege. So, I ask you again, why do you think Sam was murdered?"

She dug into her purse and pulled out a small bundle of

what appeared to be letters. "These letters are from Sam after he joined the Navy. I'd like you to read them—not now, but when you have time. I know that he wrote you a few times, too."

"Yes, he did. I kept his letters—well, they're at my parents' house in my old room."

"You might want to read those, too, to see if you see in them what I see in his letters to me."

"Certainly. I'll get them and read them along with these you've just given me."

"Well, getting back to the delicate matter. You probably know that Sam was, well...he liked boys, not girls."

"Yes, ma'am, I did know that Sam was a homosexual. He kept that very private, but he did indicate to me that he had told you. He was very much, as they say, 'in the closet.' Sam was always very masculine, and as far as I know, he kept his sexuality a secret through high school. He told me when I was about nine. We never really discussed it much after that. It was just a part of who he was, and it never once bothered me."

"Well, I don't know if the two of you ever, you know, experimented like boys will do, but that doesn't matter now."

"Well, even though it doesn't matter now, I can tell you Sam and I never experimented, as you say, and he was always one hundred percent appropriate in his friendship with me. You know I worshipped him. I would have done anything he asked, even experimented, but he never asked and, in fact, made it clear that I was not his type." At that point, I actually chuckled a bit. "Sorry for laughing, but you might enjoy this little anecdote. The day Sam told me he was attracted to boys and not girls—like I said, I was around nine or ten, and really knew nothing about sex—I asked him if he liked me like that. He laughed and said 'You're not my type.' I was actually kinda hurt, so I said 'Well, what is your type.' He laughed again and said 'Not a pip-squeak like you.'"

For the first time since she stepped into my office, Mrs. Sanders laughed. "Well, I'm glad to hear that. I figured out before he told me that he was different—mothers just know these things—but I kept hoping he would tell me. He finally did, not long before he left for the Navy. It was so hard for him to tell me. We both cried buckets. But he's, I mean he was, my son, and there was no way I was going to stop loving him."

"Of course not. And it was the same for me. Like I said, I was so naïve at the time he told me, but even then, I knew it was a secret I needed to keep. He was like a big brother to me, and I loved him with a fierce loyalty. Like you, there was no way I was going to quit loving him after he told me." I chucked again, "Though I have to admit I was a little miffed when he told me I was not his type. But, again, what has convinced you his death was more than an accident?"

"Well, you'll see when you read the letters. He thought he had found someone, someone in his outfit or crew or whatever they call them. Anyway, he thought there was another sailor interested in him, so he finally got up the courage to approach him. Well, it went badly, very badly. You'll see in the letters how bad things got for him, the awful things those other boys did to him, right up until he died. Please, just read the letters, and if you think this is just the delusion of a grieving old woman, then I'll accept your opinion and drop it."

"OK, Mrs. Sanders, I'll read these letters, and get the ones he sent me, and let's get together next week and talk about this, OK?"

"That will be fine, Clint, and thank you." She rose to leave. I walked her to the door, and as she exited, she turned back to me. "You know, he would have done anything for you. You were the little brother he never had. He loved you, too, Clint."

10.

THE LETTERS

I REMEMBER LITTLE of the remainder of that day. Mrs. Sanders' visit had shaken my foundations. Just the remote possibility that there might have been anything sinister in Sam's death filled me with dread. I wrapped up my work early, placed the bundle of letters Mrs. Sanders had left with me into my briefcase and drove to my parents' house on the off-chance one of them might be home. Neither was, and I realized I no longer had a key to their house, so I left and drove back toward downtown. After a quick stop at Angel's Diner for a take-out burger, I drove the few remaining blocks to my apartment.

As I ate a hasty dinner, I spread the letters on my dining table. There were fifteen in total. I removed each from its envelope, stapled the envelope to the corner of the letter and arranged the entire lot chronologically. My intention was to read them in order. The first letter was written on yellowed notebook paper in Sam's crisp cursive.

21 June, 1964
NAS JAX
Dear Mom,

Sorry I haven't written sooner. I just haven't had the time. The ride here from Palatka was ridiculously long. I think we stopped at every wide spot in the road. I talked with a couple of guys on the bus, but mostly kept to myself. Everybody seemed pretty nervous.

I don't know what I expected, but things are really structured here. There's a set time for everything, and really hardly any free time. We have about four more weeks of Navy Boot Camp, then we'll begin training for the specific positions for which we're selected. I don't know what my job will be yet. They test us and evaluate us, then make those assignments. We can request something specific, but there are no guarantees.

Most of the other guys are like me, right out of high school. They're from all over the country. There are even a few Negroes mixed in. I miss your cooking. The food's OK, but nothing to write home about, even though I am!

There's really nothing more to write about. All we do is run, drill, then drill and run. I've got a few minutes left, so going to try to get off a short note to Clint. I'll write more next time.

Love,
Sam

At this point I realized the incomplete picture I was likely to get from this exercise and a series of questions began to nibble at the margins of my thinking: Where were the letters Sam had received while in training? Would he not have kept them? Would they not have been returned to his mother with his personal effects following his death? Without the letters Sam had received from his mother, me, and perhaps others, the perspective I gained would be one-sided.

30 June, 1964
NAS JAX
Dear Mom,

Thanks for your letters. I can't tell you what they mean to me. Sometimes this place seems a thousand miles from home. We get news here, but honestly, I think they censor what we get and what's printed in the Navy Times. There's almost no information on base about what's going on in Vietnam. All the guys here are wondering if we'll get sent there if things continue to develop. I did hear the awful news about those three guys who disappeared in Mississippi while they were trying to sign up Black folks to vote. I bet you the Klan took them. They're probably dead. Just kids my age!

I forgot to tell you I got a letter from Clint. I guess they're on vacation this week and next. He said they were going camping at a spring down hear Ocala. Can't believe he'll be in 8th grade this fall! Hope he does OK with the 9th grade bullies since they're still keeping that grade there.

I'm making a few friends here now. I'm really taking it slow in that department. I'd like something more than just a friendship, but that's really not an option here. Plus, it's for sure hard to read other people.

Got to go for now. Miss you (and your cooking!)

Love,
Sam

---

10 July, 1964
NAS JAX
Dear Mom,

Got your last letter yesterday. Thanks. This has been a busy week. There was a big July 4th parade in downtown Jacksonville on Saturday. We had to march in formation for about three miles. It was hot as hell and nothing to drink. A couple of guys literally fell out from the heat. Then, I think our drill officers decided they needed to make up for the time we lost on Saturday (like marching in uniform in the Florida summer heat wasn't enough), so they've worked us harder than usual for most of this week.

I saw in the Navy Times where Pres. Johnson signed the Civil Rights Act. I can tell you the Black guys here were happy about that. I think it's a great way to honor Kennedy. I mean it's the right thing to do, too, but Kennedy really worked hard for this and I'm glad Johnson made it happen. I know Dr. King has to feel a great sense of accomplishment, too.

What we're seeing in the NT about Vietnam is pretty scary. It really looks like things there are on a hair trigger, like any little thing could set things off. I'm just glad I joined the Navy and not the Marines or the Army. So, what's the news from home? Anything big happen in Palatka? I'm joking, of course.

Well, I need to run, literally run. Keep those cards and letters coming!

Love,
Sam

---

30 July, 1964
NAS JAX
Dear Mom,

Sorry it's been so long since my last letter. Thanks for yours and for the clippings from the Daily News. Looks like life in Palatka is going on without me! I was really shocked and sad to see Mr. Crandell died. I really didn't know he was sick. He was always one of my favorite teachers. I'm sorry Clint won't get to have him. He made history interesting (which is hard to do). If you could send me Mrs. Crandell's address, I'd like to write her to tell her what he meant to me. You know, he's the only other person besides you and Clint who I told. He was very kind and really helped me think through a lot of things.

Here's the big news from here! Drum roll, please. I have my rating (my job)! I'm going to be training as an air traffic controller. It's what I had requested, so I guess my test score was high enough. That means I'll probably be either on a Naval Air Base or on an aircraft carrier. One of my buddies, though, got assigned to engineering, meaning he may end up in the loud, hot, cramped engine room of a ship. He is not happy.

What news there is about Vietnam in the Navy Times is not good. And I guess they never found those students in Miss. I haven't seen or heard anything about that in a while. I think they're dead. Some rednecks snatched them and murdered them I bet. Well, enough depressing talk.

Got to go. Keep those letters coming (and maybe you could squeeze a few brownies in the envelope)!

Love you,
Sam

10 Aug., 1964
NAS JAX
Dear Mom,

Thanks for your last letter and for the box of brownies! For about 10 minutes, I was the most popular guy in the barracks! They were delicious. Anytime you want to do that again will be fine.

Of course, the big news here (like everywhere) is the Vietnamese attack on the Maddox. I'm not sure we're getting the whole story, but it's got everybody here pretty worked up. It really looks like things are getting hot over there and that the Navy's going to be right in the middle of it. From what I read in the Navy Times, it looks like Congress is going to give Johnson the authority to send troops over there. This could get really ugly really fast.

I've started training for my rating (my job). I'm really enjoying it. It's a lot more technical than I thought it would be, a lot more math and physical science, plus all the operating procedures, etc. It's right up my alley, though. A lot of stuff I enjoy. Other than this, things are about the same with less PT. I did get a bump in rank. I'm now a Seaman Apprentice. The only difference is a little bit more in my pay.

The guys in my barracks have jelled into a pretty close unit. Of course, we'll all get sent in different directions in a short while. That makes it hard to make close friendships. There's one guy I really like. We're pretty close. He's from Demopolis, Alabama (yes, that's a real place) and talks like a hick, but he's really smart and funny and kind. I'm not getting my hopes up (not TOO far, anyway).

Well, got to go. Keep those letters (and brownies) coming. (Cookies would be fine, too.)

Love,
Sam

---

9 September, 1964
NAS JAX
Dear Mom,

Sorry it's been a while since my last letter. It's been crazy around here lately. It's obvious that things are heating up in Vietnam because the general activity level here has been ratchetted up. All we did on Labor Day was labor! My training is going really well. This job was made for me.

I guess you made it through the storm OK. It was not much of an event here. They closed the flight line for a day or so, but that was about it. A lot of rain and some strong gusts. I know it was worse down state, though.

Remember that guy from Alabama I told you about? Well, his name is James (not Jim!) Boatwright. We got a 6 hour pass last week, and he and I and a few other guys rode the city busses out to Jacksonville Beach. We had a great time, and it was nice to spend some time with James away from the base, uniforms, etc. He seems like he might be interested in me, but I'm not sure and too scared to take a chance. If I read his signals wrong, it could go really bad for me. He may just be a really nice guy.

Oh, by the way, we've had or formal pictures done and they'll be delivered to you. When they come, please give one to Clint for me. I've had a couple of letters from him. His mom sent cookies, too. I really miss them. I really hate not being around to keep an eye on him and keep him headed the right way. I guess I feel responsible for him in some way. He's the closest thing I have to a little brother.

Well, I guess I need to sign off. I miss you and hope to get home for Christmas.

Love,
Sam

19 Sept., 1964
NAS JAX
Dear Mom,

Thanks for your letter. I got one from Clint, too, so it was a big week for me for mail. There's really not much news to report from here. My training is really intense these days, but there's a light at the end of the tunnel. My apprenticeship in the control tower should begin in a few weeks and that should come with a new rank and a few more dollars in my paycheck (not that it matters much since there's not much I need to buy and no time to buy it anyway)! Have the portraits come yet? A couple of guys said their folks had received theirs.

I'm hoping for a pass at Thanksgiving to come home for a few days. Would it be OK if I invited James to come with me (if he can get a pass, too)? Now that we're both training for our ratings, we don't see much of each other. That one afternoon at the beach is really the only time we've spent off-base. I guess the threat of more involvement in Vietnam has the upper brass hyped up about getting us ready, but there's just not been any down time in weeks.

I saw something in the Navy Times about the Warren Commission Report. I guess they decided Oswald acted alone when he killed Kennedy. It still makes me wonder if Ruby shot Oswald to shut him up about a conspiracy, but I guess the Commission has looked at everything.

Well, on that high note, I'll close.

Love and miss you.
Sam

17 October, 1964
NAS JAX
Dear Mom,

I'm so sorry for not writing in so long. Thanks for your letters despite my lack of a reply. I know we've talked on the phone a few times, but letters are different. I'll try to do better. Also, thanks for the banana bread. It was delicious. All the guys send their love!

If things had been intense here before, they are at an even higher level of intensity now. I don't think there's any question now but that we're going into a full-out war footing.

To bring you up to speed, as you know, I'm training in the control tower now. It's very intense. We know that one mistake could be catastrophic, and the level of concentration required to do this job is enormous. I know I can do it, but sometimes I wonder how guys do this day in and day out without cracking up (particularly in a combat situation like on a carrier.)

On another subject, have you seen anything of the Coopers? I haven't heard from Clint in a long time and the last letter I had from him was really short, just a thank-you for the picture. I don't know, I think something's going on with him, or maybe he's just sort of moved on and really doesn't need me like he used to. Anyway, if you talk to his mom or grandmother, see what you can find out, OK?

In other news (as Cronkite might say) I'm not going to get home at Thanksgiving, but they've promised me I'll get a pass for Christmas. I'm pretty bummed out about it, but maybe I'll get to stay longer when I come next month.

Well, that's about all the news from here, so I'll sign off.
Love,
Sam

14 November, 1964
NAS JAX
Dear Mom,

It seems like I begin every letter apologizing for not writing more often. I know you say it's fine, but I still feel bad I don't write more often (not that there's a lot to write about).

Without going into a lot of details, I finally heard from Clint this week. The reason I hadn't heard from him in so long was because he was feeling like I was abandoning him, like our friendship didn't matter to me. At first, it made me kind of mad, but then I tried to see things through his eyes, and I realized I had probably sent him some mixed messages. In his letter, he confessed that he knew he was wrong the way he was seeing things. Anyway, I think we have things worked out now, but I really need to spend some time with him when I'm home at Christmas to just reassure him that everything's good between us.

Speaking of Christmas, my pass is supposed to start on December 18 at O-seven-hundred hours (that's 7:00 am for you non-military types). I hate to ask this, but do you think you could pick me up because the bus to Palatka doesn't stop outside the base until 11:20 that morning, and doesn't get to Palatka until 12:55? If you could be at the main gate by 7:30 it would be great. Just let me know, and if it won't work out, I'll take the bus. By the way, I have to report back to base by 7:00 pm on the 28th. Of course, all that could change. I won't really believe it until I walk out the main gate.

I guess you weren't surprised that Johnson won. It was kind of a landslide. I'm glad because there's a lot of Kennedy's legacy that needs to be finished. Not that Johnson won't have his own legacy, but you know what I mean.

85

In local news, there's a rumor going around here that the DOD is planning to close a bunch of bases. I don't think anybody really thinks NAS JAX would be one of them, but there does seem to be some concern. With everything heating up in Vietnam, that seems kind of nuts to me, but, hey, what do I know?

Well, I need to close for now.

Love you.
Sam

---

16 January, ~~1964~~ 1965
NAS JAX
Hi, Mom.

I still can't get used to writing 1965! It's been crazy here since I got back to base. It seems like, during the time I was on leave, everything here ratcheted up a few notches. There's just a tension all over the base. I can't really explain it, but I can sure feel it. It's obvious the brass are getting ready for things to get real in Vietnam. Most of the guys I hang out with went home for Christmas and pretty much all of them felt like they might not get home again for a long time.

By the way, thanks for your letter and the news from the big city. I'm really glad you're helping with the Azalea Festival this year. I know you used to enjoy doing that. Just don't try picking out one of those pretty girls for me!

I got a letter from Clint full of questions and pretty deep thoughts. The kid is really growing up. He said some really nice things about my influence in his life (almost made me cry!). He seems to be coming to terms with the fact that I'm pretty much gone from his life now. It's tough for both of us, but it's just the way things are now.

So, when I got back here, some of our regular assignments had been shuffled around and I'm now cleaning and waxing the floor in the officers' mess every Tuesday night. It has to be done after they shut down for the night, so it really makes for a long day for me. At least it's not a big room.

Everything else here is about the same. My training in the control tower is really going well. More and more, they're giving me more independence and just offering advice when I need it rather than telling me every little thing to do. As a result, I'm gaining a lot more confidence. So far, I haven't crashed an aircraft, so that's in my favor!

Well, time to go for now. Cookies? Brownies?

Love,
Sam

---

6 February, 1965
NAS JAX
Hi, Mom.

Just a quick note to catch you up. Thanks for your care package with the cookies and stuff. I really appreciate it.

I had a letter from Clint. Somehow, his uncle who works at Cape Canaveral got them a pass to a family day tour later this month and they're going to get to see where it all happens! I'm kind of jealous, but really excited for them that they get to do this.

Not much different here. I'm still fighting with that damn floor machine every Tuesday night. I don't know how much longer I'll have to do this job, but the end can't come too soon.

I'm still trying to figure out what I did wrong to get this job.

I hope you're sitting down, but I've started going to chapel. Believe it or not, I really enjoy it. It's really informal and a really different environment in which to get to know other sailors, and even some officers who seem to put their rank aside at chapel. There's also a class I'm going to on Sunday evening. It's more like a religious discussion group, but really enjoyable and really stretches my thinking about things.

Well, it's almost lights out, so I need to wrap this up. I'll try to write more later (although my life is pretty boring).

Love,
Sam

---

21 February, 1965
NAS JAX
Dear Mom,

This is hard to write, but I need to tell you about something that happened last night and get your advice. Let me get right to it. You remember my friend James, right? Well, I've really screwed up our friendship. Mom, I thought he liked me as more than a friend, so, yesterday I asked him if he wanted to catch a movie on base and he said "Sure." So, we went to the movie and as we were sitting in the dark, I reached over and took his hand. Well, he jerked his hand away and said, pretty loudly, "What's wrong with you?" Then he got up and left. I tried to follow him to apologize, but he told me to "get the hell away" from him, that he wasn't "like that" and that he didn't ever want to talk to me again.

You know this could be really bad for me if he tells anybody about this. I could even get kicked out of the Navy. I really don't know what to do. I'm hoping after he cools down he'll let me talk to him and apologize. I'm really hoping he at least cares about me as a friend and won't ruin my life and my career in the Navy. Right now, I'm just about to come unglued. I have to keep myself together and do my job and just hope this blows over, but I'm scared to death and worried sick.

Anyway, if you have any ideas, please let me know. I just wanted you to know what happened. I am going to talk to the chaplain. I really trust him and maybe he'll have some advice.

Pray for me. I love you.

Sam

---

27 February, 1965
NAS JAX
Dear Mom,

Thanks for your note. Your advice was pretty much the same thing the chaplain told me: Keep my head down and hope this will blow over. He's very understanding, but he didn't understate the realities of what could happen to me if this got bumped up the ladder. I asked him if he would help me talk to James. He said he would if James would agree.

Unfortunately, it's not looking like James is going to let this die. I tried to talk to him on Monday evening, and he pushed me away and yelled "Keep the f--k away from me, you freak!" There were other guys within hearing distance of this and it was pretty awkward, especially since he and I have been friends since we first got to boot camp. I haven't tried to talk to him again.

Also, there have been a couple of incidents this week that I know came from him. On Tuesday night, when I went to crawl into my bunk, it had been short sheeted. This is pretty juvenile, but it's not the sort of thing that goes on around here, either. Then, on Thursday morning, when I went to dress, my boots were missing from my footlocker. I found them in the yard outside the barracks.

Of course, James is completely avoiding me, and maybe one or two other guys are acting weird around me. Most of the guys are acting normal, so I don't think James has told many others. I know these two things are pretty minor, but I also know he's sending a message.

I'm just trying to do my job and avoid drawing attention to myself. Don't worry about me. I'll get through this.

Love,
Sam

---

7 March, 1965
NAS JAX
Dear Mom,

Thanks for your letter. It really gave me a boost this week. It's been a hard week, but I'm pushing through. There's at least one other guy that James has told. His name is Steve Reynolds. I know James has him working for him to make things hard for me. Wednesday evening at dinner, he walked by where I was sitting and dropped a lit cigarette right into my food. Just walked by, dropped the cigarette, and kept walking.

The other thing this week happened sometime Tuesday evening. You know I do the floors in the officers' mess on Tuesday night, so I get in late. So that night, when I got in, someone had scribbled FAG on the top of my footlocker in big letters. It was right there where everyone could see it and they DID see it. Everybody was looking at me really weirdly. It was pretty awful. I hope I'm wrong, but it seems like it's getting worse, and there's really nothing I can do about it because I can't tell anyone except the chaplain, and there's nothing he can do either.

I'm just hoping they'll get tired of making the effort to mess with me and go on to someone else. I guess the really surprising thing is I would never in a million years thought James would act this way toward another person. I always thought he was exceptionally kind. Just goes to show how wrong we can be about people sometimes.

I guess you saw the news about what happened today in Selma, Alabama. That was just awful. I just hope it makes people wake up to what's going on.

Well, I need to go.

Love,
Sam

I had come to the final letter. Knowing I was about to read the last words Sam had written to his mother, I was gripped by a dark sadness.

16 March, 1965
NAS JAX
Dear Mom,

Thanks for your letter. These days, it feels like you're the only one in my corner. I know Clint would be if he knew about all this, but I've not told him and don't intend to. It would really upset him. He has such a sense of justice, and there's nothing he could do about this.

Anyway, things are at least as bad, if not worse than they were when I wrote you last. I'm pretty much ignored by most of the guys in my barracks. The only time I really feel at ease is when I'm on the job. Nobody in the tower seems to know, or if they do, they don't care. I pretty much eat by myself now. Some guys avoid me and some I don't want to assume they want me sitting down beside them in the mess.

Last Sunday, we had an inspection by a big wig and were supposed to wear our cracker jacks (our dress blues). On Saturday, I took mine out to make sure they didn't need ironing and discovered someone had urinated on them!

Fortunately, I was able to get to the commissary and buy a new set, switch over my insignia and all, and was OK for Sunday. I didn't even bother to try to find out who did this. I'm pretty sure I already know.

I know if I can just endure this stuff until I finish training, I'll be reassigned somewhere else and get away from all this. This has been a hard lesson.

Thanks for always being in my corner, Mom. I know this upsets you, but I'm OK. It's not long until this is all behind me.

Love,
Sam

By the time I had read the final letter in the series, I was convinced Mrs. Sanders' concerns were well-founded and that there was sufficient information in Sam's letters to warrant further investigation. All the things Sam had mentioned—the incident with James Boatwright and the escalating harassment that followed—were new to me. Sam had never hinted at any of that in his letters to me. Emotionally drained, I headed off to bed, but sleep was elusive, and I tossed for much of the night, unable to clear my mind of the dread that had overtaken me.

Early the next morning, I drove back to my parents' house before I knew my mother would have left for work. After a few pleasantries, I made up some excuse to rummage around in my old room looking for Sam's letters. I found them bundled with a couple of brittle rubber bands in a drawer with old newspaper clippings. Following a hasty good-bye to Mom, I drove to my office, closed the door, and began a read-through of Sam's letters to me. As I had recalled the evening before, there was no mention of James Boatwright or the harassment Sam had received leading up to his death. I knew he had shielded me from all that, knowing how upset it would have made me.

The last letter in the stack was unlike all the others. It was the last letter I had written Sam. It had arrived at the naval base shortly after his death and had eventually been returned to me, unopened. Years before, when it was returned, I had not opened it, but placed it with his other letters to me. It remained unopened still. I picked up the yellowed envelope and looked at the address on the front—written in my eighth-grade hand. Sam's Navy address had been scratched through and a purple stamp showing a pointing hand read "Return to Sender." Below the hand was a short list of possible reasons the letter was being returned. The option that read "Addressee no longer at this address" had been checked—an explanation packed with cruel irony. Grabbing my letter opener, I sliced the top of the envelope and withdrew the letter. The notebook paper was brittle and yellowed, as was the envelope. I unfolded it carefully and began to read. A few lines into the first paragraph, I was crushed by an intolerable weight of grief and found myself sobbing.

2 April, 1965
Palatka, FL
Hey, Sam.

Hope you're doing good. I'm fine here. Will and Mom and Dad are all doing well, too. Man, I have some news for you! So, you know they have a spring dance every year at school. So, I didn't go last year, but I really wanted to go this year, and I wanted to take Christine. But I was really scared to ask her, so I talked with my mom and she basically told me there was no way around it. If I wanted her to go with me the only thing I could do was ask her. So I did on the way to school this morning. I was scared to death. My heart was beating like a mile a minute. And she said yes! So, I'm going on my first date in a couple of weeks. I have to get a new suit (nothing I have fits me anymore) and get her one of those flower things girls wear (I can't remember the name of those things) one she can wear on her wrist so it won't get smushed in all the slow dances! So, anyway, that's my big news.

So how are you doing? Do you know where you'll be going after you finish training there? Do you think you'll be able to come home anytime soon? Man, I miss you. Take care of yourself.

Love,
Clint

When I recovered some degree of composure, I folded the letter and placed it back in its envelope. I then neatly stacked the entire group of letters, placed them into my brief case and buzzed Paula to set up a conference with Mrs. Sanders as soon as possible.

11.

WHERE TO NEXT?

TWO DAYS LATER, Mrs. Sanders was back in my office. With little preamble, I got down to business. "Mrs. Sanders, I've read through all the letters, those to you and to me, and I agree with you that there's good reason to believe that Sam's death was something other than an accident. I also agree that we need to look into this further."

She sighed and visibly brightened. "Oh, thank you. I'm so relieved. You know, I've been mulling this over in my head for so many years. I was afraid I was just obsessing over things that weren't there. Thank you, Clint, for looking at this and for being willing to dig even deeper."

"You're welcome, but, after reading the letters, there's no way I would not look further into this. So, I have some questions I need to ask you if you're up for it."

"Certainly. Anything."

"OK. First, I assume all our letters to Sam are missing?"

"That's right. They weren't in his things that the Navy sent back to me. Honestly, I was in such a state at the time, I didn't think to ask about them. But, no, they were never returned."

"But in the things that were returned, were there personal items, perhaps other letters, notebooks or diaries?"

"There were a few letters, yes. No diaries or notebooks, but other personal things like his shaving kit, personal items of clothing, things like that."

"Was there anything you think might help us better understand what was going on in his life near the time of his death?"

"Nothing that I can think of, but you're welcome to look through those things. I'm embarrassed to say I've never done anything to his room. It's pretty much the way he left it. I wasn't trying to make a shrine or anything. I guess I've just always felt like keeping his room the same helps me keep a part of him. I go in there about twice a month and dust and vacuum, and cry some, but nothing's really changed. The box that they shipped his things back to me in is still sitting on his desk where it's been for, what is it, fourteen years?"

"Yes ma'am, fourteen years. And, yes, I'd like to look at that stuff if I could. Would it be convenient if I swung by on Sunday after lunch? I promised my mom I'd go to church and eat Sunday dinner with them, so I'll be in the neighborhood."

"Yes, that would be fine."

"Next question. I was thinking about Sam's funeral, and I remember three sailors sitting in the very back of the chapel. Honestly, I remember them looking very, I don't know, very uncomfortable, like they felt unwelcomed or that they shouldn't be there. Of course, it could be nothing, but it made a lasting impression on me because they didn't act like they were friends grieving the death of a friend. Do you know who they were?"

"No, I don't. I do know they were not part of the six sailors who made up the honor guard. And I also know they were not at the graveside service."

"I remember that, too. They must have left right after the service at the chapel ended. Something else, and this is a stretch, but have you had any sort of contact over the years with the chaplain who officiated the service."

"No. The last time I saw him was at the graveside. Come to think of it, I did get a nice note from him a week or so after the funeral. Would it help if I could find it?"

"It might. It would probably have his full name on it and might help me track him down. I'd like to talk with him. I know Sam shared some things with him that he might be able to discuss with me now that he's not bound by clergy confidentiality."

"Alright. I'll see if I can locate it."

"That's about all the questions I have at the moment, but I know there'll be more as I look into things."

"Where do you start with something like this, Clint? I mean, it's been almost fifteen years and everything's gone cold."

"Well, I have a call in to the base commander at NAS Jacksonville. I'm asking for a meeting with him and to see any records they have, including an autopsy report. Also, I want to see Sam's service record. I also want to meet with the JAG officer in charge at the base. Next, I'm going to try to track down James Boatright and Steve Reynolds and anyone else who was partners with them in harassing Sam. I'm also going to try to track down the chaplain. So, I've got my work cut out for me."

"Yes, I see you do. Clint, I need to be honest with you. I don't have a lot of money to spend on this. As much as I want answers, I can't afford much of an investigation."

"Mrs. Sanders, you're not paying me one cent for this. This is as important to me as it is to you, and I'm going to move heaven and earth to find out what happened. We may not like what I find, but at least we'll have some answers. But, no, this is my gift to Sam and to you, and to myself, too, to try to get to the truth here."

She teared up, hugged me, and made her way to the office door. "Thank you, Clint. I'll see you Sunday afternoon."

"Yes, ma'am. I'll see you then."

That Sunday, after an enormous meal with my parents, I walked down to Mrs. Sanders' home. She greeted me at the door and led me to Sam's room. As I stepped inside my knees buckled. The room was just as I remembered—albeit a bit tidier. Still suspended from the ceiling was the model of the Mercury launch system—the massive Mercury Redstone rocket, the crew capsule, and escape system. On the shelves were the books he had read and passed on to me to read. There, in its hallowed place, was the model of the F-86 Sabre—the plane his father had flown during the Korean War.

"The box of stuff they sent back is over there on the desk. I'll leave you alone while you look through it."

"Yes ma'am. Thank you." I stepped over to the desk, pulled out the desk chair and sat, breathing heavily, suffering from the sudden shock of feeling eight years old again—nervous, insecure, and vulnerable. After a few minutes, my breathing slowed, and I regained my emotional balance. I stood and opened the box. Inside were several pairs each of socks and underwear, a small stack of old *Newsweek* magazines, several yellowed copies of the *Navy Times,* Sam's shaving kit, about five dollars in cash and change, a rabbit's foot on a small beaded chain, and four items I found of interest—two letters from David Robinson, a friend with whom Sam had served on the County Youth Biracial Committee, a letter from Christine, and a business card for Capt. Timothy Adamson, Chaplain, United States Navy. I extracted these items from the box and sat down to look at them more closely.

The three letters were all dated during the mid-summer to mid-fall of 1964—the year Sam entered the Navy in June. The letter from Christine was simply a sweet note wishing him luck in the service. One line, however, jumped out at me and caused an audible chuckle: "Don't worry, Sam. I'll keep an eye on Clint for you."

The two letters from David Robinson were written after he had begun college at Old Dominion in the fall. They were filled with news about campus activities, his hopes that Lyndon Johnson would be re-elected, and word that he had joined the campus chapter of the Black Panther Party. There were no references in either letter to Sam's Navy life or, as they were written months before, to the hardships that preceded his death.

Chaplain Adamson's business card was the only useful artifact in the box. It provided his full name and rank at the time of Sam's death—information that might make it easier to track him down. I placed the letters back in the box, slipped the Chaplain's card into my shirt pocket and stood to leave the room. As my eyes swept the familiar space, I once again experienced the emotional dislocation that had struck me a few minutes earlier when first I entered. I found Mrs. Sanders waiting for me in the living room.

"Did you find anything in there that could help you?"

"Well, actually, I did. I found Chaplain Adamson's card that has enough information on it that I might be able to track him down."

"Oh, good. Also, here is the note he wrote me after Sam's funeral. You keep it with the other letters until this runs its course."

"Thank you, ma'am. I will."

"So, where do you go from here?"

"Well, I have an appointment on Tuesday with the JAG officer in charge of legal services on the base. The base commander sort of handed me off to him. His secretary told Paula in my office that the JAG office could offer me more help, so that's where I'm heading next. I'll call you after that meeting to give you an update."

"Thank you, Clint, and thanks for taking this on."

"You're welcome, but there's no way I would let this sit after what I read in those letters. I'll be in touch." She walked me to the door. I walked back to my parents' house and drove to my apartment. There, I opened and read the note to Mrs. Sanders from Chaplain Adamson.

14 April, 1965
NAS Jacksonville
Dear Mrs. Sanders,

It was an honor for me to officiate at the service for your son, Seaman Samuel A. Sanders. I had known Sam for several months before his death and grew to admire him greatly. As you well know, Sam was exceptionally bright and intuitive. He was always well informed on current national and global events and frequently brought his unique perspectives on those things into our Sunday evening study sessions. After Sam joined our little Sunday evening group, our discussions grew much more focused and, shall I say, passionate.

The circumstances of Sam's death were so random and unexpected that I still have trouble accepting them, as I know you must. His loss is a great loss to the Navy and to our nation. Please accept my deepest sympathies and be assured of my prayers for you as you walk through these difficult days of grief. If I can ever be of help to you, please don't hesitate to contact me. I've enclosed my card for your convenience.

Sincerely,
Capt. Tim Adamson, Chaplain
United States Navy

The card the Chaplain had provided Mrs. Sanders was identical to the one that I had found in the box of Sam's effects in his room, so I slipped it back into the envelope with the note. My sincere hope was that the path would open to me as I pressed this investigation and that the coming days would yield answers for both Sam's mother and for me.

PART III

12.

BIG IVAN

IN THE FALL of 1961, October 30 to be precise, the Soviet Union tested a thermonuclear device that remains to this day the largest explosive device ever detonated. Code named "Ivan" by the Soviets, and dubbed "Tsar Bomba"[6] by the West, the device yielded a blast roughly equivalent to fifty megatons of TNT and registered 5.0 on the Richter Scale. I was nine years old at the time and knew very few details of this event, but certainly experienced the societal aftershocks. In short, we now understood the gravity of the nuclear arms race and the tenuous deterrence keeping the superpowers from using these devastating weapons.

Even in Palatka, I began to notice changes—small signs going up around the downtown area indicating that certain structures were designated as fallout shelters. In school, teachers began showing Civil Defense films depicting the effects of a nuclear detonation and ways to shield oneself from the worst of the

[6] Tsar Bomba (a/k/a Big Ivan) was a Soviet-made hydrogen bomb and remains, to this day, the most powerful nuclear weapon every created and tested. On October 30, 1961, the bomb was detonated approximately 13,000 feet above Severny Island in the Barents Sea north of central Russia. Though the detonation was intended by the Soviets to be secret, the US had a reconnaissance aircraft aloft in the area—close enough that its paint was scorched by the blast. The resulting blast is estimated to have been 50 megatons—approximately 3,300 times the power of the atomic bomb dropped on Hiroshima near the end of World War II. The resulting mushroom cloud climbed 42 miles (67.6 km) into the mesosphere and all buildings in the village of Severny were destroyed.

blast. We began having duck-and-cover drills in our classroom, with instructions to avoid the windows in the event of a nuclear attack. All of this impressed on my young mind the certainty of an imminent nuclear exchange with the Soviets. It seemed to me that the adults in charge of the planet had decided that nuclear war was inevitable—it was just a question of when and how it would begin. I'm confident that, since that period in our history, there have been numerous studies exploring the lasting effects of this tension on developing minds, but anecdotally I can attest to its lasting effects on me—in some ways, even to this day.

That fall also brought changes to my friendship with Sam. He had entered high school that September and was suddenly much busier than he had been in the past. In the mornings, as I walked toward my school, I would often pass him going the opposite direction toward the high school. For the first two weeks of the new school year, other than those occasional brief meeting in the morning, I didn't see him at all. I began to worry and brood—has he outgrown me? Does he no longer want to be seen with a little kid like me? My concern grew with each passing day to the point that it consumed an inordinate amount of my free time.

One morning in mid-September, as I was walking toward my school, I saw Sam in the distance walking toward me. I decided I was going to confront him. As he neared, he spoke first. "Morning, buddy."

"Do you not like me anymore?"

"What? Why would you ask that?"

"Because we don't ever do anything together anymore. I figured you didn't want to hang around with a little kid anymore." At that point, I lost it, and the tears began to flow.

"Whoa, man! That is not true at all. I've just been really busy since school started. Plus, my school work is kicking my butt. I wasn't avoiding you at all. I'm sorry. I've just been busy. Come here." I stumbled toward him and he pulled me into a hug. "I'm really sorry. I didn't mean to hurt your feelings. We're still best buddies."

"OK (sniff). I just didn't know (sniff). It just seemed like you were avoiding me (sniff, sniff)."

"No, man. Just busy. That's all. Honest. Hey, let me make it up to you. You want to go to the football game Friday night? The Maroons are playing St. Augustine. You want to go?"

"Sure! I'll have to ask my Mom and Dad, but yeah, that'd be cool."

"OK, you ask them and call me. OK? I'll get us tickets after they say it's OK. Hey, I gotta run or I'm gonna miss the first bell. I'll see you later."

"OK (sniff)." Suddenly, in those few brief moments, my world was put right, everything back in place. How easily is the young heart wounded, and how quickly does it heal! Of course, my parents agreed that I could go to the game with Sam. The stadium was quite literally within sight of our front door, so all we had to do was walk a block, past Crazy Christine's house, and we were there.

I was more excited over the prospects of this adventure with Sam than I had been over anything in my life up to that point. Friday evening could not come soon enough. To make things even better, Mom had gone to J.C. Penney's and bought me an official deep burgundy Palatka Maroons football jersey in a size that all but swallowed me. (She said it was the smallest size they had.) Sam had said he would come by around 6:30. The game was to start at 7:00. So, at 5:30 I was dressed in jeans and my new jersey waiting nervously on the couch and watching Superman as a distraction. Sam had said we would get hotdogs and Cokes at the game, so Mom let me skip dinner. Determined not to move an inch from the couch until Sam arrived, I fidgeted through the local news. Right on time, Sam arrived and, after a quick word to my parents—and some cash stuffed into his hand by my dad—off we went.

As we walked past Crazy Christine's house a question that had been bothering me surfaced. "Sam, what's a maroon, anyway?"

He laughed. "Well, as I understand it, a maroon is a person stranded on an island, like shipwrecked, like Robinson Crusoe. I have no idea why they chose that name for the high school football team."

"But maroon is a color, too, right, like this shirt?"

"Yeah. By the way, it's called a jersey. But, yeah, that color is maroon too, or burgundy."

"I thought football teams were supposed to be named after strong, scary animals, like bears or tigers or something."

"Yeah. I agree. I really don't know where Maroons came from, but a lot of people at school want to change the name. They say it also means a runaway Negro slave, that a maroon could be a Black person, so they want to change the name."

"That's a dumb reason. It's just 'cause they don't like Negroes, right?"

"Yep. That's why. Anyway, tonight, they're the Maroons, so let's go yell for them!"

Maroon Stadium—the name was emblazoned along the length of the back of the west grandstand—was quite familiar to me. It was never locked, so provided a convenient playground for our neighborhood gang. However, I had never been inside at night when the field was lighted. As we entered, it seemed an altogether different place than the one in which we often played. The bright green field was striped in white. There were banners—"Go Maroons, Beat Jackets"—in burgundy and white stretched along the infield fence. The Maroon Marching Band sat in the east stands in their burgundy and white uniforms playing fight songs. On the field, the team members were warming up with practice hikes, punts, and passes. The cheerleaders were on the infield in front of the band leading the gathering students in cheers. It was all so festive, colorful, and exciting. It was also the first football game I had ever attended. Though I knew something of the game from watching NFL games with my family, this was far more exciting—and the opening kickoff was yet to come!

As we entered, we stopped and queued up at the concession stand to purchase hotdogs and Cokes, then made our way to the student section on the far side of the field. Sam spotted a group of his friends, a couple of whom I knew, and we climbed up to sit with them. Sam introduced me as his "buddy, Clint," and that seemed sufficient. I was quickly welcomed and assimilated into the world of high school, if only as something of a mascot. I'm confident the jersey helped.

There is no question but that the game was the most exciting event I had attended to that point in my young life. The cheers, the yelling, the band, the ups and downs, the sounds of contact on the field, all combined to keep my adrenaline elevated for most of the game. By the fourth quarter, however, I crashed and ended up dozing off with my head in Sam's lap. He roused me at the end of the game, and we walked home without talking— me in something of a stupor. The next weeks unfolded with a renewed familiarity, and all seemed to have been restored between Sam and me.

At some point during that previous summer, a young couple had moved into one of the new homes that had been built across the street from Sam. The young husband was a professor at the new junior college in town and his wife the new librarian at the junior high school. I don't quite remember how it began, but a group of us—Sam and Crazy Christine included—began to gather at their home in the afternoons after school to play football. The professor, who insisted we call him Adam, was right in the thick of it with us, and it was a novelty for us to have an adult playing with us. After about three weeks of this, we had managed to destroy their front lawn, so we moved our games down the street to the elementary school yard. It was there, one afternoon in late October, and in the middle of a pass play, that a formation of fighter jets buzzed our game so near the field that most of us sprawled face down on the ground.

"Something's going on," yelled Professor Adam over the deafening sound. That evening, Walter Cronkite told us the Soviets had detonated Big Ivan.

After that evening in October when Sam took me to the football game, things between us returned to normal—which is not to say that he didn't need to remind me, from time to time, that he was busier and less available to me now that he was in high school. During that fall, our time together consisted mostly of afternoon football with other neighborhood kids and Professor Adam, occasional bike rides, and dinners at each other's homes. One addition, however, was that Sam began teaching me to play chess. Though it took me weeks to simply master the movements of the various pieces, Sam was patient and brought me along to the point where, by December, I was able to look a few moves ahead. As I became more comfortable with the game, Sam began to explain to me ways I could shape his moves by carefully planning my own. At times, this seemed far too complicated for me, but gradually I began to grasp the strategic nature of the game.

One other event of note that fall was the successful NASA mission, in late November, that placed Enos, a chimpanzee, into orbit around the earth. Sam was very excited by the successful completion of this mission. He explained to me that we would next place an astronaut into orbit, and, when we did, we would catch up with the Russians. Catching up and keeping up with the Russians had, by this time, become a national obsession. Whereas the arms race was the tactical side of this competition and engendered fear in both American and Soviet citizens alike, the race to space was the element that most engendered national pride. Thus, the primate Enos took his place among the heroes of this fierce struggle to claim the stars.

The year ended with Christmas and my tenth birthday. Now that my age had entered double digits, I somehow felt much older—perhaps because I felt the age gap between Sam and me had somehow narrowed.

13.

1962, AND THE SUMMER OF BEING CONTENT

EARLY IN THE new year, Sam and I began making regular trips to the convenience store up the hill from my house. The objective of these excursions was to check out any newly arrived comic books. Sam had begun collecting them and would typically purchase one or two on each visit to the store. The comics were arranged on a large newsstand case on the opposite side from the store manager's position at the check-out counter. The manager was a young fellow who seemed oblivious to the fact that we often spent thirty to forty-five minutes behind the display reading comics and placing them back on the shelf. Sam was very selective of the issues he purchased, preferring Marvel to the other publishers. After reading his new acquisitions at home, Sam placed them in clear plastic sleeves and stored them in a large flat box under his bed. By the time he left to enter the Navy, Sam had a collection of around two hundred comics, including every comic featuring Spider-Man[7] Marvel had published up until that summer.

---

[7] Spider-Man's first appearance in a Marvel comic was in the summer of 1962 in an issue titled *Amazing Fantasy #15*. Creators Stan Lee and Steve Ditko diverged from their typical pattern of providing a teenaged sidekick for their adult superheroes and featured angst-ridden teen Peter Parker as the hero himself, struggling to understand and use his newly acquired superpowers. Perhaps the most enduring of all Marvel's stable of superheroes, Spider-Man has continued to live in comic books and has been the central protagonist in a number of highly successful films. In 2019, a single copy of *Amazing Fantasy #15* sold at auction for $1.1 million.

It was on one of these comic purchasing trips that I became acquainted with Alfred E. Neuman, the ubiquitous mascot of *Mad* magazine. On that particular afternoon, sometime around mid-January, I spied a magazine with Neuman's face on the cover. He was a round-headed, freckled, gap-toothed man-child of indeterminate age who exuded fun and mischief. I picked up the magazine and stared intently at the cover.

"You better stay away from that," Sam warned.

"Why? Does it have dirty pictures in it or something?"

"No. Nothing like that. It's just kinda, I don't know, rude. Do you know what satirical is?"

"No. What does that mean?"

"Satire, satirical stuff, is like stuff that pokes fun at important people or ideas. *Mad* is a satirical magazine. It pokes fun at politicians, at famous people, at movies, stuff in the news, and it pokes fun at adults."

"So, what's wrong with that?"

"I'm just not sure your folks would want you looking at that. I mean, it can be pretty disrespectful in the things it pokes fun at."

"So, who's this on the front?"

"That's Alfred E. Newman. He's like their mascot or something. He's on the cover of every issue and in everything inside."

"Is he a kid or an adult?"

"He's a kid, but he's the kind of kid adults would call a smart ass. Nothing's off limits or sacred to him or to the magazine."

"I don't know. Sounds like something I'd like."

"OK, I'm just warning you."

So, with a few coins from Sam, I purchased that issue of *Mad*. However, after reading a few pages, I determined that Sam was right—my parents would not appreciate the humor. As a result, while other ten-year-olds kept bootlegged copies of *Playboy* hidden in their rooms, I kept my copies of *Mad* tucked away and out of sight of my parents.

The school year wound to a close, and I completed fifth grade with better-than-average grades. As Sam wrapped up his first year at the high school, he had fewer constraints on his schedule, and our times together became more frequent. One afternoon in early June, Sam announced that he intended to go out for the track team when school opened in the fall. In preparation, he intended to begin running every morning, and wanted to know if I wanted to run with him. Though running was not something I particularly enjoyed, if it meant more time spent with Sam, I was all in. Thus it was, that on an early morning in mid-June, I walked down to Sam's for our first of what would become hundreds, if not thousands, of runs over the next few years. Though I would eventually come to enjoy running with Sam, that first morning—and, for that matter, quite a few mornings to follow—was anything but enjoyable. We set out from Sam's house and jogged down to the elementary school where the track was located. Sam's long strides made it difficult for me to keep up with him, but I was determined not to fall behind. After about half a lap around the track, my lungs were on fire, my legs felt like Jell-O, and I was absolutely certain I was going to vomit at any moment.

"Stop! Stop! I can't go on. I'm gonna puke."

"OK. We'll take a breather, but let's just walk. We don't need to stop completely."

Though Sam was breathing heavily, I was sucking long drafts of air, bent over at the waist with my hands on my knees. "Just let me catch my breath. I thought this would be fun. It's not."

"It'll get easier, I promise. We're both out of shape, but it'll get easier every time we run."

Sam was right. It did get easier, but not for several weeks of almost-daily runs. Each time we ran I could sense my stamina improving, and by about the fifth week, I did not need to stop so frequently to catch my breath. Eventually, we became bored with running the oval track and began making wide loops through the neighborhood. There were few sidewalks, so we were often forced to run in the streets, many of which were paved with brick.

In mid-July, my family took our summer vacation at Manatee Springs State Park. Although we invited Sam to join us, he decided to stay home to continue his training. I was disappointed but soon recovered as we enjoyed two weeks of swimming in the frigid spring water, canoeing and fishing on the Suwannee River, and hiking the nature trails. Of course, every evening included a campfire. It was at those times I missed my friend and often reflected on how different our lives were—him growing up without a father and me with all the benefits of two parents. And, as I drifted off to sleep with the cacophony of cicadas, Whip-poor-wills and tree frogs for a lullaby, I was gripped with dread over how my life would change were I to lose one of my parents or Will.

When we returned from vacation, Sam had decided to begin training for short distance sprints. He was particularly focused on the fifty and hundred-yard dashes, and, while I was away, had bought a rather expensive-looking stopwatch. Thus, our morning runs took on a more structured form. After a cross-country jog, we would end at the track where we would time each other running the fifty and hundred. Sam was determined to make these his races come fall and worked diligently at shaving tenths of seconds off his time.

As July drew to a close, I managed to convince Sam to spend a week with me at my grandmother's home in Campville. In order to for him to agree, I had to promise that we would maintain our training. So, on the first Saturday in August, my dad drove us to Campville. My grandmother's house was an old rambling Cracker-style home that had been expanded over the years. Originally built by my great-grandfather, my grandparents had lived there and enlarged the home as their family grew. My grandfather's medical practice had been headquartered there until his death in the late 1940's, and my grandmother had stayed on. At some point, indoor plumbing had been added, a bathroom tacked onto what was my grandmother's bedroom, and running water piped into the kitchen. Still, at that time, the old outhouse remained, and the well off the back porch still held water.

Sam and I would be sharing the "guest room." It was the largest bedroom in the house and featured a high double feather bed. The bathroom, as I mentioned, was off my grandmother's room so any needs during the night would have to be met using the "slop jar" under the bed. Sam and I agreed that this was a disgusting plan, and determined we would either hold it until morning, or pee off the back porch.

After we had settled into our room, I took Sam outside to explore a bit. I showed him the well with a functioning bucket and winch, and the wringer washing machine on the back porch that my grandmother still used every week. But what most intrigued Sam was the outhouse.

"So, do y'all use this anymore?"

"No, not for years. I guess nobody ever thought about tearing it down."

"You think your grandmother would let us tear it down?'

"I don't know. We can ask her." So, at lunch that day, we secured her permission to undertake the demolition of the old ramshackle outhouse beginning on Monday.

One significant change had occurred in Campville since the previous summer. Living with my grandmother now was her brother, my Great Uncle Albert, who had moved in with her during the winter. We called him Uncle Al. He had never married and seemed content to enjoy the free room, board, and laundry service my grandmother now provided. Uncle Al was eccentric, but quite well educated and conversant in current events. He was an avid reader, smoked a pipe, and loved playing board games—Parcheesi in particular. Although he often recruited me to play with him, I quickly learned that it was in my best interest to let him win.

Though he lived modestly, Uncle Al seemed to have some source of income—perhaps a pension of some sort. In addition, he had wrangled a little job with the Atlantic Coast Line Railroad whereby he was responsible for performing some sort of task on railcars parked along the siding in front of my grandmother's house. That first evening, after dinner, he asked if Sam and I wanted to accompany him to check the fireboxes on the railcars. Of course, we agreed. As it turned out, there were about a half-dozen railcars parked on the siding. Uncle Al said they were there to be loaded with watermelons as soon as the harvest got underway in a week or so. We walked along the siding, and Uncle Al stopped to check each coupling, noisily venting steam from each. He then checked to confirm the switches were properly set to prevent trains from entering the siding, and his workday was done. It seemed to me at the time that, whatever the railroad paid him, it was a cushy job.

Bedtime came early in Campville. With no television, evenings were quiet and typically involved reading. As neither Sam nor I had brought anything to read, we borrowed a couple of Uncle Al's *Hardy Boys* books, went to brush our teeth, and retired to our room. After stripping down to our underwear, we climbed into the feather bed to read. Sam was amazed at how the bed seemed to swallow him up, and we laughed at how neither of us was likely to move out of the trough we had settled into. After reading for a while, we both grew sleepy, turned off the bedside lamps and were asleep almost immediately.

One thing for which I had failed to prepare Sam was the passing of trains throughout the night. I had learned over the years to sleep through them, but Sam was awakened every time one came through. Then, at four in the morning, Mrs. McIntosh's rooster crowed and Sam sat straight up in bed.

"What the hell was that?" No sooner had he asked than the rooster crowed again. "What is that? Is that a rooster?"

"Yep. It's next door. Mrs. McIntosh."

"I think we need to have fried chicken for dinner tonight!"

I laughed. "I agree. Funny thing is, Mrs. McIntosh doesn't need to get up early. Grandma says she sleeps right through the crowing."

We settled back into the bed, attempting to go back to sleep, but it was not to be. I heard, more than felt, Sam moving around on his side of the bed. After about fifteen minutes of near-constant movement, he sat up again.

"I can't sleep, and I'm hot in this feather bed. I'm gonna go sit on the front porch."

"OK. I'll come with you." We pulled on our clothes and tiptoed through the living room and outside to the screened porch to the right of the front door. There were several sturdy old rocking chairs there, wearing countless coats of green paint. We each took a chair and began to rock slowly. The night sounds had diminished, and the traffic on the highway on the other side of the railroad tracks hummed along as the faintest light began to appear on the horizon to the east. We sat in silence for what seemed a long time. Then Sam spoke quietly.

"This is nice. I like sitting out here in the dark. It feels like we're a thousand miles from home and from anything that could hurt us or scare us."

"Shoot, I didn't think you were scared of anything."

"Well, you got that wrong. I'm scared of lots of things. I'm scared of the Russians. I'm scared of something happening to my mom." He paused for a while, then continued with a heaviness in his voice. "I'm scared I'll never have a family and no one will remember me. It'll be like the water, remember? Like poking your finger in the water. Nothing left to show I was ever here."

"I'll remember you. You know I will. Besides, you'll probably be an astronaut or something. Maybe the first man on the moon."

"Nope. Not that. We're gonna make it to the moon by 1970, you just watch. Kennedy's really pushing NASA."

"Well then, Mars. First man on Mars."

"Maybe so. Hey, why don't we go for a run?"

"Now? It's still dark. Well, mostly dark."

"By the time we get our running stuff on, it'll be light enough to see. Come on."

With less than enthusiasm, I agreed, and we slipped quietly back inside, changed into our running garb and sneakers and set out. Sam was right that the sky had lightened enough that we could at least make out the white lime rock road at my grandmother's front gate. We ran in silence, each of us focused on our pace and our own thoughts. Our run took us to the end of the road where my playmate Jesse lived. We then turned around and ran back, past Grandma's house, past the store, made a right and ran past the Methodist church. It seemed no one was awake or about yet. Finally circling back, we arrived at my grandmother's gate just as the newspaper delivery van was pulling away. I picked up the *Gainesville Sun* and read the frontpage headline: "Marilyn Monroe Found Dead."

On the day after Labor Day, school opened, and I began my final year of elementary school. Will was entering fourth grade, so this would be the last year, for the near term, that we would be attending the same school. For Sam and me, the summer had been the coming-of-age of our friendship—the season during which we had become keepers of each other's secrets and guardians of each other's trust.

14.

RISING TENSIONS

THE FALL OF 1962 was, in some ways, formative of the years that would follow. On October 1st of that year, African American college student James Meredith enrolled at the University of Mississippi—albeit under the protection of US Marshalls—and other Black students soon followed at other colleges and universities in the South. In our sleepy southern town, and across the rest of the region, an awareness grew that desegregation was inevitable and irresistible. In order to ease the transition to fully integrated schools, the courts permitted school districts to offer "freedom-of-choice" plans whereby Black students who chose to do so could attend white schools. It would not be until I entered high school, however, that freedom-of-choice arrived in Palatka.

Less than two weeks after Meredith desegregated the University of Mississippi, an American U-2 spy plane flying over Cuba secured irrefutable evidence that the Soviets were rapidly constructing missile facilities on that island nation just 103 miles off the southern tip of Florida. For the next ten days or so, U-2 flights continued, and the Kennedy administration amassed evidence of the Soviets' activities in Cuba. At the same time, Kennedy's team grappled with how best to respond to the growing threat, knowing full well that any misstep or miscalculation could trigger all-out nuclear war. On October 22, President Kennedy addressed the nation and announced what he termed a "quarantine" of Cuba—for all intents, a naval blockade. In addition, he voiced a demand to Khrushchev that Russia remove its missiles from Cuba and advanced our nuclear readiness to DEFCON 3. The following day, US Navy battleships took up stations 500 miles off Cuba, turning back all ships found to be carrying military materiel. On October 24, the threat level was raised to DEFCON 2—the final level of preparation before all-out nuclear war.

The fact that we, in Florida, were within easy striking distance of nuclear missiles being installed by Russia in Cuba created a low-level panic among our citizenry. Families stocked up on nonperishable foods. The construction of back-yard fallout shelters accelerated. Public buildings were prepared to house refugees in the event of a nuclear attack. Our schools held drop-and-cover drills. Households kept radios on and tuned to news programming throughout the days and nights. And every evening, we were stationed before our televisions to learn of the latest developments. Everywhere, tension was palpable. The missile crisis was on everyone's minds and lips—children as well as adults.

For our family, as well as most I knew, the threat felt very real and the likelihood of nuclear conflict very likely. Although we continued our regular activities—work, school, and church—there was an undercurrent of fear to everything we did. Without a television at home, Sam often came to our house to watch the evening newscasts. It seemed, particularly during the week after Kennedy's speech, that every day brought more ominous details. On Saturday, October 27, news broke that one of our U-2 aircrafts had been shot down over Cuba and the pilot killed. I remember sleeping very little that night, expecting at any moment the concussive blasts of nuclear bombs detonating at the Naval bases in Jacksonville. The following day, reason prevailed, and Khrushchev announced that Russia would dismantle its missile bases and remove its nuclear weapons from Cuba. Nonetheless, the US naval quarantine continued into November, when it was confirmed that the missiles were, in fact, gone.

Though tensions over the immediate crisis with Russia eased, there was no one I knew who felt the Cold War had thawed. More to the fact, it seemed tensions simply returned to their pre-Cuban-Missile-Crisis levels of fear and anxiety. Both superpowers continued to develop, test, and stockpile nuclear weapons of increasing power, and delivery systems of improved accuracy. There remained the sense that war with Russia was inevitable. Despite all that, our lives went on with a false sense of continuity—as though things would remain the same, when, on another level, we were certain they would not.

It was in the midst of this period of international tension that I discovered my voice. I had always enjoyed singing, had taken piano lessons for several years, but made little progress— it seemed my fingers simply refused to do what my brain was telling them to do—but singing was my musical forte. I had a strong, clear soprano voice, and pushed back against any smart ass who suggested I "sang like a girl." I knew enough about classical music to know that boys had sung the treble parts in the great choirs of Europe for centuries—even before women were permitted to sing in those choirs. At our church, I sang in a large children's choir and, at school, enjoyed our weekly music class. It was early that fall, after one of those classes, that my music teacher asked me to stay for a minute. After the others had left the music room, she told me the chorus director at the community college was planning to produce a short Christmas opera, and it had a part for a boy soprano. She felt I should audition. I was immediately captivated by the idea, got my mother on board and asked my church choir director to help me prepare for the audition.

On the appointed day, my mother checked me out of school and took me to the college where the audition was to be held. As it turned out, there were five boys prepared to audition, and we were to sing before the music professor and the entire college chorus. I had assumed a small room, a piano, an accompanist and the music professor. I was not prepared to audition before a room full of strangers. I was terrified! Two of the boys were from the Catholic school and each sang classical pieces in Latin. I had prepared "O Holy Night," and felt it went well. The other two boys sang hymns. Of the five of us, I thought I and one of the Catholic boys, Eugene, had performed best. As it turned out, that was also the professor's decision, so the two of us were cast as Amahl in Menotti's short opera *Amahl and the Night Visitors*.[8] There would be several performances, so each

---

[8] Gian Carlo Menotti's opera, *Amahl and the Night Visitors*, was commissioned by NBC and first performed on live television by the NBC Opera Theater on December 24, 1951. It was the first opera specifically composed for television. The opera tells the extra-Biblical story of a poor widowed mother and her crippled son, Amahl, living in the Judean countryside at the time of the birth of Jesus. The "visitors" in the title are none other than the three Magi and their page on their way to find and offer gifts to the newborn Christ. They arrive at Amahl's doorstep in the middle of the night seeking a place to rest. Amahl and his mother welcome them into their humble hut sending word to their neighbors to bring food, as they have nothing to offer their visitors. After the neighbors come and go, everyone settles in for the remainder of the night—everyone, that is, except Amahl's mother, who had been eyeing the gold of one of the Magi. Stealthily, she creeps toward the gold, clutches a handful and is immediately caught by the page who sounds the alarm. Chaos ensues as the page struggles to wrest the gold from the mother's grasp and Amahl struggles with the page to release his mother. At last, one of the Magi demands an end to the melee, insists that the mother keep the gold, explaining that "the child we seek doesn't need our gold. On love alone he will build his kingdom." In response, the mother cries "Take back your gold. For such a child I've waited all my life, and if I were not so poor, I would send a gift of my own to such a child." Then, in the most moving moment of the opera, Amahl offers his crutch as a gift, "Who knows, he may need one, and this I made myself." In that moment, the boy is healed of his infirmity, and after a celebration, joins the Magi on their quest to find the Christ-child. The curtain closes as Amahl and the Magi

of us would perform the role and serve as understudy to the other in the event of illness.

So, for weeks through that fall, as the world teetered on the brink of nuclear war, I spent hours in rehearsal at the college, missing hours in the classroom, and was having the best time of my life. The music was challenging, both vocally and harmonically. I had always had a good musical "ear," but found some of Menotti's melodies unpredictable and his harmonies dissonant. The ensemble sections with the other leads were particularly challenging, as I had to hold my own against as many as five adult singers. As a consequence of all the rehearsal and the additional vocal training I was receiving along the way, the range and strength of my singing voice grew exponentially. At the same time, I was growing socially. I had always been somewhat reserved—particularly around those older than myself. Now, I was hanging out with college kids who treated me like their kid brother. I joked with them during rehearsal breaks and shared meals with them in the college cafeteria. I began to view myself as their peer—as older than my nearly eleven years. Unfortunately, this created issues in my friendship with Sam.

Because my schedule was so full throughout that fall, I had little time to spend on anything other than school, the opera, and church. As a consequence, I saw little of Sam for weeks on end. It seemed I had scarce time for our regular runs, sometimes cancelling on him at the last minute, and, although

---

fade into the countryside leaving the mother to contemplate all that has transpired. As the NBC broadcast date neared, Menotti was still working frantically to complete the score and the singers received the final revisions only days before the first performance. The role of Amahl, though vocally demanding, is scored for a boy soprano and, as Menotti later wrote, it was his "…express wish…that the role of Amahl should always be performed by a boy." Since its premier in 1951, *Amahl and the Night Visitors* has been performed thousands of times by professional companies, college opera workshops, community theater groups, and hundreds of churches.

he was often at our house in the evenings—particularly during the missile crisis—I was typically holed up in my room trying to catch up on schoolwork I had missed due to rehearsals. On one of those evenings, sometime around mid-November, we both arrived at the bathroom door at the same time.

"Hey, Sam."

"Hey. I guess you're doing homework?"

"Yeah. It's hard to keep up, what with the opera rehearsals and all, but Mrs. Muller has really been nice to help me."

"That's good." There was a flat tone in his voice. As oblivious as I could sometimes be, I realized something was wrong.

"Hey, what's the matter? Something wrong?"

"Yeah. Something's wrong. You remember how you felt last year when I started high school and was so busy?'

"Yeah." All my neurons were firing now.

"Well, that's how I'm feeling now. You never come down to my house. You ditch me most days when we're supposed to go for a run. And all you talk about when I finally see you is how much fun you're having with all your college buddies. I feel kinda left out."

Had I been struck in the head with a two-by-four I could not have been more stunned, nor more wounded. I knew immediately, and in the pit of my stomach, how he felt—I had, indeed, felt that way the previous fall—and was crushed by guilt at having hurt him. My emotions welled and I burst into tears.

"I'm so sorry. I've just been so busy. You're my best friend. Those college guys, they're nice to me. I have fun with them, but I know I'll never see them again after the opera is over." All of this I managed to choke out between sobs and snorts—I was a messy crier.

"I know you don't mean it, you know, personally, but it really hurt my feelings, you know? You're more to me than just some little kid who lives down the street."

Now I was really going, wracked by sobs and folding in on myself. At that moment when I hoped the ground would swallow me up, Sam grabbed me and pulled me to his chest. "It's OK. I know you weren't trying to hurt me, and I shouldn't have been wearing my feeling on my sleeve. I know you've been really busy. It's OK. We're OK. Things'll get back to normal after this show is over, right?"

"Yes. Of course. As soon at the opera's over, everything will be like it was. I'm sorry, Sam, really sorry. I was an idiot. I wasn't even thinking about how I had kinda abandoned you."

"It'll be OK, buddy. Now that we've kinda cleared the air, we'll be OK. Now, I've really gotta pee, and I don't want any company in there, so you're gonna have to wait."

Laughter has such power to heal, to bridge the divide between wounded souls. I went from uncontrolled sobbing to giddy giggling in a matter of seconds. Sam laughed with me, then stepped into the bathroom and closed the door behind himself. That night, as I lay in bed thinking through that painful conversation with him, I pondered how much my life had changed as a result of his role and influence. I realized how much I truly loved him, and how deeply I ached at having taken him for granted. And I realized, perhaps for the first time in my young life, that I bore a responsibility to him—just as he did to me—to protect our friendship from all threats, including the silent threat of taking it for granted.

At last December came, and with it the short run of our production of *Amahl*. The final week before performances began found me busier than I had ever been in my life. With rehearsals every night, blocking, costuming, technical rehearsals, and long spans of boredom while the director worked with the other principles, there was little time for sleep. Each day I felt more tired than the day before. My part was demanding, and I felt myself lacking the energy necessary to perform well. Sensing that both of us playing the role were exhausted, the director ordered us to take alternate evenings off for the final four rehearsals. Only then was I able to make up some lost sleep and enter the four-show run feeling rested and energized.

Our director had decided that I would sing the performances on the first and third nights—Thursday and Saturday evenings—with Eugene singing the part on Friday evening and for the Sunday matinee. Thursday evening would be the smaller crowd, but Saturday had sold out. My family, Sam, and his mom planned to attend Thursday evening, and my parents had also bought tickets for the Saturday performance. I think I was more nervous about performing before Sam than before a full house as I realized he had never really heard me sing.

Opening night was organized chaos. I had never been involved in anything approaching this level of production—the lighting, costumes, chorus, orchestra, dancers—it was all more than my nervous system could manage. Mom had driven me to the theater for the five-thirty call time, then back home to collect Dad and Will. Curtain was at seven o'clock, and I was a wreck. I was seated backstage observing the frenzy when Sam suddenly showed up.

"What are you doing here? The show's not 'til seven."

"Yeah, I'm coming back later with Mom, but I just rode my bike over to talk you off the cliff."

"How did you know I would be scared to death?"

"I just knew. Friends know stuff about each other, and I knew how nervous you'd be. And I know part of that would be because I was gonna be here."

"You're right. I don't really know hardly anybody else who'll be out there, but I'm really nervous about messing up in front of you."

"You need to get over that. I'm gonna still be your friend even if you fall off the front of the stage and get stuck in the tuba."

"There is no tuba."

"OK. You know what I mean. Look, you just need to think of everyone out there as cabbages."

"What? Cabbages? What are you talking about?"

"Think of everyone out there with a cabbage for a head."

"That's dumb."

"I know, but it works. You won't care what a cabbage thinks about you, will you?"

"I guess not."

"There. You see. It's already working."

"You know, you're just crazy sometimes."

"Yep. I know. Hey, I gotta go. Just remember, cabbages."

"OK. And you'll be one of them. I'm gonna think of you with a cabbage for a head, too."

"That's cool. Whatever helps."

There is something electric about the half-hour or so before the curtain rises on opening night. The actors are backstage, pacing and singing to themselves, securing their costumes and props; the orchestra members are tuning, playing through difficult sections of their parts; the director is making last minute changes to lighting cues and giving final instructions to cast members; and everyone is walking on a high wire of nervous energy.

My character, a wretchedly poor shepherd boy in the Palestinian countryside at the time of Jesus' birth, begins the show as a cripple, so I was equipped with a crutch my dad had fashioned from a tree branch. In addition, young Amahl played the flute, so I had been provided a rustic-looking reed flute. Fortunately, my "flute solos" were actually played by the first oboe, so I simply had to do a convincing job of appearing to play the thing. As the show opens, Amahl is outside the little hut he shares with his mother, playing his flute and staring at an unusually bright star that has appeared in the night sky. He then must hobble inside, carrying the flute without dropping it—a feat I had not fully mastered, having dropped the damn thing in rehearsal on three occasions. So, while others were running through challenging passages in the score, I was hobbling around backstage working to avoid dropping my flute. Suddenly, the stage manager made a pass near me muttering "Places. Curtain in five." I nearly threw up.

I quickly found my place onstage and tried, with little success, to calm my racing heart. As the curtain opened, I was upstage right, seated on a large fake rock, bathed in blue light and "playing" my flute. The oboe echoed from the pit the haunting flute melody, and my stage mother sang out the first vocal notes of the opera, "A-mahl."

"Yes, mother," I replied.

"Time to go to bed."

"Coming." My voice was strong and clear and belied the terror churning in the pit of my stomach. After ignoring her and continuing to play my flute, she became frustrated and got down to business.

"How long must I shout to make you obey?"

"I'm sorry, Mother."

"Hurry in, it's time to go to bed."

Then ensued a bit of an argument, with Amahl begging to stay out a bit longer. However, as is most often the case, Mother triumphs, so I took up my crutch, clutched my flute, and hobbled into the hut without incident.

As the show unwound, I began to lose myself in the music and in my character. The footlights made it impossible to see the audience, so I didn't even need to envision them as cabbages. The opera itself runs about forty minutes—Menotti had composed it for television—so it seemed no time had passed before we were taking bows. I was the last of the actors to return to stage for the curtain call, and I could distinctly hear Sam hooting from beyond the footlights. My face was split with an ear-to-ear grin as I took center stage and bowed.

As the curtain closed, the actors all hugged and congratulated each other on a strong performance. I swam contentedly in that sea of affirmation as I headed back to the makeshift dressing room to change out of my costume. Sam met me there.

"That was amazing! You were amazing! How come I never knew you could sing like that?"

"Thanks. I don't know. I guess we never talked about my singing, and I really haven't done much singing except at school and church, so I guess there really hasn't been a time for you to hear me. Did you like the show?"

"It was great. When you said 'opera,' I was thinking, I don't know, like something at the Met or something. This was funny and sad, and joyful, and the music was pretty cool, too. I nearly cried when you got healed near the end."

"Yeah. That's my favorite part of the show." I took up my crutch and played the scene for him. "But, Mother, let me send him my crutch. Who knows? He may need one, and this I made myself." I began to walk haltingly toward him, holding my crutch in my outstretched arms. I sang out, "I walk, Mother. I walk, Mother."

He took the crutch from me and, in a surprisingly rich baritone, improvised, "What am I supposed to do with this thing?" and we both broke out in uncontrolled laughter.

After we had recovered a bit, I asked him, "Pretty cool moment, huh?"

"Yeah. Very cool. It gave me goose bumps. Is that a true story?"

"Nah. I don't know where the composer got the story, but it's not in the Bible. But I think it kinda fits with the whole meaning of Christmas, anyway. The baby Jesus come to earth to help poor and sick people."

When he replied, he sounded insecure and somewhat embarrassed. "Yeah, I guess so. I really don't know much about that—you know, about the Bible and stuff."

"Hey, that's OK. Besides my folks, you're the most Jesus-like person I know, so don't worry about it. I think you already got the important stuff figured out. So, let me get changed, and I'll see you out front."

As I had Friday evening off, my parents insisted I stay home that evening and rest. I wanted to see Eugene, the other boy cast in the role of Amahl, but we agreed that the Sunday matinee would be the time for that—after I had completed my last performance on Saturday evening. The Saturday evening crowd was larger and the performance went smoothly, but it seemed less dynamic than had opening night. I attended the Sunday matinee by myself, sitting in the audience and anticipating every challenging passage for Eugene. He performed well, and flawlessly, and I was happy for him, knowing how much satisfaction and self-confidence I had gained from performing successfully.

Christmas came and went, followed immediately by my eleventh birthday. Although I'm certain I enjoyed the gifts I received, the thing I treasured most over that holiday break was the quiet time with my family and friends. The previous weeks had been so filled with activity that the quiet days between Christmas and the New Year were a welcomed respite. Sam and I were able to return to our regular morning runs, and I became reacquainted with my other friends in the neighborhood. I remember a unique sense of contentment—of place—during those days.

15.

BE PREPARED

NOW THAT I had reached the requisite age of eleven, I joined the Boy Scouts at the first of the New Year. The troop I joined was sponsored by the local Episcopal church and was the largest and best-run in the district. Boy Scout troops are organized into smaller units called "patrols." I was assigned to the Eagle Patrol—a mixed bag of about a dozen boys led by an older scout named Joe Mike Dasher—not Joe, not Mike, but Joe Mike. He was tall and handsome and had achieved the rank of Life—one step below that of Eagle. The rumor was that Joe Mike was half native-American—his dark hair and complexion seemed to confirm that—adding to the sense of mystery that surrounded him. Joe Mike was quiet-spoken and led us by the strength of his character. Where other patrol leaders seemed to do an inordinate amount of yelling at their charges, Joe Mike gave simple, firm directions delivered in a deep, low voice. We complied—in part because we respected him, and in part because we wanted to please him.

Each Monday evening, our troop of sixty or so gathered in the church's parish hall for our weekly meeting. Following an opening ceremony and uniform inspection, we spent the remainder of the evening learning skills to help us advance in rank and earn merit badges or making preparations for upcoming events. Coming on the heels of the Cuban Missile Crisis in the fall, however, our meetings that winter often included civil defense training for what we assumed would be the inevitable nuclear attack by the Soviets. Scout leaders taught us how to duck and cover, what supplies to stockpile. We learned first aid for injuries that might be the result of a nuclear explosion and how to store food and water to prevent contamination. At one meeting, we learned how to fashion a make-shift fallout shelter using interior doors and other materials we would all have at our homes.

With each of these lessons, the underlying message was clear: The Soviets would attack the US with nuclear weapons. It was not a matter of "if," but of when. Added to that inevitability was another lesson—that our survival and that of our families depended on our adherence to the Boy Scout motto: Be Prepared. I know our adult leaders never intended to engender in us a baseline fear that our lives would likely end in a nuclear firestorm and at a young age, but that was the end result of these training sessions. I recall several arguments with my father over his unwillingness to construct a fallout shelter[9] in our backyard when it seemed so obviously the prudent thing to do.

Scouting was good for me in a number of ways. First, because of our family's history of extended camping trips, I was already well-versed in how to keep warm, dry, and well-fed in the woods. That knowledge gave me an advantage over

---

[9] The movement to construct backyard fallout shelters received the encouragement of President Kennedy in a speech on October 6, 1961. Many families heeded his call and built underground bunkers or converted backyard swimming pools, then stocked these shelters with non-perishable food items, battery-powered lights, clothing, hundreds of gallons of water, and numerous other supplies, including Geiger counters. The media took up the call with the January 12, 1962 cover of Life magazine reading "The Drive for Mass Shelters: New Facts You Must Know About Fallout." Numerous do-it-yourself pamphlets and articles appeared with instructions on how to fabricate effective fallout shelters with minimal cost. In response to Kennedy's call, Congress appropriated $169 million to stock appropriately constructed public buildings with survival supplies in the event of a nuclear attack. In some towns, even today, those rusting black and yellow Fallout Shelter signs can be found affixed to the exteriors of public buildings.

others in the troop for whom camping was new and, for some, frightening. It was also something I did that did not include Sam, so it forced me to make new friendships and work with others to accomplish common objectives. At the same time, scouting gave me experiences and skills to share with Sam where I, rather than he, was the knowledgeable one. As a result, my relationship with Sam began to change. I found that I had more to contribute to our conversations, and he began to relate to me more as a peer than as a little brother.

That spring, and for reasons I never knew, I was appointed as scribe for our troop. As such, I was responsible for keeping the records of each week's attendance and the results of the weekly uniform inspections. In addition, I received a special patch to affix to my uniform—a patch no one else in the troop had. With these added responsibilities came growth in my self-confidence and self-esteem. If others saw qualities of leadership in me, perhaps they were there.

One afternoon in mid-March, I walked down to Sam's house—unannounced, as had become my custom—and found him in his bedroom working on a model of a submarine.

"Hey, man, what you workin' on?"

"It's a model of the *USS Thresher*,[10] that submarine that just

---

10 The sinking of the *USS Thresher* (SSN-593) on April 10, 1963, with the loss of all 129 crew members onboard, was to this date, the second deadliest submarine disaster in maritime history (the first being the French submarine *Surcouf*, lost on February 18-19, 1942 with 130 crew). The second in a new class of nuclear-powered submarines, *Thresher* was designed as a submarine killer, intended to hunt down and destroy Soviet subs. Outfitted with the most advanced weapon systems deployed to-date, an advanced sonar system, and a remarkably quiet engine, *Thresher* was among the most formidable attack submarines in the US fleet. Still in sea trials at the time of her sinking, *Thresher* left port on April 9, 1963 and sailed to an area approximately 220 miles east of Cape Cod, Massachusetts, to conduct deep-dive trails. The next day, on April 10, she slowly dove deeper, running in wide circles under her rescue ship *Skylark* in order to maintain radio contact. Following set procedures, *Thresher* paused every 100 feet of depth to confirm the integrity of her hull and the operation of all systems. As she reached her proscribed test

sank." I gave him a blank stare. "Don't tell me you don't know about it? (Shrug.) Geeze, Clint, you've got to keep up with the news. There's just too much going on that you need to know about."

"OK, so tell me about it."

"The Thresher is, was, a new submarine—well, pretty new. She was finished in '60. Anyway, she was doing deep diving trials last Wednesday and sank."

"Was it the Russians?"

"No. There was some kind of accident. She went down off Cape Cod, Massachusetts. Everyone onboard was lost."

"Man, I really hadn't heard about that. How many died?"

"One hundred and twenty-nine. Everybody onboard. That's why the flags are at half-staff. President Kennedy ordered all the flags in the country to be flown at half-staff. Anyway, I got this model over the weekend. I just wanted to honor the sailors lost and have a way to remember them."

"And you're thinking about joining the Navy?"

"Yeah, but I don't want to be on a submarine. Even before this. They're just too cramped. I think I'd get claustrophobia."

"Hey, the reason I came down was to see if you wanted to camp out in my backyard Friday night. I've got a new tent for scouts and want to check it out. I want to make sure I know how to set it up before our next camping trip. It's a kinda weird design—not a typical pup tent. So, anyway, do you want to?"

"Yeah, sure. Why not?"

"Great. Mom says for you to come for dinner, so why don't we get the tent set up that afternoon, get our stuff situated,

depth, *Skylark* received a garbled message reporting "…minor difficulties…attempting to blow," and then an even more difficult to understand message that included the number "…900…" That was the last communication received from *Thresher*. Rescue operations began immediately, but by the next day it was apparent that *Thresher* had been lost with all hands aboard. Recovery operations commenced on April 12, 1963, and continued into the next year when the wreckage of *Thresher* was found in late June, 1964, at a depth of 8,400 feet (2,560 meters).

then, after dinner, we can go outside."

"Sounds good. What do I need to bring?"

"Just your sleeping bag, a pillow, a flashlight. Maybe some comic books. That's about it. My dad doesn't want us eating in the tent, but I'll sneak in some snacks."

Friday afternoon, Sam arrived about 4:30, and we began to make our preparations. My new tent was still in the box in which it had been shipped, so we unpacked it in a corner of the backyard and began to study the instructions. Instead of the typical pup tent design, this tent had a high opening at the front with the ridgeline sloping toward the back and a wider-than-typical front that narrowed toward the back. There were external poles at both ends and the sides were staked off with small cords in order to give more space in the interior. It was an unusual design, unlike any small tent I'd seen at scout campouts, and much less cramped inside. After we'd rolled out our sleeping bags and stashed our other gear—including a few snacks I'd managed to pilfer from the kitchen—it was almost time for dinner.

"You boys wash your hands before you come to the table."

"Yes ma'am," we chimed in unison. In the small hall bathroom, we jostled as we shared the sink.

"Look in the mirror, Clint."

I glanced up to see both of us reflected in the mirror above the sink. "What?"

"You're taller. Look how you're catching up with me."

"Yeah. I've grown a lot since my birthday. Mom says she can't keep up with me. She has to let my pants out all the time."

"Aw, my little brother is growing up."

I punched him in the arm.

After dinner, we were anxious to get outside. At the entrance to the tent, we slipped off our shoes, crawled inside and zipped the mosquito netting closed. It's remarkable how camping out in the backyard can produce such a sense of independence in a boy, and how sleeping outside can open the door to conversations that might otherwise never take place.

It was March, and still cool in the evenings in North Florida. Sam and I were both dressed in jeans and long-sleeved shirts. "So, Sam, you gonna sleep in your clothes?"

"No. But I'm gonna keep my jeans on 'til I get in my sleeping bag. What about you?"

"Same."

"You want to read some comics?"

"Sure. What do you have?"

"I've got the two new ones I bought the other day when we went to the store. The new Spidey one and that Dell one, the Creature. Which one you want?"

"Give me the Spider-Man. I think the Creature would give me nightmares."

For the next half hour or so we were immersed in our comics, reading by flashlight as the evening faded to dark. Outside our tent, crickets began to chirp and a dog barked in the distance.

"Sam, can I ask you something? It's kinda personal."

"Yeah, sure. You know you can ask me anything, right?"

"Yeah. I know. Well, you remember a long time ago how you told me you didn't really like girls, I mean like as girlfriends?"

"Yeah. Of course."

"Well, I guess I really didn't understand what you were really saying then. I mean, I kinda did, but I kinda didn't, you know?"

"I think so. You didn't really understand what it's like to like a girl as a girlfriend then, right?"

"Yeah. That's it. Well, anyway, I think I understand that now, and I think I understand maybe how you feel about boys, too."

"OK. Try to explain it to me."

"Well, there's this girl in my class, Paula Hendrix, and I really like her. I mean, I feel things for her I never really felt about anyone before. I want to hold her hand, and kiss her, and, you know, spend time with her and stuff. So," I hesitated. I was pushing off into deep waters. "So, is that how you feel about boys?"

"Yeah. That's pretty much it. I don't have those thoughts and feelings about girls. I mean, I like girls, and I have a lot of friends at school who are girls, but I don't want a girlfriend. I just don't have those feelings about girls."

"But you do about boys?"

"Well, about some boys. You don't have those feeling about all girls, do you? You don't feel that way about Crazy Christine, do you?" We both laughed.

"No, definitely not Crazy Christine, just Paula."

"Well, I don't have those feelings about all boys either. In fact, I've really only kinda had a crush on two boys in my life."

"Who?"

"Sorry, buddy, I'm not sayin'. But you are definitely not one of them!" He laughed and poked me. I laughed in response.

"I'm glad, 'cause that would be really awkward. Especially since I'm gonna be half naked in a little while." We laughed again, but I was not finished with this line of questioning.

"So, do you think you could make yourself change the way you feel? You know, feel that way about girls instead of boys?"

"No. Trust me, I've tried. I even prayed, and you know I'm not religious. Nothing changes. I've finally accepted the fact that you just can't change who you're attracted to, and I'm just not attracted to girls in that way."

"So, do you have, like, a boyfriend?"

"Hell, no. You and one of my teachers are the only two people in the world who know how I feel, and I intend to keep it that way. I haven't even gotten up the guts to tell my mom. If the guys on the track team ever found out, I'd be dead meat. First, I'd probably get the crap beat out of me, then no one would ever talk to me again. I would be totally alone at school. Everyone would hate me and avoid me. So, no, no boyfriend. I just admire from a distance."

"Oh, OK. That's kinda sad, really, that you can't really be with someone you like."

"It's just the way it is, and the way it has to be if I want anything like a normal life."

"OK. I understand."

"And you do understand that this whole conversation never leaves this tent, right?"

His question stung a bit. "Of course. I'm not an idiot, you know."

"I know, and I'm sorry. I wasn't trying to insult you. I just need you to know how important it is to keep this to yourself. Really, my life would be over if this got out at school."

"I understand, and I will never tell a living soul, OK?"

"OK."

"But, Sam," I snickered. "I do love you. I just don't want to kiss you."

He laughed in response. "And I love you, too. But I don't want to kiss you, either. Now, finish your comic book, and let's get some sleep."

16.

THE SEARCH

A WEEK OR two after our backyard campout, Sam proposed an adventure. He had learned from his high school history teacher of a large Indian mound in the woods across the river from Hart Point. His teacher told him that he had discovered the mound several years back but had not explored or excavated it. In our minds, Sam and I envisioned it as a burial mound replete with artifacts and, of course, the bones of the brave warrior buried there. Sam was determined we must go in search of it, and I was determined to do anything Sam wanted to do.

This adventure to find the mound would entail a water crossing—either from Hart Point or the city dock—and Sam proposed we take my family's canoe for the voyage. This presented a bit of a quandary for me: I would have to explain our mission to my parents in order to secure permission to use the canoe. In addition, we would have to work out a means by which to transport the canoe to and from our point of embarkation. Sam had recently obtained his driver's license, but we would also have to have the use of a vehicle. My parents' station wagon was the logical choice because it was equipped with roof racks. Needless to say, I had misgivings as to whether we could actually convince our parents to let us go, not to mention securing the use of the canoe and the station wagon. Whereas I had been canoeing for several years and had easily obtained my canoeing merit badge earlier that year, this adventure was on a far grander scale, and would not include adult supervision. And then there was the matter of Will. I knew he would want to go, but I also knew we could not safely take him, nor would my parents permit him to go even if they allowed me. Sam and I decided the best approach was to have the entire adventure planned out in detail and then call a meeting of all the interested parties—specifically, my parents and his mother.

For several days after school we met in Sam's room to map out the specifics of the trip. His teacher had provided him with a hand-drawn map showing the mound's approximate location. We quickly determined that we should set out from the city dock as parking and an easy launch area were both available there. Assuming a favorable wind and not much of it, we estimated we could cross that wide section of the river and arrive at the other bank after a moderate thirty-minute paddle. We prepared a detailed list of all the supplies and equipment we would take with us—canoe paddles, rope, life jackets, seat cushions, water, snacks, insect repellent, folding camp shovel, compass, hatchet and machete (for hacking our way through the jungle), and burlap sacks (for all the artifacts we would find). We determined the entire excursion would require at least two hours to execute, and that we should undertake it on either side of the noon hour in order to be assured of the best light underneath the dense tree canopy. As our plan took shape, Sam wrote down every detail to convince our parents of our forethought and preparation. Finally, after our afternoons of planning, we were ready to make our pitch. Thus it was, that one evening after dinner, Sam and his mother walked down to our house for "the meeting."

To that point, neither of us had said anything to our parents about this undertaking though the fact that we had called the meeting had clued them that we were up to something. When Sam and his mother entered our living room, she was wearing a look of concern, and Sam looked guilty—not an auspicious start. My parents seemed both curious and a bit apprehensive. Will was upset that he had been excluded. After exchanging the usual pleasantries, we got down to business. Sam began.

"Well, we know you all wondered why we wanted to have this meeting." Nods all around. "Well, we have something we want to do, and we need your help and permission." He then brought out the map and our equipment list and provided a detailed description of the trip—how the idea came to us, what we wanted to do, what we needed in order to undertake the excursion and the support we needed from them. It was a masterful presentation. He scarcely paused for a breath, and our parents did not voice a single objection or question—until he concluded. My mom was the first to respond.

"Suppose you boys get over there and get lost?"

"We'll have my Boy Scout compass so we can find our way back to where we leave the canoe. You know I know how to use it. I have the orienteering merit badge."

Sam's mother was next. "What if one of you gets hurt?"

I was ready with an answer. "We'll take a first aid kit. I have my first aid merit badge."

Then my dad surprised us all. "I don't see a problem with this. You can take our canoe. Clint is a good canoeist and should sit in the back to steer. Sam, you can drive our station wagon. I'll teach you two how to load the canoe and tie it down. My only concern is the weather. That's the widest section of the river around here and, if its windy, it can get really rough. If it's not a calm day, you'll need to wait. And one other thing. You have to wear your life jackets the whole time you're on the water. You can't just stuff them under your seat. You have to wear them."

"Yes sir, of course. Thank you!"

"Thank you, Dad."

Our mothers sat in stunned silence.

Looking ahead, Sam and I chose the next Saturday as the date, with the following Saturday as backup in the event weather precluded our plan. As it turned out, the weather was cooperative. A cool front had pushed through earlier that week, but by Friday, the wind had dropped. Saturday was forecast to be clear, cool, and windless. On Friday afternoon, after my father arrived home from work, Sam and I helped him hoist the canoe onto the station wagon's roof rack.

"Sam, I forgot to ask you if you could drive a stick shift. This wagon is a three-speed on the steering column."

"Uh, yes sir. I know how. My mom's car has a stick, but I've never driven one on the column."

"Well, up and toward you is first." Dad began to work the imaginary shift in the air to his right. "Straight down is second. Back up and toward the dash is third. Reverse is down and toward the dash. As long as you know how to work a clutch, you'll get the hang of it."

"Yes sir." I noted that Sam's response was lacking the air of confidence I was hoping to hear.

Dad then showed us how to securely tie down the canoe, then had us repeat the entire process, including loading, without his help. Once satisfied we were prepared, he left us to secure our equipment and supplies.

"I thought of something else we need to take," Sam said, as he held up a small pad and pencil.

"What's that for?" I asked.

"We need to make a record of what we find and make drawing of where things are as we excavate. That's what archeologists do. My teacher, Mr. Crandell, said it's called *in situ*."

"*In situ?* What's that mean?"

"It's Latin. It means 'in place.' You make a record of what you find and of the exact place you find it. Like if we find a skull, we make a drawing of where in the mound we find it. We include things like how deep it was buried. Stuff like that."

"Why is that important?"

"I don't really know. I guess if we find something really cool, like a skull or a pot, and archeologists decide to excavate the mound they'll know where it was found in relation to other stuff they find. I'm just guessing. I'll have to ask Mr. Crandell about that."

"Oh, OK. Hey, are you sure you can drive this thing?"

"I think so. I mean, I know how to drive a four-speed on the floor, so I think I can figure this out."

After everything was loaded, Sam went home for the night. Our plan was to meet at nine the next morning, hoping to be on the water by ten.

Saturday dawned crisp and cloudless—with what my mother called a "Carolina sky." Sam and his mother were at our house promptly at nine o'clock, and my entire family joined them on the driveway for our departure. I felt sorry for Will, who stood to the side, looking as though his dog had just died. After all the "be carefuls" and "take care of each others" we climbed into the station wagon and were off. Well, I should probably say we began the process to be off. With everyone watching, Sam cranked the station wagon and shifted into reverse to back out onto the street. As he released the clutch and began to apply the gas, the station wagon began to buck. He braked hard and tried again. Same result. By this point, both our mothers were looking very concerned and my father was laughing. Will was laughing. I was laughing.

"Shut up, Clint. This is hard enough with everyone watching

without you laughing."

"OK. I'm sorry." I made a valiant effort to stifle my snickering.

Sam tried again. This time, the wagon bucked out onto the empty street. He braked and shifted into first. As soon as he applied the gas, the bucking commenced. I could no longer contain my laughter.

"Shut up, you twerp. If you think this is so easy, you try it."

"I don't have my license."

"Very funny."

By this point, the bucking had subsided, and we began making a bit of headway down the street. Sam shifted smoothly into second and the transition resulted in only a small jolt before our progress evened out and he shifted smoothly into third. Our families faded in the rearview mirror and Sam relaxed a bit. However, at the first traffic light, the bucking returned and so did my laughter.

"Clint, shut up."

"Yes, sir."

Then he laughed. "Don't call me sir."

"Yes, sir."

"You're becoming a real smart ass, you know?"

"Yes, sir."

He punched me in the arm.

When we arrived at the city dock, the river was a sheet of glass—not a ripple on the surface—perfect conditions for canoeing across open water. Sam parked down by the boat ramp and we un-racked the canoe, loaded our equipment and supplies, and he parked the station wagon while I waited beside the boat. In short order, we set off paddling in even strokes toward the far shore. After about fifteen minutes, I realized I had underestimated the time it would take us to cross that expanse of water.

"This is going to take longer than I thought."

"How much longer?"

"Probably another fifteen minutes. Look back. We've only gotten about a third of the way across."

"Well, OK. We might not be able to take as much time at the Indian mound as we planned."

"It'll be OK. I told my parents we probably wouldn't be home before two."

We paddled on. I wasn't sure about Sam, but I was getting tired. However, I wasn't about to let him know that, so I kept at it. In due time, we arrived at the far bank. It was muddy and overgrown, and we made several aborted attempts at landing until we found a tiny cove that gave us a means to exit the canoe onto the bank without capsizing. As soon as we had unloaded everything and distributed it between us, I took a compass reading and set a direction through the forest toward where we hoped to find the mound. The woods were dense, and progress was slow as we hacked our way through. After about ten minutes, we came to an obvious wildlife trail through the underbrush.

"Deer and probably wild hogs made this," Sam explained.

Wild hogs? My imagination was immediately flooded with images of Travis being attacked by feral hogs in the film adaptation of *Old Yeller*. I was instantly anxious and wary as we proceeded. However, within a few minutes, we came upon the mound. Though we were standing on it, I did not recognize it as the destination to which we had been hiking.

"Here it is!" Sam exclaimed.

"What?"

"The mound."

"Where? I don't see it."

"We're standing on it." Rather than a high, isolated mound

of soil, what we were standing on was a large expanse of higher ground, somewhat overgrown.

"Look." Sam bent down and began to scratch in the soil. "Give me the shovel." He quickly opened the shovel and dug a small hole. Within the soil were bleached shells and small fragments of pottery. "See. This is a trash mound. See? These shells are left from them eating clams and snails and stuff."

"You mean it's not a burial mound? No skeletons?"

"'Fraid not. See how big this is?" Sam stretched out his arms and indicated the perimeter of the large, low mound. "This was where an Indian village dumped their trash. We can probably find things like pieces of broken pottery and animal bones, maybe even some broken arrow heads or pieces of flint, but there won't be human bones or stuff they would put in a burial mound."

"Oh. OK." I was disappointed, having imagined finding the remains of a native warrior with his finest weapons and provisions for his journey into the beyond. Garbage and broken pottery did not quite measure up.

"Hey, it's still pretty cool. Think about it. Hundreds of years ago, there were people living here. Hunting, fishing, trading with other settlements. When things broke, they threw them here, along with the scraps from their meals. Now, hundreds of years later, we're standing here where only a few people have stood for all those years, and we can dig up the stuff they left behind." Sam had sold me. It was, in fact, pretty cool—cool that we had found something that very few others knew about or would have ever made the effort to seek out. "Let's dig some small trenches into the mound and see what we find."

For the next hour or so, we labored to dig among the roots of trees and brush that had overgrown the mound. The mound itself was comprised largely of clam and snail shells with very little soil. In all, we dug two trenches about two feet deep and three to four feet long into the side of the mound. In that small area, we uncovered several bones of varying sizes and a number of pottery shards—a few of which were surprisingly large. My knowledge of Indian pottery was what I had seen on black and white TV westerns. This pottery was thicker, and most of the pieces had been incised with patterns and designs before they had been fired. Some appeared to have hair mixed with the clay. As we had no way to remove all the surface soil on these artifacts, we carefully placed them into the burlap sacks we had brought planning to clean and study them later.

"I'm whipped! I figure we'd better be heading back before our folks send out a search party. Can you get us back to the canoe?"

"Sure. All we have to do is go on the opposite heading than we came on. That's pretty simple."

"OK. Let's pack up our stuff and head back. I can't wait to show this stuff to Mr. Crandell. I think he'll be surprised we even found the mound, let alone all this."

When we arrived back at the little cove where we had moored the canoe, a breeze had picked up and there were waves moving across the surface of the river. Fortunately, the wind was coming from the east, meaning it would be at our backs as we paddled toward the dock. As we set out, I had to work to keep the bow of the canoe facing into the waves, but our crossing was otherwise effortless as we surfed across the open water.

After a few minutes of silence, Sam yelled back to me, "So, I know you were disappointed we didn't find an Indian burial, but didn't you think this was cool anyway?"

"Oh, yeah. This was the coolest thing I've ever done. I think I might want to be an archeologist. I can't wait to clean up the stuff we got and really look at it close."

"Me, too. This was really fun! I never really thought our parents would let us do this."

"Me neither. I couldn't believe my dad let us use the canoe and the station wagon. 'Course he may not ever let us use it again after he saw the way you drive."

"Oh, shut up! I'm getting the hang of it. The clutch feels different than my mom's car and I'm not used to the shift on the column, but I'll get it. I can't wait to teach you how to drive it, smarty pants."

"It'll be a while. I can't get my learner's permit for two and a half years. But it'll be cool if you teach me to drive, since you taught me to ride a bike!"

"Yeah. That would be pretty cool. I know it seems like a long time off, but it'll go fast. It won't be too long before you're ready."

With the wind at our backs, our return to the dock took half the time as our crossing. In short order, we had the canoe loaded on top of the station wagon and set off for home. Sam was correct in that he seemed much more comfortable with the vehicle's transmission, and we managed to pull into the driveway with no bucking. My dad was in the garage when we arrived and came out to greet us. I was surprised at his interest in the pottery shards and other items we had found. It had never occurred to me that my father might have retained something of his boyhood sense of adventure, but his fascination with the pottery was a revelation. He confessed that he thought of our expedition as nothing more than a lark and was shocked—first, that we found the mound, and, also, that we found objects within it.

The next week, Mr. Crandell taught Sam how to clean and catalogue the artifacts we had found, so we spent several afternoons using small brushes to carefully remove the dirt from the pottery shards and then affixed small numbered labels to the backs of them. We also created a map of the site and a remarkably detailed drawing of the mound showing our two excavations and, referencing the numbers on the artifacts, the approximate locations of the larger pottery pieces, bones, etc. Sam later expanded our work and submitted it as his history project. We—and I do mean we—received an A for our efforts.

17.

CONSTANT CHANGE

SOON, SUMMER WAS upon us, and in looking back, I realize those idyllic weeks represented the waning days of my childhood, and certainly of my innocence. My summers had become rather predictable—our family camping vacation, Vacation Bible School at church, and a week or two at my grandmother's in Campville. Added to this summer was a stay at Echockotee, the Boy Scout camp at Doctors Inlet near Jacksonville. The camp was to span a week and afforded an opportunity to concentrate on gaining new skills, improving old ones, and advancing in rank. We would be staying in large military-style tents with raised wooden floors and cots. We were permitted to have one tentmate from our own troop but would share the four-man tent with two boys from another troop.

On a Sunday afternoon in early June, we assembled at St. Mark's Church, loaded into a number of vehicles, and after a forty-minute drive, arrived at the camp. My father had driven our station wagon with me, three other boys, and all our gear. After unloading and a quick hug goodbye, he was off. In short order, we were assigned our tents and sent to sort out our gear before an orientation session to begin in about an hour. My chosen tentmate was a goofy kid named Ed Masters whom I knew only from scouting. Ed and I had shared a tent on a couple of weekend campouts, so we were familiar with each other's habits and were compatible. Ed was a bit younger than me but also a bit larger, or shall I say bulkier. He had an upbeat personality and was a repository of jokes, some of them quite off-color. When we arrived at our assigned tent, our two tentmates were already there unpacking their gear. They were from a troop in Lake City, around our ages, and seemed friendly. Over the coming days, the four of us became fast friends.

The week proceeded quickly, and nearly every minute of our days was filled with physical activity. As a consequence, other than the first night, there was little talking into the night as we fell, exhausted, onto our cots at the close of each day. Over the course of the week, I don't think Ed ever made it through his vast repertory of humor. Around mid-week, a team arrived from the health department to administer the first dose of the new oral polio vaccine. The other doses in the series would follow at our troop meetings over the summer.

One highlight of that week at camp was my patrol leader's induction into the Order of the Arrow (OA), a somewhat secretive honor society within scouting. Inductees into the OA are chosen by other scouts in their troops and Joe Mike was the overwhelming favorite among us. As components of the induction ritual, the inductees were required to sleep alone in the forest with limited provisions and equipment and maintain absolute silence in their scarce interactions with other scouts. The other aspects of the rituals and induction ceremonies were kept in strict confidence. This secrecy and vow of silence, coupled with Joe Mike's quiet nature and the fact that we saw very little of him for several days, made him an object of reverence. His quiet movement among us, his physical presence, his dark hair and features made him appear to us as a strong Native American brave undertaking his entrance into manhood. At the end of the week, when he reappeared wearing the Order of the Arrow sash, we peppered him with questions, most of which he refused, in his gentle way, to answer. Though he had always been an effective leader, his strength of character and leadership soared after that week of camp and we all admired him as an example of the very best of youth.

When I returned from camp, Sam and I resumed our regular morning runs. The Florida summer was in full form by then—barely-tolerable early mornings and brutally hot, humid days. The only respites were the predictable late afternoon thunderstorms that dropped temperatures for a few hours. Hanging over our mornings like the looming blanket of heat was my realization that Sam would begin his final year of high school at the end of the summer, meaning this would be our last summer, our last school year before he would move on to whatever awaited him. Each morning as we ran I was weighed down by the knowledge that there was no one in my life who could fill the void that would be left when he did, in fact, leave. I suppose Sam sensed my unease—according to my mother, I did tend to wear my feelings on my sleeve. One morning in late June, as we jogged down the middle of an old, uneven brick street behind the high school, he called me out.

"You've been awful quiet since you got back from Scout camp."

"Yeah. I guess so."

"So, what's up? What's eating you?"

"I guess I've realized how much is going to change this year. It's gonna be your last year of high school. Then you'll be going off to the Navy or college or whatever you end up doing, and I'll be kinda stuck here without you, and there's really nobody I'm close to that'll fill that hole you're gonna leave."

"Yeah, I've kinda thought about that, too. I think I've maybe kept you from having closer friends your own age, you know?"

"That's not it at all. I wouldn't trade our friendship for a hundred other friends. You've taught me so much and helped me grow so much. It's just that I worry I'll never have as good a friend as you."

"You will. You have to believe me. When you get to high school, I don't know, friendship kinda changes. Guys you barely know now will be your best friends. Once you get into extracurricular stuff, like sports or clubs and stuff, you'll make some really good friends. Just trust me, OK?"

"OK, but I hope you're right."

"I am. Now, let's pick up the pace a little. You're running like an old lady this morning."

I immediately took off in a full sprint, then waited for him at the next corner. It seemed, from that morning, my anxieties about the year to come and the looming loss of Sam's presence in my life receded somewhat to the background of my thoughts and concerns, only to return in the night as I lay awake.

In July, we took our family camping trip—that year to Manatee Springs State Park on the Suwannee River. Sam was simply too busy to join us, so Ed Masters, my tentmate from Scout camp, went along for the week. I made him promise he would not tell dirty jokes around Will or my parents. On the afternoon we arrived at the park it was raining buckets. We waited in the station wagon for the rain to let up so we could make camp, but it seemed relentless. After about thirty minutes, with no indication that the deluge would ease, my Dad ordered the three of us to change into our swimsuits. Ed was a bit embarrassed to do so with my mother sitting in the front seat, but he complied and the four of us—my Dad, Will, Ed and me—exited the car in the midst of a biblical flood and proceeded to set up our campsite in the pouring rain.

Including Ed into our family vacation produced a number of benefits, not the least of which was that Will seemed happier. Ed was never out of sorts and seemed to enjoy anything we did. He never whined, grumbled, or complained and seemed to laugh at everything. Even better, he and Will became fast friends despite the age difference, and so the three of us related more as peers than as siblings. Manatee Springs is one of Florida's magnificent freshwater springs and sits beside the Suwannee River. There is no limit to what three boys can do there—swim, fish, canoe, hike—and we made full use of it all. All too soon, it was time to pack up and head home. Exhausted after the work of breaking camp, Will and Ed slept most of the drive. I sat quietly, content in the knowledge that Will and I had both forged a friendship with Ed, and that his presence served to unite the two of us more closely than we had been in the past.

The remainder of the summer unwound quickly and predictably—VBS at church followed by a week at my grandmother's. Labor Day came, and the opening of school followed the next day.

With the beginning of the school year, I entered junior high. The changes were abrupt and somewhat disconcerting. I now changed classes, had a locker, dressed out for PE, and joined the school chorus and track club. My social studies teacher required each student in his class to report on a current event once every week. As we never knew when we would be called upon to report, I began to make it a habit to skim the evening newspaper and watch the news on television with my parents daily, so I was never at a loss for something to report when called on.

On the evening of Sunday, September 15, I was sitting with my parents as the evening newscast opened with these words: "This morning, in Birmingham, Alabama, four young girls were killed in what some authorities are calling a Klan-related bombing of a church in that southern city." The images on television showed the Sixteenth Street Baptist Church[11] with a gaping hole in one side wall where the bomb had been planted. The newsman told how the girls killed had been in a basement restroom between

---

11 In the early hours of Sunday, September 15, 1963, four members of a local Ku Klux Klan klavern—Thomas Edwin Blanton, Jr., Herman Frank Cash, Robert Edward Chambliss, and Bobby Frank Cherry—planted approximately 19 sticks of dynamite under a set of steps on the east side of the exterior of the Sixteenth Street Baptist Church in downtown Birmingham, Alabama. At 10:22 that morning, the church received a phone call in which a male voice stated "Three minutes," before hanging up. At that moment, five young girls were in a basement restroom on the east side of the building putting on choir robes for the morning worship service to come. The title of the pastor's sermon that morning was to be "A Love That Forgives." Less than a minute later, the bomb exploded, ripping a seven-foot hole in the wall near where the girls were robing. Four of those children—Addie Mae Collins, Carol Denise McNair, Carole Rosanond Robertson, and Cynthia Dionne Wesley—were killed in the blast. A fifth victim died elsewhere in the blast zone. Over a dozen other worshippers were injured in the explosion. Initial investigations of the bombing quickly led to a Klan group named the Cahaba Boys, of which all four of the coconspirators were members, but the investigation stalled due to what the FBI claimed was reluctance on the part of witnesses to talk and a lack of physical evidence. It was not until May 13, 1965 that Blanton, Cash, Chambliss, and Cherry were formally named as perpetrators of the bombing. However, no prosecutions of the four were forthcoming. Later that year, FBI Director J. Edgar Hoover formally blocked any prosecution of the four bombers and blocked the release of any evidence obtained in the investigation. In 1968, the FBI closed their investigation with no charges filed against the suspects. The file was sealed on orders from Hoover. In January, 1971, William Baxley was sworn in as Alabama's Attorney General and almost immediately reopened the investigation. His focus quickly turned to Chambliss. However, it took Baxley several years to gain access to the sealed FBI files. Finally, on November 14, 1977, Robert Chambliss stood trial for the murder of Carol Denise McNair, one of the four girls killed in the bombing. He was found guilty on November 18, 1977, and sentenced to life in prison. He died there in 1985, at the age of 81. In 1995, the FBI reopened their investigation into the bombing. In May, 2000, they announced their findings that the bombing was the work of four members of the KKK group the Cahaba Boys—Chambliss, Blanton, Cash, and Cherry. By that time, Chambliss and Cash were dead, but Blanton and Cherry were still alive and were subsequently arrested. As they approached trial, Cherry was deemed to be suffering from dementia and ruled incompetent to stand trial. Blanton's trial opened on April 24, 2001, with future Senator Doug Jones as prosecutor. The trial concluded a week later with Blanton found guilty on four counts of first-degree murder and sentenced to life in prison. He died in prison on June 26, 2020. The next year, Cherry was ruled competent to stand trial and, on May 6, 2002, his trial opened in Birmingham. On May 22, the jury returned guilty verdicts against Cherry on four counts of first-degree murder. He was sentenced to life in prison and died there on November 18, 2004.

Sunday School and worship when the explosion occurred. I sat with my parents watching and listening, stunned and not believing. I was the age of one of those girls. I thought of how carefree we children felt each week as we left Sunday School and made our way to the sanctuary of our church for worship, how we never could have conceived of anything like this happening in those brief minutes—unregulated by adults and left to laugh and enjoy the friendship of our peers. I pondered the hatred that could have moved men to undertake such a horrific act. I had no answers, no understanding. I was numb, moving in a dense fog of emotion. I went to call Sam.

"I kinda figured you'd call. You saw the story about the bombing, didn't you?"

"Yeah. I don't know. I don't understand why anyone would do that. They were just kids, like us, you know? Why would anybody do something like that? At a church!"

"I don't know, Clint. There are some awful people in this world, that's for sure. That kind of hate. I can't explain it. I can't understand it either. It makes me sick at my stomach."

"I know. I feel kinda, I don't know, kinda like I'm a zombie or something. Like I'm dead but not dead. Does that make sense?"

"Yeah. I know what you mean. Like your body is still moving, but your brain has gone somewhere else."

"Yeah. That's it. Like my brain just won't work."

"You want to come down to my house for a while?"

"Yeah. I'll be there in a minute."

My parents were still sitting on the couch immobilized by shock, watching the continued coverage of the bombing. I told them I was going down to Sam's. It scarcely registered with them.

By this point in our friendship, Sam and I seldom knocked on each other's front doors, but entered through the back doors unannounced. Within two minutes I was in Sam's room. His radio was on and the news was the same. He switched if off.

"I can't listen to any more of that right now. It's like the worst thing I've ever heard. It's worse than when the Thresher went down. That was an accident. This was on purpose. Someone put that bomb there to kill people—at a church, for God's sake—and it killed four kids!" I had never heard such anguish in Sam's voice.

"I know. One of them was eleven, just like me. They were just getting ready for church, you know, just in the bathroom after Sunday School. Who would do this?"

"The Klan, that's who. The fucking Ku Klux Klan!" I had never heard Sam use that word, but it seemed fitting to the occasion.

"So what is the Ku Klux Klan, anyway? I mean, I've heard of it, but what is it?"

"It's a bunch of rednecks who hate Black people and Jews and anybody who's not like them. They mostly just try to scare people. They burn crosses in peoples' yards and stuff like that, but they lynch Blacks too, and do other awful stuff. But this, this is way worse than the stuff they usually do."

"But why bomb a church? A church is where people go to worship God. Why bomb a church?"

"Well, that church is where a lot of folks meet to organize demonstrations and things to protest against discrimination against Blacks. I guess they thought they'd send a message like 'Stop your protesting and get back in the shadows where you belong' and Blacks would just step back quietly and stop trying to get treated like they should be treated." The anger and bitterness in Sam's voice was a bit frightening and certainly out of character for him. I wanted to understand what had happened and why, but I was reluctant to press the matter for fear of making him even more upset than he was.

"What do you think will happen? Will they catch the guys

who did this?"

"They may catch 'em, but nothing'll happen. It's Alabama. They'll never go to jail, let alone the electric chair, for killing a few Black kids."

"That's just wrong. They should be fried for this."

"I know, but that's the way it is. Especially in the South. It's awful to be anything but white if you live in the South."

The next day, as I moved through the school day, still in a fog from the previous day's news, I observed how no one else around me, other than my teachers, seemed to have an awareness of the carnage in Birmingham. Rather, I actually overheard a few kids joking about how "a few nigger kids got blowed up at some nigger church" the day before. The fact that my peers could think such things was devastating to my fundamental sense that people are, in general, good. These students voicing such thoughts had been in my classes since kindergarten. I knew them. I knew their parents. I always assumed they shared the same values with which I had been brought up. But they did not, and I was at a loss to understand how we could appear so similar on the surface but hold such different values within.

18.

MORE TRAGIC IN LIVING COLOR

ABOUT TWO WEEKS after the bombing, Sam called me early on a Saturday morning to announce that his mother had purchased a television. Not only that, but it was a color set. Whereas I was happy for him, I also feared it might limit the time he spent at our house to watch television with us. Of course, he insisted I come down to see it right away.

At the time, the only station broadcasting in color was the NBC affiliate in Jacksonville, so the set was tuned to channel 12, WFGA. The picture was a bit grainy but the contrast with our black and white set was stunning. As it was a Saturday morning, cartoons were airing, and we sat, spellbound, watching Tom and Jerry in living color. Ironically, as it turned out, I ended up spending more time at Sam's house watching their color set than he had ever spent at mine watching our flickering black and white.

On Friday, November 22, shortly after lunch, I was seated in my math class when an announcement came over the school intercom system that President Kennedy had been shot during a parade in Dallas, Texas. Our principal stated that the President had been riding in an open car and had been shot in the arm and taken to a hospital. We were shocked, of course, but not overly so, as it sounded like the President would be fine. A few minutes later, the principal again spoke. In a flat tone, devoid of his typically animated speech, he stated that school was being dismissed immediately, students who rode busses were to go straight to the loading area, students who walked to school were to leave for home immediately, and students who needed to phone parents to arrange a ride home were to come to the office. Such an abrupt dismissal was unheard of, and I knew immediately that there was more to the Kennedy story than we had been told in the previous announcement. Similar thoughts must have been in the minds of my classmates as none of us spoke but quietly collected our belongings and left the classroom. Our math teacher was visibly shaken.

As I walked toward our house, I fell in step with Crazy Christine. She was uncharacteristically solemn, lacking the usual spring in her step. "He's not just shot in the arm. They don't send us home just because the President got shot in the arm."

"I know. I think he's dead."

"Me too. So, you think it was the Russians?"

"I don't know. Could be. But there are a lot of rednecks who don't like him for what he's done for Blacks."

"Yeah. My daddy doesn't much like him for that, but I liked him, and his wife, too, and I think what he was doing was right. So, I guess Vice President Johnson becomes President?"

"Yep. Johnson becomes President."

By this point, we were in front of Sam's house, and he was coming toward us from the high school. "I'm going to wait for Sam. I'll see ya, Christine."

"OK. See ya." She continued on toward her house as Sam reached me. He looked just awful. All the color had drained from his face and tears were streaming down his cheeks.

"He's dead, you know? They've killed Kennedy."

"The principal told us he was shot in the arm, then sent us home. I figured it was more than that. Jesus, what happened."

"I don't know much. Just what our principal told us. He was

in a motorcade in Dallas and got shot. Let's go inside and turn on the TV."

At such times as this, Walter Cronkite was the newsman for much of America. His concise delivery and calming voice were what we needed in this moment. Sam switched on their set, turned the knob to channel 4, and, as the picture tube warmed up, Cronkite's image filled the screen. His face was lined with anguish. "We just have a report from our correspondent Dan Rather in Dallas that he has confirmed that President Kennedy is dead. There is still no official confirmation of this. However, it's a report from our correspondent, Dan Rather, in Dallas, Texas." Sam and I sat, staring blankly at the screen, silent and hollow inside. Time seemed to contract and expand without order or scheme. A few minutes later, a newsroom staff member rushed up to Cronkite's desk and handed him a bulletin. The always-steady Cronkite stumbled "The priest...who were with Kennedy...the two priests who were with Kennedy say that he is dead of his bullet wounds. That seems to be about as official as we can get at this time." Although he continued to stress that this was an unofficial report, Cronkite's tone and demeanor told us all we needed to know—the magic of American Camelot had been murdered on a Dallas street.

"You want something to drink. We've got some tea in the fridge."

"Yeah. Thanks." Sam went to the kitchen to get our drinks. I continued to stare at the television, horrified but unable to look away. Information was sketchy at that point, and conflicting reports were circulating. Cronkite navigated between the known and speculative with his usual grace and authority, filling the time by reviewing the President's schedule for that day. Sam returned to the living room with two glasses of sweet iced tea. He placed them on coasters on the coffee table in front of us.

"This is like a nightmare. If the Russians aren't behind this, I bet the Klan is. But my money's on the Russians. I think its retaliation for the Cuban crisis, or the Bay of Pigs."

I didn't really know what the Bay of Pigs was, but this didn't seem the time to ask. "Crazy Christine just said her daddy didn't like Kennedy because of what he did to help Negroes. It could have been the Klan."

At that moment, Cronkite was handed another bulletin. He put his glasses on and took a moment to silently read the bulletin, then looked into the camera. "From Dallas, Texas, the flash, apparently official. 'President Kennedy died at 1 PM CST, 2:00 Eastern Standard Time...'" He removed his glasses, looked at the studio clock, then replaced his glasses, looking exhausted and defeated, "some thirty-eight minutes ago." These moments are imprinted so deeply that, even as I recall them now, they play in vivid detail across my memory.

The next few days remain a fog of grief for me, lacking clear definition or detail. I remember the scene of Mrs. Kennedy, her pink suit still covered in her husband's blood, standing beside a somber Lyndon Johnson as he was sworn into office as Kennedy's successor. I assume we went to church that Sunday, though I cannot remember doing so. The television coverage was constant, with no commercial interruptions, the Navy hymn serving as its sad soundtrack. I cannot hear that hymn today without being taken back to those days. I remember watching with my family the coverage of Lee Harvey Oswald being led out through the basement of the Dallas Police Department and his sudden, surreal murder by Jack Ruby—all on live television. I remember the slow, somber funeral cortege, and the heart-wrenching scene of little John John saluting his father's caisson. We had no school for the entire week after the assassination, but there was nothing enjoyable about that time away. For me, it was a week of untold sorrow, a week when the second parenthesis—Birmingham being the first—closed on my childhood.

As if there weren't enough drama in my life, about a month after Kennedy's death, my voice broke. For boy sopranos, this is a terrifying experience. Treble boys work diligently to develop the upper range as well as the strength and quality of their singing voices. Then, quite suddenly, it ends. The clear, high notes break, then disappear, the range drops into the tenor or baritone neighborhood and the treble boy is filled with a sense of dread that, after voice change, he may be left painfully ordinary—just one average tenor or bass among millions of others. For some, this change spans months. For me, it seemed to be over in about two weeks. One week, I was singing soprano. Two weeks later, I was wedged among the second tenors. Over the next few months, my range dropped such that I settled comfortably into the bass section. Over the coming years, my voice grew and improved through formal study. However, during the fall of 1963, that could not be known, nor could it ease the anxiety as my self-assurance took such a nosedive.

As Christmas arrived, it did so with a diminished glow. The previous months had produced such horror and uncertainty throughout the nation, as well as in my own small sphere, that the Christmas season seemed somehow stripped of joy. Baby Jesus was still in the manger, but it seemed the rest of us were focused on something else. For me, I was robbed of the comfort of music that year. The previous year, I had sung the role of *Amahl*, and the story of that young boy and his miraculous healing had brought new meaning to my Christmas. This year, I couldn't even sing "O, Holy Night" on Christmas Eve because, in my thinking, my voice was gone.

19.

PITY THE MOCKINGBIRD

ON THE MORNING after Christmas, Sam called. "Hey, since it's your birthday tomorrow, and that's kinda the anniversary of our being friends, I want to take you to the movies."

"Oh, OK. Cool. So, what are we gonna see?"

"*To Kill a Mockingbird* is on at the Howell Theater. We can ride our bikes and see the one-thirty showing."

"OK. I've heard of it, but what's it about?"

"Gregory Peck plays a lawyer named Atticus Finch in a little town in Alabama. In the movie—well, in the book, too—he defends a Black man on trial on a bogus rape charge. There are a couple of kids who play major parts 'cause some of the story happens through their eyes. We read the book in my English class last year."

"I don't know. I mean, I want to go, but I don't know if my parents'll let me. It sounds like a movie for grown-ups."

"Clint, you're gonna be twelve tomorrow. You've just lived through two of the most awful things that ever happened in this country. I think you're old enough to see this movie, but check with your parents and call me back." He sounded just a bit exasperated with me.

"OK. I'll call you right back."

I found my mother in the kitchen packing up Christmas leftovers to go in the freezer. With trepidation, I posed the idea of the movie to her, and to my absolute surprise, she immediately agreed.

"I didn't think you'd let me see it," I confessed.

"Well, it's a pretty adult theme. I read the book as soon as it came out, so I know the story. But I think you're old enough, and with everything that's going on in the country these days, I think it's a good story for you to know. So, yes, I'm OK with you going to see it, but I want to talk to you about it when you get back."

"Yes ma'am."

"Is Sam going to drive you two?"

"No ma'am. We're going to ride our bikes downtown. You know it's been four years since he taught me to ride my bike, so this is kind of a celebration. He's paying my way, too."

"That's very nice of him. You boys be careful and watch out for cars."

"Yes ma'am."

The ride from our neighborhood into downtown was primarily a long downhill coast. We left about one o'clock and were at the ticket booth around one-twenty. True to his word, Sam purchased my ticket and, once inside, bought us Cokes and popcorn—all to celebrate my birthday, he said.

By my estimation, the Howell Theater had passed its heyday back in the forties. By this time, it looked a bit tired. The threadbare curtains sagged, and if you stood in one place too long, your shoes stuck to the floor. Like all such facilities in the segregated South, the Howell provided a separate entrance for "Coloreds" around the corner on the side of the building. In addition, seating was segregated, with Black moviegoers restricted to the balcony. As the cartoons ended and Harper Lee's gut-wrenching story began to unfold on the screen, I grew more and more uncomfortable at the fact that my hometown in many ways resembled the fictional town of Maycomb, Alabama.

During the trial scenes, when Atticus Finch[12] labored unsuccessfully to convince the all-white, all-male jury of Tom Robinson's innocence, a feeling of unease began to grip me—a sense that this was not going to end well for poor Tom. As Atticus delivered his passionate closing, I began to hear quiet comments and "Amens" from the balcony. Sam began to join in—not loudly, but certainly at a volume sufficient to be heard. Others on the floor level—the white section—began to turn toward us. I was embarrassed at first, but then, as Atticus laid bare the injustice that had been committed against Tom, I grew angry. After the guilty verdict was announced, the floor of the courtroom—the white section—emptied, and a defeated Atticus began to exit. As he walked toward the courtroom door, the Black spectators in the courtroom balcony stood quietly to honor him. As those on the screen took to their feet, a shuffling emanated from the balcony above us. Sam and I, as well as many others on the floor, turned to discover that those in the Howell Theater balcony were standing silently as well. Without a thought, Sam and I rose with them in silent solidarity. I was filled with both pride and apprehension at our action, but it was in that moment that I knew without question I wanted to pursue the law as a profession.

A few minutes later in the film—at the point where the Sheriff informs Atticus that Tom has been killed by a deputy as

---

12 Gregory Peck's Oscar-winning portrayal of Atticus Finch in the 1962 adaptation of Harper Lee's Pulitzer-winning novel *To Kill a Mockingbird* is, to this day, considered one of the greatest film portrayals in cinematic history. In 2003, Peck's Atticus Finch was declared the "greatest film hero of the past 100 years" by the American Film Institute. In her notes for the film's rerelease on DVD, Harper Lee said of Gregory Peck, "When I learned that Gregory Peck would play Atticus Finch in the film production of *To Kill a Mockingbird*, I was of course delighted: here was a fine actor who had made great films—what more could a writer ask for? ...The years told me his secret. When he played Atticus Finch, he had played himself, and time has told all of us something more: when he played himself, he touched the world."

he tried to escape—my pain and sense of injustice overflowed and tears coursed down my cheeks. I glanced over at Sam to see he was crying quietly as well. By the time the end credits rolled, I suppose the white audience had either forgotten our cultural indiscretion or judged us to be beyond redemption, because no one spoke to us as we exited the theater.

Once on the street, we moved toward our bicycles when we were approached by a tall Black boy about Sam's age.

"Hi. I saw you two stand and wanted to thank you. That was a pretty brave thing to do."

"It just seemed like the right thing to do. I'm Sam, by the way, and this is my friend Clint." Sam extended his hand and the other teen took it. "I guess you go to Lincoln?"

"Yeah. I'm a senior this year. My name's David, by the way. David Robinson."

"Any kin to Tom?" They both laughed.

"No. Definitely not, but a funny coincidence."

Throughout this brief exchange I had been standing to the side, somewhat spellbound at what I was observing—social interaction between two young men—one Black, one white—devoid of the paternalism that typically accompanied such interactions. At that moment, a middle-aged white man passed us and directed a comment to David.

"Boy, you need to move on, and don't be hanging around the white entrance."

"Yes, Sir," David replied to the man. Then to us, "Let's go around the corner." We stepped around the corner to the sidewalk along the side street. David continued, "So, the reason I wanted to talk to you—well, besides thanking you for standing up with us—was to ask you about something. You know, our two schools are gonna be desegregated in the next few years."

"Sure. That's inevitable. It's just a matter of time. Probably not before I graduate, but definitely by the time Clint gets there."

"Well, we're trying to form a Youth Bi-Racial Committee like the adult one the County Commission set up, but we're having trouble finding white students to be on it. Right now, we only have two white students. One is Laura Grimes. Her mother is the director of the Community Action Program for the county. The other is the pastor's son from St. James Methodist, Jimmy Williamson—probably because his father is on the adult one. That's it so far."

"Yeah. I know Jimmy. He's actually on the track team with me, but we've never talked about stuff like this. I'm really glad he's doing this."

"Yeah, he's a good guy. Well, anyway, we feel like we need to be ready for however the desegregation happens, and we think having some student leaders at both schools who've been involved in the decision-making can really help to just make things go smoother, you know?"

"Yeah. That's a really good idea. Who's sponsoring this? I mean, is it just you students, or is it more official?"

"Oh, yeah. The County Commission is setting it up. They voted and everything, so it's official. Anyway, I was wondering if you would join us, be on the committee?"

"Wow! I don't know. I'm not really a student leader," Sam replied. "I mean, I'm not in student government or anything like that. I'm not in Key Club or really any other school clubs. Just track."

"That doesn't matter. We need students who really care about these issues, and it looks like you do."

"Yeah. I do care about race relations. I think it's pretty hypocritical for us to talk about equal justice, about 'one nation under God,' when half the population is treated like second-class citizens or bombed in their churches. Yeah, these things make me pretty mad."

"That's what we're looking for—students who want to make a difference. So, will you join? Will you do it?"

"Yeah. I guess so. What do you guys do, I mean, what would I be expected to do?"

"We meet every other week on Mondays after school at the Community Action Center. We have two adult sponsors from the adult Committee who help keep us on track. Right now, we're just discussing things we can do to help our schools with the transition—things like having some joint activities or trying to get students from one school to attend athletic events at the other. Stuff like that. We also spend a lot of time talking about ways to deal with prejudice. We talk about politics a lot, too."

"OK. I'll do it."

"That's great. I need to get your phone number, and I'll call you about the details. You'll actually be appointed by the County Commission, so you'll need to attend their meeting when you're voted on."

"Oh, OK. I don't have anything to write on to give you my number. Do you?"

"No, but I'll remember it. I'm good with numbers."

"OK. It's East 57225. And it's a party line, and Mrs. Foster on our line is really nosey, so watch what you say."

David laughed. "OK. East 57225. Got it, and thanks. It was really great meeting you two." David extended his hand, first to Sam, who shook it, then to me. I shook it also. At that, he turned and walked off.

During this exchange, I had been quietly observing, wishing I were old enough to participate on the committee—old enough to do something of consequence. I turned to Sam. "Can we walk our bikes a while? I want to ask you some stuff."

"Sure. Let's go." We walked back around the corner to the

front of the theater where we had left our bicycles and began walking them toward home.

"I never shook hands with a Black person before."

"So, how was it?"

"Kinda strange."

"So, what, did you think the black was gonna rub off on you?"

"No! I'm not stupid, you know."

"I know. I was just messing with you. But really, how did it seem?"

"Not bad, just, I don't know, different. It was like doing something you're not supposed to do."

"I know what you mean. It's like we're taught in these subtle ways that we're not supposed to treat Black people like equals. I mean, no one comes right out and says it, but the message is there anyway."

"So, this club, or whatever, this thing David asked you to join—are you a little scared about doing it. I mean, there's a lot of crazy stuff going on, like Birmingham, you know. I mean even over in St. Augustine, there's been bad stuff going on."

"I know, but white people—at least white people who know that things have to change—we have to stand up. Why did you stand up during the movie?"

"I don't know. Like you said, it just seemed like the right thing to do. I guess part of it was 'cause you stood up, but part of it was 'cause I just wanted to say 'I'm with you' to the folks in the balcony—the folks in the balcony in the movie and in the theater, too."

"That's what I mean. It's just the right thing to do. You know, I think there's hope for you, little brother, even for a little squirt like you. Naw, don't punch me!"

Sam and I parted at my house, and I went inside to find my mother seated on the couch, waiting. "Sit down a minute, Son, and tell me about the movie. What did you think?"

"It was really good. And really sad. It made me mad." I then described to her how Sam and I had spontaneously stood with the Black spectators in the balconies. She was quiet for a moment, and I feared I had done something wrong.

"Did you stand up just because Sam stood up?"

"No ma'am. We both stood up at the same time. When I saw the Black folks in the balcony standing up, it just hit me that the Black folks in the movie were stuck up in the balcony, and the Black folks here in Palatka are stuck up in the balcony. It just seemed wrong, and the way to say 'It's wrong, this whole thing is wrong' was to stand up with them. Sam and I were the only white people who stood up, and the others were staring at us, but it just felt right. I was scared, but it just felt right."

"That was a very brave thing for you and Sam to do. Maybe a bit dangerous, but I'm proud of you for doing it. If white folks don't begin to take a stand in this civil rights movement and confront the KKK and other hate groups, the hate is going to win."

"Yes ma'am. The white people in the movie, the Ewells, they lied about what they said Tom did to Mayella. Tom was innocent, but they found him guilty because he was Black. He had a messed up left arm, and Atticus proved he couldn't have hurt Mayella, but the jury just ignored all that. And then, he got killed trying to escape. It was all just wrong. And Sam and I cried when the Sheriff told Atticus Tom was dead."

"It's a really sad story, but it pretty well shows the way things are for Black people here in the South. Now, I know it'll be hard to do, but try to put it out of your mind for a while. Do something physical like play outside or go for a run or something like that."

"Yes ma'am."

For some reason, I wanted to be alone for the remainder of the afternoon. However, Will wanted to play basketball—he was picking up the sport and was already better than me—so we played several games of Horse on the driveway. The effect was to temporarily distract me from the avalanche of thoughts that had cascaded through my mind during and since the film. By bedtime, both my mind and body were exhausted, and I slept soundly on that, the eve of my twelfth birthday.

20.

1964, "A REALLY BIG SHEW"

1964 WAS THE year Crazy Christine went, well…, crazy. She who had always been rough and tumble, who could stand up to—and often triumph over—any boy in the neighborhood, became absolutely obsessed with a young pop quartet from Liverpool, England. In January, the Beatles' first album was released in the United States, and somehow a copy of that release fell into the hands of the biggest tomboy in Putnam County. By the time the Fab Four appeared on the Ed Sullivan Show for the first time in February, Christine was a full-on devotee. Perhaps, in looking back, we all needed a diversion from the horrors of the previous year. If so, the Beatles certainly provided it.

Ed Sullivan's Sunday evening variety show was a staple at our home. On the evening of February 9, we sat in our living room as the show began with Sullivan's understated lead-in and his distinctive articulation of the word "show." Then, as they say, all hell broke loose. When the Beatles began their set, the audience—packed with teenaged girls—went temporarily insane—screaming, crying, jumping up and down in their seats, pulling at their hair. At the same time, the quartet on stage bumped and gyrated, shook their long manes—at least certainly longer than my crew cut—and unquestionably changed the course of popular music for decades to come. As for me, I sat staring and confused. I simply didn't understand the lure. To me, their songs seemed trivial and the lyrics trite.

All the hysteria from the audience was completely lost on me.

By this time, my musical tastes had been shaped by the influences of Sam, who was a fan of Bob Dylan, Woody Guthrie, and Pete Seeger, and my cousin Carol, who had introduced me to the folk trio Peter, Paul, and Mary. To me, these folk singers sang songs and ballads with history and context, meaning and substance. I found the Beatles' music shallow and rather pointless. So, as I watched the Beatles that Sunday evening, I kept looking for something of value—and simply found nothing. Though I would later come to enjoy and appreciate their music, on that night, I went to bed questioning my own musical preferences as well as the wisdom of my generation. The next morning, I met up with Christine as we walked to school.

"Oh, Clint," she screeched, "Did you see them last night on Ed Sullivan."

"See who?" Of course, I knew who "who" was.

"Don't be an ass. You know who I mean. The Beatles, you dummy. Did you see them?"

"Yes, I saw them."

"Weren't they fabulous? I mean, they're just so perfect, and they sang like they were singing to me 'I want to hold your hand.'" She actually began singing it as we walked to school.

"OK, OK. I get it. Actually, I don't get it. What do you see in them? I think their music is dumb. It doesn't say anything. 'She loves you, yeah, yeah, yeah...'" Now it was my turn to sing.

"Clint, you're the one that's dumb. They're just dreamy."

"Dreamy? What does that even mean. 'They're dreamy.' More like a nightmare."

At that point, Crazy Christine punched me in the upper arm—hard, I might add—and ran off toward school yelling as she went, "All boys are stupid, and I'm never going to speak to you again."

I do not recall being disappointed at the time by that threat.

Though less cataclysmic than Beatlemania, another event occurred in my life early that year that centered on Will and my mother. Will had joined the Cub Scouts the previous year, and, at the New Year, my mother became his Den Mother. Simply put, that meant she was responsible for a group of about eight or ten Cubs who met at our house each Saturday morning. As a matter of convenience, I was appointed Den Leader for that Cub Pack. The Den Leader is a Boy Scout who assists the Den Mother with activities and acts as something of a role model and recruiting agent for the younger Cubs. Because Sam and I had been running regularly for several years, it seemed to me that I could best help my mother by taking the Cubs down to the track at the elementary school for a period each week and running out some of their energy. As it turned out, this worked quite well and gave my mother an opportunity to prepare for the next activity without a living room full of squirming eight-to-ten-year-olds. It also seemed wise to me to recruit Sam to help me with this activity. He did so somewhat reluctantly as, he claimed, he really didn't have any experience working with kids. In rebuttal, I reminded him that he had taught "this kid" how to ride a bicycle, how to run, and how to be a relatively decent human being, so his argument was without merit.

Because the high school track team used the track daily, Sam knew how to mark off a fifty-yard course and we began to time the boys running the fifty-yard dash. But before we timed their sprints each week, we sent them for a slow warm-up jog around the full track. Sam had drawn up a chart on graph paper and we recorded each boy's time as the weeks progressed. On the Saturday after my encounter with Christine over the Beatles, as the Cubs ran the track, I probed Sam for his take on this Beatle hysteria.

"So, Christine has gone nuts over the Beatles. She actually

punched me Monday morning for saying I thought their music was dumb. What's with this Beatles thing, anyway?"

"I'm not sure. I think it has something to do with non-conformity."

"What? What is non-conformity?"

"It's like doing stuff that doesn't fit with what's expected. Like their long hair. Most guys have crew cuts like you and me, but the Beatles have long hair. It doesn't conform to what most people think is right. And like the way they kinda move around on stage, it's not like singers and musicians usually do. So, they don't conform to peoples' expectations. Does that make sense?"

"Yeah. I get that, but why be that way? Why be, what did you say, non-conformity?"

"Non-conforming."

"OK. Why be that way?"

"Because the old way isn't working. The old way puts Blacks at the back of the bus." Sam grew more agitated as he continued. "The old way goes to war when the rich arms manufacturers and their bribed politicians say so, like what's happening in Vietnam. The old way meant kids were seen and not heard. None of that is working anymore. So, non-conformity is the new wave. The way we can say 'Things have to change.'"

I was taken somewhat aback. "So, you see all that in the Beatles' long hair?"

"Yeah. I do. It's their way of saying 'We're not gonna do things the way they've been done before.'"

"Maybe I misjudged them. I don't know. This is all a lot for me to take in. I still think their music is dumb."

"Yeah. I do too. Give me Dylan or Woody any day."

"Yeah. Me, too. I like their music 'cause it's got a message to it."

"Yeah, but if you listen to it, it's the same message: Things have to change. You know, like '...how many times can a man turn his head and pretend that he just doesn't see?' There are big changes coming, Clint, big changes. People who've been ignored are tired of being ignored."

By that point in our conversation, several of the boys had completed their circuit of the track, so we began their timed sprints. Still, Sam's explanation played like a loop in my mind and I began to listen for that message he claimed was embedded in my music—things have to change.

As the brief Florida winter slipped unnoticed into spring, an undefined unease gripped me. I became somewhat melancholy as the end of the school year approached. Then, one day in early May, it struck me right between the eyes: Sam was graduating, joining the Navy, and leaving, probably forever. Now that it had a name, my depression deepened. One afternoon, about two weeks before the end of the school year, I walked down to Sam's house. I found him in his room, trying on his cap and gown. I stepped into his room, saw him in his gradation attire and immediately burst into tears.

"Holy crap, Clint, what's the matter? Did your dog die or something?"

"Not funny, Sam. You know I don't have a dog." I sniffed and snorted. "Seeing you in that means you're gonna be leaving real soon and I'll hardly ever see you again." The tears returned.

"Whoa, man. It's not like I'm goin' away forever. I don't enlist until the middle of June, so we'll have some time after graduation to hang out. Plus, I'll be home on leave sometimes."

"Yea, but by the time you come home on leave, you'll be like an adult. You won't want to hang out with a kid like me. You'll want to do grownup stuff."

"Not true. I'll still want to go for bike rides and go running. We can go camping and stuff like that. It'll work out. I promise you. I want you to be proud of me and happy for me, Clint."

"I am, and I will, but I'm gonna miss you so bad." At that, I flung myself at him, wrapped my arms around him and wailed like a love-sick tomcat. He just hugged me, and we rocked side-to-side for a while until my sobbing eased.

"You OK now? I hope you didn't get snot on my gown."

I laughed and wiped my eyes. "Yeah. Sorry. I hate being such a baby."

"It's OK, man. I know how you're feeling. I'm kinda sad about leaving my whole life behind—you, my mom, my school friends—but I'm pretty excited about what's to come. I really hope you can be excited for me. You know, that's what friends do for each other, they share each other's excitement."

"I am excited for you, but I'm scared for you, too. There's something about Vietnam on the news nearly every night. Everybody's saying we're going to be at war in a year. I just worry about you being in the Navy."

"Look. I'll probably be assigned to a huge ship. It's about the safest place I could be if we really end up in the war. North Vietnam doesn't have much of a navy or many planes. It's not like in World War II when the Japanese took out so many of our ships. It'll be different. Plus, it may not even come that that. This could all be just a bunch of saber rattling."

"What's that mean?"

"Just kind of a pissing contest between the US and North Vietnam. Unless the Chinese get involved, then it's a whole different ball game, but I don't think it'll come to that. Anyway, let's talk about something else. Like, how do I look in this get-up?"

"You look pretty cool, for a guy in a dress."

"It's not a dress, dummy. It's my academic regalia." He said this with a feigned air of snobbishness.

"OK. But it still looks like a dress. What's the gold rope for?"

"It means I'm an honor graduate—that I have a good GPA."

"What's a GPA?"

"It means grade point average. It's like they give you a number for every A you make, every B, and so forth. You get four points for an A, three for a B. So, they add up all your grades for the whole time you're in high school, then divide that total by the number of grading periods and that gives you your GPA. The highest you can get is a 4.0."

"That seems pretty confusing, if you ask me. So, what's your GPA?"

"Three point eight."

"So, I guess that's pretty good, then, huh? Mostly As, right?"

"Yeah. Mostly As. That's why I get to wear the gold cord. You have to have a 3.5 GPA to be an honor grad."

"Gee, I didn't know you were smart," I laughed. He began chasing me around the room, threw me on his unmade bed and began to tickle torture me to the point I nearly wet my pants. "OK, OK! I'm gonna pee my pants. I take it back. I knew you were smart. You're the smartest guy in town. Now, let me up."

"OK, but first you have to say 'Sam is the smartest person I've ever known' three times."

"OK. OK. Sam is the smartest person I've ever known. Sam is the smartest person I've ever known. Sam is the biggest smartass I've ever known." The tickling resumed. I did need to change my underwear when I got home.

On Friday evening, May 29, my family sat with Sam's mother in the stands at the football stadium for his graduation. After the high school principal made a few opening remarks, he announced dramatically, "Ladies and gentlemen, I present to you the Palatka Senior High School graduating class of 1964." The crowd applauded and rose to their feet as the high school band began playing the oft-used section of Edward Elgar's *Pomp and Circumstance*. From the north end of the football field the line of graduates began processing toward the rows of seats set up mid-field. The honor graduates entered first, and I immediately spotted Sam. Dressed in his burgundy cap and gown and wearing the gold-braided cord, he towered above most of the other graduates. As he passed in front of us, he quickly glanced up and smiled. I waved enthusiastically, though I was not certain he had seen me. Absentmindedly, I began counting the graduates—thirteen honor graduates and 184 others, for a total of 197. The line progressed and, in orderly fashion, filled the chairs. When all were in place, the band came to a cadence and ended, an area minister took the podium and pronounced an invocation, the graduates sat, and the ceremony began.

By the time the salutatorian had concluded her speech I was bored. But as the principal began to award the diplomas, I perked up—particularly since the honor graduates would be recognized first. Sam was fourth in the line after the valedictorian, salutatorian, and one other girl. When the principal called out "Samuel Adams Sanders," the others in our entourage applauded politely, but I was on my feet clapping wildly, yelling "whoo hoo!" This Sam heard, and glanced my way with a broad smile on his face. My mother tugged on my pants leg urging me to sit, which I did reluctantly. The remainder of the ceremony was of no interest to me, so I brooded in silence over the fact that Sam would be leaving in less than a month.

We caught up with Sam briefly after the ceremony. By this time, he had removed his cap and unzipped his gown. "Mom, would you take this stuff? I'm gonna ride to the grad night party with Jimmy Williamson and I don't want to fool with it." He then slipped off his gown and handed it, his cap, and his diploma to his mother. Looking at me, he smiled, "Hey, I heard you yell for me. Thanks."

"Sure. I was really proud of you. Hey, I never knew your

middle name was Adams. It's Adams, right, with an S, not Adam?"

Sam's mother chuckled. "That's right, Adams with an S. His father really admired Samuel Adams, so Sam was named after him."

I assumed Samuel Adams was someone I should know, or would perhaps learn about in high school, so I responded as though it made perfect sense. "Oh, OK. So, you're going to a party?"

"Yeah. The Kiwanis Club throws a party for all the grads so we won't go out drinking and do something stupid. There's a dance with a bunch of refreshments, then we go to a movie—a double feature—about two in the morning, then they serve us a huge breakfast at the Methodist Church. By the time it's all over, the sun's coming up and all we want to do is go home and go to bed. It's actually a pretty smart idea."

"Jimmy Williamson's that guy in that racial committee thing you're on, right?"

"Yeah. We've gotten to be pretty good friends. We think the same way about a bunch of stuff. His dad's the pastor at the Methodist Church where we'll have breakfast tomorrow morning. Well, listen, I've got to go. Thank you all for coming. It really meant a lot to have you all here."

My dad responded for our family. "We were proud to be here, Sam. You're really a member of our family, and we wouldn't've been anywhere else tonight. Congratulations." My dad extended his hand and Sam shook it.

"Thank you, sir. Well, I'll see you all later." And he was off. And I went home and pouted until I fell asleep in my bed feeling very small and alone, and very sorry for myself.

21.

"YOU'RE THE ONE WHO'S GOIN' AWAY, WHY AM I AFRAID TO SAY I'LL MISS YOU WHEN YOU'RE GONE?"

SAM WAS SCHEDULED to enlist in the Navy on June 17, meaning I had a little over two weeks to spend time with him. I knew, of course, that he would have a hundred things to accomplish prior to that date, including spending time with other friends, so my time with him would be limited. Thus, I hatched a plan to carve out some quality time as our last outing together.

My grandmother in Campville lived on a large lot, the back acre of which was wooded and uncleared. I proposed to Sam that we go on a two-night campout in those woods, that we cook our own meals and not rely on my grandmother for anything. He agreed, though with serious questions about the use of a latrine. So, we began to plan our trip. The first challenge was securing transportation. Sam and his mother had only one vehicle, so we needed to convince my parents to let us use one of theirs. When I floated the idea, I was surprised that they agreed immediately and even worked out a means for both of them to get to work in order for us to take my father's station wagon.

So, on the Friday morning before Sam would enlist the following week, we made the drive to Campville. When we arrived, my grandmother insisted we eat lunch with her. We did, then began carting our equipment back into the woods behind her house—tent, cooler, sleeping bags, folding chairs,

Coleman lantern, and more. After we had chosen our campsite and cleared the underbrush, we pitched my tent, tossed our gear inside, dug a latrine, and began to scour for firewood. Fortunately, my dad had sent a bundle of fat pine with us to make fire-building easier.

During my twelve years, I had spent a good amount of time in the Florida scrub. I was comfortable with the out-of-doors and most of the creatures that inhabited it. However, I remained—and do so to this day—quite uncomfortable around snakes. As Sam and I probed the thick woods for dry firewood, we came upon a small, sun-dappled clearing no more than ten feet across. We moved into the clearing, looking down and paying little attention to our surroundings when we suddenly found ourselves less than three feet away from an enormous rattlesnake. The snake was coiled and basking in a patch of sunlight. Sam, I, and the snake, all became aware of each other at the same moment. The snake coiled more tightly and began to rattle. Sam and I froze.

"Holy shit, Clint! Look at that thing! What do we do?"

Though I had never encountered a rattler in the wild, I had been taught in Scouts how best to deescalate an encounter with one. "Don't move a muscle. We're gonna freeze for a few seconds to let him know we won't come any closer. Keep your eyes on him." My heart was pounding and I was terrified, but I knew I had to keep both of us still and calm. After about twenty seconds, the rattling stopped, but the snake remained coiled and ready to strike. "Now, we're gonna take one big step backward. Really slow. Like slow motion." Very slowly and deliberately, we stepped back. The snake resumed rattling.

"Jesus, Clint! Why did he start that again?"

"He's not sure what we're doing. He's scared of us, too."

"No way he's as scared as me. No way."

After what seemed like a month—again, no more than twenty seconds—the snake stopped rattling, but still stayed ready to strike. "OK. We're gonna take another big step back. Slowly. Slow motion, remember." This time, the snake remained silent, but also coiled, as we slowly stepped back. "OK. Let's take two or three more steps back this time but keep watching him." Three more slow steps back and we were now about ten feet from the snake. He remained coiled but did not sound. "OK. Now we can turn around and get the hell out of here!" We turned and sprinted about thirty yards before stopping to catch our breath.

"Jesus, that was scary. I don't know if I can sleep out here knowing that thing's out here, too."

"I don't think he'll bother us. Especially once we get a fire going. Our camp's a good hundred yards away. But just to be on the safe side, I think we should clear another five feet of brush around our campsite."

"OK, but if he shows up again, we're packing up. OK?"

"OK."

"By the way, you really handled that well. I was scared shitless, but you really kept calm and got us away. I'm impressed."

"Thanks, but don't think I wasn't scared. I thought my heart was gonna bust out of my chest. I've never seen a rattler in the woods. It's pretty scary when you just come up on one like that. I'm just glad he rattled. Sometimes they don't—they just strike."

We continued walking toward our campsite, still carrying the armloads of firewood we had collected before our encounter with the rattler. "So, what do you do if you get bitten by one?"

"Well, we learned in Scouts to try to suck the poison out, tie a tourniquet between the snakebite and your heart—that's if you get bitten on your arm or leg—and get to a hospital quick." I began to chuckle.

"What's so funny?"

"One time in one of our Scout meetings they were teaching us first aid for snakebites, and the Scoutmaster was telling us how to suck the poison out, and this kid asked 'What do you do if you get bit on the butt?' And the Scoutmaster said 'That's when you find out who your friends are.'"

Our laughter helped to distance us from the terror of the past few minutes. We arrived at our campsite, dropped our loads of firewood, and immediately busied ourselves with expanding the clearing around our site.

"Let's take all this underbrush we've chopped down and make a boma," I suggested.

"So, what's a boma?"

"It's what they do in Africa to keep their animals safe at night. They make this circle of underbrush like a little stockade to keep out things like lions."

"How about rattlesnakes? Will it work for them?"

"Not really, but it'll make us feel safer, anyway. Plus, it'll be fun to make."

After about an hour, we had carefully placed the cut underbrush around the perimeter of our campsite. The effect was to separate us from the woods beyond and afford a sense of security and privacy our site had been lacking. By this time, it was late afternoon, and we had yet to build a fire or make any preparations for dinner.

The geology of north Florida is devoid of rocks, by which I mean there are no rocks lying about on the surface anywhere. Consequently, we dug a pit into the soft, sandy soil, scraped the ground of weeds and combustible materials for about three feet around the pit, and commenced building a fire. With the fat pine kindling my dad had sent, the fire started quickly. Dinner for this evening was to be Hobo Stew, a Boy Scout standard—packets of heavy-duty aluminum foil packed with stew beef, cut potatoes, onions, and carrots, and seasoned with my mom's secret ingredient—Lipton Onion Soup Mix. After the fire had burned down, we carefully placed our dinner packets atop the coals and waited.

"You know a lot about this stuff, don't you?"

"Yeah, I guess. I mean, we've been family camping for ages and I've learned more stuff in Scouts."

"But you're, I don't know, I guess comfortable is the word. You're comfortable out here with all this. Even the rattlesnake. I mean I know you were scared like me, but you kept your cool. You really saved our asses."

"You can bet I was scared alright. I mean, I come across snakes all the time in the woods when we're camping, but that's the first time I've seen a rattlesnake. When we froze, all the stuff I had been taught came back to me—keep your eyes on the snake, no fast movements, back off slowly, wait, back off more. All that was right there in the front of my brain. I guess my Scoutmasters would be happy some of that stuff stuck."

"You have to tell them about today. They'll be proud of you."

"Yeah. I'm kinda one of the nerds in our troop, but the funny thing is, I know a whole lot more about camping and staying in the woods than a lot of the cool guys. This'll definitely improve my reputation!"

By this point, we could hear sizzling coming from our foil packets, and the escaping steam brought a delicious aroma to our noses.

"Man, those things smell great. I'm starving. Can we break out a couple of Cokes while we wait?"

"Sure." I reached over to the cooler we had brought and extracted two cold canned Cokes. "Man, these are freezing!" I handed one to Sam.

"Thanks. Hey, how do we know when those are done?"

"You can pretty much tell by the smell. When you start smelling the vegetables, then it's about ready. We usually let 'em go about forty-five minutes, just to be sure."

We continued to talk about trivial things while our dinners cooked. Sam told me about the graduate party, how he danced with a few girls but mostly hung out with Jimmy Williamson, about the second-rate movies they screened for them at the Howell, and the massive breakfast meal at the Methodist Church.

"So, do you kinda have a thing for Jimmy Williamson?"

"Nah. He's a nice guy and all, but we're just friends. He's kinda awkward in big crowds and I am too, so we just find ourselves thrown together sometimes. You know I've gotten to know him in the Youth Bi-Racial Committee and he really takes on leadership there, but it's a small group. He's really smart—especially about history and politics and stuff—but, no, I'm really not attracted to him that way. We're just two misfits who feel more comfortable in each other's company."

"Oh, OK. So, do you think you might meet somebody when you join the Navy?"

"Man, that's a bad idea, really. If the Navy had the slightest idea I like guys, they'd toss my ass in a New York minute. Homosexuality is cause for immediate dishonorable discharge. So nope, I'm not looking for a boyfriend in the Navy."

"I don't know, it's kinda sad that you can't, you know, have somebody special like everybody else does. It just seems wrong."

"Clint, you're just saying that because you know me. Not too many people can put a face on homosexuality because they don't know anyone who's gay."

"Gay? What do you mean by gay?"

"It's a word we use to describe ourselves. It's simpler than saying homosexual, and we don't want to call ourselves queers."

"Jeez, no. When somebody at school calls somebody else

a queer it's like a cuss word. They usually end up in a fight. No, queer's a bad word. Gay works. But now I'll never be able to hear someone say they're gay without thinking something else!" We both laughed at that. "Hey, dinner's ready."

We carefully lifted the foil packets out of the fire, placed them on metal meal trays, opened them, and began to eat.

"Oh, man, this is delicious! I was kinda worried about how this was gonna turn out, but it's great."

"Yeah. This is our typical Friday evening dinner at weekend Scout campouts. It saves a lot of time that first night when you're trying to get camp set up and all. It's easy and quick. Course there's always some kid who forgets to bring his, so I always end up sharing mine, but that's OK. My mom always packs too much in mine anyway."

After we had eaten, we built the fire back up and sat quietly for a while. Darkness came early in those thick woods, and the night began to sing with crickets, cicadas, and an owl in the distance.

"If my dad was here, he'd call that owl right up to our campsite."

"You're joking, right?"

"No, really. It's pretty amazing. He can sound just like an owl, and he calls to them, and they fly over and light in a tree close by and then they talk to each other."

"That's pretty cool." A heavy, unexpected silence hung between us. "I guess I missed out on a lot of stuff by not having a dad around."

I was uncertain how to respond and hesitated a bit. "Yeah. I guess you're right. I never really thought about it. I guess I take my parents for granted. I mean, sometimes they tick me off, but they're really great, and my dad is so much nicer than a lot of other dads I've met."

"Yeah. Your folks have always been great to me. I remember that summer I went with y'all to the mountains. That was the first time I ever went camping. Your folks really made me feel like I was a member of your family. But it was kinda sad, too, because I realized for the first time what I had missed—two parents and maybe a little brother or sister. It's just been me and Mom for as long as I can remember. Then, I was like in this big family with a mom and a dad and two little brothers. It was great, but sad at the same time. Does that make sense?"

"Yeah. It does, and I'm really sorry about your father. But, hey, if you want a little brother, you can have Will." That bit of humor parted the clouds of sadness that had gathered around us, and we laughed together.

"Hey, Clint, why don't you sing something?"

"What? Man, I don't know. I guess I could sing a folk song. I wish I played the guitar."

"No. That's cool. Sing a folk song. I haven't heard you sing since the opera thing."

I grabbed a pitch out of thin air and began to sing.

You're the one who's goin' away,
Why am I afraid to say
I'll miss you when you're gone?

I paused.

"Hey, why'd you stop? And when did your voice change?"

"I want you to sing with me. And my voice changed a long time ago."

"I don't know that song at all. But, hey, you sound really good. I like your new voice."

"Thanks. So, this song is real old. I learned it from a scratchy old 78 my Grandma had, but it's really easy. Come on, try it."

"OK, but you have to promise to never tell anybody about this. I don't sing."

"Did you ever try?"

"No. But that's beside the point. Anyway, keep going."

"OK, but I'm gonna start over."

You're the one who's goin' away,
Why am I afraid to say
I'll miss you when you're gone?
There's a train a-comin' down the track,
And all you own is on your back.
I'll miss you when you're gone.
Don't know why you have to go,
Don't believe you once said so,
I'll miss you when you're gone.

Sam joined with a rich baritone that, I think, surprised us both. He sang on pitch and picked up the simple tune quickly. We sang all the verses together, and it seemed the owl may have joined us.

"I thought you said you couldn't sing."

"I didn't think I could. I never really tried it before." We sat quietly for a few minutes, drawn in by the flames dancing in the firepit.

I had something I needed to say, and now was the time. I cleared my throat and began. "Sam, you're gonna be leaving next week, and I got something I need to tell you."

"OK. Shoot."

I forged ahead. "Besides my parents, you're the best person I've ever known. I don't know how my life would be if you hadn't taken me down to the track that day to teach me how to ride my bike. You're my best friend and I love you like you were my big brother, maybe more, and I just needed you to hear that before you go away." By this point tears were coursing down my face. "I really didn't want to cry, but I can't help it. I'm just gonna feel lost without you down the street. Just lost."

"Hey, it'll be OK. Really. I promise I'll write to you. But you have to write me back. And we can still talk about stuff in our letters, OK?"

"Yeah. But you know it won't be the same." By now, I was at the "fully-engaged" stage of crying.

"Hey, come here. It's time for a hug." I crashed into him, his chair tipped backward and deposited both of us onto the ground, whereupon we both began laughing hysterically.

Once our laughter subsided, Sam righted his chair and we sat quietly as the fire died and the night pressed in. "I'm tired. You ready to turn in?"

"Sure. What about the fire?"

"It'll be OK. We cleared around the pit real good. It'll just burn itself out." We made our way to the tent. I zipped open the mosquito netting. "Remember…"

"Shoes off at the door. I remember."

Once inside, we stripped down to our underwear, turned off our flashlights and lay on top of our sleeping bags. The night was still and not particularly cool. The only light was an orange glow from the dying fire. I glanced over at Sam and couldn't help but both admire and envy his toned body. "Man, you are really in shape. I don't think you've got an ounce of fat anywhere on you."

"Thanks. It's all the running, you know. You don't look too shabby yourself—for a little kid."

"Hey!" Thus began a pillow fight of the first order. After that had run its course, we were both overheated and completely exhausted. We lay quietly, listening to the night sounds. Within minutes, I heard Sam's breathing change and knew he was asleep. I followed closely after.

Sometime during the night, the air cooled to the point that I crawled into my sleeping bag. I awoke as the earliest morning light seeped into the clearing. Sam was still breathing deeply, so I lay still, listening to the birds singing and calling to each other—sounds I rarely heard at home. After a few minutes, Sam stirred and looked at me, grinning. "Well, we're both still here, so I guess the rattler didn't get us. What's for breakfast?"

"Oh, man, you're gonna love this. I'm gonna cook us eggs and bacon in a paper bag."

"What? What do you mean?"

"Just what I said. I'm gonna cook eggs and bacon in a paper bag."

"You're gonna waste some good eggs and bacon. That's what you're gonna do."

"You just wait. You'll be amazed. But first, we have to get the fire going and then let it die down to a good bed of coals."

"Then let's get to it, 'cause I'm starving!"

We pulled on our clothes and shoes and began to stir up the ashes in the firepit. "There's enough coals left from last night to get this going again." I added a few pieces of the fat pine, followed by a few small pieces of hardwood, and in minutes, the fire was burning well. After adding a few larger pieces of hardwood, we let the fire burn down.

"I gotta pee."

"Me, too."

When we had dug our latrine the day before, we had located it well beyond the campsite. It was now outside our boma. We quickly removed the brush that formed the doorway to the boma and made our way to the latrine. Sam and I had known each other well for about five years, but we had never stood side by side to pee. It was a bit awkward at first and we both laughed a bit nervously.

"Well, this is a first for us. Just don't be jealous, OK?"

I laughed and then responded. "I was about to tell you the

same thing. Don't be jealous of what you see, man. We can't all be blessed like this."

"I don't plan to see. Probably couldn't see if I looked."

If I hadn't been in mid-steam by that point I would have punched him. Instead, we both laughed, finished our business, and returned to camp.

"The fire looks about right. OK, you ready to be amazed?"

"I'm ready to watch you ruin our breakfast."

"Just wait. I've got to get a few things ready, then you're gonna have to eat your words." I busied myself with setting out the things I would need—a large paper grocery bag, a stout forked stick I had cut from a sapling the day before, a package of bacon and a carton of eggs. "There's orange juice in the cooler, if you want to pour us some."

"OK. What about coffee?"

"Oh, man, I'm sorry. I didn't even think about that. I don't drink it, so I didn't even think you might want some."

"It's fine. Orange juice is fine. I don't really need to be alert today, anyway."

"OK. Now watch and be amazed. I learned this at Scout camp last summer. When the guy who showed us first told us what he was going to do, we were all 'No way! That's nuts!' But it works. We do it all the time now at our campouts." I carefully rolled down the first few inches of the top of the grocery bag, then pierced it with the two sharpened prongs of the forked stick. Next, I laid strips of bacon covering the bottom of the sack and held the entire assembly above the bed of coals in the firepit.

"That's gonna catch on fire!"

"Not if I do this right, and I've done it a bunch of times and the bag never caught on fire."

"How is that possible?"

"Well, the guy who showed us at camp last year said the

main thing it to keep the bottom of the bag high enough above the coals. You know, paper has to get pretty hot to burn."

"Yeah, I know. Like 451 degrees. That's where the title of the book comes from. *Fahrenheit 451*."

"That's a book?"

"Yeah. It's a great book by Ray Bradbury. You'll probably read it in high school."

"Anyway, the secret's keeping the bag high enough, so it doesn't get hot enough to catch fire, but low enough to cook the bacon and eggs. Look." By this point, the bacon in the bag had warmed and the grease was soaking into the bottom of the bag. "The bacon's already cooking."

"I'll be damned. You're right. I can hear it sizzling! It smells pretty good, but is it gonna taste like a paper sack?"

"No. It'll taste perfect. Just wait. Hey, you could get out some paper plates for us to put this on."

Sam opened the wooden storage box with our dry food and kitchen supplies and extracted a couple of paper plates. Within minutes, the bacon was done, and I used a pair of tongs to remove it from the bag, placing three slices on each plate. Next, I cracked four eggs into the bottom of the grease-soaked bag. "You want the yokes broken?"

"Yes, please. I can't stand runny eggs."

"Me neither. Now you have to cook the bacon first, so the bag gets soaked with the grease and the eggs don't stick, but it's the same deal. You keep the bag at the right height so it doesn't burn but the eggs cook." Within a few minutes, I was lifting the cooked eggs out of the bag and onto our plates. "So, are you impressed?"

"I would never have believed in a million years that you could cook breakfast over a fire in a paper bag. And this tastes great! Do we have any salt and pepper?"

The best thing about cooking in the paper bag is the clean-up afterward. We finished breakfast, threw our plates and "cookware" into the fire pit, where it immediately burst into flames, and the clean-up was done.

"Man, I don't know about you, but I stink, and I can't wear these clothes another day. I smell like a campfire with bad BO. You think we could sneak over to your Grandma's and wash off under the hose?"

"No, man. We said we were gonna live off the land—not rely on Grandma for food or a bathroom or anything. So, we need to go over to the clay pits and go swimming and wash off."

"I didn't bring a swimsuit."

"You don't need one. We can skinny dip."

"OK. Let's do it."

From our bags we took towels, soap, and a change of clothes and made our way toward the clay pits. This entailed a bit of a hike through the woods toward the area where the pits had been dug years ago to extract clay for making bricks. As we walked, we both unconsciously scanned for snakes.

"So, one time I was here staying with Grandma and playing with this kid named Jesse who lives down the road from Grandma. We came out here to these pits and there were some Black boys skinny dipping. Jesse and I were watching them from behind this hill, but they saw us. They yelled at us and started chasing us, and we ran for our lives."

"So, did they catch you?"

"Nah. I really don't think they chased us very far. They were a lot bigger than us, but they were naked, you know. I think they just wanted to scare us off. But we never really looked back to see if they were still back there. We just high tailed it back to his house. I was scared, though. I didn't know what they'd have done if they'd caught us."

"Probably nothing. And you're right, they probably just wanted to scare you off. I hope we have the place to ourselves, though."

"Yeah. Me too. I'd hate to put anybody else to shame besides you when they see my manhood."

"In your dreams, little man. In your dreams."

We did, indeed have the place to ourselves. As I'd never swum in these pits, I was unsure of the depth. The water had an opaque blue cast to it, I assume from algae bloom, but otherwise looked clean. We found an old log on which to lay our clean clothes and towels and stripped. I felt awkward doing so but didn't want to make it seem obvious.

"Please don't lust after my body, Sam." We both laughed.

"Like I told you years ago. You're not my type."

"I don't know how deep this is—you can't see bottom—but those Black kids were out there about waist deep. I think we just walk out slowly 'til we know what the bottom's like."

"I agree. You don't think there are alligators or anything like that in here, do you?"

"I wouldn't think so. There's really nowhere for them to lay out in the sun and I don't think there's much around here for them to eat."

"Except skinny-dipping kids."

"Well, yeah."

We tip-toed out like two giggly girls at the seashore. The water was surprisingly cold.

"This is freezing!"

"Yeah. I hadn't expected that. It's not as cold as the springs, though."

The bottom was soft and sandy, but not mucky, and seemed to slope away gently from the shore. About fifteen feet from the edge we were in waist-deep water. Comfortable that we were unlikely to sink in the mud or step off into the abyss, we began to horse play, splashing each other and trying to pull each other under. After about ten minutes of that we were tired and cold.

"We better wash off. I need to get out and warm up. You can wait here. I'll go get the soap." Sam sloshed back to shore and returned shortly with a bar of soap. "I figured we could just share and not get two bars of soap wet."

"Good idea."

We passed the soap back and forth, washing our buzz-cut hair and upper bodies. We waded into shallow water to wash our lower halves, then back out to rinse. Once clean, we dried off and quickly changed into clean clothes. When we arrived back at our campsite, we added a bit of wood to the fire and played Gin Rummy until it was time for lunch.

After sandwiches, chips, and Cokes, we decided we needed a nap. Sunlight on the tent made it uncomfortably warm inside, so we pulled our sleeping bags and pillows outside and stretched out on the soft ground. Within minutes, we were both asleep. Waking later, we decided to go for a run. This entailed returning to the measure of civilization afforded by the limerock streets of Campville. After changing into our running shorts and sleeveless shirts, we walked back to my grandmother's house and out to the road that paralleled the railroad tracks. The road was uneven and uncomfortable on our feet, so we soon shifted to the more even grassy shoulder.

"So, are you going to keep this up after I leave?"

"Yeah. I plan to go out for track when I get to high school. Plus, I'm in the track club now, so, yeah, I'm gonna keep running. I think I'm better at sprints, though, than distance running. But then, I kinda like cross country. I just don't like running long distances around the same track. Cross country is more interesting."

"I agree. Cross country's different at every meet. Sometimes, you run through neighborhoods, sometimes through the country. One time at a meet in Hastings we ran through a cow field. That was interesting, dodging the cow pies."

"I bet. You know, we should've done this before we took our baths. We're gonna stink again."

"You're right. We may have to go swimming this evening, just to cool down and rinse off."

"Great idea. Hey, did you bring any money with you?"

"You mean now, like on this run? No, but I've got some back in the tent. Why?"

"'Cause Dyess' Store is open, and we could get a snack. Also, the mail comes in around 3:00 and that's fun to see."

"OK. When we finish our run, let's just go get some cash and go to the store."

Twenty minutes later, we jogged up to the front porch of Dyess' Store. Dyess' was a typical country store. My guess would be that it was built sometime near the turn of the century. Just inside the double screen door, the Post Office was to the right. There, a battery of brass post office boxes went from floor to ceiling with a small, barred window set in the middle. In the mysterious realm behind that window, one of the Dyess sisters held court. She was the Postmistress, whereas her sister was the proprietor of the store. I don't know that either of them ever married. Their father, Old Mister Dyess, had years before fallen victim to dementia, and was often seen walking in the area behind the store talking to everyone and no one in particular.

Inside the store, there were shelves on all the outside walls with a counter running the full perimeter. Merchandise was displayed on the shelves with the shopkeeper working behind the counter to bag the items selected by the customer. In the center of the store was an ancient pot-bellied stove that kept the place warm in cooler weather. There was a large cooler filled with soft drinks and a large pickle barrel stocked with enormous dills. Sam and I made our way to the cooler.

"I'm having a Yoo-hoo. They don't have those at our store, you know?"

"So, what's a Yoo-hoo, anyway?"

"It's a chocolate drink, but it's not carbonated. It's really good."

"Alright. I'll try one."

I fished two Yoo-hoos from the cooler and set them on the counter beside the register. One of the sisters—Mary or Arlene, I could never tell them apart—was there. "Anything else for you boys?"

"No ma'am. No, wait I'd like a PayDay, please. You want something?"

"Yeah, I'll take a PayDay, too."

"Two PayDays comin' up. So, who's your handsome friend here, Clint?"

"Oh, this is my friend Sam. He's about to join the Navy."

"Good choice, sailor. Girls love a man in a uniform. OK, that'll be fifty-two cents with tax."

Sam was flustered and too busy blushing to retrieve any cash from his pocket, so I placed fifty-five cents on the counter, and Sister Dyess handed me the change.

"Has the mail come in yet?" I asked.

"Nope. Should be about ten minutes. You boys gonna bring in the mailbag?"

"Yes ma'am."

"Just tell Miss Arlene in the Post Office so she won't go out and get it."

"Yes ma'am."

"And Sailor Sam, come back to see us when you get that uniform, OK?"

"Yes ma'am."

Sam was, by now, a deep shade of crimson, and it was all I could do to keep from laughing. As we passed the Post Office window, I told Miss Arlene that we would retrieve the mailbag. We then took our drinks and candy bars outside and dragged two rocking chairs to the far end of the porch. In my best Miss Mary voice I crooned "Girls just love a man in uniform. And Sam, come back and see us when you get that uniform." I then broke out in uncontrolled laughter.

"Clint, let me ask you something. Have you ever had a PayDay bar stuffed up your ass?"

"No." I was still laughing and gasping for breath. "But it sounds like fun."

By now, Sam was laughing with me. "You little shit. You better sleep with one eye open tonight."

At that moment, the train whistle echoed from the Orange Heights crossing about five miles north.

"Mail train's coming!" I yelled excitedly.

"So, they just throw a bag of mail out the train as they whiz by?"

"Yep. Then we run out and get it and take it inside."

"So, how does mail go out?"

I pointed to a strange-looking pole standing beside the railroad tracks. Suspended within a large C-shaped bracket mounted to the pole was a mailbag. "There. See the mailbag? That's the mail that's going out. There's a guy in the train who has this hook thing, and he snags the mailbag."

"Does he ever miss?"

"Oh, yeah."

"So what happens? Do they stop the train?"

"Nope. The mail just doesn't go out that day. Hey, we need to get ready."

We placed our half-drunk Yoo-hoos on the porch railing and

made our way toward the track. By now, the train was nearing Campville and began sounding its whistle again. The rumbling grew louder, and suddenly, the train appeared. Only four cars long, it passed us going full throttle. From the last car, an arm extended a hooked pole from a window and skillfully snatched the outgoing mailbag from the bracket. Off the rear deck of that last car, another man tossed a mailbag toward us. It landed in the tall weeds between the road and the tracks. Sam and I ran out and picked it up.

"That's pretty cool. I've never seen anything like that. I guess I just assumed little towns like this got their mail by truck or something."

"I know. Sometimes there are a half-dozen kids here to run out to get the mailbag. It's kind of a contest to see who gets it."

We walked the mailbag back into the store and Miss Arlene came through a door in the little Post Office and took it from us, thanking us for our help.

"So how long before people can pick up their mail?"

"I guess about thirty minutes, depending on how much there is. When I was little, Grandma and I would walk down here so I could try to get the bag. Then we'd wait for Miss Arlene to put up the mail before we went home."

"Should we wait and get your grandmother's mail?"

"Nah. It's kinda the highlight of her day. Everybody waits until they hear the mail train, then comes down here to visit and wait for it to be in the boxes. It's kind of a social event here in Campville. Everybody stands around and talks."

"OK. Life is kinda different here, isn't it?"

"For sure."

We reclaimed our rocking chairs and continued to sip and munch. Within a minute or two, folks began to arrive from every compass point around Dyess' Store. The few Black residents of

Campville who lived, quite literally, across the tracks, stood together and a good distance back from the store. The white residents congregated in front of the store and on the porch. My grandmother arrived minutes later, waved to us and struck up a conversation with a couple of neighbors.

Sam commented in a hushed tone, "Look how the Black folks are staying way over there and not coming close to the store."

"I know. It's always that way. They wait until the white folks have gotten their mail and wandered away before they come over here. Sometimes my grandmother talks with them because my grandfather used to be their doctor. They all know her."

"That's cool that your grandfather treated Blacks. I guess all doctors do that. I don't know."

"Me neither. I guess it's part of their oath or something. Like they're supposed to treat anybody who's sick or needs them. Anyway, my grandmother said that when my grandfather died that all the Black folks were really upset 'cause they didn't know who would take care of them then."

At that moment, Miss Arlene called out from inside the store, "Mail's up."

"That was fast. Must not have been much in that bag," Sam commented.

"It did feel pretty light."

Slowly, the crowd in front of the store began to disburse as each person checked their mailbox and sauntered back home. When most of the whites had left, the small cluster of Black residents moved toward the store. As they approached, one older woman broke away and walked toward where Sam and I were sitting.

"Young man, you're Doctor Henry's grandson, aren't you?"

"Yes ma'am. But I didn't know him. He died before I was born. This is my friend, Sam."

"Pleased to meet you, Sam."

"You, too, ma'am."

"Your name's Clint, right?"

"Yes ma'am."

"Clint, you grandaddy was a good man, a good man."

"Yes ma'am. That's what I've heard."

"You know, he was the onliest doctor 'tween here and Gainesville, and the only one what would treat colored folks."

"Yes ma'am."

"He delivered all three'a my babies, and one time, he saved my husband's life. He got real bad sick, burnin' up with a fever, and throwin' up. An I brought him to your grandaddy, and he looked him over, and poked around, and says 'He's got appendicitis. We got to get him to the hospital in Gainesville right now.' An we didn't have no car, so you grandaddy loaded him and me in his car and drove us to Alachua General. They operated on him, and he was just fine. Lived another seventeen years. Yes sir, you grandaddy was a real good man."

"Thank you, ma'am. I really appreciate you telling me that story. All I know about my grandfather is what my dad or other relatives tell me."

"Well, all us older colored folks around here knew him and loved him. You tell you grandmama hello for me. I'm Ms. Wilson, Althea Wilson. Well, you young men have a nice afternoon."

"Thank you, Ms. Wilson. You, too." She walked toward the door and entered the store.

"That was a pretty cool story," Sam said, "how your grandfather took them in his car to the hospital."

"Yeah. I'd never heard that. It's nice to hear it from somebody he really helped. I know he had a drinking problem. I think he came home from World War One kinda shell-shocked."

"Was he a soldier?

"No. He was an army doctor, and, from what I've heard, he treated a lot of really messed up soldiers in France. It kinda messed him up, too. I don't think him and my dad had a very good relationship because of it. My grandfather used a horse and buggy for making house calls, and when he'd finish, he'd drink on his way home, pass out, and the horse would bring him home. My dad was the oldest, so he'd go out and help get him in the house. It's nice to hear a story like Mrs. Wilson's to kinda balance out some of the other not-so-good stuff."

"Yeah, I guess so. Hey, are you finished?"

"Yeah. We can go. We need to gather some more firewood before it gets dark."

"Oh, fun, fun. I hope we can avoid our friend from yesterday."

"Me, too. We need to be more careful, that's for sure."

We jogged back to my grandmother's house. She was sitting on the front porch. I relayed the greeting from Mrs. Wilson, and then Sam and I walked back into the woods, picking up deadfall as we went. After about thirty minutes, we had gathered a sufficient pile of dry firewood. It was now late afternoon, and time to make preparations for dinner. The menu for the evening included hotdogs, chips, Cokes, and brownies my mother had made and sent with us.

There was a stand of palmettos bordering our campsite and just outside our boma. I cut two long fronds, stripped off the leaves, and sharpened one end of each. These would serve for roasting our hotdogs. As we had done the night before, we first built up the fire, then waited for it to burn down to provide us even heat for cooking. I suppose the activity of the day had left us both with healthy appetites as I ate two hotdogs and Sam consumed three. By now, the sun was low on the horizon, and dark was gathering in the thick woods where we were camped.

"If we're gonna wash off, we probably need to go pretty soon. I'm gonna fire up the lantern so we have some light when we come back."

"Good idea. I'll get our towels and soap while you do that."

I set the Coleman lantern atop our wooden equipment box, filled the tank with fuel, pumped it up, and lit it. I then hung it from a low tree branch over our campsite. With flashlights in hand, Sam and I hiked toward the clay pits for our evening baths. Once again, we were alone. We quickly stripped off—avoiding the awkwardness of the morning—and set about the business of washing away the afternoon's grime. I suppose we were both tired—or it could have been the gathering darkness—but there was no horseplay on this evening. By the time we began our walk back to camp, the woods were dark, and the night's serenade had begun. As we neared our temporary home, the light from the Coleman lantern served as a welcoming beacon, lighting up the interior of our boma.

"Mom sent the stuff for S'mores. Wanna make some?"

"Oh, yeah. We had those on the camping trip in the mountains. Sure. Let's do that."

Once again, we built up the fire and waited. After about thirty minutes, the fire had burned down to a glowing bed of coals. Using the same palmetto sticks on which we had cooked dinner, we began to indulge in one S'more after another. When we had eaten ourselves into a sugar-induced stupor, we put away the makings, rebuilt the fire, and sat back to listen to the crackle and the night sounds beyond our safe enclosure.

"I could really get used to this, you know?"

"I know what you mean. No parents, no pesky little brother. We'd have to pack a lot of hotdogs, though?"

Sam laughed, "You got that right. We really did some damage this evening."

"I know. Plus, I ate too many S'mores. I feel like I could puke."

"Well, aim it the other way, please."

"No. I'm OK. I just feel like I might explode." After a pause, I changed the direction of our conversation. "So, Sam, does it bug you when people say stuff like 'Girls really like a man in uniform.' I mean, since you really don't care much what girls think?"

"Nah, not really. I mean, I just kinda laugh it off inside my head. I kinda think, 'Man, if they only knew.'" We both chuckled at that remark.

"So, I'm kinda curious—and you don't have to answer this if you don't want to—but, how do you see the future? I mean, if you meet some guy and you both really like each other, it's not like you can get married or have kids or anything. I mean, what do gay guys do for the rest of their lives?"

Sam took a while before he answered, and I wondered if I had crossed a line. "Well, some gay guys form life-long partnerships. They live together, buy a house, do most things married people do, but you're right, we couldn't have kids."

"That really stinks 'cause I think you'd make a great dad."

"Me, too. And I'd really like to have kids. Maybe, someday, they'll let gay folks adopt. But all that's way in the future. For the next few years, while I'm in the Navy, I'm gonna be the straightest-acting guy you ever saw."

"Well, it's not like you act, I don't know, girly now. You know how some guys act sissy? You don't ever act that way. So nobody'll figure it out. I mean, if you hadn't told me, I'd never have guessed."

"Yeah, I know what you mean. I mean, I'm a guy, so I act like a guy. It's all I know how to do. Besides, I'm really not attracted to guys who act feminine."

"Well, OK. Thanks. I appreciate you being straight with me." At that, Sam chuckled. "What's so funny."

"You're the straight one. Not me."

"What?"

"Never mind. Anyway, it's OK. I know you're curious. I've always tried to be honest with you, and you've always done a good job of keeping my secret."

"I promised you I would, and I will. Always."

"Thanks. Hey, speaking of romance, you never said much more about that girl you had a crush on. What was her name? Paula something."

"Paula Hendrix. Yeah, it never really went anywhere. She kinda went ape over Kent Browning and really never gave me another look. I got over it."

"So, anybody else catch your eye?"

"Nah. Not really. I'm keeping my options open." We both laughed at that. "So, on another subject, what happens when you enlist next Wednesday? I mean, is there a ceremony or something?"

"Nah. Technically, I guess I've already enlisted. I mean, I signed the papers and already took the oath. All that happens Wednesday is they pick me up at the Post Office with some other guys from Palatka and take us to the Naval Air Station in Jacksonville. After that, I really don't know much. I guess we get our uniforms and stuff and get assigned to a training unit. One thing I do know—I won't be making many decisions for myself after that."

"Yeah, I guess not. They kinda own you after that, don't they?"

"Yep. I'm their property for three years."

"Man. I know it's gonna be a big change for you, but it's gonna be a big change for me, too. I mean, who am I gonna hang out with, Crazy Christine?"

"Maybe so. I've got a prediction."

"Don't even say it."

"No, really. You know how Christine's gone nuts over the Beatles?"

"Well, yeah. They're about all she talks about. It makes me wanna puke."

"OK, but hear me out. You notice how's she's dressing more feminine, fixing her hair and stuff?"

"Yeah. Now that you mention it."

"OK. So, here's my prediction: By the time you get to high school, she's gonna be cheerleader material. By senior year, Homecoming Queen material."

"No way, Jose! Crazy Christine? No way."

"You just wait."

"OK. If you say so."

By now, the fire had burned down, the darkness had seeped into our enclosure, and the night sounds were calling us.

"I'm beat. You ready for bed?"

"Yeah. Let me turn off the lantern, and we can turn in." I removed the lantern from where it hung over us, set it on the wooden storage box and turned it off. In the fire glow and dying light from the lantern we made our way into the tent, undressed and lay atop our sleeping bags. Hardly a word was exchanged before we were both asleep.

The next morning, we were all business. After a quick breakfast, we began to break camp. As soon as the sun dried the morning dewfall from the tent, we swept it out and carefully rolled it up for storage. We then began hauling our gear out to the station wagon. After several trips, we were ready to load and go.

"What about the boma. Should we take it down?"

"Nah. I wanna leave it up. When I come to see Grandma, it'll be my special place to be by myself. You know, it'll be the last place you and me did something special, so I want to leave it here."

"Oh, OK. Well, let's load up and hit the road."

About that time, my grandmother came out to see us off.

"Well, it was sure nice to have you boys here," she laughed. "I'm only joking. I know you boys wanted to be by yourselves, be self-sufficient. Looks like you survived."

"Yes, ma'am. We did OK. Clint's a pretty good cook. He even cooked us bacon and eggs in a paper sack."

"Well, that sounds interesting. Never heard of such a thing. So, Sam, I want to wish you luck in the Navy. I don't know much about Navy life—the Doctor and both my boys were in the Army. Well, Clint's father started out in the Army Air Corps, but ended up in the new Air Force toward the end of the war. But, anyway, none were ever in the Navy. I imagine life on a ship is quite different."

"Yes, ma'am. I'm sure it is." During this conversation, we had been loading our equipment into the back of the station wagon.

"Well, I won't keep you boys. I know you have 'miles to go before you sleep,' as Mr. Frost would say. Again, very best of luck to you, Sam."

"Thank you, ma'am."

"Now, you both come here and give me a hug before you shove off." After hugs all around, we were off. The ride home was quiet. I was lost in self-pity, and I imagine Sam was thinking of how dramatically his life was to change in a few short days.

My parents insisted I not bother Sam the first two days of that week, reminding me he was packing and spending his final hours with his mother. I was not happy with this directive but accepted it as reasonable.

Mid-morning on Wednesday, my grandmother drove Will and me down to the Post Office to see Sam off. The bus was to arrive around eleven o'clock, so my mom planned to take an early lunch hour and meet us there. My dad was working the counter inside, so planned to step out briefly when the bus arrived. We pulled into the parking lot around ten thirty, and Sam and his mother arrived about ten minutes later. I ran over to him as he unloaded a large duffle from the trunk of their car. He looked anxious.

"Hey. So, you ready for this?"

"I don't know. Now that it's here, I'm pretty nervous. The time I went with you guys to the mountains is the longest I've ever been away from home. My mom is a wreck. I mean, she's trying to be strong, but I can tell she's torn up inside. I think it'll be better once I get on the bus."

We walked toward an area where several other young men around Sam's age had congregated. There were other parents there, including my mom who had arrived by this time and was standing with my grandmother and Will. Sam, his mom, and I joined them.

"Thank you all for coming to see me off. I really appreciate it."

"Sam, you know we think of you like a member of the family. We all wanted to be here to send you off." At that moment, a large chartered bus pulled into the parking lot, and, seconds later, my dad walked around the corner of the building to join us. The other young men began to say their goodbyes.

"Well, I guess this is it." I could tell Sam was near tears, and I was barely keeping it together. "Let me hug you all." He began to make the rounds of our little group, hugging Will, then my Mom, next my grandmother, then shaking hands with my dad. Then he looked at me and I completely dissolved into tears. He wrapped me in a tight hug, and spoke quietly in my ear, "It'll be OK. We'll be OK. You write me and I'll write you back, OK?"

"Yeah. OK. I love you, Sam."

"I know. And you know I love you, too, right?"

"Yeah."

He released me, and put an arm around his mother's shoulders, walking her away from us and toward the bus. My mother was crying now, Will was crying, my grandmother was crying, I was falling apart, and I'm fairly certain I saw a tear make its way down my dad's cheek. My mom spoke under her breath, "This is so hard for her. She's going to feel so alone."

We watched as Sam lifted his mom off the pavement in a strong embrace, picked up his duffle, and joined the short line of young men boarding the bus. As he mounted the first step, he looked back and waved, then continued into the dark interior of the bus. It seemed most of the window seats were already taken. I strained to make him out as he walked down the center of the bus and took an aisle seat. He leaned forward and waved again. The bus door closed. The bus belched black smoke and drove off.

22.

NOW IS THE SUMMER OF MY DISCONTENT

THE NEXT FEW days were something of a blur. I felt empty and somewhat out of place with Sam gone. I moped about the house until the weekend when my dad insisted we go fishing. On that Friday evening, he came home from work with a bag of live minnows and placed them in the refrigerator. The next morning, long before sunup, he rousted Will and me from sleep. We pulled on our clothes and met him in the back yard where our fishing boat was already hooked up to the station wagon. Apparently, the specks were biting at Lake George, so off we went.

Arriving at the lake just as a bit of light was breaking to the east, we launched the boat, motored out to a spot just off the bank, and began dropping our baited hooks into the water between the lily pads. Within seconds, we began catching fish. So active was the bite, it almost became ridiculous. Of course, Will and I wanted to keep every fish we caught, but Dad ruled we had to return the smaller ones to the lake. For about three hours, we caught one right after another. With a cooler full of enormous specks, Dad called an end to our expedition around ten o'clock. We motored back to the boat ramp, loaded the boat, and headed home.

The fishing trip was an effective therapy for my sad spirit—which, I'm confident, was the precise reason my father had planned it—and, by the time we arrived home to show our remarkable catch to Mom, I felt more like myself than I had in days. Dad and I spent about two hours cleaning the fish and placing them in plastic bags. Most went into the freezer, but we set plenty aside for dinner that evening. Will was still a bit young to be trusted with the sharp filet knives my father reserved for cleaning fish, so just the two of us worked at the small fish-cleaning shelf he had attached to a large pine tree in the back yard.

"Thanks, Dad."

"Thanks for what, Son?"

"You know, for taking us fishing this morning. I kinda needed that."

"I know. That's one reason we went. Plus, I didn't want to miss that crazy speck bite everybody at the Post Office had been talking about. You know we've gone before, but we never hit it like that."

"It was a blast! I never caught that many fish in my life! It was like every time I dropped my hook in the water, I caught a fish."

"So, how are you doing with Sam gone? I know you've been down since Wednesday."

"Yes, sir. I'm pretty bummed out. It's not just that he's gone, it's—I don't know how to explain it—it's like I know things have changed forever. I mean, he's always been there, down the street, and we've had this friendship that was so different, you know, like the age difference didn't matter. And now I know it'll never be like that again. I mean, we'll always be friends, but it's like he's all of a sudden an adult, and I'm still a kid."

"But Sam's always been like a big brother to you, and that'll never change. Right now, the age difference seems like it all of a sudden matters because all of a sudden he's doing a very adult thing—joining the Navy. But in a few years, you'll catch up with him. Then you'll both be young men, doing things young men do, and things will fall back into place. Does that make any sense?"

"Yes, sir. I think so. I guess I've got about five more years before Sam and me'll be kind of at the same place in life. I mean, he plans to go to college after he gets out of the Navy, and I'll be going to college, so it'll be like we're the same age because we'll be doing the same thing. Maybe we can even be college roommates!"

"That's right. It's not so much the age difference between you two. I mean, you've both been at pretty much the same stage of life—going to school and living at home. All of a sudden, Sam's stepped into the next stage of life, and you're still back here going to school and living at home. But, trust me, these years'll go by fast, and pretty soon, you'll step into that next stage of life, and Sam will be there, too."

"That makes sense. Thanks, Dad."

"Sure. Now, let's get finished here and get showered up. We both smell pretty fishy and I don't think your mother'll be too happy until we get cleaned up."

The next day, Sunday, while my family sat in our all-white Southern church, three young men—James Chaney, from Meridian, Mississippi, together with Andrew Goodman and Michael Schwerner, from New York City—were in the tiny Mississippi hamlet of Longdale, speaking with the congregation of a Black church that had been burned. These three were among an interracial group of young adults—college students mostly—spending their summer in the segregated South in an effort to register African-American voters.[13] As they left

13 21-year-old Andrew Goodman and 24-year-old Michael Schwerner were New Yorkers who had planned to spend the summer of 1964 in Mississippi participating in a project known as Freedom Summer or the Mississippi Summer Project—a volunteer campaign aimed at increasing voter registration among Black citizens in the state of Mississippi. In addition to voter registration, the project established Freedom Schools and other organizations in small towns across Mississippi to assist the Black communities in those towns and to educate them on matters of racial justice and voting rights. Twenty-

to return to Meridian, they were arrested in Philadelphia, Mississippi, for speeding, held in the local jail until around 10:00 pm, and then released. As they drove out of Philadelphia toward Meridian, they were followed by officers and others, pulled over again, abducted, taken to a remote location, and murdered. Their bodies were then buried in an earthen dam that was under construction. Their disappearance triggered a massive search and investigation by the FBI that ended with the discovery of their bodies five weeks later, on August 4. The investigation into the disappearance and murder of these young men consumed the news cycle for most of that summer, running alongside the personal drama of my acceptance of life without Sam.

The week after our fishing trip was a busy one. We were scheduled to leave on vacation the following Saturday, so there was quite a lot of preparation. Earlier in the spring, my parents had purchased a new Apache Golden Eagle pop-up tent camper. This would be our first trip using it, and our first extended camping vacation without a traditional tent on the ground and all the drama that sometimes accompanies tent camping in Florida's summer monsoons. As expected, my father had spent

---

one-year-old James Chaney was a young Black Mississippian and activist with the Congress of Racial Equality (CORE)—one of the sponsoring organizations of the Mississippi Summer Project. Though Goodman, Schwerner, and Chaney were murdered as a direct result of their work for the Mississippi Summer Project, they were by no means the only victims of violence targeted at the volunteers. Civil rights workers were arrested on trumped-up charges, and churches where volunteers met with Black congregants and homes that hosted the volunteers were targets of racial violence. Over the course of that summer, over 1,000 project volunteers were arrested, 80 were beaten, 37 Black churches were bombed or burned, 30 Black homes or businesses were either bombed or burned, four volunteers were killed, four were seriously wounded, and three Black Mississippians were murdered because of their activism. Though the objective of registering large numbers of Mississippi Blacks to vote was not achieved, the Summer Project brought significant media attention to the plight of Black southerners and had lasting influence on the course of the Civil Rights Movement.

much of his spare time during the month of May engineering precisely how our other camping gear would fit into the new camper, designing and constructing new storage boxes and a new kitchen box—with Mom's input, of course. Will and I were given specific dimensions into which all our clothing must fit, and we each began the task of selecting what we would take. This was much easier for Will, as he was content to spend two weeks in the same shorts and T-shirt with a couple of changes of underwear. I, on the other hand, was much more concerned about my wardrobe—there was now the off-chance of meeting a cute girl—so the small space Dad had afforded me presented a significant packing challenge.

About mid-week, a letter arrived from Sam. I read it over several times, then placed it for safe keeping in a Hav-a-Tampa cigar box in my closet. There I would place all subsequent letters from him—those same letters I reread years later after his mother visited me at my office and rattled the pillars of my universe with her suspicions about the nature of Sam's death.

21 June, 1964
NAS JAX
Dear Little Brother,

How are you doing? It was sure hard leaving all of you standing at the Post Office. The bus ride was long and boring. I mostly kept to myself and all the other guys on the bus seemed as nervous as me. Things are fine here. I'm beginning to get used to the routine—wake up in the dark, go run a few miles, eat breakfast, go drill a while, eat lunch, go to some classes, go run a while, eat dinner, go study a while—you get the drift, right? I'm just glad we did all that running together. At least I was in pretty good shape. Some of the other guys in my unit puke every time we run.

How is your summer vacation going? Is your family going camping this summer? Where to? Tell me all about it, OK?

There's a lot of guys here my age—most just out of high school. They're from all over the country, and some have some really strange ways of talking. Especially the guys from New York! There are a few Black guys here, too. Things are really hard for them. I'm trying to be friendly so they don't think all white guys are complete asses.

Hey, got to go for now. Please write me back. Mail is the only thing to look forward to! Maybe I can send you a picture of me in my uniform.

Your Big Brother,
Sam

Though I had never written a letter to anyone, I immediately set about the task of doing so. Everything I wrote about seemed uninteresting. How could anything in my present life be of interest to a Navy sailor? At dinner that evening, I expressed my frustrations to Mom. She assured me that the objective was just to let Sam know I was thinking of him and remind him that his connection to home was still intact. So, that evening after dinner, I completed my first epistle highlighting the very mundane goings-on in my very mundane life.

The remainder of the week went by quickly and, on that Saturday morning, with the new camper hitched to the station wagon and our canoe strapped to the roof rack, we set off for Alexander Springs in the Ocala National Forest.

Alexander Springs is one of Florida's largest natural freshwater springs. Its crystal-clear water—at a constant 72 degrees—fills a large sand-bottomed lagoon before flowing east to finally merge with the St. John's River. Among my favorite places to visit, our family enjoyed swimming in its gin-clear waters, snorkeling, fishing, canoeing, and hiking through its pristine old growth wetlands. In fact, our little troupe was equipped for taking advantage of everything the park had to offer.

The drive from Palatka took about an hour and a half—most of it through rural landscapes and national forest land. Along the way, we passed through the town of Salt Springs, where a unique mineral spring flows east to empty into Lake George. From there, we left behind anything that resembled civilization and drove through dry, sandy scrub land until we arrived at Alexander Springs. After checking in at the guard house, we drove through the camping area, selected our site, and began to set up camp. Everything was different now that we had the pop-up, and nothing seemed to be where it had been previously. As a result, it took over an hour to complete what in the past would have taken us thirty minutes. With our home for the next two weeks ready for occupation, Mom laid out provisions for lunch.

"Can we go swimming after lunch?"

"Yes, Will. After you wait thirty minutes." This thirty-minute rule was unassailable in our family. The theory was that swimming immediately after eating could cause muscle cramps leading to drowning. Whether there exists any scientific data to support this claim mattered not a sliver to my mother. The rule was iron-clad—no swimming for thirty minutes after eating.

"After we go swimming, can we take the canoe down to the run and maybe do some fishing?" I asked.

"Yeah! That would be great!" Will responded.

"Do you think you two can haul the canoe down there by yourselves?" asked Dad.

"Yes sir. I think so. Will's a lot bigger this summer than he was last."

"I can do it."

"OK. You remember the one rule?"

"Yes sir. Life jackets. Don't sit on them, wear them."

"That's right. OK. Sure, you boys can take the canoe down."

After lunch, we hastily changed into our swimsuits, grabbed towels, our masks, fins, snorkels, and flip-flops and began the excruciating wait until Mom granted the official reprieve at the end of the required thirty-minute jail time. Will and I had been swimming since we could walk and had taken Red Cross swim lessons every summer for years, so our parents were comfortable allowing us to swim unsupervised. The expectation, of course, was that we never swam alone and kept a close eye on each other. Even so, my dad loved swimming in the bracing spring water, so he decided to join us. The walk from the camping area to the spring took only a few minutes, but as we walked along the unpaved campground roads, we noticed that they had very recently been improved by a thick layer of white, bleached shell material.

"Hey, this looks like the stuff the Indian mound was made of. Remember when Sam and I went to that Indian mound across the river? The mound was made of this stuff." We began to glance down as we walked, and within seconds, I spied something familiar—a shard of pottery. "Oh my gosh. Look at this!" I squatted down and picked up the shard. "This is Indian pottery. Look! See, it's even got a pattern carved in the clay."

"Let me see!"

"Hold on, Will. Look, Dad." My father took the shard from my hand and turned it over in his.

"I'll be darned. You're right, Son. It is a piece of Indian pottery. Did they just bulldoze an Indian mound to pave these roads?"

"How could they do that? That's like destroying history." I was incredulous when faced with the likelihood that was precisely what had been done. "Why would the Park Service do a thing like that? When Sam and I found that Indian mound, we wrote down what we found and drew maps and stuff to show where we found the stuff we took. Sam used it as a project for his history class and everything had to be researched and written up like a real archeologist would do."

By the time the unpaved campground road ended at the swim area parking lot, I had found three more pieces of pottery of varying sizes and Will had found one. Though excited by our finds, still, I was troubled by the obvious fact that what should have been regarded as an historic site had been so cannibalized for paving material—and by a state agency, no less.

For those unfamiliar with swimming in 72-degree water, you might assume it would feel cool and refreshing—and you would be wrong. It is, in fact, bone-chillingly cold. To enter it, there are essentially two methods: one, you make a dash from shore and dive headfirst; or, two, you slowly tiptoe out on the false assumption that entering the water slowly will somehow mitigate the full-body spasms that result from employing method number one. My dad was a devoted proponent of method one. He would run full-speed into the water and dive head-first as soon as the depth would permit. Will and I had developed a hybrid technique employing components of both methods. We would tiptoe out, squealing as we went, to about mid-thigh, then dive headfirst to end the agony.

"OK, Will. Let's go get wet, then come back and get our masks and stuff."

"OK. I hate this part."

"I know. Let's get it over with." So we did. The water was numbing. We scuttled back to shore, shivering, and donned our masks, fins, and snorkels, then duck-walked back into the water.

The experience of snorkeling in crystal clear spring water makes the slow but inexorable loss of body heat tolerable. Looking toward the springhead itself, the water takes on a clear blue tint as the depth increases. The white sand bottom reflects the ripples on the surface. Fish dart about and turtles forage in the aquatic vegetation around the edge of the vast pool. As we neared the spring itself, the bottom fell away quickly to a depth of perhaps twenty-five feet. Floating on the surface and looking down at the cave system where the water emerged, we watched older teens and adults free-dive to the bottom and even swim through some of the openings in the rock formations. In coming years, I would enjoy doing the same.

Will and I were both thin with virtually no body fat. As a result, we became chilled quickly. Our ability to tolerate the water was limited to about twenty minutes, after which we would have to get out, shivering, dry off, and sit in the sun to recover. True to form, we soon agreed it was time to go warm up. Dad then borrowed my mask and snorkel and went back out to enjoy the underwater panorama. After about an hour at the spring, we headed back toward our campsite, finding several more pottery shards along the way. Mom seem much less excited about our finds than we were but, as would any good mother, she made a valiant effort at showing interest.

After sitting in the sun for a half-hour, Will and I had recovered sufficient body heat to energize us for canoeing. The challenge before us was to get ourselves, our life jackets, paddles, a small anchor, and fishing gear, plus the canoe to the launch at the same time. After arguing about several ways to accomplish this, we decided we could wear the life jackets down to the launch. Dad then volunteered to walk with us and take the remaining gear.

The preferred method for two-man portage of a canoe is overhead. Each canoeist—one at the bow and one at the stern—grasps the gunwales, hoists the canoe overhead, then, if possible, rests the gunwales on their shoulders and off you go.

The height difference between Will and me, and the fact that he might not be able to see where he was going with his head inside the hull of the canoe, suggested that he should handle the stern with me at the bow. After two attempts to hoist the canoe, we managed to get it positioned and began walking toward the launch. About half-way there, I could tell Will was tiring.

"You OK back there?"

"Yeah. This thing's killing my shoulders and I can't hold it up for very long."

Dad spoke up, "Do you want me to relieve you, Will?"

"No sir. I can make it, I think." His determination renewed, we forged on and soon arrived at the launch area.

"So, how do we get the other stuff back to camp without you, Dad?"

"When you get back in, one of you stay here with the canoe while the other takes the paddles and fishing stuff back to camp, then comes back here so the two of you can bring the canoe back."

"OK. That'll work."

"I'll stay with the canoe, Clint. You can take the other stuff back."

"OK. That's fine."

"OK. I'm going to leave you boys with it. Remember the rule?'

"Yes sir. We wear our life jackets the whole time."

"Right. Have fun."

"Thanks, Dad." As he walked away, Will and I readied the canoe, loaded the paddles and fishing gear, and pushed off, with Will at the bow and me at the stern. The spring creek—called a spring run—flowed clear and gentle, with patches of lily pads and low-growing tree branches overhanging the shoreline. We paddled out into midstream, dropped the small anchor, and began casting small jigs into the open water at the edge of the lily pads. The water was clear as air and we could see small panfish swimming about, darting in and out of the underwater vegetation. After about twenty minutes, we had caught nothing.

"We should'a brought some dough balls," Will opined.

"Yeah. These little bream sure aren't interested in these jigs we're casting. Let's up the anchor and try over closer to the bank." We stowed our small spinning rods and I raised the anchor. Before we could get our paddles in the water and get underway, the current caught us and pulled us toward the shore and a large overhanging oak tree. By the time I could begin to right our course, the bow of the canoe—with Will in it—had run up under the overhanging tree. At that moment, a small water snake dropped out of the tree branch and landed right in the middle of the canoe between us.

"Holy shit!"

"Get it out! Get it out!" Will was frantic, and I was trying desperately to scoop the snake up and over the side with my paddle. "Get it out, Clint!"

"I'm trying! Relax, Will. It's just a little water snake."

"How do you know? It could be a moccasin."

"It's not a moccasin. I told you, it's a water snake." About that time, I managed to flip the terrified snake over the side where it gratefully swam away from us toward the shore. "There, it's gone. Are you happy now?"

"Yeah. But I'm tellin'. You cussed."

"If you ever want me to do anything with you ever again, you better keep your mouth shut. So, I cussed. I was just surprised. It's not like I go around cussin' all the time. Besides, if you tell Mom and Dad I cussed, I'm gonna tell all the guys in the Cub pack you peed your pants over a little water snake."

"I didn't pee my pants. Besides, I'm wearing a bathing suit."

"Who you think they'll believe, me or you? Now, do we have

an understanding?"

"Yeah. OK. I won't tell. But you have to promise you won't say I peed my pants."

"As long as you keep your side of the deal, I'll keep mine."

"OK. Deal."

"OK. Now, have you had enough of this? 'Cause I don't think we're gonna catch anything without worms or dough balls."

"Yeah. That's fine. Let's go."

We paddled back to the landing and beached the canoe. I hauled all the gear back to camp, quickly relating to Mom and Dad story of the water snake—and leaving out any mention of my slip of the tongue—and went back for Will and the canoe. Will was tired and grumpy by now, so the trip back to camp with the canoe required two breaks along the way.

After resting for a while, I decided to walk along the campground roads looking for more pottery shards. With a small bag in hand, I spent about thirty minutes along the roads and found a number of shards as well as some animal bones with obvious butcher marks on them. Returning to camp, I showed my finds to the family. My father remarked that the shell mound material must have been spread along the roads very recently, otherwise the pottery pieces would have been crushed by vehicle traffic.

"Maybe the rangers would tell us where this stuff came from and we could go find the mound and maybe dig in it some."

"You can ask them. My guess is it came from somewhere pretty close—maybe even somewhere along the spring run. I'm sure Indians would have had settlements or camps near the spring or along the run, so I bet this stuff came from nearby."

"That'd be so cool. Can I walk over to the rangers' office and ask them?"

"Sure, but don't be surprised if they won't tell you."

"OK."

Five minutes later, I was at the ranger's office. There was a young park officer seated at a desk just inside the door. I told him what I had found and my assumption that they had dug the road material from a shell mound. He was straightforward, acknowledging that I was correct and admitting that he felt it was a bad idea and a bad example of how to treat such sites. I then asked him if he knew where the mound was. He responded that he didn't know exactly, but that it was somewhere near where county road 445 crossed the spring run about a mile east of the park entrance. I thanked him for the information and returned to camp. By this point, it was late afternoon and Mom had begun preparations for dinner. As we ate, I related to the family the information I had gleaned from my conversation with the ranger and elicited from my dad a promise that we could try to locate the mound.

After dinner that evening, we all walked down to the spring. By this time, the day visitors had left and only the overnight campers remained. The sun was low in the sky, and there were a few individuals standing near the edge of the water. About ten feet from shore was a large alligator lying stationary on the surface of the water. As we approached, we realized the persons there were throwing slices of bread to the alligator and he was languidly eating the bread.

"That's not a good idea," Dad said under his breath.

"How come?"

"Alligators are wild animals and they're usually about as scared of us as we are of them. Feeding them makes them not as scared of us. It also makes them associate food with people, and I don't want an alligator associating me with food. Does that make sense?"

"Yes sir. That makes perfect sense. I thought it was against the law or something to feed gators anyway."

"I think it is, but this guy here has probably been coming up into the spring for who knows how long because folks have been feeding him. I really don't know why the rangers haven't stopped this."

We watched from a distance as the folks feeding the alligator tossed it their last few slices of bread and moved on. It seemed the gator then turned his gaze toward us expecting us to offer him the next course.

"I don't think I want to go swimming here anymore."

"He won't be around here during the day, Will. There are too many people. He's just gotten used to coming up into the spring in the evening and being fed by folks who ought to know better. At some point, he's gonna come out of the water and grab some tourist's little dog, and then the fun will be over."

"Man, I'd like to see that."

"No, Son, you wouldn't."

Each of the remaining days of our vacation unfolded in similar fashion—eating, swimming, hiking, canoeing, fishing—there was really little else to do in the center of a National Forest, and that was fine with us. Although we did make an effort to find the shell midden where the paving material had been excavated, we were unsuccessful. However, by the end of our two weeks, Will and I had collected well over a hundred pottery shards—many with inscribed designs in a wide variety of patterns.

One of the advantages, as well as disadvantages, of camping—at least then—was that we were completely cut off from the outside world with no access to news. Thus, on returning home on July 12, we were shocked to learn that the three young Freedom Riders who had disappeared in Mississippi weeks before, had yet to be found. The front page of our local newspaper and the opening minutes of every evening newscast led with this story for much of the remainder of that summer.

In the pile of held mail Dad brought home from the Post Office that Monday was a letter from Sam.

30 June, 1964
NAS JAX
Hey, Clint.

Got your letter last week. Thanks so much for writing. I didn't write right back since I knew you all were on vacation. Sounds like fun! Watch out for rattlesnakes, though! Hope you all had a good time. Be sure to tell me all about it.

It's more of the same here. Drill, run, eat, class, and a little bit of sleep. I can't say I'm enjoying everything, but I'm learning a lot. We've got to march in a July 4th parade in Jacksonville on Friday. It's going to be hot as you-know-where! The food here's pretty awful. I can't wait to get home and have a home-cooked meal.

Man, I can't believe you'll be in 8th grade in September. Time really flies, doesn't it? Hey, on the serious side, you need to keep up with that story in Mississippi about the three guys that went missing. They were there to register Negroes to vote. It looks like the Klan took them and probably murdered them. Anyway, it's an important story, so pay attention to it. OK, enough big brother advice.

That's about all the news from here. Write back, please. I miss you.

Your Big Bro,
Sam

I read Sam's letter quickly, then set about writing him back.

At least I had something to write about this time—an alligator, Indian pottery, and another snake story. After I had finished the letter and began to reread it, I began to question whether Sam would find any of it interesting. He was now a young adult, in the Navy and engaged in all sorts of challenging and interesting adult things each day. Would he even care about the rather ordinary happenings of my life? Nonetheless, I folded the letter and stuffed it into an envelope, addressed it to Sam the precise way Mom had shown me, and took it into the kitchen for Dad to take to work with him the next morning. Mom was in the kitchen.

"Did you write Sam back?"

"Yes ma'am, but I don't know if he'll like it."

"What on earth do you mean? Of course he'll like it. Did you tell him about our vacation?"

"Yes ma'am, but I'm wondering if he'll be interested in all that now that he's, you know, in the Navy and all."

"Clint, I can assure you he'll enjoy hearing all about your life. I can tell you from experience that, when you're in the service, any letter from home is a treasure. You read and reread every word. Even news of the most ordinary things is so meaningful."

"How is that possible? He's doing all these exciting, new things—important things—and I'm just picking up broken pottery from the campground road."

"Clint, the fact that you took the time to write him is what's most important. Also, those things you think of as ordinary help Sam stay connected to the people he cares about, the people who are most important to him. You remember I was in the Marine Corps during the war?"

"Yes ma'am."

"Well, the letters your Grandmother wrote me were about the most ordinary, everyday things you can imagine. I remember she once wrote me about going to Anderson's—it was a store downtown—to try to find some thread to match some fabric she had. She must have written three paragraphs about that— how she had to trade ration coupons with your aunt before she could put gas in her car, how little traffic there was downtown, how there was nothing in the store to buy. I hung on every word because it was all so ordinary, so normal, and my life in the Marines in DC was so abnormal. Can you understand that?"

"I'm not sure. I guess it's good for Sam to see that what he's doing lets us go on with our normal lives."

"That's right. But the important thing is that you sat down and took a pen and paper and your time to write to him—that you were thinking about him when there were other things boys your age could have been doing."

"OK. Thanks, Mom."

"You're welcome. I'm glad we had this little talk." She laughed and returned to her work. I went outside to see if anyone was doing any of those things boys my age do—like playing baseball across the street on the high school athletic field. About ten days later, a letter arrived from Sam.

23 July, 1964
NAS JAX
Hey, Clint.

Thanks for your letter. It was great to hear from you. Thanks for telling me about your vacation. Sounds like you all really had a great time. The thing about people feeding the alligator is crazy. I've never seen one in the wild. Also, what you said about the stuff they used to pave the roads in the campground is crazy too! I can't believe they can just dredge up an Indian mound and use that stuff to pave roads in the park! Not exactly the way we excavated that mound across the river, was it? It's cool that you and Will found pieces of pottery and bone though. I'd like to see that stuff sometime, maybe if I get home at Christmas.

Hey, I told you to watch out for snakes. Remember? I think I'd have peed my pants if one had dropped in the middle of the canoe. Yeah, I know it was a small one, but a snake is a snake as far as I'm concerned! I think Will took it pretty well, if you ask me!

Things are about the same here—drilling, classes, PT, etc. I've made a few friends. Most guys are friendly, but there are some jerks here, too. And, no, nobody special, but thanks for asking!

I guess the big news here is that we will get our job assignments in a couple of weeks. They call them ratings. I don't know why, but they're our jobs. Anyway, then we'll start another round of training to learn those jobs. I'm really hoping for something in aviation or communications but we'll see. As long as I don't get stuck in the galley (that's the kitchen on a ship)! Once I get my rating, I should also get a bump in rank. Again, we'll see.

Well, gotta go for now. Please write when you can. I miss you and your family. Tell them all "Hi" for me.

Your Big Brother,
Sam

As my very ordinary life continued on its course that summer, half-way around the world, events were unfolding that would shape the course of our nation's history for decades to come. On August 2, the *USS Maddox*, a Navy destroyer patrolling the Gulf of Tonkin, was shadowed by three North Vietnamese torpedo boats. Though the US government significantly inflated the significance of these events at the time, what apparently transpired was an exchange of fire precipitated by the *USS Maddox*. According to material declassified years later, four Vietnamese sailors were killed in the exchange, whereas, on the *Maddox*, there were no casualties. In immediate response, Congress passed the Gulf of Tonkin Resolution granting President Lyndon Johnson authority to deploy US troops to defend South Vietnam. The long and costly Vietnam War had begun.

23.

A NEW FRIEND

AROUND THE MIDDLE of August, on a Saturday morning, Will and his Cub Scout pack were meeting at our house, and, as had become our routine, Mom had me take the boys—about eight of them as I recall—down to the clay track at the elementary school to time them running the one hundred yard dash. We had begun these timed runs back before Sam left and I was determined to keep them going. When we returned to the house, several of the boys began talking about things they had heard regarding the planned desegregation of our schools. They were using a word that was not permitted in our house to describe Black persons and Mom was becoming weary of correcting them. At some point in the conversation, I blurted out "Yeah, but we're gonna have to shower with them after PE." More than anything, it was an attempt by me to enter the conversation as the cool older boy.

My mom, however, was having none of it. She pulled me aside and, as she would have described it, gave me a tongue lashing. "Don't let me ever hear you say anything like that again. These boys look up to you, and you need to set a good example." I was crushed and humiliated, but I was also taught a powerful lesson. When, a few days later, a letter from Sam arrived, and I read his words about the murders of the three young civil rights workers in Mississippi, my guilt was compounded.

20 Aug., 1964
NAS JAX
Hey, Clint.

Great to hear from you, buddy. Thanks for your letter and PLEASE tell your mom thanks for the delicious cookies. They made me one very popular seaman! I guess you're getting ready for eighth grade! I'm really proud for you, but I can't believe you're that old. Seems like just a week ago I was teaching you to ride your bike.

I'm doing fine here. I'm really enjoying my training. I can't remember if I told you I was going to be an air traffic controller. It's a lot of responsibility and pretty high-pressure, but it's one of the jobs I really hoped I might get, so I'm pretty happy about it. It's a good fit for me (and sure better than being a gunner or a cook).

Clint, let me get serious with you a bit. There's a lot of stuff happening in the world that's not good. It looks like we're going to war in Vietnam, and that could change a lot of things. Also, there's some really awful stuff happening with race relations in our country. I hope you'll watch the news and keep up with what's going on. I guess you heard they just found the bodies of those three civil rights workers who were kidnapped and murdered in Mississippi. All they were doing was trying to get Black folks to register to vote. The Klan took them and murdered them. I'm sure of it. They were my age. That could have been me! I know you'll be having Black kids coming to your school pretty soon. I hope you'll be kind to them and welcome them because a lot of the kids in school with you won't. OK, enough heavy stuff.

Are you going to stay at your Grandma's like you usually do? If you do, check out our boma and see if it's still standing.

Well, I need to go. Tell your mom she can send cookies anytime she feels like it! I miss you, buddy.

Your big brother,
Sam

Summer was drawing to a close, but I was to spend one of the remaining weeks at my paternal grandmother's home in Campville. So, on a Sunday afternoon in late August, our family made the drive for a visit and to leave me at Grandma's for the week. When we arrived, Uncle Al was rocking on the front porch and stuffing tobacco into his pipe. He stood to greet us and Grandma came out with hugs all around. Aware that the next hour would be filled with adult conversation, I grabbed Will and took him back into the woods to show him the boma Sam and I had built earlier in the summer.

"So, what is it you want to show me?"

"It's a shelter Sam and me built. It's called a boma. You make it out of brush and stuff and make like a ring around your campsite. The natives do it in Africa to protect their animals from lions and stuff at night."

At times, Will regarded me as an unschooled child. This appeared to be one of those times. "There aren't any lions out here, Clint."

"I know that, but it was fun to build and it made it feel like we were in our own little world or like we were in the middle of the jungle or something. Besides, we'd just come up on that rattlesnake right before we decided to build it. It just kinda made us feel safer."

We tromped through the undergrowth, which had thickened substantially over the summer, at last arriving at the boma. It appeared undisturbed and in surprisingly good condition.

"This is pretty cool. Is there like a door?"

"Yeah, kinda. Come around here." We moved to the opening,

still covered with the brush we had left in place when Sam and I vacated. As I thought back to that day, it seemed like years had passed. "Here. Help me move this stuff aside. There, see. We can just walk right in now."

The interior of the boma appeared just as Sam and I had left it. The firepit still held the charred remains of our campfire, and it was still possible to make out the area where we had set up my tent. I pointed them out to Will.

"Yeah. This is cool. It does feel kinda safe in here. But, hey, there's no bathhouse out here. Did you all go to Grandma's house to pee and take a shower?"

"No way. We really roughed it. We dug a latrine for peeing and stuff, and we went to the clay pits and took our baths. We skinny dipped."

"You got naked right out in the open?"

"Yep. There was no one around. It was just Sam and me. We took our towels and soap, stripped off and took our baths in the clay pit."

"I don't know if I could do that. Hey, will you take me to the clay pits? I've never been there."

"Sure, they're not far, but we have to go through the woods, so keep an eye out for snakes."

"OK."

We left the boma, carefully closing off the entrance, and hiked through the woods toward the clay pits.

"So, you saw Sam naked?"

"Well, yeah. I told you we skinny dipped to take our baths."

"Like I said, I don't think I could do that."

"Sure you could. It's kinda awkward at first, but you get used to it. We're all guys, you know?"

"Yeah. I know. I just don't think I could get naked in front of a stranger."

"Will, Sam's not a stranger. He's more like our big brother."

"Yeah. I guess you're right."

After a few more minutes, we arrived at the clay pits and stood atop one of the hills created by the removal of the surface soil, looking down into the pits.

"Wow! The water's blue, but not like at the springs. It's kinda cloudy. Are there alligators in here?"

"I don't think so. I think the minerals in the clay make the water that color. You can't see the bottom, so we were really careful when we first went in. We just kinda shuffled our feet and went real slow till we knew how deep it was and where it dropped off."

"Is it cold?"

"Yeah, but not as cold as the springs, that's for sure. There's just not much sunlight under all these trees. Hey, we probably better head back."

Ten minutes or so later, we arrived back at Grandma's house. The adults were still on the porch, drinking coffee and eating pound cake.

"Would you boys like some pound cake?"

"Yes ma'am, but I don't like coffee."

"You can have some milk, Will. Milk for you, too, Clint?"

"Yes ma'am."

"Clint, go with your Grandmother and help her bring your cake and milk out."

"Yes ma'am."

A few minutes later I was back with two servings of cake. Grandma followed with our glasses of milk. Will and I ate our cake in silence as the adults talked about the gathering clouds of war and the murders in Mississippi. In the past, I had tuned out their conversations, but on this afternoon, sitting in the still, muggy Florida afternoon, I hung on every word. Perhaps

I was moving toward adulthood. Perhaps I was interested because of Sam's influence, or perhaps it was in knowing how this talk of war was so relevant to the direction Sam's life might be taking in a matter of a few months. A half hour or so later, my parents and Will left for home. I accompanied Uncle Al on his duties for the railroad, and, by the time we returned to the house, Grandma was preparing dinner. I joined her there and we talked as she busied herself about the kitchen.

"I don't think I had mentioned that your cousin Kevin is coming for a visit."

"No ma'am, you hadn't."

"Yes. He said he'd be here about mid-week, so you boys will have a few days to spend together."

I didn't know Kevin well at all and wasn't certain how I was related to him. I had met him only twice before and didn't remember spending any time with him outside the accompaniment of adults.

"I really don't know him too well. He's a lot older than me and I really don't understand how he's my cousin."

My grandmother chuckled. She had this contagious sort of laugh that drew you into the humor she found in so much of life. "Well, it's a bit confusing, so it's no wonder you don't understand the relationship. Kevin is the grandson of my sister, Elizabeth, in New Orleans."

"That's Aunt Bess, right?"

"Correct. She's your great aunt. Have you ever met her?"

"No ma'am. I've just heard Mom and Dad talk about her."

"Well, her daughter, Ophelia, died in childbirth, giving birth to Kevin. Kevin's father was in graduate school at Tulane, so your Aunt Bess and your Uncle Bob took care of baby Kevin. Well, Kevin's father met a girl at school. They fell in love and he asked her to marry him. She agreed, but with one condition:

she refused to raise Kevin. So, your Aunt Bess and Uncle Bob raised Kevin like he was their son."

"Wow! They just abandoned him? I mean, his father just abandoned him?"

"That's essentially what happened, yes. I was so angry at Kevin's father at the time, but Bess and Bob actually seemed pleased to have Kevin, so I never said too much about it—at least not around them. Anyway, to make this long story shorter, Kevin's father became a successful businessman. He got into oil in New Orleans and made a lot of money. So, I guess to assuage his guilt at abandoning Kevin, he always gives him expensive gifts at Christmas and for his birthday."

"So, how old is he?"

"Kevin?" I nodded. "He's about seventeen or eighteen. I know he's old enough to drive. He just finished high school and his father gave him a car. He's driving himself here from Louisiana. He used to come on the train. Even when he was little, maybe eight or nine, Bess would put him on the train and send him here for a visit. But he's driving himself this time."

"Well, he's younger than I remembered. He's about Sam's age. So, what's he like? I mean, is he like angry all the time 'cause his father didn't want him?"

"Not at all. Kevin is the sweetest most polite boy you could meet. However, he's very independent, and I think Bess and Bob have indulged him. But he's not spoiled. You'll enjoy getting to know him. He doesn't seem at all bitter about how his life began, his mother dying bringing him into the world and then his father not stepping up to raise him. Bess and Bob have given him a good life, and he's turned out well. You'll like him."

"OK. I hope he's not expecting a lot of excitement here in Campville."

She laughed again. "Oh, he knows what to expect here. I

actually think he enjoys the change of pace. New Orleans is a strange city. Not at all a place I'd want to live. I think Kevin enjoys the quiet, simple life here."

"Is he gonna stay in my room?"

"Yes. Is that alright with you? That's a double bed, and you don't take up much room."

"Yes, ma'am. That's fine with me. I hope he doesn't snore, though."

She chuckled again. "Well, I don't know about that."

Evenings at my grandmother's were always quiet. She had no television, and only played the radio in the mornings to catch up on the news. As there was no overhead lighting, her home was lit by table lamps, so the living room took on a golden glow as though from candlelight. My Uncle Al sat quietly in his recliner reading his mysteries. Grandma sat across the room from him, also reading. So, I played my part, but often retired early to read in bed.

Well before daylight the next morning, Mrs. McIntosh's rooster greeted the new day and woke me. I lay in bed a bit, wondering what Sam might be doing. I laughed aloud as I recalled that first morning here when that same rooster had awakened him. After a few minutes, I pulled on shorts, a t-shirt and my running shoes and stepped into the early light for a run. When I returned, Grandma was sitting in her chair sipping coffee and reading the *Gainesville Sun*.

"Would you like some coffee?"

"No ma'am. I don't like it."

"I understand. How about some of the paper?"

"Yes ma'am. Thank you."

She handed me the B section—State and Local News—and there I read about a hurricane that had struck Guadeloupe the previous day. "Says we might have a hurricane late this week or next."

"I saw that. But a lot can change in the coming days. I'm not too concerned about it."

"Me neither."

After breakfast, I decided to go out to the boma again. For some reason, I felt I might sense Sam's presence there. It had been a special place to us—the place where we had spent the last and best days of our friendship. As I made my way through the woods, I thought of our time here a little over two months previously and how dramatically things had changed for us in the weeks since. Moving aside the brush that concealed the entrance, I stepped into that sheltered space. It was still, quiet and empty. Sam was not there, and I could not sense him. In that moment, I could not look ahead to a time where we might occupy this space again. Sam had moved on and I was left behind. I was suddenly overtaken by grief and self-pity and crumbled to the ground sobbing.

I don't know how long I sat on the bare earth beside the cold firepit, but at some point, I began to upbraid myself for my self-indulgent feelings. I began to gain or regain perspective. Sam and I were friends—friends for life. Nothing could rob me of that. I remembered my mother's words to me that I would, within a few years, catch up to him, that we would then share that stage where education and profession are pursued, where relationships are confirmed, where the gateway to adulthood is pried open. There would be good times again. Drying my tears, I dusted myself off and returned the way I had come, but not before carefully replacing the dried brush across the entrance to the boma.

The pace of life in Campville was measured not by the calendar, but by the unique or special events that marked the days. Tuesdays meant the arrival of the Bookmobile. My grandmother was an insatiable reader, often consuming four or five books each week. I recall a time when I was a young adult, mentioning to her that I had been reading James Clavell's monumental series on Asia, beginning with *Shōgun*. She laughed and acknowledged that she had read *Shōgun* as well and confessed, "I never enjoyed reading anything so much that I probably shouldn't have been reading." So, on that Tuesday afternoon, we walked down to Dyess' store to await the arrival of the Alachua County Library Bookmobile. At precisely 2:00 pm, the large van turned off the county road and parked in front of the store. Grandma and I were the only readers waiting at that moment so we made the place our own. I remember choosing two books—under the likelihood that it might be a slow week in Campville—one of which was Pat Frank's *Alas, Babylon,* set in a sleepy Florida town during a nuclear apocalypse. Coupled with the underlying fear generated by drop-and-cover drills, the Cuban Missile Crisis, and the ever-present assumption that nuclear confrontation with the Soviets was inevitable, the book scared the bejeebers out of me. Since I had no library card in Alachua County, I gave my selections to Grandma and stepped outside to wait for her. From across the highway, several Black residents arrived to make their selections. Among them was Mrs. Wilson who had spoken with me about my grandfather when Sam and I were visiting in June, and a boy about my age whom I assumed to be her grandson.

"Hello, Mrs. Wilson."

"Well, hello young mister Clint Cooper. Back for a visit I see."

"Yes ma'am."

"Your grandmother inside the bookmobile?"

"Yes ma'am. She loves to read."

"So do I. I'm a slow reader, but I don't forget nothin' I read. Did you pick out something?"

"Yes, ma'am. I picked out two books. Grandma doesn't have a TV and things can get kinda slow here."

She laughed. "Don't I know that! This here is my grandson, Jacob." She indicated the handsome, lanky boy beside her, staring at the ground.

I extended my hand to the boy. "Hi, I'm Clint."

Hesitantly, he took my hand and responded, "Hi, I'm Jacob, but you already knew that." We both laughed.

"You boys visit while I go pick out some books."

"Yes ma'am," we both chimed in unison.

"So, how old are you, Jacob?"

"I'm thirteen. How about you?"

"I'm twelve. I'll be thirteen in December. Where do you go to school?"

"I go to school in Melrose, but our school only goes through eighth grade, so next year I hope I'll go to Hawthorne High, if they integrate. What about you? Where do you live?" Jacob took the rocking chair next to me as we continued our conversation.

"I live in Palatka. I'll be stuck at the junior high until tenth grade 'cause of overcrowding at Palatka High. So, where will you go if they don't integrate the high school in Hawthorne?"

"I'm not really sure. Most colored kids around here just quit after eighth grade, but I want to go to college, so that's not a good plan for me. There's no Negro high school in Melrose. The closest ones are in Palatka and Gainesville. Either one, and it would be three hours on the school bus every day. I live with my Grandma, and she says I can go to Jacksonville to live with my aunt and finish high school up there. I don't really want to do that, but if I have to, I will."

"Man, that really stinks. I hope they go ahead and integrate the school here so you don't have to spend your life on the bus or go to Jacksonville."

"Thanks. Me, too. I've never lived anywhere but here, and this is nothing like Jacksonville." We both laughed at that.

"You got that right. Palatka's pretty small, but it's like New York City compared to Campville."

"I hear you, brother."

"Hey, you want to hang out some this week? I'm all by myself and kinda bored."

"Uh, I don't know. I mean, that would be great, but there's not a lot of mixing here. I mean, this that we're doing now—meeting at Dyess'—this is about all the mixing that happens around here. I mean, if you really want to, I'll ask my grandmother."

"Cool! Do you have a phone? I'd give you my grandmother's number, but I don't know it."

"We don't have a phone, but the family next door does. You could leave a message with them if you want to meet up."

At that moment, Grandma exited the van, followed by Mrs. Wilson.

"I see you boys are getting to know each other."

"Yes ma'am. We've been talking about school and stuff. We're gonna hang out some this week while I'm here."

"I think that would be a wonderful idea."

Mrs. Wilson added, "You two just need to be careful. There's some folk around here who don't think much of mixing. Just be careful where you go and what you do."

"Yes ma'am. Grandma, would you give Mrs. Wilson your phone number and could you write down the number for their neighbors so we can call each other about getting together?"

"Certainly. But you boys need to listen to Mrs. Wilson. Thank goodness, things are changing, but people are slow to change around here."

"Yes ma'am."

Grandma took a small note pad and pen from her purse and

began the exchange of phone numbers with Mrs. Wilson. From the north, a train whistle sounded.

"Sounds like the mail train is early. Do you boys want to bring in the mailbag?"

"Yes ma'am."

"Clint, go inside and tell Miss Arlene."

"Yes ma'am."

I quickly ran inside, gave notice to Miss Arlene in the Post Office, then rushed back out just as the train began to sound for the Campville crossing.

"Let's go!" I yelled to Jacob over the noise of the passing train. The hook extended from the caboose, the hanging bag was snatched from its bracket and a mailbag was tossed off the back of the train. Within seconds, Jacob and I arrived at the spot where the bag had landed. He picked it up and handed it to me.

"Here. You probably better take this in. They really don't like Black kids doing this. It's kind of a white kid thing."

"That's just dumb. Let's take it in together. You hold it on one end, and I'll grab the other." So, in we went, carrying the mailbag as though it required two boys to bear its weight. Miss Arlene thanked us, and we exited the store feeling proud that we had struck a blow for racial equality in the sleepy little hamlet of Campville. Parting ways with Jacob and Mrs. Wilson, Grandma and I walked back down to her house as they crossed the tracks to the other side of the highway.

"He's a really nice kid. I like him."

"He's a fine boy, and, from what Mrs. Wilson says, does very well in school."

"But he told me that unless they integrate the high school in Hawthorne, he'll have to ride the school bus to Palatka or Gainesville or go to Jacksonville to live with an aunt if he wants to finish high school and go to college."

"I know. It's really so unfair to colored kids who want to excel. Things will change a great deal during your lifetime, but not quickly enough for a lot of Black young people."

"I know. Sam and I talk about that sometimes. He got put on a biracial committee for the county and he's made friends with the Black students on the committee. I hope I can hang out some with Jacob. I've never really had a Black friend before."

"I hope so, too. Just remember that Kevin's coming tomorrow. He probably won't get here until dinner time, but tomorrow might be the only opportunity you and Jacob have to play together."

"Grandma, kids our age don't play. We hang out."

"Oh, I see." We both laughed at the need for such a distinction.

Dawn was reluctant to arrive on Wednesday morning, and, when it did, it was gray and breezy. I went out for a quick run but cut it short as a brief shower blew past. After I changed out of my damp running clothes, I went into the kitchen where Grandma was preparing breakfast.

"Need any help?"

"I think I have this under control. Go tell your Uncle Al that breakfast is ready. And would you run out and grab the newspaper. He usually gets it, but it was raining."

"I didn't see it out there when I came in, but I'll run out and check."

I walked through the living room and relayed to Uncle Al that breakfast was ready, then stepped outside to find the newspaper on the porch. After breakfast, we all sat in the living room sharing the morning's *Gainesville Sun*.

"Looks like that hurricane is heading our way, Grandma. Says here it hit southwest Haiti on Monday with hundred and fifty mile-an-hour winds."

"Well, I guess we might better check what the radio's saying about it."

"It'll miss us." Uncle Al opined. "They always do."

"Not Donna."

"You're right. Not Donna. Your grandmother's right. We'd best check what they're saying on the radio."

Grandma turned on the radio and, as it warmed up, we heard the voice of the announcer in mid-report. "...struck the southwestern peninsula of Haiti on Monday with sustained winds of one hundred and fifty miles per hour. After crossing the mountains of Haiti, Cleo lost intensity and emerged into the Caribbean on Tuesday as a Category 1 hurricane—a minimum-strength hurricane. Cleo is expected to continue on a westerly course throughout the day today, likely skirting the southern coast of Cuba. However, forecasters at the National Hurricane Center are predicting a northerly shift in Cleo's path, perhaps as early as this afternoon. After that, they say, the storm will likely cross Cuba, weakening further, and head north. From there, Cleo's path is less certain, and forecasters say the storm could move north along a path somewhere between the Gulf of Mexico off Florida's west coast to a path more northerly or northeasterly over the state of Florida or just offshore to the east of the state. Stay tuned for hourly updates on Hurricane Cleo on this station, WGNV, Gainesville, 1090 on your dial." Grandma switched the radio off.

"Like I said. It'll miss us."

"Regardless, Clint, if you want to pla...hang out with Jacob, today will be your only chance. Not only will Kevin be here from this evening on, but the weather's likely to be turning nasty for the next several days."

"Yes ma'am. Can I have that number Mrs. Wilson gave you? I'll go ahead and leave a message for him with the neighbor."

Grandma opened her purse and took out the notepad on which she had written the phone number. I dialed it and a woman answered. "Hello."

"Hello. I was wanting to leave a message for, uh..." I realized I didn't know Jacob's last name. "Uh, Jacob, Mrs. Wilson's grandson."

"Who is this and what you want with Jacob?"

"Uh, this is Clint Cooper, Doctor Henry's grandson."

"Oh, yes, of course. Jacob said you might call. Alright. What's your message for him?"

"Would you please tell him that I'm free for most of the day today if he wants to do something together. Uh, he can call me back, or just come down to my grandmother's house."

"Alright. I'll give him the message."

"Thank you."

"You're welcome. Goodbye."

Now the waiting began. I picked up a section of the newspaper but was preoccupied by other thoughts. I had never had a Black friend. In fact, I had never had the occasion to play with or spend time around Black kids. I was anxious that I might say or do something to offend Jacob, concerned that he might be ill at ease around me. Then, I began to wonder what we might do with our time together. About that time, the phone rang. It was Jacob who said he was on his way. I went out on the porch to meet him, and, within ten minutes, he came jogging up the road.

"Hi." He was a bit out of breath.

"Hi, yourself. Did you run the whole way?"

"Mostly. I figured if some honkey wanted to run me off, I'd at least make him chase me up here to your grandma's house."

"Good idea. So, did you meet any honkeys on the way?"

"No," he laughed. "I did get chased by the Dyess' dog, but that stupid mutt chases everybody, so I figured it wasn't because I was Black."

"Cool. So, what you want to do?"

"I don't know. What do white boys do?"

"Pretty much what Black boys do I expect. Dang! I wish I'd told you to bring a bathing suit."

"Really? I didn't know your grandma had a pool."

"Very funny. No, but we could go swimming in the clay pits."

"It's not exactly swimming weather, but we could just go in our skivvies if you want to go swimming."

"Sure. That's cool. Let's go in and grab a couple of towels."

"I'll just wait out here, if that's OK."

"Suit yourself. I'll be right back." I went inside, grabbed a couple of old towels and was back out within half a minute. We walked toward the back yard and the woods beyond. "Before we go to the pits, I want to show you something."

"Oh, OK. What is it you want to show me?"

"Something me and my friend Sam built earlier in the summer."

"Oh yeah. My Grandma said she met a friend of yours last time you were here."

"Yeah. He's like my best friend and my big brother. He's in the Navy now, so I don't get to see him. Maybe at Christmas." By now, we had entered the thick woods on the back half of my grandmother's property. "Anyway, I wanted to show you our boma."

"What's a boma?"

"Actually, it's African."

"So you think I should know what it is?"

"No, that's not what I meant. I just thought it was cool that it's from Africa, and you're, you know. Never mind."

"I get it. Since I'm kinda from Africa, I should know about African stuff, right?"

"That's not what I meant. I'm sorry. I didn't mean to say something stupid."

"Man, we're cool. I was just messin' with you. Don't get too worked up about it, OK?"

"OK."

"So, again, what's a boma?"

"It's this kind of temporary thing African farmers use to keep their livestock safe at night, like when they're out in the bush herding their cattle or something. I learned about it in Scouts. We had this missionary speak to us and show slides and all. He works with farmers in Africa helping them make their farms better, and he told us about bomas. Anyway, we're here." Jacob looked around but failed to understand what he was seeing.

"What am I supposed to be seeing. This big pile of dead brush?"

"Look here." I stepped forward about six feet and removed the brush from the entrance. "Now, come inside." We stepped into the enclosure and Jacob turned slowing taking it in.

"Wow! This is pretty cool. It's like your own private world in here. I'd never have spotted this if you hadn't shown me."

"I know. It just blends into the woods. See, over here's our fire pit, and over there, where the grass is smooshed flat, is where we set up my tent."

"So, you and your friend camped out here?"

"Yeah, for like three days and two nights. It was so cool. We cooked our food over the fire and washed off in the clay pits. It was the most fun Sam and I ever had. He left for the Navy the next week, and I haven't seen him since."

"That's too bad. I mean, I guess it's good for him, but not so good for you."

"Yeah. I really miss him, but we've been writing to each other. Anyway, so maybe sometime when I'm over here, you and me can camp out here, too."

"That would be cool. I've never camped out, but it would be fun. We'd be like in our own little world."

"Yeah, where the rednecks can't bug us."

"Right on!"

We stepped back outside the boma and I replaced the brush across the entrance. We then began walking toward the clay pits.

"So, your neighbor with the phone kinda gave me the third degree."

Jacob laughed. "Yeah, she's kind of bossy. Likes to be in charge."

"I wasn't sure she was gonna give you the message, but, obviously, she did."

"Yeah. She's actually good about that. I wish we had our own phone, but Grandma really pinches pennies."

"So, you ever swim out here, in the clay pits?"

"All the time. It's the only place in walking distance around here to go swimming. I really don't know who owns this land, probably some timber company, but nobody ever bothers us out here."

"I was out here a long time ago, playing with Jesse something, I don't remember his name."

"Oh, yeah. I know who you're talking about. They own the dairy down toward Hawthorne."

"Yeah. I guess they moved or something."

"Yeah. They built a house at the dairy."

"So, anyway, me and Jesse were messin' around out here, and we went toward the clay pits. We heard voices, so we kinda snuck up and looked over one of those giant piles of dirt and there were some Black guys skinny dipping."

"Was that about three years ago?"

"Yeah, why?"

Jacob laughed. "'Cause my cousin Abe was one of them. He told me a couple of little white boys were spying on them and they chased them off."

Now I was laughing. "No way! That's too funny. Yeah, me and Jesse took off running and never looked back. I don't know how far they chased us, but we didn't stop running 'til we got to his yard."

"I can't believe that was you. Abe's a good guy. They wouldn't of hurt you. Besides, they were butt naked. It's not like they were gonna chase you very far."

"I know, but at the time we were scared stiff. Besides, we were little kids, you know?"

Minutes later, we arrived at the clay pits. We stripped down to our underwear and placed our towels, clothes and shoes on the same log Sam and I had used for that purpose weeks earlier.

"Jeez, this is cold. I forgot how cold this water is," I remarked.

"Yeah. I think it's easier just to go in all at once and get the shock over with quick."

"OK. Let's go!" With that, we rushed out into waist-deep water and began splashing each other. This quickly devolved into horseplay that lasted until we were both chilled to the bone.

"I'm freezing. Let's get out and warm up," I suggested.

"OK. I'm with you. My teeth are chattering. It would help if we had a little fat on us, but you're as skinny as me."

"I know. Hey, let's take our towels up on that little hill over there. See, there's a patch of sunlight there. We can lay there and warm up."

"Good plan."

Once we had climbed to the crest of the hill, we laid our towels in the sun and stretched out on them, side by side.

Jacob yawned, "Man, this feels fantastic."

"Yeah. The sun feels great. Maybe our underwear'll dry out, too. I hate wearing wet underwear under my clothes."

"You do that a lot?" he teased.

"No, but, you know."

"Yeah. I know."

"So, I'm not trying to be nosey, but how come you live with your Grandma?"

"It's a long story, but we've got time, so here goes. My mama was real young when she got pregnant with me. She was fifteen, and my father was twenty-one."

"Oh, man."

"Yeah. So, they eloped to Georgia and got married before I was born. Then, they came back to Campville, left me with my Grandma and ran off to Chicago."

"You mean they just left you?"

"Well, the plan was, they were gonna get jobs up there and then come back to get me, but that never happened. Not long after they got up there, my father left my mother and took up with some other woman. My mother ended up livin' on the street with no money and froze to death in a cardboard box the first winter."

"Holy shit! Pardon my French, but that's awful. How come she didn't just come home?"

"I don't know. I've wondered that a lot. Maybe she was embarrassed or thought he'd come back to her. I don't know. Maybe she was too proud to ask my Grandma for bus fare. She was still a kid, you know. Only about seventeen then. It makes me sad for her, you know?"

"Yeah. It makes me sad just to hear about it. So, did your father ever try to come get you?"

"Nope. Never seen the guy, and don't want to. If I ever saw him, I think I'd spit in his face, kick him in the nuts and walk away. Unless I had a gun."

"I get it. Man, I'm sorry."

"Don't be. I guess I've had about as good a life as a Black boy livin' in the sticks can have. My Grandma is the best mother I could hope for. My Grandpa died when I was about five, so it's just been Grandma and me. We're poor, but we don't lack for anything. Grandma pushes me to work hard in school, and I plan to go to college one way or another and make a better life for her and me."

"Man, I hope it works out for you, but I don't know, it sure seems like life has given you a raw deal, you know?"

"Yeah, but there are plenty of folks worse off than me. Being Black can be hard, but I think Dr. King is gonna bring some change. I think things'll get easier for Black folks from here on out."

"I hope so, too. My friend, Sam, really likes Dr. King. You know, you're the first Black friend I've ever had."

"Well, it's not like I have a lot of white friends. I ride the Negro bus to school, go to a Negro school, and live across the tracks from the only white kids for five miles, so there's not much chance to make friends with any white kids. Plus, folks around here are pretty redneck."

"I understand. They're pretty redneck in Palatka, too. You know, when the Klan bombed that church in Birmingham and killed those four little girls, some kids at my school thought it was funny! Can you believe that?"

"Yeah. Yeah, I can believe that."

"Man, I'm gettin' too much sun. I'm gonna get a sunburn."

"Well, I'm not too worried about that." We laughed, stood up, picked up our towels and walked back down to where we had left our clothes.

"Well, at least my underwear is dry on the front."

"Yeah. Mine, too." We dressed and began to walk back through the woods toward my grandmother's house.

"So, what you want to do now?"

"I don't know. I think we've taken in all the attractions in Campville."

I laughed in agreement. "You ever played Parcheesi?"

"Nope. How do you play?"

"It's a board game. My Uncle Al loves to play it. We could see if he wants to play a game."

"You mean inside the house?"

"Well, yeah."

"You sure that's OK?"

"Yeah. I'm sure that's OK. Just one thing, though."

"What?"

"Do not, under any circumstances, beat my Uncle Al."

"Oh, OK. I'll remember that."

We found Uncle Al on the front porch, smoking his pipe. When I proposed a game of Parcheesi, he readily agreed. I went inside and brought the game box out and we set it up on the table on the porch. Jacob mastered the game within five minutes and we ended up playing three games. Interestingly enough, Uncle Al won all three, although Jacob came dangerously close to taking the final game. By the time we finished playing, the weather had taken a turn for the worse. Jacob decided he needed to head home, but Grandma insisted he join us for lunch before leaving. After lunch, I walked him down to Dyess' store and we said our goodbyes. We promised to get together again the next time I was visiting Grandma. As I walked back toward Grandma's a squall line hit, drenching me with a tepid rainfall that signaled tropical weather on the way.

24.

I DIDN'T MUCH LIKE CLEO, EITHER

THROUGHOUT THE AFTERNOON, the weather deteriorated. I lay in bed reading *Alas Babylon* while Grandma fretted, worried about Kevin driving through the worsening weather. For his part, Uncle Al sat calmly in his recliner reading with his unlit pipe in his mouth.

Around dusk, I heard Grandma call out, "Kevin's here!"

I crawled out of bed, looked in the mirror, brushed my hair, and scurried out to the porch to meet this cousin I scarcely knew. Parked in front of the house was a fire-engine-red Chevrolet Corvette. It was the most beautiful car I'd ever seen. Unfolding from the driver's seat was a tall, stocky, older teen with a broad smile on his face. Grandma rushed out into the nasty weather to wrap him in an embrace. Uncle Al and I prudently remained under the shelter of the porch.

"Aunt Rose, don't come out here. You'll get drenched. I can get my stuff. You go back to the porch."

Grandma called to me, "Clint, come out here and help your cousin get his things out of the car."

"Yes, ma'am."

"No, you don't, Clint. Stay up there. I can get my stuff, and there's no sense in all of us getting wet." I was in a bit of a quandary, having received conflicting orders, but chose to listen to my older and obviously wiser cousin. Within seconds, Kevin bounded up the steps and lifted me off the porch in a bear hug. "I'm so glad you're here, Clint. I've really been looking forward to this ever since Aunt Rose told me you'd be here."

"Yeah. Me, too. I know I've met you before, but it's been a long time ago, and I really don't remember it."

Kevin greeted Uncle Al, after which Grandma ordered us all into the house and out of the weather. "Did you drive through a lot of bad weather, Kevin?"

"No ma'am. Not really. It didn't start getting squally until I was around Tallahassee. It's been getting worse since then, but still, not too bad. That car hardly feels the wind. It just cuts right through the squalls."

"And I'm sure you were driving under the speed limit."

"Well, yes ma'am, sometimes."

Uncle Al chimed in, "That's a pretty fancy car you're driving. Did your worthless father give it to you?"

"Albert! We'll have none of that!" Grandma scolded.

"Yes sir. My dad gave it to me for graduation. This is really the first road trip I've made in it. It drinks gas, but it's sure fun to drive."

"Kevin, I hope you don't mind, but you'll need to bunk in with Clint. His folks are picking him up on Saturday, so you'll have the room to yourself after that."

"No, ma'am. That's fine with me if it's OK with you, Clint."

"It's fine with me. The bed's plenty big, and I'm pretty skinny. We'll be fine. You don't snore, do you?"

"Well," he chuckled. "I don't know. I guess you can tell me."

"Can I see your car?"

"Sure. Let's hold off and see if we get a break in the rain and I'll show it to you."

"Great!"

Grandma had fixed a pot roast and vegetables for dinner. Added to that were homemade biscuits and pear preserves from the ancient tree outside her back door. It was all delicious, and Kevin put away as much as the rest of us combined. When dinner was over, I glanced outside to see that it was dark and raining even harder.

"I guess we can wait 'til tomorrow to see your car."

"That's probably a good idea. Hey, if it's OK, I'm going to go take a shower. I left New Orleans at daybreak and I need to get cleaned up."

"That's fine. There are clean towels on the shelf above the toilet. Remember that it takes a while for the water to get hot."

"Yes, ma'am. Thanks, Aunt Rose."

It occurred to me that I hadn't showered since Jacob and I swam in the clay pits that morning. "I'll go after Kevin."

"That's fine. You'll want to wait about twenty minutes for the water heater to catch up."

"Yes, ma'am. Can I turn on the radio and check on the hurricane?"

"That'll be fine."

I switched on the old set and, as the tubes warmed up, Satchmo was singing. When he finished, the seven-thirty bulletin began. "Here's the latest bulletin from the National Hurricane Center. As of 7:00 pm this evening, the center of Hurricane Cleo was over open water in the Florida Straits and strengthening over the warm waters of the Gulf Stream. Over the past twenty-four hours, Cleo made landfall on the southern coast of Cuba, crossing quickly over the island nation overnight. Shortly after 7:00 am this morning, Hurricane Cleo moved offshore of Cuba and took a northerly track, which, unless the storm deviates, will bring it onshore south of Miami, Florida, in the early hours of tomorrow morning. Reports of damage and casualties in Cuba are, understandably, sketchy, but it appears the weakened storm caused minimal damage while over the island. Now that Cleo has moved back over open water, forecasters expect the storm to re-intensify to a Category 2 hurricane, with sustained winds near one hundred miles per hour, before making landfall in south Florida. Those with interests in the South Florida area should pay close attention to updates on this dangerous hurricane. The next bulletin will be issued at 11:00 pm tonight. Stay tuned to this station, WGNV, Gainesville, 1090 on your dial, for the latest on Hurricane Cleo. We now return to our regular programming." I turned off the radio and went to get clean clothes in anticipation of my shower.

It seemed we were all ready for bed early that evening, Kevin having driven since before sunrise, so he and I turned off the light around nine o'clock and talked quietly in the dark.

"So, Clint, how do you keep yourself entertained when you're here in Campville?"

"Good question. Mostly, I read. I go for a jog every morning. Play Parcheesi with Uncle Al."

"You know not to ever beat him, right?" We both laughed knowingly.

"Oh yeah. I learned that a long time ago."

"So, what else do you do?'

"Well, you know, we go down to Dyess' for the mail. That's about it. But my friend, Sam and me, we camped out back in the woods for three days. We went swimming in the clay pits, cooked all our food over the fire, and built a boma. That was a blast. But he's in the Navy now."

"So he's about my age, then?"

"Yeah. He graduated this year, too. He's eighteen, though. You're seventeen, right?"

"Yeah. I started school a year early. I think my Grandma wanted to get me out from underfoot. It's pretty cool that you have a friend my age. Maybe that's why you seem more comfortable around me, more like a peer than a younger kid."

"What's a peer?"

"It's someone who's kind of at the same place in life as you are. Like a similar age."

"Oh, OK. Yeah, Sam's been like my best friend and my big brother forever, well, not forever, but you know what I mean."

"Sure."

"Anyway, that's probably why I feel comfortable talking to you and can, you know, kinda relate to you like a..."

"Like a peer?"

"Yeah. Like a peer. So, anyway, I made a new friend this week, and we went swimming in the pits today and hung out for a lot of the day. He nearly beat Uncle Al at Parcheesi even after I warned him! His name's Jacob, he's thirteen and he's Black."

"Well that's cool. I never really had a Black friend."

"Me neither. His grandmother knows Grandma, and Granddaddy Cooper delivered her babies. He's smart and funny and I really like him. He wants to go to college."

"That's great. Hey, I was thinking we might go into Gainesville tomorrow and see a movie. What do you think?"

"And ride in your car?"

"Well, of course."

"That'd be great. What movie are we gonna see?"

"Well, have you seen *Becket?*"[14]

---

14 Released in 1964, *Becket* is a film adaptation of Jean Anouih's play *Becket or the Honor of God*. Starring Richard Burton as Thomas Becket, Peter O'Toole as King Henry II, and Sir John Gielgud as King Louis VII of France, the film was nominated for 11 Academy Awards and won the award for Best Adapted Screenplay. The film opens with King Henry receiving a penitential flogging and addressing the departed spirit of Thomas Becket. Then, the story rewinds to the past where we find Becket in his role as loyal cohort to Henry and facilitator for his limitless trysts. Determined to keep Becket as a trusted confidant, Henry makes him Lord Chancellor, in part so that he can control his actions in that position. Instead, he finds Becket increasingly at odds with decisions that he, as King, chooses to make. Amid growing distrust and disdain for Becket by the nobility, as well as others of the Royal Family, Henry nonetheless continues to trust and rely on him to arrange

"Nope. What's it about?"

"Well, it's based on a play, we read it in my English Lit class. It's about this English guy, Thomas Becket, who's friends with King Henry II. The king is a, well, a ladies' man."

"You mean he's a playboy, right?"

"Yeah."

"I know what you mean. I'm twelve, but I'm not a dummy."

"Gotcha. So, anyway, Becket and the King do a lot of partying, but the King gets in this big disagreement with the Church—the Pope was incredibly powerful and he could tell royalty what to do—so, anyway, Henry is in this big disagreement with the Church and, when the Archbishop of Canterbury dies—he's the head of the Church in England—so, when he dies, the King decides to appoint Becket as the Archbishop because he thinks

---

diversions from what Henry views as the oppressive demands of court and his loveless marriage. When Henry seeks to tax church properties in order to raise funds to support his military campaigns in France, he butts heads with the aging Archbishop of Canterbury, the head of the Church in England. When the Archbishop dies, Henry appoints Becket to fill his place—against Becket's advice—assuming he can better control the church and, in particular, receive Becket's blessing to tax church properties. However, Becket takes his new position seriously and morphs into a sincerely spiritual man frequently invoking the "honor of God." Siding with the church and against Henry in several significant matters, Becket is eventually forced to flee to France, where he is welcomed by King Louis VII, who perceives Becket as a means by which he can further antagonize Henry. From France, Becket travels to Rome to implore the Pope to release him from his position as Archbishop and allow him to live out the remainder of his life in a monastery. However, the Pope refuses and instead sends Becket back to England with the admonition to stand firm against the King on matters of civil interference into ecclesiastical matters. With no real way out of the situation, Becket asks Louis to arrange a meeting with Henry wherein they agree to a fragile truce. But Henry's obsession with Becket's perceived disloyalty, coupled with the constant urging of his queen and mother to do away with Becket, drives Henry into a state of drunken despondency. Spiraling downward, and in a fit of rage, Henry yells to a group of his faithful noblemen "Will no one rid me of this meddlesome priest?" Acting on what they perceive as the King's orders, those barons do precisely that, and murder Becket in the cathedral at Canterbury. The film ends as it began—with Henry's flogging as penance for his role in Becket's murder. As to the historicity of the film, it—and the play on which it is based—takes significant dramatic license and those inaccuracies will not be explored here.

he can control the Church through Becket. The only problem is, Becket takes the job seriously, and so he and Henry become almost like enemies. Becket loves Henry, but he loves the Church more, so Henry...well, I'm not going to tell you how it ends."

"OK. It sounds confusing."

"It sounds more confusing than it is. It's got a lot of action in it. I think you'll like it.

"OK. So, you think maybe my friend Jacob could come?"

Kevin paused before he responded quietly. "Clint, you know he can't sit with us, right? He'd have to sit in the balcony."

"Jesus, I completely forgot! What was I thinking? That's just so wrong. He's my friend. We should be able to sit together at the damn movie." By now, I was speaking loudly, bordering on shouting.

"Hold on, man. I know, I know. It stinks. I wish it wasn't like this, but it is."

"Well, it needs to change!"

"I agree, but we live in the South, and it's not going to change overnight. You know about those three students that were murdered in Mississippi?"

"Yeah. I know. Sam wrote me all about that."

"Well, one of those guys was Black, but the other two were white, and those Klansmen still killed the white boys. I know Florida isn't Mississippi, but Louisiana sure is. You really have to be careful where you go and what you do. If we tried to get Jacob into the movie with us, in the white section, it could get real ugly real fast."

"I know you're right, but when is this gonna stop? When can I have a friend who's Black or brown or purple and nobody give a damn?"

"I don't know. I think things are changing, but there's so much resistance and so much hate from a lot of white people.

It's gonna take a long time."

"Right now, Jacob doesn't even know how he'll go to high school if they don't integrate the high school in Hawthorne. He may have to go live with his aunt in Jacksonville just so he can get a diploma. That's just wrong. He should be able to go to high school without having to leave home."

"I know, man. And I really feel for your friend. He's lucky to have you in his corner. Keep being his friend, but just be careful, OK?"

"Yeah. OK."

"Hey, I hate to be a party pooper, but I'm bushed. I need to say goodnight."

"OK. Goodnight, Kevin."

"Goodnight, Clint."

Within less than a minute, Kevin's breathing became deep and regular and it was apparent he had drifted off. As for me, I lay awake, listening to the occasional rain on the tin roof, angrily pondering how absurdly unfair life was that I couldn't even take a friend to a movie simply because of the color of his skin.

The next morning, the weather seemed unchanged from the evening before. The sky was completely overcast with occasional rain squalls passing through. I slipped out of bed, pulled on my running togs and managed to get soaked on my abbreviated morning run. When I returned to the house, Kevin was dressed and he and Uncle Al were seated, sharing the morning paper. Grandma had breakfast well underway.

"Clint, go get out of those wet clothes before you catch your death. Hang those things on the back porch."

"Yes ma'am." After I had changed and hung my dripping clothes on the clothesline, Grandma called us to breakfast. She had prepared a large spread and I was intrigued by the fact that Kevin poured ketchup on virtually everything on his plate—

eggs, sausage, and even grits.

"The news in the paper about the hurricane is a day old," Kevin remarked.

"We'll catch the latest on the radio after breakfast."

"Yes, sir. By the way, Aunt Rose, Clint and I are going to drive into Gainesville and catch a movie today, if that's OK."

"In this weather? Are you sure that's a good idea?"

"Well, it's likely to be worse tomorrow, and Clint leaves on Saturday, so this is really our only chance. It's not a long drive, and, besides that car handles a wet highway like a race car."

"That's because it is a race car, son."

"Well, yes sir. I guess you're right."

After breakfast, Kevin and I cleared the table, then he insisted that Grandma relax while he and I cleaned the kitchen and washed the dishes. When we were finished, we took seats in the living room and Uncle Al switched on the radio.

"Hurricane Cleo made landfall overnight last night south of Miami, Florida, as a Category 2 hurricane. Sustained winds at the time were near one hundred miles per hour, with gusts up to one hundred and thirty miles per hour. Cleo weakened as it moved north over land on a path to the west of the greater Miami area. By 7:00 am this morning, the storm was centered to the north and west of Miami. Throughout the day today, Cleo is expected to continue a northerly track twenty to thirty miles inshore of the east coast of Florida with the center of the storm expected to be near Cape Kennedy by evening. Preparations are well underway at the Space Center to safeguard America's launch facilities from the anticipated impact of Hurricane Cleo. The storm is expected to pass our area overnight tonight, with the center passing between Palatka and St. Augustine. In terms of potential local impact, the National Hurricane Center is warning citizens in our area to prepare for heavy rains and sustained winds of forty to fifty miles per hour overnight with gusts up to sixty miles per hour. The formation of tornadoes is possible with the passage of Hurricane Cleo. We will interrupt regular programming in the event of any tornadic activity in our area, otherwise, stay tuned for regular updates on Hurricane Cleo on this station, WGNV, Gainesville, 1090 on your dial." Uncle Al switched off the radio.

"Kevin, if you boys are going to go to a movie, you need to take in a matinee. It sounds like you'd better be back here before evening."

"Yes, ma'am. We'll do that. Let me check the movie times in the paper." Kevin scanned the morning newspaper until he found the movie listings. "There's a showing at 1:30. I think that's the one we should go to, Clint. How about we head over early and grab lunch at McDonald's. It'll be on me."

"That sounds cool. We don't have a McDonald's in Palatka. The one in Gainesville's the only one I've eaten at, and only one time before. Thanks."

From that point, it seemed the clock froze. The morning dragged past as I anticipated riding in Kevin's red Corvette, eating at McDonald's, and going to a movie. It would be such an adult excursion—the sort of thing college guys might just as well do with a free afternoon.

Around 11:30, we left for Gainesville in a light rain. Riding in Kevin's Corvette was unlike anything I had experienced to that point in my life. The powerful engine rumbled and the car was alive with pent-up energy. Sitting so close to the roadway, I felt a part of every curve and rise in the pavement. The interior seemed more like the cabin of a spacecraft with a futuristic instrument panel and seats that surrounded us. I don't know how fast Kevin drove, but I'm confident it was well above the limit.

When we parked at the McDonald's, others stared at us, and

I felt like a celebrity arriving at a red carpet event in Hollywood. Kevin, however, seemed unaffected by the attention his vehicle garnered, as though he had just pulled up in a beat-up station wagon. After lunch, we drove the short distance to the theater, purchased our tickets, and found seats about midway back. The previews included trailers for *Mary Poppins* and *My Fair Lady*, and I remember wondering at the time how incongruous those upbeat movie musicals were with the very real crises that seemed to be enveloping America. Then the feature began.

Becket opened with Peter O'Toole, as Henry II, kneeling in a church about to endure a penitential flogging, addressing the obviously dead Thomas Becket, "Well, Thomas Becket. Are you satisfied? Here I am, stripped, kneeling at your tomb, while those treacherous Saxon monks of yours are getting ready to thrash me. Me—with my delicate skin. I bet you'd never have done the same for me." Kevin was certainly correct in his assessment—I was immediately and fully captivated by the film and the dramatic story it told. The conflict that grew within Becket between his loyalty to Henry and his determination to fulfil his ecclesiastical duties with integrity was exhausting to me. By the time the film ended, I felt I'd been flogged myself.

As we exited and walked toward the car, Kevin asked for my assessment. "So, what did you think?"

"It was...I don't know how to say it. It hurt to watch. I mean, the movie was great—maybe the best movie I ever saw next to *To Kill a Mockingbird*—but it just kinda rips your heart out. I mean, they were such good friends, and then Becket tries to do the right thing and Henry hates him for it. It makes me wonder if I could have been that strong, you know? Would I be able to do the right thing even if it cost me my best friend?"

"Exactly. Man, you got it. You really understood the main theme of the film. You're a pretty smart kid, you know?"

"Thanks. I think it comes from hanging around Sam. He's always making me think about stuff, making me dig below the surface, you know?"

We arrived at the car and climbed in. No sooner had Kevin cranked the engine than a blustery squall hit. "We got in just in time. So, Sam must be a really good friend."

"He's the best friend a guy could ever have. He doesn't treat me like a little kid. He teaches me about important stuff, and he doesn't let me get off easy with my ideas. He's the one who taught me to ride a bike. He's the one who got me started running. He's been like a big brother and a best friend rolled into one."

"That's great. I never really had a friend like that when I was younger, or even now, for that matter. I mean, I have good friends, but nobody who sounds like Sam."

"Yeah. He's pretty special. Our whole family loves him. His dad was killed in the Korean War, so it's just him and his mom. I think my dad feels kinda responsible for him. He's like a member of our family, you know?"

"That's cool."

As we drove back out to Campville, the intensity of the storm increased measurably. By the time we parked in front of Grandma's house, it was pouring and the wind was blowing steadily on a horizontal plane. "Let's make a run for it, but we're still gonna get soaked." And we did.

While Kevin and I had been in Gainesville, Grandma had made an enormous pot of vegetable soup. That was accompanied by grilled cheese sandwiches for dinner. Afterward, Kevin and I did the dishes and then took seats in the living room for the evening storm update.

"Throughout the day today, Cleo has kept to the forecast track up the peninsula of Florida, losing strength as it went.

Earlier today, after passing through Dade County, Cleo was downgraded to a tropical storm but continues to pack tropical storm force winds and produce significant rainfall. As of seven o'clock this evening, the eye of Cleo was situated near the Space Coast of Florida, and there have been reports of a possible tornado in the Titusville area. Cleo is expected to continue moving north overnight on a path that will bring the center of the storm near St. Augustine around daybreak tomorrow. Here in the north central Florida area..." At that moment, the electricity went out.

"Holy crap! I can't see a thing!"

"Everyone just keep your seats," said Grandma. "I've got some candles ready over here on the buffet. I figured this would happen. Just give me a minute and we'll get some light in here."

"I've got my flashlight right here by my chair, Rose. Let me get the candles lit." Uncle Al shuffled into the dining room by the light of his flashlight and, one by one, brought several lit candles back into the living room. The wind raged beyond the windows, rain pelted the tin roof, but the interior of the house was bathed in a soft, warm glow that seemed to belie the discord outside.

"I sure hope Mom and Dad and Will are OK."

"I'm sure they're fine, Clint," Uncle Al responded. "Your house is concrete block. If this old place can stand up to another hurricane, I'm sure your house in Palatka will do just fine. You can call them if the phone line's not down."

"Oh, OK." I walked over to the telephone, but the line was dead. "It's dead."

"I'm sure they're fine."

I was unconvinced, having heard clearly that the eye of the storm would be passing close to St. Augustine—a mere thirty miles from Palatka. With the power out and the phone lines down, I began to feel isolated, trapped, and helpless, unable to monitor the progress of the storm, and unable to check on my family. The candles provided sufficient light to avoid bumping into objects and people, but certainly not enough light by which to read. Anxiety and boredom—seemingly incompatible partners—marched in lockstep around my gut. I began to pace about the room.

"Clint, will you sit down. You're making me nervous."

"I'm sorry, Uncle Al. I need to move around. I feel like I'm gonna explode. I'm worried about my family, and with the power out, we won't be able to listen to the radio. They said there was a tornado somewhere."

"Titusville. That's a long way from here."

"Alright. But what if one comes here? We won't get any warning."

"Tornadoes are usually here and gone before there's a warning, anyway. If one came through here—and I mean *if*—we wouldn't know until it was here and gone. This storm is a force of nature, son. There's not a thing we can do to alter its course. We just have to ride it out."

"Yes sir." I returned to my seat, no more confident or assured than I had been, but knowing there was no point arguing with Uncle Al. It was somewhat like playing Parcheesi with him—you appear to give it your best effort, knowing all the while you will let him win.

"Hey, we could play cards or something," Kevin suggested. "We can do that by candlelight."

"That's a good idea, Kevin. I'll take the tablecloth off the dining table and we can play in there."

Nearly two hours later, after untold hands of Rummy 500, the decision was made to retire for the night. Surprisingly, Uncle Al lost all but a couple of hands yet seemed altogether nonplussed—something to remember for the future. Kevin and I carried a lit candle into our room and prepared for bed.

"Hey, thanks for everything today—McDonalds and the movie and getting to ride in your car. It was great."

"You're more than welcome, man. Happy to do it. Honestly, I don't really have much family. It's really just my grandma and me, so it was fun to hang out with you today."

"So, do you ever see your father?"

"You know about my family situation?"

"Yeah. Grandma told me. Hey, if you don't want to talk about it, it's fine." We pulled back the covers and crawled into the bed from opposite sides. Kevin blew out the candle and the room was suddenly, impenetrably dark. "Whoa! I can't even see my hand in front of my face."

"Yeah. Maybe our eyes will adjust in a few minutes. But, no, I don't hardly ever see my father. Just around my birthday. He has a family, so I don't see him at Christmas, and I've never really spent more than a few hours with him at a time."

"Oh, man. That really stinks."

"It's OK, really. I mean, it's all I've ever known, so I don't expect any more from him. I mean, I love him, but he's not a big influence in my life or anything. He gives me stuff, like the car, but I think it's to make him feel better. I don't resent him. I don't hate him. It's just the way things are."

At that moment, a strong gust hit the house and the tin roof sounded as if it were being peeled off. "Damn! What was that?"

"It's the roof."

"It sounded like it was coming off or something."

"No. It just kinda buckled when that big gust blew across it. Let's just hope the roofing nails hold."

"What do you mean?"

"Well, the tin's nailed onto the roof trusses. If those nails pull out, well, there goes the roof."

"Oh, man. That would be bad. Really bad."

"Yeah, but I don't think that's gonna happen. You know anything about this house?"

"No, not really. Except it's old and none of the floors are level."

He laughed. "That's for sure. But, no, this house was built by your great grandfather, Aunt Rose's father, sometime back in the late 1800s. It's been through a lot of hurricanes, so I don't think this little storm's gonna take the roof off."

"Yeah. I guess you're right. We went through Donna a few years back and the roof stayed on then, and that was a really bad one."

"There you go. See. Nothing to worry about. Now, let's get some sleep."

"OK. Goodnight." I held my hand up before my face again and still could not see it. The darkness was absolute, the rain continued to fall in sheets, the wind raged, and the roof continued to buckle. I lay awake in the noisy darkness, worrying about my family and praying the roofing nails would hold. At some point, sleep overtook me.

25.

"THE STORM IS PASSIN' OVER,
THE STORM IS PASSIN' OVER,
THE STORM IS PASSIN' OVER,
HALELU!"
AFRICAN-AMERICAN SPIRITUAL

THE FIRST DAWN following the passage of a hurricane is an eerily quiet event. The winds have subsided, leaving only the occasional gust; the rains have all but abated, but other sounds are absent as well—birds in particular. They have not left but remain sheltered in their safe places unsure of the wisdom of venturing out. Traffic is practically non-existent, as only the most stalwart choose to leave their homes. And the morning light is an otherworldly golden glow, as though one has been transported to some distant, Mediterranean beach at sunrise. As I came awake the morning after Cleo, that was the silent, glowing world I found. Kevin was sleeping, and the house was still. I slipped out of bed, pulled on a pair of shorts and a t-shirt, and, carrying my running shoes, tip-toed into the living room and laced them on.

As I stepped out into the morning, I was struck by the chaos left by Cleo. The two enormous pecan trees astride my grandmother's walk had been stripped of leaves, and branches of all sizes littered the yard. Across the railroad tracks, highway 301 was empty. The usual parade of eighteen-wheelers was absent and not a single vehicle appeared in either direction.

As I began a slow jog down the lime rock road, I realized I was going to be spending an inordinate amount of my run dodging fallen debris. But since I had cut it short the morning before, I was determined to make the best of the situation on this morning. As I neared Dyess' store, there were several sheets of roofing tin lying in the road. Glancing up at the roof of the store, their source was apparent. As I continued, there was more evidence of Cleo's visit, but I saw no other damage to houses or buildings. As I returned to the house, I saw the newspaper deliveryman's pickup and watched as he tossed the paper toward my grandmother's porch. Uncle Al, newspaper in hand, met me outside as I came up the walk.

"You're pretty disciplined about your running, aren't you?"

"Yes sir, I guess so. I want to make the track team when I get to high school. Plus, I'm in the running club at my school, so I need to keep it up. By the way, Dyess' lost some of their roof in the storm."

"That's not good. Did you see any other damage around town?"

"No sir. Just lots of branches down. And there's a big tree blown over down by where the dairy family used to live, but it didn't hit anything."

"Good. Well, your grandmother's got breakfast underway. Good thing we have gas, because the power's still out. Why don't you go wake up Kevin."

"Yes sir."

I found Kevin already up and getting dressed. "I didn't even hear you get up."

"I'm pretty stealthy. Hey, I think we need to spend the morning picking up outside. There's a ton of branches down all over the yard."

"Sure. That's a good idea."

After breakfast, I checked the phone, but found the service

272

still out. Then, Kevin and I put on jeans and began collecting the storm debris from Grandma's yard. We made a large pile of it on the edge of the woods behind her house, but it was too wet and green to burn.

"Hey, I want to check on the boma."

"I heard you use that word the other day. Just what, exactly, is this boma thing?"

"So, Sam and I camped out back in the woods at the first of the summer and we built a boma. It's a shelter made out of brush that you build around your campsite. In Africa, farmers build 'em to keep their animals safe at night. So, I want to see if it survived the storm."

"Oh, OK."

We made our way back through the woods. Everything was dripping wet, and we were as well after only a minute. Arriving at the campsite, it was apparent the boma had not fared well.

"Oh, crap. It's ruined." I tried to hide the empty sense of loss I felt but did a poor job.

"Hey, Clint, it's OK. We can fix it, can't we?"

"Yeah. I guess. Most of the brush is scattered around here, and we could cut some more. Why would you help me do this?"

"Well, it's pretty obvious this was important to you, and it's not like we have plans for the day."

"Yeah." I chuckled. "I guess you're right. But, yeah, this is a special place to me. That camping trip was the most fun Sam and I ever had together, and the boma was kinda the last place we spent any time together, so, yeah. It is pretty important to me. Thanks. We're gonna need to get some knives or something for cutting fresh brush. Sam and I had a hatchet, but I don't think Grandma has such a thing."

As it turned out, I was wrong about the hatchet. Grandma did, in fact, have an ancient wooden-handled hatchet she said she used for chopping kindling back in the days she cooked on a wood stove. So, right after lunch, Kevin and I returned to the woods and spent about an hour restoring the boma. When we finished, I felt as though my world had been put right as well.

"Thanks, man. I really appreciate you helping me with this."

"Happy to help. So, I guess you can tell Sam the boma's still standing."

"Yeah. I'll write him. In fact, I have a lot to write him about now—meeting Jacob, you coming, riding in your 'Vette, the movie, the hurricane. Yeah. It's gonna be a long letter!"

When we reached the house, the power had been restored as well as the phone service. I phoned my family in Palatka and found they were all fine and had sustained no damage from the storm. My mom confirmed that they would be over the next morning to collect me and visit with Kevin. Later that afternoon, I borrowed writing paper from Grandma and began a letter to Sam.

Around ten o'clock Saturday morning, my parents and Will arrived. My dad seemed particularly glad to see Kevin and, while they visited, I took Will out to let him sit in the Corvette. He was appropriately impressed. Grandma insisted they stay for lunch, after which we loaded my things and set out for Palatka. I kept up a running monologue all the way home. Of course, I wrote Sam a long letter detailing my stay in Campville and received his reply the week school began.

3 Sept., 1964
NAS JAX
Hey, Clint.

It was great to get your letter. It was sure a fat one! What, no cookies? Just joking, kind of! Man, your visit to Campville sounds pretty exciting, what with the storm and all. Cleo didn't do much here on base. Just a big blow for a day or so. They shut down the flight line and we tied down all the aircraft just to be safe, but it really didn't amount to much.

Your cousin Kevin sounds cool. I can't believe he's my age and has a Corvette! Wow! It must have been something to ride in that. I'm really glad he helped you fix the boma. I sure hope we can camp out in it again someday. Hey, your friend Jacob sounds like a nice guy, too. I'm really proud of you for making friends with a Black person.

Hey, I really appreciate you telling me about the thing with the Cub Scouts. Man, your Mom really ripped you a new one, buddy! She was right, though, and I'm glad you realized it. Those little guys look up to you, and they're going to try to follow your example. Honestly, I've thought a lot over the years about my influence in your life, and I've really tried to set a good example for you (except for teaching you to cuss! Don't tell that to your Mom!).

I guess school starts after Labor Day. Are you excited? Are you planning to do any extracurricular stuff? Are you still going to do the track club and chorus. I just hope you don't get Miss Denham for 8th grade English. That woman is a psycho!

Well, got to go. Lights out in a few minutes. I'll try to get this in the mail tomorrow. Take care of yourself.

Your Big Bro,
Sam

School began the day after Labor Day, and, very quickly, my life took on a predictable routine. Eighth grade was something of a let-down—neither here nor there. Because the ninth grade had been moved to the junior high to ease overcrowding at the high school, it felt as if those of us in eighth grade had been denied our rightful place at the top of the junior high food chain.

One rather surprising change in my world occurred on the morning of the first day of school. As I walked toward the school, I spied a girl walking about fifty yards ahead of me. She wore an emerald-green pleated skirt with a wide belt that served to accentuate her figure and a pale green long-sleeved blouse. Her sun-streaked dark blonde hair was pulled back in a ponytail and she walked with a confident sashay. I did not recognize this girl and assumed she was newly arrived over the summer. Quickening my pace, I was intent on catching up with her, but didn't want to appear too obvious in doing so. Running a fast calculation in my head, I determined I could close the distance by the time we both arrived at the elementary school playground and still retain some semblance of my feigned disinterest.

As I walked toward her, I rehearsed my opening. "Hi. You must be new here. I'm Clint." That might work—simple, but sincere. "Hello. Are you walking to the junior high." No, that one was just dumb. Obviously, she was walking to the junior high. "Hi. I think you're heading the wrong way. The high school's back that way." No, no, no. That was just too pathetic. As I closed the distance, my anxiety increased until I was only about four feet behind her when she spoke.

"Hi, Clint. I know it's you. I recognize your walk."

I was dumbstruck. It was Crazy Christine! How in God's name could this be the same girl I'd grown up with? What had happened over the summer to transform the roughshod tomboy I loved to hate into this... this junior high beauty? After a couple of hopeless attempts, I finally found my voice.

"Uh, hi Christine. How was your summer?"

"It was perfect. I spent the summer with my grandmother in Atlanta, and she enrolled me in this amazing charm school. I learned about fashion and makeup, how to walk and all kinds of stuff. So, what do you think of the new me?"

"Uh, you, uh, you look great. I mean, I didn't recognize you at first. Yeah, you look great. I mean, you look pretty."

"Thank you. That's what I was going for, you know. But don't be fooled. I can still beat your ass."

"I have no doubts about that." She followed with what could only be described as a condescending giggle that seemed to say "I'm now completely out of your league." And I believed her.

"So, did they teach you how to cuss like a Southern lady in that charm school?"

She giggled again, without the attitude. "No. That was definitely not on the syllabus." We were now walking side by side. "So, Clint, what did you do with your summer?"

"Well, Sam and I did a camping trip right before he left for the Navy. Then, Will and me went fishing with my dad."

"Will and I."

"Right. Will and I went fishing. Then our family went camping at Alexander Springs for two weeks, and a snake fell in the canoe with Will and me...with Will and I."

"No, you were right. It's the object of a preposition, so it's 'with Will and me.'"

"Oh. OK. I can never get that right. Anyway, after that, I went to stay with my Grandma in Campville, and my rich cousin from New Orleans came in his brand new red Corvette and took me to Gainesville in it to see a movie. Then Hurricane Cleo came through. That's about it. That was my summer."

"Sounds busy, and a lot of outdoor stuff, too."

"Yeah. I love being outdoors, camping and fishing and stuff. You like that stuff, too, don't you?"

"I do, but I have other interests, now, too."

"Like what?"

"Well, like fashion and makeup and..."

"And boys?"

"Well, yes, and boys. But not boys our age. Not boys your age, so don't even think about it. No, I'm more interested in boys like John, Paul, George, and Ringo." She spoke their names with a sexy softness in her voice that made me strangely jealous.

"So, you're still on the Beatles, eh?"

"Most definitely." By this point we had arrived at school and parted to go to our individual homerooms. As it turned out, we began walking to school together most mornings, and I found myself enjoying the new Christine.

19 September, 1964
NAS JAX
Hey, Clint,

Got your letter on Thursday, just had to wait until the weekend to write you back. I'm still laughing about your meet-up with Crazy Christine the first day of school! Don't you remember me telling you to watch out for a big transformation in her? I just didn't think it would come this fast! Maybe she's getting an upgrade so one of the Beatles will propose! Here's my next prediction: She won't be one bit interested in junior high guys (unless it's one of the 9th grade guys). She'll have her sights on high school guys from here on out.

So, my condolences on getting Miss Denham. Man, she made my life miserable. Just keep your head down, do all the reading, and try not to piss her off. Remind me to tell you about what she did to me one time in front of the whole class. (It's too long to write it all out.) Anyway, maybe she'll like you. She either loves you or hates you. There's no in between. She really hated me.

So, anyway, things are pretty much the same here. I have about two more weeks of intensive training for my rating (my job) and then I'll start an apprenticeship in the control tower. Depending on how that goes, I should get a bump in rank to Seaman and maybe even be a PO3 (Petty Officer 3rd Class) by Christmas. Unless I screw up and crash a plane into the tower or something!

By the way, we had our official portraits taken last week. They're sending them to my mom, but she'll get one to you. It should help keep roaches out of your room!

Hey, got to go for now. Write back soon. Miss you and your folks, and Will, too.

Your Big Brother,
Sam

As promised, in early October Mrs. Sanders called to say the portraits had arrived and invited me to come down and get one. Within minutes I was knocking on her door. She ushered me in and presented me with a framed eight-by-ten of the most handsome sailor I'd ever seen. Ramrod straight, a thin, knowing smile on his lips, his uniform impeccable—he looked as if he were bound for a recruiting poster. But the thing that struck me, that undermined my confidence in our friendship, was the fact that the young man in the portrait was just that—a young man. He was no longer the older boy who had been my mentor and friend. He was now a man, with friends who were men, doing a man's job. I left the Sanders' home clutching the portrait and wondering where I now fit in Sam's world. I placed the framed portrait in a prominent place in my room and, on Mom's firm instructions, wrote a thank-you note to Mrs. Sanders and a brief note to Sam. Two weeks later, I received a reply from him.

10 October, 1964
NAS JAX
Hey, Clint.

Got your note, and you're more than welcome for the portrait. You didn't have a lot to say in your letter. Is everything OK with you? Is school going OK, and is Miss Denham loving you yet? How are your folks and Will?

Things here are about the same. My formal training is wrapping up and I should begin working in the tower pretty soon. The mood on base is kind of tense. I think everyone, and particularly the upper brass, are worried about getting us ready for war if this mess with Vietnam keeps heating up. Hey, did you see that Dr. King is getting the Nobel Peace Prize? That's pretty cool, but it's going to make a bunch of rednecks pretty unhappy.

Hey, I might be able to get home for a quick visit over Thanksgiving. I've turned in a request for a pass. If I can come, I might bring a friend with me. I hope we can all hang out some.

Well, not much else to report. Please write when you can. I really enjoy hearing from you.

Your Big Brother,
Sam

Sam's mention that he might bring a friend with him should he visit at Thanksgiving served to fuel my insecurities about our friendship. If we were still friends—and, as he said in his letter, he wanted to hang out when he was home—why did he need to bring someone with him? As I dwelt on this, I began to feel as though I had been replaced, that I no longer held a special place in his life. Stirring those feeling into the simmering stew of early adolescent hormones and emotions resulted in a growing despondency within me. I didn't write him back, nor did I write him again for weeks to come. I stayed busy with school, track club, chorus, and Scouts and these activities seemed an anesthetic to the pain I was experiencing at feeling sidelined by him.

26.

THE RUSTING RELIC IN THE WOODS

IN EARLY NOVEMBER, we made a Sunday afternoon trip to Campville to visit my grandmother. The day before, I had called Jacob's neighbor and left a message that we were coming the next day and asking if he could hang out for a while. After visiting with Grandma and Uncle Al for a reasonable period, I phoned Jacob's neighbor to ask if she would let him know I would meet him at Dyess' store in about fifteen minutes. Will was bored with all the adult conversation and anxious to go with me, so he and I walked down to Dyess' to meet Jacob. Just as we arrived at the store, he was crossing the tracks and wading through the tall weeds to meet us.

We shook hands. "Hey, man. How've you been? I think you've grown a foot since the summer. This is my brother, Will."

"Hi, Will. I'm Jacob." He extended his hand and Will shook it enthusiastically. "Man, you've got a strong handshake for a little guy."

"My brother said to always shake hands strong."

"Well, that's a good plan." Turning to me, he asked, "You've shot up, too. So, what we gonna do?"

"I don't know. But I want you to meet my parents, so why don't we go back to Grandma's house."

"And then, can we go in the woods and maybe go to the clay pits?" Will asked, hopefully.

"Yeah, Will, we could do that. I want to check on how the

boma's doing. But no skinny dipping, OK?"

"No! I don't want to go skinny dipping. Besides, it's too cold now."

"You're right, Will. Definitely too cold for skinny dipping." We laughed at Will's expense.

"Anyway, that sounds cool. I'd like to meet your parents and see your Grandma and your Uncle Al again, too."

We walked down to Grandma's and found the adults on the porch talking. I introduced Jacob to my parents and he politely greeted them and said hello to my Grandma and Uncle Al. We then walked around the house and into the woods.

"So, Jacob, is there any word on whether they're going to integrate the high school in Hawthorne next year?"

"Doesn't look like it."

"Man, that stinks."

"I know. I've pretty well adjusted to the fact that I'm going to have to go to Jacksonville for high school. My aunt and uncle live about two blocks from Raines High School, so I can walk to school. Plus, it's one of the best Negro schools in the state, so I feel like it will get me ready for college."

"That actually sounds good."

"I know. Now that I've accepted the idea, I'm kinda excited. Nervous, too. Jacksonville's a big city."

"Yeah. It's for sure bigger than Campville." We laughed. "So, do your aunt and uncle have any kids?"

"Yeah. They have one daughter, Janice, who's in college now, and a son, Ulysses."

"Ulysses? Really?"

"Yeah, I know. Anyway, he'll graduate from high school next year. They both went to Raines, I mean went and are going to Raines. Janice is doing great in college—Dean's list, whatever than means—and Ulysses is smart, too, and already looking at colleges. So, I think they'll be like an inspiration to me to work hard and maybe get a scholarship."

"That really sounds great, but I'll miss getting to see you every now and then."

"Well, I'll be home for the summers, so we can hang out then."

"Cool!" By now, we had reached the boma. It looked much as it did when Kevin and I had left it back in August.

"Wow! This looks bigger or something," Jacob remarked.

"Yeah. My cousin, Kevin, and I added more to it. Actually, the hurricane pretty much destroyed it and Kevin and I rebuilt it and added more brush to it. It's held up good."

"Can we go inside?" Will asked.

"Sure, Will. Hang on. Help me move this stuff over the door." Once we had moved aside the dry brush hiding the entrance, we stepped in. The firepit was still visible, but grass and weeds, turning brown as winter approached, had grown up to obscure any other features. As I stood in that space where Sam and I had spent such a memorable few days, a wave of intense grief washed over me such that it was all I could do to keep my emotions in check. In that instant, I realized how much I missed him and how unfair I had been to judge him at a distance. I felt small and childish for wanting to deny him a special relationship with someone else and resolved to write him as soon as I returned home that evening.

Will's voice called me back to the present. "Cool. I love this place!"

"Me, too, Will. Me too."

"Hey, maybe next summer you and me and Jacob can camp out here. That would be so cool."

"Yeah. That would be cool. You up for that, Jacob?"

"Sure. Is your tent big enough for the three of us?"

"It would be a bit tight, but we can hang Will on a hook

above us."

"Hey!"

"Just joking, buddy. Yeah. The tent's big enough. You and me are both skinny, and Will's even skinnier. We'll all three fit."

"Cool! Do we have to skinny dip, though? I don't think I want to skinny dip."

"Get off it, already! You don't have to skinny dip if you don't want to, Will. You can bring a bathing suit for when we go to the clay pits."

"Or do like me and Clint did and go in in your underwear."

"OK. I just don't, you know, want to be naked in front of you guys."

"It'll be fine, Will. I promise. OK?"

"OK."

After we closed up the boma, we tromped through the woods to the clay pits. On the way, we came across an enormous, rusting piece of equipment.

"Whoa! What is this thing?"

"I don't know. Jacob, have you ever seen this? Do you know what this is?"

"No man. I can't believe I've been coming over here all my life and I've never seen this. I mean, it looks ancient, like it's been here for years. You know, it kinda looks like an old bulldozer, or like some blown up tank from World War II or something. I wonder why they just left it out here to rust."

We spent several minutes climbing up and over the relic but could not get a clear sense of what it might have been or why it had been abandoned to time and the elements.

Leaving the mystery behind, we went on to the clay pits, spent a few minutes trying to skip rocks across the surface of the water, and decided we should return to my Grandma's. We arrived just in time for pound cake. Afterward, my dad announced we would be leaving soon. Jacob said his goodbyes to my family and Will and I walked him back down to Dyess'. We promised to keep in touch and to get together over Christmas if possible. We also agreed to take up with Uncle Al the mystery of the rusting relic in the woods.

The drive home seemed interminable—anxious as I was to begin a long letter to Sam. As soon as we pulled into the drive, I bolted from the car, rushed to my room, grabbed pen and notebook paper, and began writing. The letter ran three full pages, ripe with guilt, confession, and mundane details of my life. I sealed it in an envelope, addressed it, and placed it on the kitchen table for Dad to take with him to the Post Office the following morning. That night, I could barely sleep. Had I said the right things? Did I sound childish? Would he be angry with me that I had been angry with him? Several times during that long night, my doubts reached such a pitch that I nearly retrieved and destroyed the letter. But, thankfully, it remained where I had placed it and, when I awoke from my restless sleep on that Monday morning, it and my Dad were gone.

The next few days were absolute misery. I worried constantly over how my letter would be received by Sam. Would he be angry, hurt, both? Would he view me as a sniveling baby with whom he should probably part ways? I was so preoccupied and distracted by these thoughts that my mom determined I might be "coming down with something," and my grandmother prescribed an iron tonic that I barely avoided by demonstrating clear proof that I was not running a fever. On Friday afternoon, when he returned from work, my father brought a letter from Sam. I rushed to my room and, with deep trepidation, opened it.

11 November, 1964
NAS JAX
Dear Clint,

I got your letter in today's mail and decided I needed to write you right back. I really don't know where to start, so I'll just jump in. I have to be honest. I was kind of pissed off at first when I read your letter. How could you think that I was throwing our friendship out the window? But, as the day went by and I had time to think about things, I began to see how you could have thought that. It sure explains why you haven't written in so long.

You're right. We are in different places in life right now. You're still in school and I've moved into the next phase of life: life after high school. But that doesn't mean we grow apart or that we don't care about each other anymore! I still love you like the little brother you've always been. That will never change. In a few years, you'll catch up to me when you go on to college, but you'll still be my little brother. You will always be my little brother.

At the same time, I think you really showed a lot of maturity to think through things the way you did and to realize where your thinking had been wrong and where your feelings messed up your thinking. Not too many guys your age can admit when they're wrong and try to make things right like you did in your letter.

But I don't know what I was thinking either when I thought about bringing James home for Thanksgiving. (As it turns out, I didn't get a pass, anyway.) I want to spend what little time I have at home with my Mom and with you and your family. I mean, James is great, but I see him every day. I'm really sorry I even thought about taking time from seeing you. Anyway, I'll be home at Christmas and I WON'T BE BRINGING ANYBODY WITH ME! OK? Think about stuff you want us to do together and I'll be 100% on board.

Now, let's move on, OK? Thanks for updating me about what you've been up to. I'm glad the boma is still standing. I guess it'll be too cold at Christmas to camp out, but maybe we can build a campfire and roast hotdogs or something. I really want to meet your friend Jacob. He sounds like he's a smart kid with a lot of determination. And we need to figure out what that thing is you guys found out in the woods. I love a mystery!

Well, I need to wrap this up, but let me say this one more time: YOU'RE MY LITTLE BROTHER AND YOU'LL ALWAYS BE MY LITTLE BROTHER AND I LOVE YOU.

Your Big Brother,
Sam

Given my propensity to shed tears at the drop of a hat, I had dissolved into a sniveling mass of guilt and relief by the time I had finished Sam's letter. Of course, with exquisite timing, Will chose that moment to come bounding into our room.

"Hey, what you...what's wrong with you? Why are you crying? Did your dog die?"

I couldn't help but laugh at his wit at quoting me to myself. "Very funny. You know I don't have a dog." I snorted and wiped my face. "I just got a letter from Sam and it made me really sad and happy at the same time."

"How can you be sad and happy at the same time?"

"I can't explain it. You just can."

Years later, as I sat in my office the morning following Mrs. Sanders' visit and reread that letter, I was once again awash in guilt and grief. With remarkable clarity I was taken back to the first few hours after I had learned of Sam's death, and the debilitating sorrow that accompanied that news. How could it be possible, after all that time, that pain of such intensity could resurface? Does such pain simply lie dormant in our memories only to return at the most random provocation? And what sort of power does such pain command that it can bring with it sorrow of other sorts? It was apparent, as I reread that letter as an adult, that my relationship with Sam had been, in that moment, at great peril, and could have been altogether lost had he not responded to me with grace and a wisdom that belied his years.

27.

HOME AGAIN

THANKSGIVING WAS, AND remains, my favorite season of the year—in part because it revolves around wonderful food, visits with family, college football, and the Macy's Parade. The frantic pace that characterizes Christmas and the material excesses of over-the-top gift giving are absent, and it's possible to see more clearly the things that truly matter.

Our Thanksgiving followed a prescribed set of rituals that seemed constant from year to year. We had a gluttonous Thanksgiving Day meal with my maternal grandmother, aunts, uncles, and cousins on that side of the family, watched the Macy's Thanksgiving Day Parade on television, and ended the day with an SEC football game and leftovers. Then, either on Friday or Saturday of that long weekend, we enjoyed a similarly gluttonous meal in Campville with my father's side of the family. However, since Grandma Cooper did not have a television, there was no football and substantially more "visiting"—which, to us children, meant a substantially greater measure of boredom.

On this particular year, we assembled in Campville on the Saturday after Thanksgiving. Gathered there were my grandmother, Uncle Al, two sets of aunts and uncles with five cousins among them, plus my immediate family—eight adults and seven kids of which I was the eldest. But, unlike in the past, this year Will and I had a plan to mitigate the boredom of interminable adult conversation about politics, the looming war, and the general decline of civilization. We had the woods, the boma, and the clay pits, plus the Mystery Machine. So, after dinner, I announced that Will and I would lead an excursion into the woods including any kids who wished to accompany us. Immediately, my Aunt Ida, who was obsessively overprotective of her two boys, began to pepper me with questions and misgivings.

"Are there lots of bugs and mosquitoes?"

"Not too many."

"You know Jeremy is very allergic." It was a statement, not a question.

"Yes, ma'am. We'll put on some Off before we go out."

"What about snakes?"

"Yes, ma'am, some." I conveniently failed to mention the encounter Sam and I had with the rattler, and Will seemed to understand that was classified information.

"It sounds dangerous."

"Will and I have been out there lots of time and never died." At that statement, my father gave me the eye, but with a slight smile on his face.

"Have you ever gotten lost out there?"

"No, ma'am. Never."

Eventually, my uncle intervened and gave his approval for the boys to accompany us, so, off we went—a troop of seven kids tromping into the woods. The boma was our first stop. They seemed, as a group, rather unimpressed. Next, we visited the clay pits where we threw rocks into the water and I tried, unsuccessfully, to keep my youngest cousins out of the mud. Finally, we wandered around a bit until we came upon the Mystery Machine. The rusting hulk of whatever it once had been was, by far, the most popular attraction of the adventure. We climbed over and around the machine, sat in what remained of the operator's seat, toyed with the rusting controls, and invented a war game that saw us driving the newest war machine in America's arsenal behind the German lines to rescue downed Allied pilots. At last, our mission successful, we marched back to Grandma's far dirtier than when we'd left. My Aunt Ida was not pleased.

After the aunts, uncles, and cousins left to return to their south Florida homes, Will and I took the opportunity to ask Uncle Al if he knew the story behind the Mystery Machine—what it was and why it had been left to the elements. He replied that he had heard years ago that an excavator of some sort had broken down out there, that they had been unable to repair it, and had simply abandoned it. That explanation was a far less engaging story than the one we kids had concocted earlier that day. Will and I determined to stick with our story of courage and valor instead.

That stretch on the calendar between Thanksgiving and Christmas is filled with breathtaking anticipation for most children—will Santa bring what I want? For me that year, the anticipation of Sam coming home for a visit far eclipsed all other expectations for the season and was almost palpable. I held it close to me each day, marking the days until it would become a reality.

One afternoon in the middle of December, Mrs. Sanders phoned to ask if I would like to go with her to Jacksonville to pick up Sam for his holiday leave. As it turned out, his pass was to begin the morning of Friday, December 18—the last day of school before our Christmas break began. I reluctantly told Mrs. Sanders that I doubted I'd be able to skip school that day to accompany her, but that I would be back in touch with an answer one way or the other. As was so often the case when it came to my parents, they surprised me again with an immediate green light. As my father explained, "It's the last day before Christmas break. You all won't be doing any work anyway. If you don't mind missing the cupcakes and Kool-Aid, you're free to go with Mrs. Sanders."

The intervening days seemed to drag by, and I was terribly distracted. Finally, Friday arrived. Sam's leave was to begin at 7:00 am, and Mrs. Sanders wanted to be waiting at the gate for him at that precise hour. That, of course, required a departure from home at 6:00 am. Bleary-eyed, I walked down to the Sanders' home at 5:45, and we left immediately.

Traffic up US 17 to the Naval Air Station was surprisingly heavy at that time of the morning. Mrs. Sanders explained that many who worked in Jacksonville lived elsewhere and commuted each day. This, to me, seemed like an absurd idea. Why not live near your work rather than waste hours each week commuting?

The main gate of the base was located directly on 17 at Yorktown Avenue. The Marine guard at the gate directed us to a parking area just inside the entrance where we could wait for Sam. There were a number of other families parked there waiting to collect their sailors, and the number grew as 7:00 am approached. The waiting seemed interminable and, from that vantage point, there was little of the Naval base to be seen. Mrs. Sanders and I stood outside her car, staring in the direction from which we assumed Sam would come. At about 7:15, I saw in the distance a sailor hefting a large duffle rambling toward us with a walk I could have recognized anywhere.

"Here he comes! Geeze, he looks huge!"

"I do believe he's put on some weight, Clint. It looks like it's all muscle. He looks good from this distance, doesn't he?"

"Yes, ma'am. He sure does." I realized I had not seen Sam since that sad day in June when he had boarded the bus that had taken him to the Navy. I was suddenly gripped by a wave of anxiety and self-doubt. He was bigger, stronger, more a man of the world, and I was still the same boy as when he left.

At that moment, Sam spied us, waved, and broke into a run. I did the same, and we closed the distance quickly. When we met, he dropped his duffle, grabbed me in a bear hug and easily lifted me off my feet.

"Holy, shit, Clint! You've grown a foot. I can hardly pick you up. I'm so glad you came with Mom to get me!"

With our arms across each other's shoulders—a bit of a reach for me—we walked back toward his mom.

"You're the one who's grown! You have muscles on top of your muscles!"

"That comes from hours of exercise just about every day. When I look in the mirror, I hardly recognize myself. I feel like the Incredible Hulk sometimes, without the green skin."

"You look great in that uniform, by the way." At that moment, Mrs. Sanders rushed forward to embrace him.

"Look at you! You're so handsome in that uniform."

"And I can't wait to put on some civvies."

"What are civvies?"

"Civilian clothes. Like regular clothes. We call them civvies."

"Cool."

The drive back to Palatka seemed far shorter as I peppered Sam with questions about life in the Navy, the job he was learning, the food, where he thought he'd be sent when he completed training. Suddenly, we were turning onto Kate Street and into their driveway.

"Hey, Clint, come in and help me unpack."

"I can't. My mom told me to come straight home so you and your mom could have some time together."

"OK. Well, come down after lunch, if you can."

"Sure. Hey, you want to go for a bike ride, like old times?"

"That would be great. I'll make sure my bike's OK and the tires haven't gone flat. I'll see you then."

The remainder of the morning seemed to stretch out like a country road. Finally, after a quick lunch, I rode down to Sam's. It was a typical early-winter day in north Florida—clear and cloudless, cool enough to wear a light jacket but warm enough to break a sweat with the slightest exertion. I found Sam in their garage, tinkering with his bicycle.

"Hey. You look smaller in civvies. You sure that uniform doesn't have padding in it? How's your bike?"

"OK, funny man. Don't make the Hulk mad, remember?" We both laughed. "Yeah, the bike seems to be in good shape. The tires were a little low, but they look OK. So, where do you want to go?"

"Everywhere! Let's ride down to the river, then back by the Ravines. If you feel you can make it that far, seeing as how you're an old man and all."

"Alright, smart ass, you're on. And we'll see who drops by the wayside first."

The ride down to the river was an easy one, as it's essentially one long downhill grade. When we arrived at the city dock, there was a large sailboat moored there.

"Wow! Look at that boat! It's beautiful."

"*She's* beautiful. Ships are called 'her' and 'she,' but, yeah, she's beautiful. About thirty-five feet and sloop-rigged. Let's go look at her closer."

We walked down the dock to where the boat was moored. On the stern, in script, the word "*Runaway*" was painted, and underneath, in small block letters "Cornwall, Ontario."

"What's that mean, '*Runaway*'?"

"That's her name. Holy cow, they sailed her all the way from

Canada!"

"No way!"

"Sure did. Look, it says the boat is registered in Cornwall, Ontario. That's in Canada, my friend."

"Whoa!" At that precise moment, an older man appeared through the companionway and greeted us.

"Good afternoon, gentlemen."

"Hello, sir. Welcome to Palatka. You've come a long way to get here."

"That we have. Left Cornwall in early October, after the hurricanes were finished, and took our time down the East Coast. We decided to tuck in here for Christmas and then head on down to the Caribbean." He then called back into the cabin. "Helen, come up top and meet our visitors." Then, turning back to us, "And whom do I have the pleasure of addressing?"

"I'm Seaman Sam Sanders of the US Navy, home on leave, and this is my friend, Clint Cooper."

"A Navy man! Splendid! I'm Walter Hemingway—no relation to the writer—and my wife, as you know, is Helen." As if on cue, Helen appeared at the companionway and made her way on deck. "Helen, this is the official Palatka welcoming party, US Navy Seaman Sam, and his friend, Clint." We exchanged greetings with Helen, who insisted we join them for lunch on deck. Though we had both eaten earlier, we enthusiastically agreed.

Within minutes, Walter had, with our help, set up a teak table and chairs on deck and Helen reappeared with a number of things I had never before eaten—cucumber sandwiches among them. Over lunch, Walter and Helen—they insisted we call them by their first names—plied us with tales of their trip down the coast. They had sold their small hardware store in Cornwall and spent most of what they made purchasing and outfitting *Runaway*. Walter laughed that they had arrived at the name because their two adult children had accused them of running away from everything. Their intention was to spend three or four years sailing the Caribbean—flying home once or twice each year—then to sell the boat and return to Cornwall to fully retire. To me, it sounded idyllic. After an extended lunch, Sam and I excused ourselves and continued our ride.

Whereas the ride to the river was mostly downhill, the trip back to the Ravines was quite the opposite—a long uphill climb. By the time we reached the gates into the park, I was breathing heavily and trying my best to hide the fact from Sam. He, on the other hand, seemed almost refreshed.

"So, you ready to quit yet?"

"Kiss my ass, old man!"

"Whoa, where did you learn such language, and such an attitude? We'll just have to press you harder, young man."

One small bit of information I had not shared with Sam was the fact that I had been riding the Ravines on a regular basis as a component of my endurance training. By now, I knew every dip, every hillock and every pothole, and I could finally pedal the entire perimeter without stopping. As we began the circuit, I sensed him matching my pace. In every respect he stayed with me and together we reached that little streamside oasis where we had rested so long ago. Sitting again in the thick grass beside the same cool stream, I thought back to the first time we had stopped at that spot.

"You remember the first time we stopped here?"

"Kinda. It was a while ago, you know?"

"Yeah, but it was really a huge thing to me."

"How so?"

"Well, I was this shy little kid and you were this big teenager, and we were talking like equals. Like you weren't talking down to me, but treating me like someone your own age, and it was,

I don't know, it was really important to me. Do you remember we had this funny conversation about whether you could poke a hole in the water with your finger?"

"Oh, yeah. I do remember us talking about that."

"Remember how you said there was no way to tell your finger had been in the water when you took it out? And then you said it was kinda like your dad, that he lived and then he was gone and there was hardly anything left to show he had been here."

"Yeah. I do remember now." Sam's countenance clouded over and he sat silent for a long moment.

"I'm sorry. I was dumb to bring that up."

"No. It's OK. It's just that I don't think about him very often anymore, and then when I do, I feel guilty for not thinking about him. It's just like the water thing. I'm proof that my dad lived because he lives in the things I know about him, but even that proof is fading."

Our conversation had taken a sudden, serious tack. I stared at the ground in front of me, nervously plucking blades of grass. "I didn't really know what you were talking about that day. But I kept thinking about it, like I had to figure it out, you know? And then, one day, it kinda hit me. Unless you're famous, about the only way anybody in the future will know you existed is if you have kids, you know? Like you live on through your kids and your grandkids. But since you won't have kids, 'cause you won't get married 'cause, well, you know, then me and Will, we have to make sure you're remembered." I glanced up to catch Sam wiping his eyes.

"That's a really, really nice thing for you to say. I'm for sure not going to be famous, unless I do something really stupid like make Air Force One crash into the runway or something. So, yeah, I'm gonna be like poking a hole in the water. Here, gone, forgotten."

In response, my voice came from some unknown place and left my lips with a tone and timbre I did not even recognize. "Never. You will never be forgotten. At least not by me. You hear? Never."

"Whoa. Yeah, OK, then. I believe you. So, enough of this heavy talk. Let's get going so I can shame you some more."

"Some more? What do you mean, 'some more'?"

We completed our ride and parted ways for the evening. I had a full day the next day with final rehearsals for our church's Hanging of the Greens the following evening. Will and I were both singing with our respective choirs and I was to perform a solo. Sam had said he wanted to attend, and I was excited that he would be among the congregation.

Sunday was full as well, with services in the morning and final preparations for the pageant during the afternoon. As it turned out, both Sam and his mother were in attendance. All went smoothly, including the humorous behaviors of the smallest participants as they tugged at the red bows tied around their necks and waved at their parents in the audience. I sang *Gesu Bambino* with the church organist and an oboist accompanying me. Other than our informal hootenanny around the campfire, it was the first time Sam had heard me sing since *Amahl*, and since my voice had settled into a smooth baritone range. After the program, both Sam and his mother were effusive in their compliments—almost, but not quite, to the point of embarrassment.

I was anxious for Sam to meet my new friend Jacob and hatched a plan for us to take a drive to Campville. I contacted Jacob through his neighbor to confirm he was free, and the trip was planned for Tuesday. Will asked to go, and so the four of us planned to have a campfire in the boma, eat lunch there, and hang out for the afternoon. I was also determined to take Jacob a small Christmas gift and Mom suggested we wrap up a box of school supplies for him. It seemed to me a bit impersonal, but also a practical gift.

On Monday afternoon, before our scheduled trip on Tuesday, Sam and I rode our bikes downtown to Couver's Office Supply and picked out an assortment of things Jacob could use for school. We then circled back by the city dock to say hello to Walter and Helen. During our brief visit with them that afternoon, they mentioned that they planned to up-anchor early on Christmas Day, then motor back to Jacksonville and out into open water. We exchanged addresses with them and wished them well, as we feared we might not see them again before their departure. As Sam and I rode back toward home, I floated an idea.

"Hey, what if we sneak onto the boat Christmas Eve and leave some Christmas presents for them? Maybe our moms would bake some stuff and we could wrap it up and leave it for them."

"I think that's a great idea! Let's maybe put up a little decoration, too."

"What about a little Christmas tree?"

"I don't know about that. We're gonna have to be really quiet so we don't wake them up."

"What if we get a little bitty cedar tree and decorate it ahead of time and then we could just sit it in place really quick? We could get one tomorrow out in the woods behind my Grandma's."

"That might work. We could decorate it with stuff that would rot or that fish would eat 'cause they'll probably have to throw it overboard at some point. I mean, they won't have room for it on the boat."

"What kind of stuff?"

"Like strings of popcorn and cranberries. Stuff like that."

"Cool. Let's do it!" It was shaping up to be a busy week.

28.

BACK TO THE BOMA

THE NEXT MORNING, Will and I walked down to Sam's house. I carried a small daypack containing my Scout hatchet, some fat pine kindling, and a box of matches, as well as a colorfully wrapped package containing the school supplies for Jacob. Will and I each carried two small folding camp stools my dad had suggested we take.

Sam's mom had agreed to make lunch for the four of us and to let Sam take her car for the trip. We were to meet Jacob at Dyess' store at 10:30, so we left Sam's house around 9:50 to allow plenty of time for the drive. Will was so excited to have been included, he chattered the entire way, asking Sam all sorts of questions about his new life in the Navy. For his part, Sam patiently answered each question put to him. As we pulled into the parking area in front of Dyess', Jacob was waiting in one of the rocking chairs on the porch. I hopped out and led him back to the car. After making introductions, we drove down to my grandmother's and parked in front of her house. She was on the front porch waiting for us.

"Hello, boys." She graciously embraced each of us. "Sam, it's so good to see you again. How is the Navy treating you?"

"Pretty well, ma'am. Good to see you again, too."

"And Jacob, how are you?"

"I'm good, ma'am. Just trying to get good grades and stay out of trouble."

"Your grandmother tells me you'll be going to high school in Jacksonville next year."

"Yes ma'am. That really ended up being the best choice. Especially since they won't integrate Hawthorne High."

"I'm so sorry about that. I do wish things would move quicker in that area. Well, I know you boys have big plans, so I won't keep you. I've got a pound cake in the oven, if you want to stop by for a slice before you head home." That proposal met with universal approval.

As we made our way into the woods, Sam seemed on high alert.

"You scanning for snakes?"

"Hell, yeah. One encounter like that last one is one too many."

"What are y'all talking about?" Jacob asked.

"When Sam and I camped out here in the summer, we walked right up on a huge rattlesnake."

"It scared the crap out of me, I have to tell you. Clint here, mister woodsman, knew what to do and it worked out fine, but I didn't stop shaking for a week. So, yeah, I'm scanning for snakes."

"Hey, we need to scan for a small cedar tree, too," I reminded him.

"What for?"

"We're gonna sneak it onboard our friends' yacht on Christmas Eve," I replied.

"What are you talkin' about?" Jacob asked.

"I'll explain when we get the fire going."

We found the boma much as I had left it in early November. With many of the trees now leafless, the brown underbrush from which we had constructed the shelter was more visible as we approached. Inside, the weeds that had grown up over the summer were now dead and brown. We set about clearing the area around the firepit, then began to gather wood for a campfire. Once the fire was burning well, we opened the camp stools and circled up around the fire. Although the weather was sunny, there was still a chill in the air and the fire was particularly inviting.

"Man, this feels great. I was getting a little cold," I commented.

"Me, too. What are we eating for lunch?" Will asked.

"Will, I swear, all you think about is food."

"Do not."

"OK. Whatever you say. Anyway, Sam's mom fixed our lunch, so I don't know what we're having."

"Well, I hope you guys like meatloaf sandwiches, 'cause that's what we're having."

"I never ate a meatloaf sandwich, but I'm up for anything," Jacob said.

"So, when are we eating?" Will asked.

"Will! Good grief! Are you that hungry?" I responded.

"I'm starving!"

"OK. We'll eat in a little while."

"Mom packed a jug of iced tea and some potato chips, too. Plus, there are a couple of extra sandwiches, Will, so I think we can fill you up," Sam laughed.

"Cool."

"So, Jacob, I take it there isn't a high school around here you can go to?" Sam asked.

"Yeah. That's pretty much it. I could go to Gainesville or Palatka, but I'd spend half the day on a bus. Plus, I'd have to get up around 5:00 to catch the bus. I have an aunt in Jacksonville, and they live about two blocks from a really good Negro high school, so that seemed like the best idea for me. I really hate to leave home, and Jacksonville's so big."

"Every place is big next to Campville, Jake," I joked.

"You're right. So, when did you start calling me Jake?"

"Like right now. Is that OK?"

"Yeah. It's cool. I like it. Nobody else calls me that, so, yeah, it's kinda special. So, anyway, Raines—that's the high school I'll be going to—it's really good and a lot of kids go on to college from there. That's my goal. I want to go to college and get a good job and help out my Grandma."

"That's great," said Sam. "You're really smart for wanting a college degree. It really opens a lot of doors. When I get out of the Navy, I plan to use the GI Bill to pay for a lot of my college. There was really no way my mom could save for college for me, so the Navy seemed like a good plan."

"Can we eat now?"

"Yes, Will. We can eat now."

Other than Sam, meatloaf sandwiches were a novelty to the rest of us—thin slices of cold meatloaf wedged between soft white bread slathered with mayonnaise and ketchup. What could better satisfy the Southern palate? Suffice to say, they were a big hit, with none leftover. As we ate, and afterward, conversation ebbed and flowed, sometimes into areas of controversy, other times centered on simple things about which boys are interested. I was pleased with the level to which Will remained engaged in our discussions—even those subjects that required a more mature perspective than that of the typical eleven year old. Sam was particularly interested in probing Jake for his thoughts on and experiences with growing up Black in the American South. For his part, Jake was insightful and expressed his thoughts with clarity and honesty. At times, as he spoke, I felt guilty for having been born white, but there was no acrimony in his words and I never felt our budding friendship was in jeopardy.

"So, Clint, you were going to explain the thing about the

cedar tree," Jacob reminded us.

"OK yeah. Well, last week, me and Sam were down at the city dock and we met this old couple living on a sailboat. They had sailed all the way from Canada. So, we've kinda become friends with them, but they're leaving early on Christmas Day, so me and Sam got this idea of sneaking on their boat and leaving a little Christmas tree."

"Can I come?" Will asked, hopefully.

"It'll be pretty late. We have to wait for them to go to bed. We'll ask Mom and Dad. If they say it's OK, you'll have to be really, really quiet. We want to surprise them, not wake them up."

"I can be really quiet."

"OK. We'll ask. So, anyway, we need to find a small cedar to cut and take with us."

The winter sun slid quickly down the west, and soon it was time to put out the campfire and pack up our gear for the trip home. As we made our way out of the woods, we found the perfect little cedar. I used the hatchet to cut it at the ground, and we loaded it in the trunk of the car. However, before leaving, we paused at Grandma's front porch for slices of warm pound cake and cold milk. After saying our goodbyes to her, we walked back to the car for the trip home.

"I can just walk from here. You don't need to drop me."

"Naw. Hop in, Jake, we'll drop you at your house."

"Oh, OK."

"Besides, I've got something in the car for you. Will, you sit up front with Sam, and Jake and me'll sit in the back so he can open his Christmas present."

"Whoa, man! I didn't get you nothin'."

"And I didn't expect you to. It's really not much. Just some stuff I thought you could use. Hop in and you can open it on the way to your Grandma's." We climbed into the car and waved to my grandmother as we pulled away.

"Jake, remember I don't know where you live, so you'll need to give me directions."

"Sure. Just go up to Dyess', then cross the railroad tracks and 301, then go straight for a while. I'll talk you through it."

"OK."

I drew the brightly wrapped box for Jake from behind the seat where I had placed it on the drive over. "Here. Merry Christmas."

"Man, thanks. I really didn't expect this, but thanks." He began to carefully unwrap the box. "I can probably use this paper to wrap up what I made for my Grandma, so I don't want to rip it." After he opened the box to reveal the neatly-arranged school supplies, I felt it might have been a poor choice, but he put me at ease immediately.

"Oh, man! This stuff is great. I can really use all of this. Oh, wow! My own protractor! Thanks, man. I really appreciate this."

"You're welcome. I just wanted to get you something, and my mom suggested this kind of stuff. Sam helped me pick it out, so thank him, too."

"Thanks, guys. You have no idea how much I can use this stuff. There's nowhere around here to shop for school supplies, and we really don't have money for much of this kind of stuff anyway. Thanks. Oh, Sam, stay on this road to the stop sign, then turn right."

Several minutes later, with Jake's directions, we stopped in front of a small wood-sided house painted a brilliant aqua. Surrounded by a well-kept yard, the house looked like photos I had seen of homes in the Caribbean.

"Man, this is a long walk from Dyess'. You never said it was this far."

"Clint, I walk everywhere except to school, so this really

isn't far for me. Besides, Dyess' is the closest place we can buy milk or bread, so we're used to the walk. Hey, do you guys have a minute to say hi to my Grandma?"

"Sure."

Sam killed the engine and we climbed out of the car. By the time we started up the walk, Jacob's grandmother came through the front door. "Well, Lawd, Lawd, look what the cat dragged up! Young Mister Cooper, young Navy man Sam, and who is this?"

"Hello, Mrs. Wilson. This is my little brother, Will."

"Yes. I can see that now. He's like a small version of you. Pleased to meet you mister Will Cooper." Mrs. Wilson extended her hand and Will took it.

"Thank, you, ma'am. Pleased to meet you."

"Do you boys have time for a visit?"

"They've got to get back to Palatka, Grandma, but look at the stuff they gave me for Christmas." Jake displayed the box of school supplies and his grandmother's eyes began to dance.

"Boys, this is so nice of y'all. I know Jacob can use all these things. Thank you for thinking about him."

"You're welcome, ma'am. We just wanted to get him something for being such a good friend."

"Well, thank you again. I wish you all could stay a bit, but I understand. Thank you for stopping by and for these nice things."

"Yes ma'am, of course."

Jake gave each of us a hug and we piled back into the car for the drive home. Within minutes, Will was asleep. Sam and I conversed little on the drive, each caught up in his own thoughts.

29.

MISSION IMPROBABLE

ON WEDNESDAY AFTERNOON, Sam walked down to our house and he, Will, and I strung popcorn and cranberries while my mom baked zucchini bread for us to leave as a gift for the Hemingways. Sam's mom had agreed to bake an apple pie. My father had fashioned a tree stand for the tiny cedar from a coffee can painted red with rocks placed around the trunk to stabilize it. We then decorated the tree and set it in a corner of the garage. Christmas Eve was the next day and I found myself more excited about this little project than what I might be receiving for Christmas. Will, too, was excited as our parents had agreed to let him stay up and go with us to deliver the tree and gifts.

Christmas Eve was always a frenzy of preparations—wrapping, cooking, cleaning, last-minute decorating—but I could hardly concentrate on anything other than thinking through how we might sneak onto the Hemingways' boat without waking them. I weighed numerous scenarios but finally arrived at the conclusion that only one of us should actually board the boat. The others could pass the tree and food gifts to him in order to reduce the risk of being caught. Although Will was smallest, I feared he might also be less agile and, thus, make more noise. Since I weighed less than Sam, perhaps I should be the one to climb aboard *Runaway*.

We had agreed to leave at 9:00 that night and park where we

could observe the boat at a distance. Our thinking was Walter and Helen might turn in early in consideration of the early start they had planned for Christmas Day. As we pulled into the parking lot at the dock, Sam cut the headlights and we found a dark parking spot with a good view of the boat. It was about 9:15 and the boat was already dark. There was no movement that we could detect.

Sam whispered, "It looks like they've already gone to bed."

"Yeah, but what if they just turned off the lights?"

"We need to wait a while to make sure everything's quiet."

"I kinda need to pee," interjected Will.

"Will, for heaven's sake! Why didn't you do that before we left the house?"

"I didn't need to go then."

"You're probably just excited. Can you hold it a while?"

"Yeah. I can hold it."

The waiting was exhausting. Sam and I both watched the dashboard clock willing it to move faster.

"I really need to pee."

"Good, Lord, Will. OK. Open your door real quiet. Don't close it. Just step over there by that bush and pee." Will slipped out the back seat, did his business, and slipped quietly back into the car. "Don't close the door all the way. Just pull it to."

"OK."

Time crept along like a classroom clock on the last day of school. At 9:45, Sam decided it was safe to mount our operation. "OK. Here's how this needs to happen. When we get out of the car, don't close the doors all the way. Will, you'll carry the bag with the baked stuff in it. I'll carry the tree. Clint needs to have his hands empty so he can get onto the boat quietly. Then, I'll hand him the tree. Last thing, Will, you'll hand him the bag. Absolutely no talking, not even whispering. Everyone understand?"

"Yep."

"Yes."

As though we were infiltrating enemy lines, we began to execute the mission. The night was chilly with a slight breeze off the river. The sky was dark with a new moon, but there was enough ambient light from the parking lot for us to find our way. My heart was in my throat. As we reached the dock, the sound of the waves lapping the dock pilings masked our footfalls. We moved silently, each determined to avoid the slightest sound. Once we reached the spot where *Runaway* was moored, Sam raised his hand to signal us to stop. Then, he motioned me ahead.

The boat was rocking gently on the waves and I took a moment to gauge the regular movements. Up. Down. Up. Down. I nodded to Sam and began my approach. Negotiating the stanchions and lifelines was to be my biggest challenge. With my right foot still on the dock, I stepped over the lifeline, took hold of the nearest stanchion to balance myself, and placed my left foot quietly on the deck. I then swung my right foot off the dock to join my left on the deck. I was aboard the boat. Sam gave me a thumbs-up. I nodded and pointed to the tree. He placed the tree stand into my outstretched hands and I set the tree carefully in the nearest corner of the cockpit. I then nodded to Will who handed me the bag containing the baked items.

Everything was going smoothly until, at that moment, a large rat scurried down the dock directly toward us—and Will in particular. I glanced up, and his eyes were the size of dinner plates. He was frantically pointing at the rat, and I could tell from his panicked expression that it was only a matter of seconds before he would lose what little remaining composure he had. Sensing the crisis, Sam lifted him from the dock, held him aloft and took about three steps to the side, reducing the likelihood of a direct encounter with the rat. I quickly concluded my tasks onboard and deftly stepped back onto the dock. By now, the rat had moved beyond where we had been standing and the crisis was averted. All remained quiet in the boat's cabin. Our mission complete, we silently made our way back to the car.

"Don't slam the doors," Sam whispered. "Just hold the doors closed 'til I get out of the parking lot." He cranked the engine, which sounded to my ears like a locomotive, and slipped out of the parking lot with the headlights off. Once we were on the street, he gave us permission to close the doors. He then switched on the headlights and we drove home chattering with excitement.

"I can't believe we pulled that off!"

"Me neither. But that rat scared the crap outta me! Thanks for rescuing me, Sam."

"I could tell you were about to lose it, buddy. All I could think to do was just pick you up and get us out of the rat's path."

"There for a minute, I thought you guys were gonna leave me on the boat by myself!"

"You think they'll know who that stuff is from?" asked Will.

"I put a tag on the zucchini bread with our names on it, so, yeah, they'll know," I answered.

"They probably would've guessed anyway, but I'm glad they'll know for sure," Sam commented.

Looking back, I can't remember a single gift I received the next morning, but I will never forget the experience of gifting the Hemingways the little cedar tree. About three weeks later, a note arrived from Walter and Helen addressed to Sam and me— they had no way of knowing of Will's involvement—thanking us for the gifts and for making their Christmas morning such a delight. The envelope bore Bahamian postage stamps.

The day after Christmas was a quiet blur of leftovers and college football. Most of the kids in the neighborhood were outside, riding new bicycles and showing off new toys. I spent some time at Sam's half-watching football and talking. The following day was my thirteenth birthday, and it dawned cold and rainy. We attended services that morning but stayed in through the afternoon. That evening, we celebrated my birthday with Sam in attendance. My mom had made an angel food cake and decorated it. My parents gave me my own stereo and the Peter, Paul, and Mary *In Concert* album, Sam gave me a copy of James Weldon Johnson's *God's Trombones*, and Will gave me a bobble-head statue of the Peanuts character Schroeder. Although I was excited to have become a teenager, the fact of Sam's imminent return to base tempered the celebration.

For his return trip to the Naval Air Station in Jacksonville, Sam had insisted he would take the bus. So, on that gray, blustery Monday morning, I walked down to say goodbye before his mother drove him to the bus station.

"So, this'll be your first full day as a teenager. How's it feel?"

"I don't know. About the same, I guess. I thought I'd feel more grown up, but it still feels about the same. Maybe next year, when I get my learners' permit, it'll feel different. So how do you feel about going back to the base?"

"Kinda like you, I guess. I think the word's ambivalent. I'm looking forward to what's ahead, but this time at home has really reminded me of how different my life is now."

"Do you miss it?"

"Yeah. I miss my time being my own, you know? We just don't have much say in what we do, where we go, who we spend time with. Most of that stuff's decided for us. Being home, it was great being able to do what I wanted to do when I wanted to do it. Plus, I really miss you and my mom, and your family, you know?"

"Well, we really miss you, too. Me especially. I miss having you around to talk to about stuff, you know? I don't know. Some stuff I just don't want to talk about with my parents."

"Well, I know it's not the same, but you can always write me."

"I know, but I'm a terrible letter-writer."

"Aw. You're not so bad, for a rebellious teenager, you know?" Sam seemed always able to dispel my melancholy, and did so that morning, too.

Mrs. Sanders entered the conversation with, "Sam, we'd best get going."

"OK, Mom. Well, kiddo, until next time." We hugged. Sam and his mom climbed into the car and pulled off. Though I couldn't know it at the time, it would be the last time I saw him.

30.

REVELATIONS

THE RESUMPTION OF school was still a week away, and the first few days after Sam left were gloomy and cold, closely mirroring my mood. For the most part, I stayed in and was both bored and anxious. There seemed to be something buzzing in my brain that was undefinable yet bothersome—an unease, a sense of being out of place. As I struggled to understand these feelings, I came to realize that they were born, in part, by the fact that Sam's role in my life had, for the most part, come to an end—that I was now somewhat on my own. This realization left me feeling vulnerable and adrift, uncertain of how to navigate even the immediate future. My perceptive mother noticed the cloud hovering over me. Early on New Year's Eve, she pulled me aside for what I recognized was to be a serious conversation.

"Clint, I can tell something's bothering you. Is it about Sam leaving?"

"Kinda. But it's more than that, I guess."

"I know it's hard, but can you tell me what you're thinking, what you're feeling?"

"Umm. I'll try. I guess I just feel, I don't know, kinda cut loose. Sam was like an anchor for me, and I realize he's pretty much out of my life now, and I know I have to work some things out for myself, like the kind of person I want to be and stuff like that. Like I've kinda been in his shadow for all these years, so I didn't have to be myself. I'm not explaining this very well."

"No. Actually, I think you're doing really well. Are you worried about being more on your own now?"

"Yes ma'am. I mean, Sam's taught me so much, but now I have to work stuff out for myself. In a way, I'm excited about that. I mean, it shows I'm growing up. But in another way, I'm kinda scared."

"What scares you about growing up?"

"That I'll mess up. That I'll make the wrong decisions or chose the wrong side, you know?"

"Clint, that fear is a part of being an adult. I know you probably think adults have everything figured out, like we always know what to do. Well, we don't. Your dad and I struggle sometimes to know the right way to raise you and Will. We want you to be responsible young men who are fair and honest, who care about other people and who know how to choose the right path, but sometimes we're not sure how to guide you that way. The fact that you're struggling within yourself with how to be a good person shows you're on the right path to being a good person. Does that make any sense?"

"Yes ma'am. I think I understand what you're saying. But if you and Dad have trouble figuring things out sometimes, how am I supposed to get it right?"

"You won't always get it right. Sometimes you'll make the wrong decision. But you'll learn something when you do, and hopefully, you won't make that mistake again. Also, you do have other people around you who can help. Besides your dad and me, you have teachers at school, Dr. Parham at church, and you still have Sam. You can write him, you know?"

"Yes ma'am. I know that, but I also want to learn to think for myself. To make my own decisions. I mean, I want to make the right decisions, but I want them to be my decisions, you know?"

"Yes, I do understand. And, Clint, don't sell yourself short.

The fact that you want to make your own decisions and that you're having trouble deciding how to do that tells me you are more mature than you're giving yourself credit for being. I know you'll work this out. It won't always be easy, but you have a good heart and a good mind, so I'm sure you'll make the right decisions most of the time. Just remember that your dad and I are here any time you need to talk, OK?"

"OK, Mom. Thanks."

Thus, the first few weeks of 1965 were a reckoning of sorts for me. I entered the year as a fresh teenager—the age Sam had been during the early part of our friendship. That fact wormed its way through much of my thinking in the days following my conversation with Mom. I thought of how mature he had seemed—adultlike even—when first I had met him, whereas I, in comparison and to my own thinking, seemed much less so. Yet, as I began to find some peace within these conflicts, I was determined to pattern myself more after the thirteen-year-old Sam I remembered. I made a conscious effort to be more responsible, more intentional in my studies, and to be a better older brother to Will. At the same time—though I did not understand it in these terms—I was determined to be less dependent on Sam's friendship for affirmation of my own worth.

As a manifestation of this new me, I committed myself to becoming better informed regarding the events in the world beyond Palatka. Much as Sam had done for me, I endeavored to explain these events to Will and to lead him to better understand their implications for the future. I knew that our area schools would likely be fully integrated by the time he reached high school, and I was determined that he should be a force for good in that process. I also wanted him to see the global crisis represented by our nation's escalations in Vietnam, realizing that both he and I could be drafted into that conflict in years to come.

As a result, my correspondence with Sam took on a more serious tone as I posed questions to him and weighed his responses.

As school resumed the Monday after New Year's, I again fell into the pattern of walking alongside Christine. (I had, by that time, abandoned the appellation "Crazy" prefacing her name.) Though it was sometimes challenging, I often managed to steer our conversations toward topics other than the Beatles. At such times, I found her to be brighter and more aware of the issues facing our nation than I had assumed. I recall one particular conversation in mid-January that challenged my earlier perceptions of her.

It was a crisp, clear morning—the sort that assures Northerners will continue to move to Florida. We had chatted about nothing in particular when I decided to take our conversation on a different tack.

"So, you know, when we get to high school, there are gonna be Black kids in school with us."

"Of course I know that, Clint. I swear, sometimes you act like I'm a moron or something."

"I didn't mean it that way. I'm just wondering how you feel about that."

"Well, how I feel about it is that I think it's OK. I mean, if they think they can get a better education at a white high school, well, I'm OK with them coming to our school."

"So, do you think you can be friends with Black kids?"

"What a ridiculous question! Of course I can be friends with them. I'm not some redneck from Alabama, you know. I think we need to learn to get along. You can see where things are headed, you know? I'm not saying it'll be easy, but I think we need to work this out. Our parents' generation is not going to get this done so it's up to us, don't you think?"

"Yeah, I do. I mean we're all people. So, yeah, we've got to do better than our parents' and grandparents did. You know I have a Black friend, right?"

"Yes. That boy who lives near your other grandmother, right? Jacob, right?"

"Yeah. I call him Jake. He's really smart, but there's no high school for him to go to, and the white one in Hawthorne isn't integrated, so he's gonna have to move to Jacksonville and live with an aunt just to go to high school."

"Now, see, that's just wrong. It shouldn't have to be that way. So, yeah, I'm fine with going to school with Black kids. Who knows, maybe you can improve your musical tastes."

"What does that mean?"

"Clint, the only music you like is folk music. That's the only kind of music you ever talk about. Do you ever listen to soul? Next to the Beatles, it's the best music on the planet. Maybe you can broaden your musical horizons if you hang out with Black kids."

"What's wrong with what I like?"

"Nothing's wrong with it. It's just that you don't listen to anything else."

"Well, I thought you only listened to the Beatles."

"Clint, my musical tastes are much more eclectic than that."

"Eclectic? What's that mean?"

"It means varied. My tastes are varied. I love the Beatles, of course, but I like the Stones, The Supremes, The Temptations, Wilson Pickett, just a whole lot of other groups besides the Beatles. That's being eclectic."

"Oh. OK." I decided that morning to become more eclectic.

16 January, 1965
NAS JAX
Hey, Clint,

It was great to get your letter, but wow! You really stepped up your letter-writing game. I'll try to respond to all the stuff you mentioned but may have to save some stuff for next time.

First, I couldn't stop laughing about your "talks" with Christine on the way to school. If I didn't know better, I'd think you might have a crush on her. (Actually, I don't know better!) You remember me telling you to watch that one? I told you one day you'd look and she'd be a beauty. So, she's smart, too? My advice: take it real slow. Smart, pretty girls can do some real damage to your heart (not that I have a lot of experience in that area).

The stuff you said about my influence in your life really meant a lot to me, and I'm really proud of you for wanting to be a better big brother for Will. He's a great kid and he looks up to you. You're right that it's time for you to reach down to him.

I know what you're saying about growing up in a small town, especially one in the South. Things are so different here. The guys here are from all over the country. They're black, white, even some guys who look Chinese or Japanese. There are all sorts of accents and all sorts of opinions about things. Most of the guys from the North think us guys from the South are complete hicks. They seem surprised I have a full set of teeth! They also think we're all prejudiced against anybody different from us, Blacks especially. Frankly, I think they're pretty arrogant. They haven't been brought up here and listened to all the racist crap we hear all our lives. I think it's easier for them to be more open-minded, but I keep that opinion to myself.

Well, I need to write Mom, so I better close this out. Please keep writing whenever you can. I miss you.

Your Brother.
Sam

31.

STATE SECRETS

MY UNCLE DAVID—married to my somewhat obsessive Aunt Ida—was my father's younger brother. After his service in World War II, he attended the University of Florida, where he obtained a graduate degree in some area of engineering. As the US space effort advanced, he landed a civilian job at Cape Canaveral[15] and found himself working on the team designing the next generation of spacecraft—the Apollo capsule. All of this work was highly classified, of course, and we had learned to avoid the subject when the family gathered. However, one evening in late January, my father announced over dinner that the Cape was to be open to family members of employees on

---

15 Cape Canaveral, the site of both the Cape Canaveral Air Force Station and the Kennedy Space Center, was chosen as a missile test and launch site in 1949, with initial construction begun the following year. The Cape's southern location allows launch vehicles to take advantage of the increased linear velocity of the Earth's east-to-west rotation—stronger at the Equator—as well as the Atlantic Ocean to the east where aborted launches are far less likely to impact human activity than would launches over land. It should be noted that Cape Canaveral was originally planned as a test and launch site for ballistic missiles, as the quest to launch humans into space had yet to begin. The first rocket launched from the Cape was a V-2 rocket—a German design by Wernher von Braun from World War II, and the scourge of London during the war—from Launch Complex 3 on July 24, 1950. The first ICBM launched from the Cape was a Titan on February 6, 1959. Between 1963 and 1973, the entire Cape was named Cape Kennedy. In 1973, the nomenclature was changed such that the Cape Canaveral Air Force Station retained its name, the space launch facility took on the name Kennedy Space Center, and the geographical island formation on which those two are located retained the name Cape Canaveral.

one Saturday in February, and that Uncle David had obtained a pass for us for that event.

I was absolutely beside myself with excitement. Would we meet the astronauts? Would we see the rockets? Would there be a launch that day? I peppered my father with questions for which he had no answers. All he knew was that we were to line up at the gates that morning, and that our pass and detailed instructions would be coming by mail.

6 February, 1965
NAS JAX
Dear Clint,

I got your letter on Tuesday. I AM SO JEALOUS! I can't believe you're going to get to visit the Cape! That's one of the most top-secret bases in the whole country. I really can't believe they're letting you all visit it. They may have to kill you afterward, you know? Just joking. Kind of. But, yeah, I'm so envious. I'd give anything to be able to see that. You have to tell me everything you do and see.

Things here are about the same. My formal training is nearly finished and they're giving me a lot more independence in the tower. Of course, they watch everything I do, but they're not telling me every little move to make now. So far, so good. I haven't crashed anything yet!

One thing that changed when I got back to base was one of my duties. I am now responsible for keeping the floors clean and waxed in the officers' mess. I don't know how I got this job and I really don't enjoy it. I have this ancient floor machine I have to use. It's noisy and hard to operate. At least I only have to do this once a week. I guess it's better than cleaning toilets!

So, this will shock you. I've started going to chapel. You know I've never been religious but going to chapel is a way to meet other sailors in a different kind of environment. There's a worship service on Sunday morning that's very informal, then I go to a study group on Sunday evenings. It's kind of a Bible study, but more of a philosophy class. We discuss a lot of different ideas and religious teachings and try to see how they relate to modern life. It's really pretty interesting. Sometimes we really get into some heated discussions.

Well, I need to close so I can write Mom a short note. Take care of yourself and take good notes at the Cape so you can tell me all about it.

Your brother,
Sam

About a week later, Dad came home with a large envelope that had arrived addressed to him via US Registered Mail. The envelope contained our official visitors' pass onto the Cape Canaveral facility on Saturday, February 13, 1965. Included with the pass were instructions and a list of things we could and could not do, among them: where to line up for entry; what identification to bring; and instructions to follow the vehicle in front at a safe speed and distance, to avoid stopping at any point during the tour, and under no circumstances to exit our vehicle.

The intervening days dragged by. All Will and I could think of was the coming visit to the Cape. Nothing else mattered. Nothing even came close. When the day finally arrived, Dad roused us in the dark hours of the morning and we were on the road by 5:30 am. Mom had packed both breakfast and lunch, anticipating that the lines might be long to enter and we might need to eat as we waited. The drive down US 1 to the Cape seemed interminable, but we arrived just as the sun was coming up. The day dawned clear and the eastern sky was painted along the horizon with a smudge of pink and orange as if in a highwayman's landscape.

At the intersection with Old Highway A1A, a police officer was stationed directing traffic. As we turned east toward the Cape, the rising sun was in our eyes. About two miles down the road, cars were already lined up along the eastbound side of the highway as far as we could see. The gate was not to open until 8:00 am.

Stoically, Dad pulled into the line and cut the engine. It was going to be a long morning. At that point, the line was stationary, so Mom decided it would be a good time to eat breakfast, after which, we were faced with the dilemma that Will and I both needed to pee. My father's solution was to open both passenger-side doors, for us to stand between them and aim for the ditch. I was mortified, but Will seemed to take it in stride—he who was emphatic he would never go skinny dipping! Nonetheless, the call of nature was strong, and, bolstered by my dad's assurance that I would never see any of these people again, I did what needed to be done.

Around 7:30, a Jeep with four uniformed airmen pulled up beside our car. They exited the Jeep and each moved to a vehicle waiting in line. My dad rolled down his window to speak with the one who was now standing beside our car.

"Good morning, sir, and welcome to Cape Canaveral."

"Good morning, Airman...Hutchins, right?"

"Yes sir. Hutchins, sir. Thank you." The young airman handed Dad a small booklet. "Sir, this booklet provides information about the sites you will see on your tour today. There are a total of fifteen sites. Each is clearly numbered with a large sign beside the road. The numbers correspond to the entries in this booklet."

"Do we need to show our pass?"

"Yes, sir, but not now. They'll check your pass and ID when you reach the gate. Please have those ready for the guards there."

"OK."

"Do you understand that you are to remain in line, follow the vehicle in front of you, not stop for any reason, and not exit your vehicle for any reason?"

"Yes, sir. We're clear on all of that."

"Very good, sir." He then glanced at the rest of us. "Folks, enjoy your visit."

"Thank you," we all chorused, and he was off to the next vehicle.

About an hour later, the line began to move. Following the car in front of us, we pulled onto the highway and crept along for at least another thirty minutes before we saw the gate ahead. As we neared the gate, we noticed two heavily armed guards stationed on either side and two others wearing side arms who were obviously checking visitors' passes and identification.

"Wow! This is like getting into Fort Knox or something," I remarked.

"Son, there's a lot of classified and top-secret stuff on the other side of these gates. Honestly, I'm pretty surprised they're letting us in. This is probably one of the most closely guarded bases in the world."

Within minutes, we were stopped beside the guardhouse. Dad rolled down his window, and one of the guards approached.

"May I see your visitors' pass and identification, please?" Dad handed over the requested items. The guard took them into the guardhouse and returned within seconds.

"Everything's in order, sir. I know you've been told you are not to stop, but this tour is kind of stop-and-go, so be prepared to take it real slow. Some folks are already having problems with their engines overheating. If you have trouble, pull to the shoulder and wait in your car. Do not get out. Someone will come to help you in a matter of minutes. Is all of this clear, sir?"

"Yes, airman. I understand."

"Very good, sir. You may proceed." Dad pulled ahead slowly and fell in behind a green sedan. Mom picked the booklet off the dashboard and opened it.

"OK. Let's see what this says. You boys start looking for the signs with the numbers on them. Hon, this says we're to turn right onto Pier Road."

"I'm following that guy up there, and he's following the guy in front of him." Dad chuckled. "Let's hope the guy in the first car paid attention to the directions. OK, we're turning right. Yep, Pier Road. So far so good."

"OK, boys, start looking for the first site."

"What is it?"

"OK. Let me read it to you. 'The first site on your tour will be Launch Complex 5/6, and it will be on your left.'"

"There it is! Up there!" Will screeched excitedly. "See the big sign with the number one on it?"

Mom continued to read from the booklet. "'This complex, comprised of two launch pads, was constructed in 1955 and '56, and was the site of the launch of the first Mercury capsule on 21 November, 1960. In addition, space chimp Ham launched from this complex on 31 January, 1961. However, this site is best known as the complex from which Alan Shepherd launched on 5 May, 1961, for the first US manned space flight.'"

"Whoa! That's the one we stayed home from school to watch. Do you remember that, Will?"

"Yeah. I remember it didn't launch and Dad finally sent us to school. But then we watched it in the library. This is so cool!"

"The booklet says Gus Grissom also took off from here for

the second US manned space flight on the 21st of July, 1961."

"'Launched,' Mom. Not 'took off,'" I said. "It's 'launched' for space flight."

"I stand corrected."

The endless line of cars lurched forward at an excruciatingly slow pace—we certainly could have walked faster. We passed several more sites, mostly dedicated to development and testing of missile defense systems rather than space flight. Mom decided she, Will, and I should take turns reading the information in the booklet, so we struggled with such terms as "aerothermodynamics," for which none of us had a working definition. Will was reading as we neared the fourth site.

"'4. Immediately past Launch Complex 31/32, and also to your left, you will notice what appears to be an airport runway, and, in fact is. However, this runway is called the Skid Strip, so named for the reason that the early finned Snark missiles were reused, brought back to earth, and skidded to a landing on this concrete runway.' That's weird. Here, Clint, your turn."

"OK. 'Number 5. Immediately past the skid plate, and, again on your left, you will see the oldest structure on the Cape: The Cape Canaveral Lighthouse.'"

"There it is, up there."

I continued reading. "'Constructed in 1868 to replace an older, shorter lighthouse, it was moved to this location in 1894.' Mom."

"Let's wait a minute 'til we get past the lighthouse." We sat in silence as the line of cars lurched forward. Shortly, we spied the large sign for the sixth site. Mom took up the narrative. "Number 6. 'Directly in front of you is Launch Complex 2, including Pads 1, 2, and 3. Constructed in 1951 as a launch area for Snark and, later, Matador missiles, this site was deactivated in 1962 and now serves as a staging area for rescue operations for both Mercury and Gemini projects.' Hon, this says we're to turn left onto Central Control Road then right onto ICBM Road. I know, you're just following the guy in the green sedan."

"Yep."

The road we were now on paralleled the coast, and we could see the Atlantic just a short distance off to our right. All the launch facilities along this road appeared to have been constructed between the road and the shore, and most had been designed to accommodate the massive Atlas launch vehicle. It was Will's turn to read as we approached the ninth site.

"'Number 9. Launch Complex 13 was constructed over two years, from April 1956 to April 1958, and specifically designed to accommodate the newest generation of the Atlas rocket. On 15 February, 1960, an Atlas Able exploded on this site during an engine test.' Whoa! That must have been cool!"

"Some people might have gotten killed, Will. Maybe not so cool. Keep reading."

"Yeah. OK. 'After repairs, launches resumed on 11 October, 1960.' How come they write the dates like that, anyway, with the day before the month?"

"It's just the way the military does it. Sam does it that way in all his letters and I do it in my letters to him. Keep reading."

"OK. OK! 'On 10 November, 1961, the space monkey Goliath was launched from this site aboard an Atlas E rocket. Unfortunately, the mission failed.' So, does that mean the monkey got killed?"

"Uh, yeah."

"Poor monkey."

"Keep reading."

"OK. Geeze, you're impatient. 'During 1962-63, this complex was converted to accommodate the new Atlas Agena rockets to be used in space exploration. Since that time, there have been three successful launches of satellites and also the NASA Mariner

3 probe on 5 November, 1964.' Your turn." Will handed me the booklet. I scanned the next entry and passed the booklet to Mom.

"Mom, will you read the next one? I really want to look at this one."

"Sure. 'Number 10. By far the most historic site on your tour today is Launch Complex 14. Constructed in 1956-57, it was designed to be the launch site for manned Mercury missions employing the Atlas launch vehicle. Cleary visible from your vantage point is the 154 foot 8 inch service structure used to prepare the Atlas for launch. Also present at this site is a 92 foot ramp rising 22 feet above ground used to bring the rockets to the pad. From this site, four successful manned orbital Mercury missions were launched: Friendship 7, carrying astronaut John Glenn on 20 February, 1962; Aurora 7, with astronaut Scott Carpenter aboard on 24 May, 1962; Sigma 7, bearing astronaut Walter Schirra into space on 3 October, 1962; and Faith 7, on 15 May, 1963, with astronaut Gordon Cooper aboard. On 10 November, 1964, the Mercury 7 Memorial was dedicated. You will pass the memorial right beside the road as you near the entry road into the Launch Complex.'"

"There it is. Up there. I can't see it very good."

"Clint, switch places with Will so he can see better. You can see over him."

"Yes sir." Mom continued as we neared the memorial.

"It says here, 'The monument, constructed of titanium, shows the numeral 7, honoring the original seven Mercury astronauts, inside the astronomical symbol for the planet Mercury. Mounted on the slab is an inscribed tablet describing the achievements of the Mercury program. Beneath the slab is a time capsule to be opened in the year 2464 containing memorabilia from America's first explorations of space.'"

"2464? I'm pretty sure we'll have blown ourselves into

oblivion by then."

"Clint, don't say things like that."

"Well, it's true, Mom. Look at all the missile sites we've passed today. There've been hundreds of missiles launched from here, and most of them were for carrying atomic bombs. At some point, Russia and us are gonna attack each other and the whole world'll be destroyed. I mean, all this space exploration is really cool, but if we're just trying to beat the Russians to the moon so we can launch missiles at them from there, then it's not really about science. It's just about preparing for all-out nuclear war." I had worked myself up into a bit of a frenzy by that point and Will was looking at me as though I had lost my mind.

"Hold on, son. You do understand we have to stay ahead of the Russians so they never think they have an advantage, don't you?" Dad asked, seriously.

"Dad, I know about deterrence. But I also know about mutually assured destruction, MAD. We've already got enough bombs to wipe Russia off the map. And they've got enough to do that to us. Why do we have to keep making more and bigger ones?"

"I guess because they are."

"Well, somebody needs to yell 'Stop!' because we're gonna destroy everything if we don't."

"Can we get back to the tour, please?" Will interjected.

"Yes, Will, we can. What's next?"

Next, it seemed, were two launch complexes constructed to accommodate Titan I and II missiles—the primary delivery vehicle for nuclear weapons in America's arsenal. I kept my peace and didn't even mention this fact.

As we neared the thirteenth site on our tour, it was Will's turn to read. "Number 13. You will notice a great deal of activity at this site, Launch Complex 19. This is currently the most exciting place to be on the entire Cape, as it will be the launch site for the first manned Gemini flight in a few short weeks. Astronauts Gus Grissom and John Young are scheduled to pilot the Gemini 3 spacecraft atop a Titan II rocket and make three orbits of the earth before splashdown. The flight, intended to test the Gemini's Orbital Attitude Manure...Man...' What's this word?"

"Maneuvering. Orbital Attitude Maneuvering System," I read.

Will continued. "Orbital Attitude Maneuvering System, enabling the astronauts to control their orbit and re-entry, will last nearly five hours.'"

Though I was excited to see the complex where Grissom and Young would launch within weeks, I was still cooling down from my tirade about nuclear war, pouting, and at the same time, feeling a bit embarrassed. We were nearing the end of the tour. The route looped back south through the Cape Canaveral Air Force Station and past the final site—the Mercury Control Building well off to our left. From that point, the line of vehicles gained speed and we were soon waved through the gate.

"Thanks, Dad. That was pretty amazing. Really cool," Will said.

"Yeah, Dad. Thanks. And thanks for breakfast and lunch, too, Mom," I responded.

"You're welcome, boys," Mom replied.

Will and I slept most of the drive home. Upon arriving, I went directly to my room and began a letter to Sam. I wanted to report back to him on our visit to Cape Canaveral, but also wanted to gauge his thoughts as a "military man" on nuclear warfare. I received his reply within a few days.

20 February, 1965
NAS JAX
Hi, Clint.

I got your letter mid-week but haven't had a chance to write back until today. Man, it really sounds like your tour of the Cape was amazing. You realize you and Will are possibly the

only kids in Palatka to have seen that stuff first-hand, right?
You should have a lot of material for school assignments in
the next few months. I think the most exciting things you saw
were launch pad 14 where so many of the Mercury missions
launched and pad 19 where they're getting Gemini III ready
for launch. You saw history in the making, Clint!

You asked my opinion about nuclear weapons. Wow! That's
a heavy subject. I guess I never thought too much about the
right or wrong of them until recently. I mean, they've just
been something we lived with and I guess I always figured
that, at some time in the future, there'd be a nuclear war
with the Soviets. Anyway, you remember I told you I was
going to this study group at the chapel on Sunday evenings,
right? Well, it so happens we've been talking about something
called Just War Theory. Short version: Just War Theory is
this way of looking at a war to see if it's the least bad way
to fight it. Not good, just the least bad way to fight a war,
or if there's an ethical way to wage war. I don't know if I'm
explaining this very well. Anyway, it's based on the teachings
of a bunch of philosophers and religious scholars. So, we've
been studying it and discussing how it relates to past wars,
like WWII, and what's going on in Vietnam now. So, two
weeks ago, we got into a discussion about whether you can
fight a "just" war with nuclear weapons. (This is getting too
long, but I'm nearly there.) So, one of the principles of JWT is
that you don't attack civilians, only soldiers. So, the chaplain
said that the bomb we dropped on Hiroshima in WWII killed
somewhere around 100,000 civilians. So, he asked, "Can we
fight a just nuclear war?" Most of us said "No." So, then we
talked more and decided that nuclear weapons should never
be used and that we should never fire first if it came down to
an all-out war with Russia. Anyway, I don't know if any of

this answers your question, but that's kind of my thinking these days. Enough of this!

I had a care package from my mom a couple of weeks ago. It had cookies, socks, deodorant, writing paper, envelopes, and stamps in it. It's amazing how such simple stuff makes me so happy!

I hope you're keeping up with the news. There's just a lot of stuff happening these days, especially with civil rights and Vietnam. I really think things are going to get worse before they get better.

Well, I need to wrap this up. Thanks for writing.

Your brother,
Sam

32.

BLOODY SUNDAY

THE EDMUND PETTUS Bridge carries US highway 80 across the Alabama River at Selma, Alabama. Constructed of steel and concrete in 1940, it hardly seemed the sort of place where history might be made, or the course of American history forever altered. As 1965 dawned in Selma, the voter rolls there were comprised of 99% white voters, despite the fact that the state of Alabama was 30% African American. That February, tensions in nearby Marion, Alabama escalated between civil rights demonstrators demanding voting rights and armed whites and state troopers determined to deny them. In response, leaders, including Dr. Martin Luther King and James Bevel, formulated a plan for a peaceful march from Selma to the state capital in Montgomery to demand access to the ballot box for African American citizens.

The proposed route for this action required that the marchers cross the Pettus Bridge to access highway 80 to Montgomery. On Sunday, March 7, 1965, the march began, with young John Lewis and Hosea Williams in the lead. Due to the high arched design of the bridge, the marchers, approaching from the north, could not see the south end of the bridge until they reached its apex. There, waiting for them, were dozens of armed police officers. Yet Williams and Lewis continued leading the marchers toward the foot of the bridge. Once there, they were met with a brutal and violent response from the police, leaving seventeen hospitalized and many others injured. That evening, the network newscasts led with shocking images of the brutal beatings inflicted on the peaceful marchers. The day would become known as "Bloody Sunday," and the stunning brutality of the police response would provide impetus for Congress to pass the Voting Rights Act.

On that Sunday evening, I came into the living room after completing my homework, switched on the television, and dropped onto the couch. Mom was in the kitchen preparing dinner. Dad and Will were elsewhere. As the set warmed up, the first images I saw were of police with night sticks beating mostly Black civilians. The scene was horrific, but I had no context. As the newscaster continued to describe the violence, I began to pick up details—somewhere in Alabama...peaceful unarmed marchers...demonstrating for voter rights.

"Mom, you've gotta come see this!"

"What is it, Clint? I'm in the middle of fixing supper."

"Please come now."

"Alright, alright." She entered the living room, wiping her hands on her apron. "Now, what was so important that..." She stopped mid-sentence as her eyes locked onto the images on the television. "What is this? Where is this happening?"

"Somewhere in Alabama. They were marching somewhere for voting rights and the cops attacked them." Mom took a place beside me on the couch as the voice on the television continued.

"Organizers say dozens of marchers were injured, seventeen so badly they required hospitalization. Among those seriously injured in the violent attack was Student Nonviolent Coordinating Committee leader John Lewis, who, together with Rev. Hosea Williams, led the marchers across the bridge and into the violent clash with police."

"I've heard of John Lewis. He's not much older than Sam, Mom. Jesus, look how they're just beating them!"

The newscast continued: "The unarmed and peaceful marchers were attempting to walk all the way to the state capital in Montgomery to demand an end to voter suppression in Alabama, when they were stopped almost before they began."

"This is horrible. How can they do this to people who are just trying to claim their right to vote? How can they just beat people so unmercifully who haven't done anything?" Tears were now streaming down my mother's face as she continued to address the television. "They're going to kill some of these people. Look at that woman bleeding in the road!"

The broadcast returned to the newsroom and the anchor continued. "The march, beginning in Selma, Alabama, and intended to end at the steps of the state capital in Montgomery, was planned with the counsel of Dr. King and James Bevel, active in the Southern Christian Leadership Conference and a local civil rights leader in Selma. The stated objective of the march was to shine light on the barriers placed in the paths of African American citizens in Alabama to secure their access to the ballot box. On the heels of the violence today, leaders are already calling this 'Bloody Sunday,' and vow to continue the struggle to guarantee the right to vote for all Alabamians. Elsewhere in the news..." Mom switched off the television and we sat for a moment in stunned silence, she daubing her eyes with a tissue and me sitting slack-jawed, still staring at the dark screen.

"Clint, I'm sorry you had to see that."

"That could have been Sam and his friend David, you know? I mean, who knows, it could have been me and Jake. I mean, if we lived in that hick town in Alabama, maybe we'd have all been out there marching. Those folks didn't go out looking for a fight. They just wanted to make a statement. I mean, this is

America. Everyone's supposed to be able to vote, right?"

"Yes, Clint. But a lot of really prejudiced whites are afraid if Blacks start voting in big numbers they'll actually have some power to make changes."

"What would be so bad about that?"

"Nothing. But they're acting out of fear. Plus, they see Black leaders like Dr. King gaining a lot of influence, and they see public opinion shifting to support the civil rights movement, and they're scared of losing power and their place in white southern society."

"I just wish they'd all just, I don't know, go away or die or something. Sometimes I wish Blacks would do like the KKK and just go out and hang these rednecks. Hang the Klansmen. I hate them. They all need to die!"

"Clint, that's not the solution."

"Well what is? If the Klan and all their redneck followers were gone, things would be a lot better."

"I agree, but violence is just not the way to change things. You keep watching. I'll bet you, over the next few days there's going to be a real outcry from people all over the country, white and Black, about this horrible thing today in Alabama. This is going to change a lot of peoples' thinking about what Black folks go through just to live a simple life and enjoy the rights that white folks take for granted."

"I hope you're right. Mom? Can I call Jake?"

"Of course. Go ahead and call the neighbor and leave a message for him to call you back collect. And Clint?"

"Yes, ma'am?"

"I know this was awful to see, but I'm really proud of you for knowing the right side of all of this."

"Thanks, Mom."

I quickly placed the call to Jake's neighbor, asking that

they give him the message to call me back as soon as possible. Within ten minutes, the phone rang.

"I'll get it. It's probably Jake. Hello?"

"I have a collect call from Jacob Wilson. Will you accept the charges?"

"Yes, operator. Jake?"

"Hey, Clint. Man, what's up? You sound upset."

"Yeah. Did you see what happened in Alabama today?"

"You mean those marchers getting beat on that bridge? Yeah, I saw that on the news."

"It's awful. I'm really sorry."

"What do you have to be sorry about, man. It wasn't you doin' the beatin'."

"Yeah, I know, but I feel, I don't know, responsible somehow. All those cops were white, and most of the folks gettin' beat were Black. I'm just ashamed, I guess."

"Clint, man, you got no shame in this. You're not like those rednecks. You'd never have done somethin' like that."

"I know, but sometimes I'm ashamed for being white. I wish we could've been there. You and me and Sam and his friend David. I mean I don't want to get beat up, but I just feel like I need to be a part of something like that to say 'Hey, I'm not like these white bigots. Not all white people are like this.' You know?"

"I know. I think that, too, sometimes." He chuckled. "But there aren't a lot of demonstrations going on in Campville these days."

"Yeah. I guess not. Not much happening in Palatka, either. Some stuff in St. Augustine, but that's about as close as it gets. Do you think all this'll make a difference? Will things change?"

"I'm not sure, but I think some things'll change. I sure hope so. I'd hate to see all this pain count for nothing."

"Me too, man. Me too."

"So, have you heard anything from Sam lately?"

"Yeah. I got a letter from him a couple of weeks ago. I had asked him what he thought about nuclear war, and he wrote me back some really interesting stuff about something called Just War Theory and how nuclear war is immoral. It was pretty deep, but I understood most of it. Come to think of it, I need to write him back."

"Hey, man, this is costing you money, you know?"

"Yeah, I know. I just needed to talk to you after what happened today."

"I really appreciate it. It means a lot to me that you called about this. Sometimes I feel like I live on the far side of the moon or somethin', you know? Like nothin' that happens anywhere else ever gets here."

"Yeah, I know what you mean. I mean, Palatka's a lot bigger, but still, it's pretty quiet here. Well, I guess I better go before I spend all my allowance paying my folks back for this call."

"Right. Hey, thanks for calling. Hope you get over this way soon."

"Me too. See you soon. Bye."

"Bye."

Later that evening, I wrote to Sam, venting my anger at the injustice of Bloody Sunday and proposing that when he returned from the Navy, he, David, Jake, and I form a secret group to pursue Klan members in the dark of the night and exact judgement for their decades of evil. Strangely, and so out of character for him, Sam did not write back immediately, and I waited a couple of weeks for his reply—and for what would turn out to be my last letter from him.

27 March, 1965
NAS JAX
Hey, Clint.

I'm sorry for not writing sooner. There's been a lot going on, and things have gotten really rough here the last few weeks.

Yes, I saw the news about the march in Selma, Alabama. It was awful. There was no reason for the cops to beat those folks the way they did. Some were kids. I'm glad you talked with Jake about it and tell him "Hi" for me. I've kind of fallen out of touch with my friend David. We exchanged a couple of letters right after I left, but we haven't written to each other since then. I've got to look him up next time I'm home. I'm telling you this to tell you to keep in touch with Jake. Interracial friendships are really important these days. So, if the four of us form a secret society to punish the KKK, what would we call it?

I'm counting the days until I finish my training here and get a new assignment. I don't even care if it's on a carrier in the Gulf of Tonkin, I just want to get as far away from NAS JAX as I can! There's really nobody here I'll miss, except Chaplain Adamson.

Hey, sorry this is so short, but I need to get going. Thanks for your letters. They really mean a lot. I'll write more next time.

Your Brother,
Sam

Three days after Bloody Sunday, Will turned eleven and, thus, became eligible to join Boy Scouts. I'm not sure who was more excited, Will or Ed Masters, with whom Will had forged a friendship on our vacation several years prior. By this point, Ed was easily twice Will's size and they made an odd-looking Laurel-and-Hardy, as they seemed inseparable at every scouting event. Whereas scouting had been for me one tick on my clock, for Will it became all consuming. He enthusiastically pursued every possible means for advancement and, by summer, had already achieved the rank of First Class. It was apparent, even then, that he would far surpass me in rank and accomplishment.

Spring meant the Spring Dance at my junior high. Whereas I had avoided the event the previous year—in part because I have two left feet—this year, I was interested in attending, particularly if a certain formerly crazy neighbor girl would accompany me. The real challenge was in mustering the courage to ask her and the risk to my fragile ego if she said "No." Thus, I resorted to accessing my only resource on all things female—my mom.

"So, I want to ask Christine to the Spring Dance, but I'm scared she'll say 'No.'"

"Does she have a boyfriend or anyone else you think she'd want to go with?"

"I don't think so. I mean, we walk to school together every morning, and she never says anything about a boyfriend. I don't see her hanging out with a guy at school. Nobody talks about her like she's with someone. So, no, I'm pretty sure she doesn't have a boyfriend."

"OK, then. What do you think is the best way to ask her?"

"I don't know. I guess I could ask her on the way to school. But if she says 'No,' then it would be really awkward for us to walk together from then on. Maybe I should write her a note?"

"No. Not a note. She needs to see you have the courage to ask her in person. Look, son, you've known Christine most of your life. I know for a fact you've had plenty of disagreements with her over the years."

"Yeah. She used to beat the crap outta me."

"Right. So, what I'm saying is, this won't change your friendship if she doesn't want to go to the dance with you, or if she already has plans to go with someone else. I've never understood why kids your age think they have to have a date to go to these things anyway."

"We just do. It's just really uncool to go without a date. It's better to not go than to look like a loser."

"OK, then. So, if you ask her, and she says 'No,' how will that make you feel?"

"Kinda dumb. Embarrassed."

"So, is there someone else you would want to ask if Christine turns you down?"

"No, ma'am. Not really."

"So, how will you feel if you never muster up the courage to ask her?"

"Like a coward. Like a failure."

"So, which is worse, asking and being turned down, or not asking and feeling like a coward?"

"Not asking her and feeling like a chicken."

"There's your answer."

"Why don't I feel more confident about this now?"

"Because there's no easy solution. You just have to do the hard work and ask her. Until you do, none of the small questions matter. Like, what will you wear? Should you get her a corsage? Until the big question is settled, you're not going to feel confident. There's no way to feel any more confident about this until you just go ahead and ask her."

"OK. Thanks, Mom, I think."

She laughed. "Always happy to help."

Needless to say, I barely slept that night. All night long I played out one scenario after another of me asking Christine to the dance. In some, she agreed. In others, she turned me down. After each, I mused on how I might feel—elated or crushed, emboldened or humiliated. It seemed a problem without a solution. I just had to ask her. There was no other way to know. There was no other way to move beyond this conundrum. At some point, I drifted off into a fitful sleep and awoke feeling as though, once again, Christine had trounced me.

As we did every morning, I waited on our back porch for

Christine to pass, then fell in step with her to walk to school.

"You look kinda tired this morning."

"I didn't sleep very well last night." My heart was drumming so loudly in my temples I was certain she could hear it. I couldn't string this out. It was now or never.

"Uh, Christine, can I ask you something?"

"Well, of course."

"Uh, would you, I mean, if you aren't already going with somebody, would you, I mean, I understand if you don't want to or something, but would you..."

"Clint, are you trying to ask me to the Spring Dance?"

"Yes! Yes, that's what I'm trying to ask. Will you go with me to the Spring Dance?"

"Yes. I'd like that."

"Really?! You'll really go with me?"

"I said I would. How many times do you need me to say it? Yes, I'll go with you to the Spring Dance. Now, can we move on?"

"Yes, yes, we can move on. Yes."

Now, those other questions needed to be answered, but I had Mom to help with that. That evening, we talked, with Mom deciding I needed a new suit for the occasion and a cymbidium wrist corsage was required. My assignment was to find out the color of Christine's dress so the corsage could be made to match. The mysteries of dating were beginning to open to me. So momentous was this occasion that I wrote Sam a letter that evening. Several weeks after his funeral, it was returned to me unopened and stamped "Return to Sender."

The morning of April 7 broke cool, crisp and cloudless. Walking to school that morning, I was successful in learning that Christine's dress for the Spring Dance was to be lavender with purple trim. I had no idea of the relevance of that information with respect to flowers for a corsage, but I was confident in the fact that Mom would. Since the morning I had posed the question to Christine—well, in all fairness, she had known my intentions before I could mumble the invitation—things had been quite ordinary between us. We talked about school and music. She asked about Sam. I asked her about her plans for the summer and whether they included another round of finishing school in Atlanta. The school day was ordinary in every respect. Christine and I rarely walked home together, so I was alone as I rounded the corner of our house and spied my mother's car uncharacteristically parked in the driveway.

33.

REQUIEM FOR A BROTHER

THE FOLLOWING DAYS unfolded in a gray fog of numbness and despair. Sam's funeral was to be on Saturday at Johnson-Davis Funeral Home. Chaplain Adamson from the Naval Air Station would preside. Mrs. Sanders had asked me to sing and to share a few words. I felt totally incapable of doing either of those things, but agreed, nonetheless. I owed it to Sam and to our friendship.

Once I had chosen the song I would sing, I set about trying to write the things I wanted to say. Mom had suggested that she type my remarks as my handwriting could, at times, be a challenge to decipher, even for me. All day on Friday I fretted over the task. What could I say that could possibly do justice to my love for Sam and my gratitude for his role in my life? Would my words simply serve to make the day even more tragic for Mrs. Sanders? Would I come across as childish and shallow? Still, I was determined that my words would be my own. I did not want guidance or direction from anyone. I needed to do this myself.

By dinner time that evening, I had reached a point of marginal satisfaction with my eulogy. After we had eaten a quiet meal, Mom set about typing my remarks. I sat nearby to provide translation for my scrawl. Other than a couple of grammatical changes, she made no suggestions and I began to wonder if what I had written was so mundane and juvenile as to be a distraction to the mourners. About halfway through, I noticed her wiping her eyes. A few minutes later, she said. "I need a break, Clint. This is beautiful, but it's breaking my heart. Give me a few minutes."

"Sure, Mom. So, you don't think it's bad, do you?"

"Hardly. It's one of the most heartfelt things I've ever read. I knew you loved Sam, but I guess I never realized how mature your love and admiration for him were. You've expressed your feelings in a very mature way in what you've written. I just hope you can get through it without falling apart."

"Oh, I've been crying all day. But tomorrow, I'm going to use the Sam method to deal with my feelings."

Mom laughed. "And what, pray tell, is the Sam method?"

"Well, remember when I was doing *Amahl*, and Sam came to see me backstage before opening night? I was a nervous wreck. He told me to think about everybody in the audience with cabbages for heads. So, that's what I'm gonna do tomorrow."

"OK. Well, that's an interesting approach. But, you know, if you have to stop and pull yourself together, it'll be fine. Just take your time. Everyone will understand, and they'll probably be crying right along with you. I know I will."

Mom completed the transcription, pulled the page from the typewriter and placed it in a folder for me. "I made a carbon copy for Mrs. Sanders. I know she'll want to keep it."

"I hope it doesn't make her even sadder."

"Clint, it will make her so proud. It will mean more to her than you can imagine."

"OK. Thanks, Mom."

"You're welcome. And Clint?"

"Yes ma'am?"

"I'm really proud of you for doing this."

"Thanks, Mom."

J. Neil Sherouse

Saturday morning was clear and cool. The funeral was to begin at 10:00, but I wanted to get to the funeral home well ahead of time to meet with Joe Mike Dasher, my patrol leader from Scouts, who was to accompany me on guitar. Dressed in my new suit—the one we purchased for me to wear to the Spring Dance—I was dropped at the funeral home at nine o'clock by Mom, who then went back home to return later with the rest of the family. Joe Mike was waiting for me. We ran through the song a couple of times, and then I sought out Chaplain Adamson to confirm the order for the service. By nine thirty, I was waiting in the foyer for my family. Christine and her family entered, and she and I spoke a few words. She was visibly upset and had been crying. Then, to my surprise, my Grandma Cooper waked in with Jake, who was wearing a dark suit, white shirt, and tie. I hugged my grandmother, then Jake.

"Jake, man, I'm so glad to see you! It really means a lot that you're here."

"Hey, wouldn't have missed this, and I'm not, thanks to your grandma. But I'm not sure where Black folks sit at a white funeral."

"I can tell you where you're gonna sit. You're gonna sit with me and my family."

At that moment, Sam's friend from the Youth Bi-Racial Committee, David Robinson, came in. I introduced him to Jake, and insisted he sit with us. Within minutes, my family had arrived. We all signed the guest book, then took seats near the front. I sat on the end of the row so I could slip out easily when my time came to sing and speak. Joe Mike and his guitar had taken up a position to the side of the podium behind several large floral displays. Jake was seated beside me with rest of our group filling the remainder of the pew. As I scanned the growing crowd, I noticed a number of young men, several of whom I recognized as friends of Sam's from the track team at school. I caught Christine's eye and she smiled at me. Also, seated in the back, were three young men in Navy uniform. They appeared to me uncomfortable to be there.

Sam's open casket was at the front of the chapel, and some guests were walking up to stare at his body. I had no intention of doing so, nor did anyone else in our family group venture forward. The organist was playing hymns on the Hammond organ with every bit of vibrato the old instrument could summon. I couldn't help but think "Sam would hate this!" A few minutes before the hour, the funeral director and another member of his staff walked down the center aisle, closed the casket, and spread the Stars and Stripes over it. He then asked us all to stand and Mrs. Sanders entered, escorted by Chaplain Adamson. After Mrs. Sanders was seated on the front row, the chaplain directed us to sit and the service began.

After a prayer and a reading, the chaplain called on me. My heart was in my throat and my temples throbbed. I feared I was going to be sick but managed to get myself up to the podium. I was to share my remarks and then sing. I placed the folder containing my typed eulogy on the podium, opened it, nervously cleared my throat, looked out at the cabbage-headed congregants and began to read.

I'm Clint Cooper. I'm a friend of Sam's. I knew Sam Sanders most of my life, but I didn't really get to know him until right after my birthday when I turned eight. My birthday is right after Christmas, and I needed help learning to ride the bike I had gotten for Christmas. Sam took me down to the track at my school and spent a couple of hours teaching me to ride. The only thing he didn't teach me was how to stop, so I kind of crashed when I rode back home. Everybody but me thought that was funny.

After that, Sam and I became really good friends. We rode our bikes around the Ravines lots of times. We went crabbing on the river. He went on vacation with us to the mountains, and he and I went camping together at my grandmother's in Campville. One time, we paddled our canoe across the river to look for an Indian mound. He took me to my first Maroons football game.

We did all kinds of things together, but we also talked a lot about important things. Sam taught me about growing up, about how white folks need to treat Black folks better, about why countries go to war and why they should try not to. Sam was like a big brother to me, except better because we never fought. He was always teaching me things and helping me become a better person.

I guess we looked kind of funny together, big tall Sam and skinny little me, but he never seemed to mind. Sam's friendship with me gave me a lot of self-confidence to try things I never thought I could do. He made me feel special and important to him. He didn't have to hang around with me, but he didn't do it for him. He did it for me. He knew I needed him in my life. He was just good like that.

Besides my family, Sam was the most important person in my life, and I loved him like a brother. One time, when we were down in the Ravines, we got to talking about how most people live their lives and then no one remembers them after they're gone. I promised Sam that I would never forget him, that I would remember him for the rest of my life. Of course, I thought we would both live to be old men and still be friends. I never thought he would die so young. But I will still remember him the rest of my life and miss him every day. Thank you.

Somehow, I made it through reading those words without falling apart. Others, including my mother and Mrs. Sanders, did not fare so well. I then moved across the dais to where Joe Mike was standing with his guitar. I nodded to him, and he began to finger-pick the opening chords. Pushing aside my grief, I sang to Sam. I sang for Sam.

> *All my trials, Lord,*
> *Soon be over.*
> *I've got a little book with pages three;*
> *And every page sings hope to me.*
> *All my trials, Lord,*
> *Soon be over.*
> *If heaven was a thing that money could buy,*
> *Well, the rich would live, and the poor would die.*
> *All my trials, Lord,*
> *Soon be over.*
> *Too late now brothers;*
> *Too late to change your mind.*
> *All my trials, Lord,*
> *Soon be over.*
> *There grew a tree in Paradise,*
> *Believers call it the Tree of Life.*
> *All my trials, Lord,*
> *Soon be over.*
> *If I had wings, I sure would fly*
> *To be with you in the by and by.*
> *All my trials, Lord,*
> *Soon be over.*
> *Too late now brothers;*
> *Too late to change your mind.*
> *All my trials, Lord,*
> *Soon be over.*[16]

16 The folk song "All My Trials," was popularized by a number of singers during the 1950s and '60s, though its origins are somewhat clouded in mystery. Although

I really didn't know if others would like the song or think it appropriate, but I knew that Sam would like it, and that's all that mattered to me that day. As I took my seat beside Jake, he reached over and squeezed my arm boosting my confidence and affirming my efforts. After the service ended and we filed out to drive to the cemetery, several attendees thanked me for my words and the song. We then drove in silent procession to Oak Hill Cemetery. Once there, the hearse was met by a Navy honor guard of six uniformed sailors who bore Sam's casket to the open grave. What followed was a brief internment officiated by the chaplain. Then, two of the honor guard folded the flag that had been draped over Sam's casket and presented it to Mrs. Sanders. A bugler nearby began to play "Taps" and I fell apart. All the determination I had mustered to make it through the service collapsed around me and I sobbed inconsolably. Surprisingly, it was my dad who rescued me, led me to our station wagon and tucked me into the back seat to cry in private.

"You did good today, Son. I'm really proud of you, and Sam would be too. You had to keep it together when the rest of us didn't have to. Now, you need to let it out. Let your tears flow, Son. Get it out."

And get it out I did. While my parents visited with Mrs.

---

ethnomusicologists have meticulously documented the histories of many American folk songs, "All My Trials" is not among the catalogue of their work. The first known recording of the song was in 1956 by Bob Gibson under the title "Bahamian Lullaby." The following two releases of the song—by Cynthia Gooding in 1957, and Billy Faier in 1959—credit Erik Darling as having passed it on to them. Gooding claimed that the song had originated as a "white spiritual" that made its way to the British West Indies and then returned to the states with a gentle island rhythm. Joan Baez, who released the song as "All My Trials" in 1960, suggested it began as a pre-Civil War gospel song, traveled to the Bahamas, and was forgotten in the US until being rediscovered during the American folk music revival of the 1940s through mid-60s. Others who have recorded variations of the song include Peter, Paul, and Mary, the Kingston Trio, Pete Seeger, The Seekers, Paul McCartney, and Ray Stevens. Needless to say, there are numerous versions of both the text and tune. The text, as used here, was adapted for inclusion in this novel.

Sanders and others in attendance, I sat in the car and sobbed. After about ten minutes or so, when my well of tears had run dry, the car door opened, Will climbed in and just sat beside me and hugged me. He never said a word, just comforted me in his own way. After I had regained my composure, Will and I returned to the dwindling crowd and I was able to visit with Jake and Sam's friend David. Just before we left to return home, Chaplain Adamson sought me out.

"Clint, you did today what a lot of adults would have had a hard time doing. I know it meant a lot to Mrs. Sanders, and Sam would have been so proud of you."

"Thank you, sir. You knew him, right?"

"Yes, I did. I had gotten to know Sam pretty well over the past couple of months. He was an exceptional young man and an exceptional sailor. I learned even more about him today through what you shared about him. I just wanted to thank you and wish you the very best. Like you said, I know you will keep Sam with you for the rest of your life. In that way, his life will continue in you."

"Yes sir. Thank you."

The following days were lifeless for me. I returned to school on Monday, but simply stumbled through the week with no thought but to put one foot in front of the other. Christine and I walked together each morning but spoke little. At school, some friends and teachers said kind words to me, others seemed to avoid me for lack of anything helpful to say. Slowly, I began to regain emotional balance, life began to be enjoyable, laughter returned, the Spring Dance came and went, and the years unrolled before me—high school, college, law school—all in the blink of an eye.

PART IV

34.

*YOU SHALL KNOW THE TRUTH, AND
THE TRUTH SHALL SET YOU FREE.*
-JESUS, JOHN 8:32

MY APPOINTMENT WITH the JAG officer in charge of legal services at the Naval Air Station in Jacksonville had been set for 10:00 am on Tuesday, January 16. To this point, 1979 had begun with the life-altering visit by Mrs. Sanders and her very credible assertion that Sam's death had been something other than an accident. This had led me down a rabbit hole of investigation in an attempt to piece together the last weeks of his life, fourteen years in the past. As I drove the long-familiar route north on highway 17—the same route I had taken with Mrs. Sanders in December 1964, when we picked Sam up for his Christmas leave—I was struck by how little things had changed. The ramshackle old buildings along the way remained, looking only slightly more ramshackle. Yet I was so dramatically changed from that day so long ago. As I turned into the base entrance, I was suddenly seized by the same emotions that had filled me on that long-ago day—excitement, anxiety and uncertainly. The guard at the gate confirmed my appointment and gave me directions to the Legal Services Building. After parking and entering, I was met by a young officer who escorted me to the office of Lieutenant Commander Ezra Lightner, senior JAG officer for the base.

"Mr. Cooper, please come in. I'm Ezra Lightner, JAG officer

in charge here." He extended his hand, we shook, and he directed me to a chair. "I know a little about why you're here, but please fill in the details for me."

"Certainly, and thank you for seeing me. Here's my card." I placed my business card on his desk and sat back down. "I know you're busy, so let me just jump in. In April, 1964, a young seaman by the name of Sam Sanders died here on base in what was, at the time, ruled an accident. He was running a floor machine in the officers' mess late at night and was somehow electrocuted. They didn't find him until the next morning. I should tell you that Sam was a good friend of mine and that I represent his mother as her attorney. At any rate, a couple of weeks ago, Mrs. Sanders, Sam's mother, came to see me. Long story short, she made a very strong case that Sam's death was not accidental."

"I see. So, what was the basis of her claim?"

"Commander, Sam was a homosexual and very much in the closet. He really wanted to serve and knew he had to keep that fact hidden."

"Certainly. It would have meant immediate dishonorable discharge if that fact had become widely known."

"Exactly. And Sam understood this. However, he thought he had found another sailor who was interested in him. They went to a movie together here on base and Sam tried to take his hand. The whole thing went sideways, and that other sailor, and at least one other, undertook a campaign of harassment against Sam. Mrs. Sanders brought me a trove of letters Sam had written her about the incident and the harassment that followed. I read them over very carefully, and I agree with her that Sam's death could have been the last incident in that escalating series directed at him."

"I see. Forgive me, Mr. Cooper, but that's pretty sketchy evidence to support such a charge. And I don't mean to sound like an ass, but is it possible that you're not quite as objective as you might otherwise be if Sam hadn't been your friend?"

"I understand. And no offense taken. Frankly, I've asked myself that same question a dozen times over the past two weeks, 'Am I letting my personal feelings hijack my objectivity? Am I pursuing this because Sam was a close friend?' Honestly, Commander, I'm pretty confident my questions about the circumstances of Sam's death are justified by a reasonable measure of doubt based on what I read in Sam's letters to his mother."

"Alright. I'm willing to accept that on face value, but I need to make it clear that my office will not pursue this matter. I'm willing to offer you some support if you want to continue to look into this, but, as far as I'm concerned, I will not recommend that NCIS look into it. It's just too cold a case and there doesn't appear to be much to go on other than a few old letters."

"I fully understand your position, Commander. All I was hoping for was that you might be able to give me access to some information so that I could continue my own investigation."

"Exactly what sort of help are you wanting?"

"Well, sir, I was hoping to be able to see the military records of Sam as well as two other sailors—the two who were harassing Sam before his death. If that's not possible, I would appreciate any contact information for them or their parents that might be available. Also, I was hoping to have access to Sam's autopsy report."

"Alright, Mr. Cooper, let me see what I can do. I'll need the full names and ranks of the sailors involved." He grabbed a pen and legal pad and prepared to write down the information he had requested.

"Certainly. They are Seaman Samuel Adams Sanders, Seaman Apprentice James Boatwright—I don't have a middle name—and Seaman Apprentice Steven Reynolds. Again, I don't have a middle name. I do know that all three enlisted in the summer of 1964 and trained together here from then at least until Sam's death in April 1965."

"That should be enough to go on. As to the autopsy, I just don't know. I'll see what I can find out."

"Oh, and one other thing."

"Yes."

"There was a chaplain serving here on base at the time. He counseled Sam and also officiated at his funeral. I'd really like to speak with him. I don't have much to go on, but I do have his card from back then." I fished Chaplain Adamson's business card from my jacket pocket and handed it to him. He wrote the information on his pad and handed the card back to me.

"Again, I'll see what I can do."

"Thank, you sir. I really appreciate it. One other question."

"Yes?"

"I have to confess, I'm not very familiar with the UCMJ. Assuming I uncover enough evidence to convince you to have NCIS investigate, is there any provision in the code to charge discharged personnel under military law?"

"Well, yes, but—and it's a big 'but'—Article 3 of the UCMJ allows for the reactivation of a former service member who is discovered to have committed a crime while in the service so that he can face courts martial under the code. This rarely happens, and only under extreme cases. So, that being said, don't hold out for that, even if you do find convincing evidence that one or both of these seamen were involved in Seaman Sanders' death."

"I understand. And again, thank you for your time and for your help in this."

"You're welcome. I'll contact you within the week with what

I've been able to uncover."

"Thank you." I rose, we shook hands again, and he walked me to the entrance of the building.

About a week later, I received a call from Commander Lightner. Surprisingly, he had a good bit of actionable information for me. First, he had obtained copies of all three seamen's military records. In reviewing them, he found that Sam's record was impeccable up until the time of his death. His reviews were all positive and there was no hint of any suspicion regarding his sexual orientation. Seaman James Boatwright had been assigned to a swift boat crew in Vietnam. He was killed in action on February 13, 1966, when his boat was attacked in the Mekong River Delta by Vietcong forces. His death benefit was paid to his parents in Demopolis, Alabama. Commander Lightner provided their address. Seaman Steven Reynolds became a Corpsman on a hospital ship. He was discharged in July 1967, and his final pay and discharge papers sent to an address in Valdosta, Georgia. Again, the commander provided that address.

The one piece of disappointing news was that there had been no investigation of Sam's death and no autopsy. The medical examiner's report listed the cause of death as an accidental electrocution and the matter was closed. Finally, Lightner told me that Chaplain Adamson had retired several years ago and was now living in Jacksonville. As it turned out, the current chaplain on base knew him well, and stated that Adamson was now serving as an assistant rector at San Jose Episcopal Church there in the city.

As soon as I hung up with Commander Lightner, I phoned Mrs. Sanders to tell her what I had learned. She was pleased that we now had some direction to the investigation, and also pleased that Sam's military record was untainted. I next phoned the church in Jacksonville where Chaplain Adamson was on staff. He was surprised to hear from me and readily agreed to meet the following Monday morning. After that call, I asked Paula to clear my calendar for the following week. A road trip was in the works.

I debated within myself whether to phone Seaman Boatwright's parents to probe for information or simply to show up on their doorstep. Despite the extra driving it would require, I decided the element of surprise might be of benefit, particularly if they chose to withhold information from me. Then again, what if I drove all the way to Demopolis and they were out of town—on vacation or visiting relatives? I finally concluded that it was worth that risk to simply knock on their door unannounced. Having settled that matter, I began to plan my itinerary. My first stop would be to talk with Chaplain Adamson. Then, I would make the long drive to Demopolis, followed by a loop back to Valdosta, and home. In preparation for my pilgrimage, I drew up lists of questions for each of those I hoped to interview.

35.

THE LONG ROAD HOME

ON MONDAY MORNING, January 29, I left my apartment and drove to Jacksonville. I found San Jose Church easily, parked, and followed the signs to the church office. Chaplain Adamson was expecting me.

"Clint Cooper. I never expected to see you again. Welcome, and how you've changed! I still tell folks about the remarkable eulogy you gave at Seaman Sanders' funeral. How old were you, fourteen?"

"Thirteen, sir, and it's good to see you again."

"Let's take a little walk. I want to show you my favorite place here for serious conversation." We walked along a colonnade toward the sanctuary. The chaplain spoke in a hushed tone. "Given the reason you're here, I just thought a more out-of-the way spot might be good for us to talk. The little chapel here is very quiet and very private." We made our way across the transept of the main sanctuary to a small adjoining chapel.

"This is an unusual room."

"You see why I like it? It's constructed entirely of coquina rock."

"I see that."

"A fellow named Jim Russell built it. He also built a small community of houses out of this rock. Every one of them is different. Somehow, the porous nature of the stone absorbs sound. Did you notice how quiet it got when we stepped in here?"

"Yes, as a matter of fact, I did." We took seats in one of the wooden pews at the front of the chapel.

"Clint, you mentioned on the phone that you wanted to ask me about Sam, and I understand you're his mother's attorney."

"That's correct. Chaplain, I know that he shared with you some of what was going on with him in the last few months of his life. I know that normally clergy confidentiality would prevent you from discussing any of what Sam shared with you, but I hope you'll feel that limitation died along with Sam."

"That is a bit of a conundrum for clergy. Just when and under what circumstances are we released from that obligation? I want to help you and Mrs. Sanders, but some of what Sam shared with me was very confidential and I don't know that he'd want me to reveal it, even in death."

"Maybe this will help. When I was nine, Sam told me he was a homosexual. He also told his mother before he enlisted. In addition, we are both aware of the incident with Seaman Boatwright and the harassment that it triggered. Does that help you with your conflict of conscience?"

"Yes, it certainly does. Alright, then, what can I fill in for you?"

"Sam and I carried on a correspondence during the time he was stationed at NAS Jacksonville, but he never told me about the incident with Boatwright nor about the harassment he received. I learned about all that by reading his letters to his mother. In those letters, he mentioned that Boatwright and another sailor, Steve Reynolds, were the main perpetrators of the pranks against him. Are you aware of any others who were involved?"

"No. Those were the only two Sam mentioned. He did say that a lot of the others in his barracks started avoiding him, but honestly, I think that was more because they didn't want to be targeted by whoever was doing these things. I didn't get the sense that Boatwright had told very many people. Do you plan to talk with him?"

"I can't. He was killed in Vietnam less than a year after Sam died. I have his parents' address in Alabama, and I'm heading there after I leave here. I'm really just pulling on loose threads, to be honest."

"I understand."

"Did Sam ever mention that he felt he was in serious physical danger from Boatwright?"

"No, but he did say he felt like the pranks and harassment were escalating, and I agreed with him. It started out with his shoes being tossed into the yard, then escalated to someone urinating on his dress uniform. I know they wrote 'fag' on his footlocker. There were a few other things, too. Honestly, it all seemed pretty juvenile, but of course there was no way he could report any of it because he would have to have revealed what had triggered it. Or, if Boatwright or Reynolds were questioned, they would certainly have destroyed his career in the Navy."

"Exactly. So he really had no option but to endure it. He couldn't retaliate, and he couldn't report. Chaplain, did you ever question whether Sam's death could have been the result of this escalation?"

Adamson drew a deep breath. "Frankly, yes. I did wonder about it. But his death was ruled an accident. I don't think there was any sort of investigation. They just determined the floor machine shorted out and killed him. Still, I wondered."

"You're right. I met with the head JAG officer two weeks ago. He was very helpful but found out there was no investigation and no autopsy. The medical examiner just ruled it accidental electrocution and they looked no closer at it. I guess they really had no reason to do so. One thing that I don't know, and I don't know why I didn't think to ask Commander Lightner, was the condition of Sam's body when he was found. Do you know anything about that?"

"A little bit. They found him early the next morning when the kitchen crew reported to begin prepping for breakfast. From what I heard and what I remember—I mean this was a major incident, at least for a few days anyway—he was lying in a pool of water beside the floor machine. It was tipped over. There were burn marks on both his hands and one of his shoes was off. They determined the jolt had literally blown the shoe off his foot. That's really all I know."

"Jesus! Sorry."

"Not to worry. I say his name frequently, and not always out of devotion."

We both chuckled. "Do you know if there were any marks on his body, like maybe he had been hit or beaten?"

"No. I don't know about that, but I think I would have heard if such were the case. And I suppose they would have investigated further if it looked like there was any foul play."

"Sure, that makes sense. Well, I guess that's it. I really appreciate your time. It's been good to see you again."

"Clint, I don't know where this is going to end for you. Personally, I hope Sam's death was an accident. If it wasn't, this whole incident is much more sinister and there's at least one person who's kept a terrible secret for fourteen years. I'd like to say good luck, but I don't know what that means."

"I know. I'm just looking for answers, for an alternative explanation, if there is one. Mrs. Sanders needs some resolution, and now, so do I. Thank you again."

"You're welcome, and I hope some of this has been helpful. Please let me know what you find out, OK?"

"Will do."

"Can you find your way out? I think I'll stay here a while."

"Sure. I was a Boy Scout." We laughed, shook hands and I exited the way we had entered.

Interstate 10 runs east to west from Florida to California. The stretch through the panhandle had been fully completed just within the last year, so I had determined to drive it to Mobile, Alabama, before heading north on US 43 to Demopolis. This route is, for the most part, rural. I once passed a dead alligator on the shoulder that had obviously had an unfortunate run-in with a vehicle. To say this drive was boring would be understating the obvious. I arrived in Mobile that evening feeling dull and travel-weary, found a room at a cheap motel, and slept soundly until six the next morning. After a shower and breakfast, I was on the road again, driving north through western Alabama.

Demopolis, Alabama, is a river town settled atop a high chalk embankment at the convergence of the Black Warrior and Tombigbee Rivers. I arrived there around ten that morning and made my way to River Road, easily locating the Boatwrights' house. The modest but well-kept home backed up to the Black Warrior River. There were two vehicles parked to the side of the house—a well-used pickup and a later model sedan. My assumption was that both Mr. and Mrs. Boatwright were at home. My stomach was in knots as I exited my car and walked up their front steps, knocked on their front door, and waited. Within seconds, the door was opened by a fiftyish woman wearing an apron.

"May I help you?"

I adopted my most honey-dipped Southern accent. "Yes ma'am. My name's Clint Cooper. I'm an attorney from Florida and I'm looking for the Boatwrights, the parents of Seaman James Boatwright." She was immediately on guard.

"I'm Erma Boatwright. Jimmy was my son. What's this about?"

"Mrs. Boatwright, may I come in, and is your husband home?"

"Yes, come in. My husband is out in the shed. I'll get him.

Please have a seat in the parlor. I'll be right back." She ushered me into a comfortable room nicely furnished with antiques. I perched on a spindly settee that looked as if it might support my modest weight and waited uncomfortably for her return. Toward the back of the house, I heard muffled conversation but distinctly made out the words "lawyer" and "Jimmy." Within seconds, Mrs. Boatwright returned followed by an enormous man in a flannel shirt and overalls. He extended his hand.

"Mr. Cooper, is it?"

"Yes sir."

"I'm Jim Boatwright. Erma tells me you're a lawyer from Florida askin' about Jimmy?"

"Yes sir. I apologize for just showing up like this. I'm on something of a road trip trying to get some information for a client of mine."

"Well, let's us sit down and you please explain what this is all about."

"Yes sir." Jim and Erma took seats across from me and I jumped into my less-than-straightforward explanation. "My client is a Mrs. Sanders. Her son, Sam, trained at the Naval Air Station in Jacksonville with your son James."

"We always called him Jimmy, but he told us he was goin' to be James in the Navy. You do know he's gone, don't you?"

"Yes ma'am, I do, and please accept my condolences. As I understand it, he died a hero in Vietnam."

"Yes sir, he did. He was on a boat on patrol in the Mekong River and they were attacked. The VC hit the boat with an RPG and the boat went right down. Only two of the crew made it."

"I'm so sorry, Mr. Boatwright."

"Thank you, sir. Now, how can we help you?"

"Well, I'm actually trying to locate a mutual friend of James and Sam Sanders, a sailor named Steve Reynolds. He trained with the two of them. Did James ever mention him or Sam to either of you?" Now that I had established the nature of my visit, both the Boatwrights became noticeably less anxious.

Jim continued, "I don't think I ever heard him mention a Sam Sanders. Did you, honey?"

"No, I don't think I've ever heard that name." Their responses were so slathered in polite Southern that I couldn't accurately gauge their veracity.

"But he did talk about Steve Reynolds. In fact, he left us some instructions to let Steve know if anything happened to him when he was in Vietnam."

"Really? What did he ask you to do?"

Erma picked up the conversation. "Well, around the middle of the summer he shipped out, that was '65, we got a letter from him with an envelope addressed to Steve Reynolds in Valdosta, Georgia. Jimmy's letter said that if anything happened to him in Vietnam, and we took that to mean if he was killed, to please mail the letter to Steve. We thought it was kinda strange, but, of course, when Jimmy got killed, we sent the letter."

"So, the letter was addressed to Steve in Valdosta, right?"

"Yes sir."

"Did you by any chance write down the address and did you happen to read the letter that was inside that envelope?"

"Yes sir," Erma responded. "I did write down the address in case I needed it for some reason, but we didn't open the envelope."

"We didn't think it was any of our business," Jim commented.

"Certainly. Mrs. Boatwright could you possibly locate that address?"

"Oh yes, it's here in the desk. I have every letter that Jimmy wrote us, too." She left her seat and walked across the room to a beautiful cherry fold-top desk, opened it, and retrieved an index card from a small basket inside.

"I know its presumptuous of me, but could I possibly read the letter from Jimmy that the letter to Steve was enclosed in?" Of course, I wanted to read all of James' letters, but couldn't devise a credible reason for asking to do so.

"Well, yes, I suppose, if that would help you."

"Thank you. It might give me another clue to go on to find Steve." She returned to the desk and withdrew an envelope, then handed the index card and the envelope to me.

"1113 Toombs Street in Valdosta. Let me jot that down." I withdrew a pen and small notepad from my jacket pocket and made a show of writing down the address. It simply confirmed the address already provided me by Commander Lightner. I then opened the envelope and drew out the letter from James. As I began to read, a sadness overcame me.

23 July, 1965
NAS JAX
Dear Mama and Daddy,

Like you know, I'm heading to Vietnam in just a few days and wanted to get this to you before I go. Inside here is a letter to my buddy Steve Reynolds. This letter is to him but it's addressed to his parents' house. If anything happens to me, please mail this letter. It's important because Steve needs some information from me that I can't give him right now. I know this sounds weird, but it will make sense to Steve.

Please don't worry about me. I'm going to be on a boat. You know I know how to drive boats better than I know how to drive cars, so I'll be fine on the water.

I know I haven't always been the best son. I've tried to do things right, but I've messed up some, too. But I'll try to make you proud fighting for America. Just remember that

I'll always love you.

Love,
James (aka Jimmy)

"Are you alright, son?"

"Yes sir. Sorry. There were just so many young men who must have written letters to their parents like this one."

"Yes, I'm sure there were," Jim nodded. "Jimmy was just one of them, I suppose."

"Jimmy was always a good boy," Erma commented. "Smart. Done well in school."

"We was hoping he'd go to college, but he wanted to see the world. Growin' up here on the river, I guess the Navy seemed like his ticket outta here. Was there anything in the letter to help you?"

"No sir, I don't think so, but thank you both so much for letting me invade your privacy by reading it. Again, I'm so sorry for your loss."

Mrs. Boatwright was teary-eyed as she responded. "Well, we sure hope this helps you find Steve. If you do, please ask him to get in touch with us. We'd like to hear his stories about Jimmy. And what about Mrs. Sanders' son, Sam? Do you think he'd talk to us about Jimmy?"

"I'm sorry, ma'am. Sam died about a year before Jimmy."

"In the war?"

"No sir. It was in an accident on base. Well, I've taken up enough of your time. Thank you both again for your help."

"We're happy to help. Would you like something to drink before you go? Maybe a glass of tea?"

"No ma'am, thank you. I probably need to get on my way to Valdosta."

"So, your next stop is Steve's parents?"

"Yes sir. That's my plan. Again, thank you." I stood and

began to make my way toward the front door. I was in the grip of conflicting emotions, walling me in on every side. I needed to get away, and quickly.

"Well, best of luck to you, Mr. Cooper. And, if you locate Steve, please ask him to get in touch with us."

"I certainly will."

"And please give Mrs. Sanders our condolences."

"Yes, sir."

I was out the door and down the steps. They stood on the porch and waved as I drove away. My heart was pounding, my temples throbbed, my breathing came in gasps. I gripped the wheel as though I could barely control the car. Careening back up River Road toward town, tears began to overflow my eyes, such that I had to pull into the parking lot of a Piggly Wiggly to avoid veering off the road. I parked and dropped my head to the steering wheel sobbing uncontrollably. What the hell was wrong with me? Why was I in such a state? As my breathing slowed and I regained my composure, I began to understand the genesis of my meltdown. The Boatwrights were good people, and James was likely a good person, as well. Their grief was justified, and they suffered the loss of a child as did Mrs. Sanders. What had most rattled and disoriented me was that I had experienced an emotion I had never anticipated. I had felt sympathy for James Boatwright.

My visit with the Boatwrights had taken only about a half hour. It was nearing lunch time, but I had no appetite, so I began the long drive to Valdosta. When I planned this fact-finding trip, I had failed to realize that my route from Demopolis toward Valdosta would take me along US highway 80, through the town of Selma and across the Edmund Pettus Bridge. My planned route would then follow that taken by the marchers in March 1965, on their way to Montgomery. This fact eluded me until I hit the outskirts of Selma. Then, it struck like a bolt from the blue.

Highway 80 runs due east from Demopolis, but in Selma, makes a hard-right turn to the south. After that turn, and in less than five miles, the high arch of the bridge loomed ahead of me. I was entering a pilgrimage route, sacred and soaked with the blood of those valiant citizens who chose to leave their very ordinary lives to take up a very extraordinary cause. Chills coursed through me. My eyes misted over. Near the foot of the bridge, I found a parking spot, got out and started walking up the bridge toward its center. I remembered reading that the marchers could not see the opposite end of the bridge—could not see the law officers amassed to beat them—as they began their peaceful walk on that fateful Sunday. Now I understood why. The arch of the bridge is steep and, coming from the north, it is impossible to see the highway beyond the apex of the bridge.

When I reached the center of the arch, I gazed toward the other end. Traffic was moving; commerce was alive. There were no memorials, no historical markers that I could see. To the good citizens of Selma, it was as if nothing of significance had happened here. As I stood, transfixed by the irony of the place, it occurred to me that I was likely within a few yards of where Rev. Hosea Williams had asked twenty-five-year-old John Lewis, upon seeing the assemblage of evil at the foot of the bridge, if he knew how to swim.

After a few minutes, I returned to my car, drove across the bridge, and continued my own pilgrimage. An hour or so later, I stopped for a late lunch and gas, then continued on, passing through Montgomery mid-afternoon. I still had at least five hours ahead of me and exhaustion had taken hold, so I pressed on a couple more hours and stopped for the night in Eufaula, Alabama on the border with Georgia.

The next morning, I took my time leaving Eufaula as the drive to Valdosta would only require about three hours. I didn't want to arrive at lunch time, so delayed my departure until mid-morning. When I had made the decision to arrive at the Boatwrights' front door unannounced, I had made a similar decision regarding the Reynolds in Valdosta. Around two o'clock that afternoon, I parked on Toombs Street in front of a craftsman-style house in need of a fresh coat of paint. Immediately, those old anxieties returned. I mustered my courage and knocked on the door. Mrs. Reynolds opened the door to me within seconds.

"Hello. Can I help you?"

"I hope so. I'm looking for the Reynolds, the parents of Seaman Steve Reynolds."

"I'm Lavonia Reynolds, Steve's mother. My husband is deceased. Is everything alright? Is Steve alright?"

"Yes, ma'am, as far as I know. Let me explain myself. My name is Clint Cooper. I'm an attorney from Palatka, Florida, and I'm trying to locate Steve. He was in the Navy with the son of my client, Mrs. Sanders. Her son's name was Sam, and they were also friends with a sailor named James Boatwright. Are either of those names familiar to you?"

"Yes. I know the name James Boatwright. What's this all about?"

"Yes ma'am. I'm sorry to be confusing. Would you mind if I came in, or if we sat here on the porch a bit?"

"No, of course. Please come in." We stepped into the front room of the house and took seats across from each other. "Mrs. Reynolds, let me explain why I'm here. As I said, my client is a Mrs. Sanders. Her son, Sam, was a mutual Navy friend of your son, Steve, and James Boatwright. Both Sam and James are deceased and I'm trying to get some information on Sam for Mrs. Sanders. Yesterday, I visited with James Boatwright's parents in Alabama. They actually provided your address, so I drove here to speak with you."

"I see. You said you were looking for some information. What sort of information are you looking for?" Her defenses were up as though she sensed a sinister purpose to my visit. I needed to put her at ease quickly.

"Mrs. Reynolds, both Sam Sanders and James Boatwright are dead. They died while serving in the Navy within a year of each other. Both Mrs. Sanders and the Boatwrights know very little about their sons' lives in the Navy, and they all are hoping Steve can fill in some of the gaps for them. The Boatwrights asked me specifically that, if I found Steve, to ask him to contact them. They and Mrs. Sanders just want to know more about their sons' time in the service."

"I see. I guess that makes sense. I guess if something had happened to Steve while he was in the service I'd want to know more. Probably want to talk to some of the fellows who served with him. Like I said, I know of James Boatwright, but I never heard Steve mention a Sam Sanders."

"Yes ma'am. When I visited with the Boatwrights, they told me that James had left a letter with them that was to be sent to Steve here at home if anything happened to him, to James, during his tour in Vietnam. Do you remember that letter?"

"Yes, I do. When it came, Steve was still overseas, so I didn't open it. The next time I wrote him, I told him about it. He wrote back and asked me keep the letter until he got out and got home. He said he was pretty sure he knew what it said, but to please not open it. I really didn't ask him anything else about it. I figured it was some pact they'd made to look after something if either of them got killed. Frankly, I really didn't want to know. When he got discharged that summer, Steve came home and stayed here while he looked for a job. He got the letter then."

"I see. Mrs. Reynolds, where is Steve now?"

"He lives in Macon. He was a Corpsman in the Navy, and he still works in the medical field. He works at Macon Hospital in the x-ray department."

"Would it be possible for me to talk with him?"

"Well, I suppose. I mean, I can give you his phone number."

"That would be great. Could I also have his address in case I need to write him?"

"Yes, certainly. I'll write those down for you. Give me just a minute. Can I get you something to drink? I have some fresh ice tea made."

"A small glass of tea would be great, thank you." She left me briefly while she poured my tea and wrote down Steve's phone number and address. I had no doubts she would phone him about my visit and that could very well make it impossible for me to get any useful information from him. My mind was racing. Assuming he worked a day shift at the hospital, she would likely be unable to reach him until he arrived home from work. If I could be waiting for him at his home, I might be able to intercept him before his mother warned him off. I knew I was probably two hours south of Macon by Interstate 75. If I got away from Valdosta soon and drove the speed limit, I could make it to Steve Reynolds' home before he returned from work. Mrs. Reynolds returned with a glass of tea and a slip of paper with Steve's information written on it.

"I brought some lemon in case you wanted some."

"Thank you, Mrs. Reynolds. I do like lemon in my tea."

"Here's Steve's address and phone number. He's married with two little girls. They're the joy of my life, those two."

"I bet they are."

"My husband died when Steve was in junior high. It sorta took the starch out of him. He lost motivation at school. Lost interest in just about everything. I worked in the registrar's office at the college for thirty-seven years. I always assumed Steve would go to school there, but he just wanted to get out of Valdosta as soon as he graduated from high school."

"Sounds very similar to James Boatwright's and Sam Sanders' stories. The Navy provided a doorway to something else for all three of them. Well, I guess I need to be on my way. Thanks, again, for this information and here's my card if you ever want to contact me."

"Mr. Cooper, how did those boys die, Sam and James?"

"Well, James was on a boat crew in Vietnam. His boat was attacked and he and most of the crew were killed. Sam actually died in an accident on the Naval base in Jacksonville. A piece of equipment shorted out and electrocuted him."

"Oh, my. That's terrible. I guess if I lost my son in the military, I'd rather it be in combat, but I guess it hardly matters to a mother how you lose a child."

"No, ma'am. Probably not. Well, Mrs. Reynolds, I'll be on my way. Thanks for the tea and for taking the time to talk with me. I really appreciate it."

"You're welcome, Mr. Cooper. I hope you can talk to Steve and that he can give you some details that will be of comfort to those boys' folks. It's so sad, and I feel so blessed that Steve made it home OK. Of course, he saw a lot of terrible things, other boys in real bad shape, but he never really talks about it."

"I understand. Again, thank you ma'am."

She walked me to the door and stood in the doorway as I drove off. I made my way to the interstate and headed north. About an hour later, I stopped for gas and picked up a map of Macon. After some squinting at the street list on the map (could they possibly use a tinier type face?) I found the block in which Steve Reynolds' home was located. An hour later, I was parked on his street about a hundred yards from his front door. It was just after five in the afternoon, and there was no activity at the Reynolds' home. Sitting there, staring forward, I felt like a cop on stakeout in some B movie. Something about what I was doing just felt sleazy and underhanded.

Within minutes, a late-model Toyota sedan pulled into the driveway and a young woman and two elementary-aged girls got out and entered the house through the side door. The knots in my stomach returned. Steve arrived in a small Toyota pick-up about fifteen minutes later. He was dressed in scrubs and made his way to the side door. I exited my vehicle, walked briskly to the front door and rang the bell. The younger Mrs. Reynolds answered.

"Hello."

"Hello. Mrs. Reynolds?"

"Yes. Can I help you?"

"I was wondering if I could speak with your husband." I passed her my business card. "I'm Clint Cooper, an attorney from Florida, and I'd like to talk to your husband about a Navy acquaintance of his."

"I see. He just got home. He may have already jumped in the shower. Please come in and let me see if he can talk right now."

"Thank you." She showed me into what appeared to be a family room with an overstuffed couch and console TV. She returned in less than a half-minute.

"Steve hadn't gotten in the shower yet, so he'll be right here. Can I get you something to drink?"

"No, thank you. I'm fine." Steve Reynolds appeared within seconds. I stood and extended my hand. My heart was racing such that I feared he might hear it. My tongue stuck to the roof of my mouth as I began to speak. "Mr. Reynolds, I'm Clint Cooper. I'm an attorney from Florida and was hoping to ask you a few questions about a couple of sailors who trained with you in Jacksonville."

"I see. OK." He took a seat to the right of the couch where I had been sitting. I sat back down and turned toward him. "Who did you want to ask me about?"

"I wanted to talk with you about James Boatwright and Sam Sanders." He blanched, then drew in a long breath.

"I figured somebody'd come around someday to ask about them."

"Then you know why I'm here?"

"Yeah. Pretty much. What do you want to know?"

"First, let me tell you who I am, what I know, and what I'm looking for. I'm Sam Sanders' mother's attorney. I also grew up with Sam. He was my best friend. His death devasted me and still haunts me. So, you need to know that I'm looking for the truth here, and I fully expect to get to it. I want you to know that I've met with the senior JAG officer at NAS Jacksonville and with the chaplain who was assigned to the base and knew Sam. I know that Sam was a homosexual, that there was an incident between James and him, and that you and James set about to make Sam's life a living hell after that. I met with James Boatwright's parents yesterday and they gave me your mother's address. I visited with her earlier today. I know that James had a letter sent to you by his parents after his death. I'm pretty confident it had something to do with Sam's death. I don't think Sam's death was an accident, and I think you know something about the circumstances under which Sam died. So, how am I doing so far?'

I paused for a breath, amazed at how forceful and angry I had been in my brief diatribe toward Steve Reynolds. It seemed to have rattled him to the core, which had been my intention. He sat silent, visibly shaking. Tears began to flow down his reddened cheeks. Then, the phone rang. I heard Steve's wife answer the call. She then stepped into the room where we sat in silence. Steve was facing me with his back to her.

"Steve. It's your mother. Shall I tell her you'll call her back?"

He cleared his throat. "Yes, please. Tell her I'll call her later." He then looked directly at me. "I knew this would come out sometime. I've been looking over my shoulder for nearly fifteen years. I'll tell you what you want to know and damn the consequences. I can't carry this any longer."

Mrs. Reynolds appeared in the doorway again. "Steve, she said it's important."

"Tell her I know why she's calling and it's OK. Tell her I can't talk now, and I'll call her later."

"OK."

I then spoke to him in a softer tone. "So, Steve, now that you know what I'm here for, why don't you start at the beginning. If I have questions, I'll interrupt you, but I need to hear your explanation of what happened to Sam."

"OK. So what happened with Sam and James—I mean, they had been best buddies up until then—was that they went to a movie and Sam tried to hold hands with James. It really freaked James out and he got up and left the movie. When he got back to the barracks, he told me about it. He said he was gonna get Sam for what he did."

"OK. That fits with what I know. So, did James threaten Sam's life? What did he say he was going to do to him?"

"No. He didn't say anything like 'I'm gonna kill him,' he just said he was gonna get him back. So, a day or so later, we swiped Sam's boots and threw them out into the drill field. Then, I walked by him in the mess hall and dropped a cigarette into his food tray. It was stuff like that. You know, fraternity prank stuff."

"From Sam's letters to his mother, it seems like you guys

escalated the pranks, though."

"Yeah. I guess James was wanting Sam to react, you know, to fight back or something. I mean we knew he couldn't report what we were doing because James could probably get him kicked out of the Navy. But Sam just kinda took it, so we did some other stuff."

"Like what?"

"Like we wrote 'fag' in big letters on his footlocker with a magic marker. Then James got Sam's dress uniform and we peed on it. That was kind of the line for me. After we did that, I told James I was done. This was gettin' out of hand and I wanted out. James was pissed at me and called me a queer. Then he said he had something special planned for Sam."

"He used those words, 'something special?'"

"Yeah."

"What was that? Did he tell you what he had planned?"

"No. He was still kinda pissed at me, so he quit talking to me about any of it for a few days. Then, Sam got electrocuted by the floor machine when he was doing the floor in the officers' mess. They didn't find him until the next morning." Steve choked on that last sentence and struggled to keep his composure. That ironic sympathy I had felt for James returned, directed toward Steve.

"OK. Take your time. When Sam was killed, did you think that James had something to do with it?'

"Yeah. I thought that the minute I heard about it that morning. I was at work at the base hospital, so I couldn't talk to James. I didn't see him 'til late that afternoon. He was a basket case. He was—I don't know how to describe it—he was scared shitless, and when we got away from people to talk, he was crying and babbling on about not meaning to hurt Sam."

"What did he say exactly?"

"He said he just wanted to scare Sam, to send him a message.

He told me he had messed with the floor machine so it would short out and maybe give Sam a good jolt. He was crying and blubbering about how sorry he was and that he never meant to hurt Sam, that he didn't even really hate him. Then he made me promise to never tell anyone."

"And you agreed? You agreed to keep it a secret? You agreed to protect James?"

"Yeah. I know it was wrong, but he was my friend, and I really believed it was an accident. James was normally a good guy. This thing with Sam just, I don't know, pushed him over some cliff or something. No, I really believed he was telling the truth when he told me he didn't mean to hurt Sam. So, yeah, I agreed to keep quiet about it. It wouldn't bring Sam back, anyway, and I figured James and I would get court martialed for what we did."

"So, how did James act after that? What was he like?"

"It was like he was dead inside. He just went through the motions, you know. About a month after Sam got killed, we were together, and he said he was volunteering for a swift boat crew. He said he hoped he got killed in action so his parents would get his death benefit. He was real depressed. That's when he got the idea for the letter."

"OK. Tell me about that letter. Do you still have it?"

"Hell no. I burned that thing as soon as I read it. So, James said he was giving his parents a letter addressed to me at my mother's house that his folks were supposed to mail me when and if he got killed in Vietnam. I mean, he really just wanted to die. I think he woulda killed himself except that his parents wouldn't have gotten the death payout."

"So, what did the letter say, exactly?"

"So, the letter said something like 'If you're getting this letter, I'm dead. From this time on, if somebody asks you about what happed to Sam Sanders, you can tell them. Tell them I never meant for him to die. I'm releasing you from your promise to me to never tell anyone.' That was it. That's pretty much all it said and pretty much the words he used."

By this point, Steve seemed to have relaxed. Though it sounds cliched, it was apparent by his demeanor that he had unloaded a heavy burden he had carried for a very long time. I felt he had been honest with me and, in some way, had welcomed the opportunity to tell this story.

"Steve, why did you stay quiet all these years? Did you ever tell anyone about all this?"

"No. I never told anyone. I never told my mom and I never even told Michelle, my wife. I guess I figured there was nothing good that could come of telling anyone."

"Did it ever occur to you that Sam's mother had a right to know?"

"I did think about that. But I didn't know if she knew that he was, you know, a homo, and I didn't want to tell her that if she didn't know. It was the excuse I gave myself for not looking her up and telling her."

"I have a couple more questions."

"OK."

"There were three sailors at Sam's funeral. I saw them sitting in the back. Do you know who they were?"

"Jesus. That was you that sang and did the talk about Sam! Jesus! Yeah. I know. It was me, James, and another guy who knew Sam, a guy named Larry Thatcher, but he didn't know anything about who was messing with Sam or how he really died or any of that stuff. He just went to the funeral with us because he liked Sam."

"OK. I had a feeling that it was you and James. I saw you guys before the service started and you looked really uncomfortable."

"It was pretty awful. James said we had to go, like it was some way to say 'I'm sorry' to Sam. Honestly, when you talked, it tore me up. James, too. He was just sittin' there and sobbing."

"One more thing. Sam's mother and I both wrote him pretty regularly. When Sam's stuff was returned to his mother, none of those letters were with his personal effects. Do you know what happened to them?"

"Yeah, I do. Of all the guys they could've asked to pack up Sam's stuff, they asked James. See, most everybody thought they were still good friends, so they asked James to box up Sam's stuff to send to his mom. So, anyway, when he was doing that, he found all those letters, and he was afraid that there was something in them about him and me that could really lead back to him and why Sam died. So, he took them and threw them in the garbage dumpster outside the mess hall."

My stomach heaved. Through all the days since I had reread the letters Sam had written to his mother and me, I had held a paper-thin hope that ours to him might somehow be found in the process of my investigation. Now I knew that that would not be.

"So, what happens next? What's gonna happen to me?"

"I don't know, Steve. I'll be honest with you. When I spoke to the JAG officer about all this, he all but told me the Navy was not interested in pursuing this. I agreed that I would report back to him my findings, but, given the fact that James is dead, there's really no one to prosecute. You conspired to conceal the facts of Sam's death, but I honestly doubt the Navy wants to pursue that, and you've told me that you had nothing to do with rigging the floor machine to short out."

"And I didn't. I swear."

"And I believe you. James, who did, is dead. Right now, I see no value in telling his folks about any of this. They're good people and their final memory of their son is that he died a hero. I don't see any value in taking that away from them. Frankly, it would just be cruel and spiteful."

"Yes, sir."

"I'm going to report back to Mrs. Sanders everything I've discovered—the circumstances under which Sam died, the roles you and James played in his death and in hiding the truth all these years. I think she deserves to hear this from you, too, but what you do is really up to you."

"Yes. I'd really like to talk with her, to apologize."

"I think that would mean a lot to her. She's not an angry woman. She lost her husband in combat in Korea and lost her son in circumstances that have haunted her for years. She deserves some peace, Steve. I think it would be good for you, too, to talk with her and apologize."

"Yes, it would. I've carried this for all these years, and it's been eating at my soul." He began to weep again. "I need to make this right. I need to feel clean of this."

"It looks like you have a good life here. You're in a helping profession. You have a beautiful wife and two cute kids. You need to tell Michelle about all this, too. She deserves to know what has been gnawing at you all this time. Believe me, she knows there's something there."

"She does. I always just tell her it's all the awful stuff I saw when I was on the hospital ship. But you're right, she deserves to know, too. How do I go about talking to Mrs. Sanders?"

"I'll leave you her phone number and my card, too. Give me a few days to talk with her first. Maybe give it a week, then call her. Can I tell her to expect to hear from you?"

"Yes, please."

"After I talk with Commander Lightner, the head JAG officer on the base, I'll phone you and tell you his reaction. Honestly, Steve, other than clearing your own conscience about your role in covering up the truth about Sam's death, I think you're in the clear here. Mrs. Sanders is not a vengeful person. She just wants and deserves answers."

"Yes. Thank you. I know it sounds strange, but in some ways I'm really glad you dug into this and came here today. Like I said, I've been carrying this for a long time. I needed to get it off my chest."

"I appreciate you being honest with me. I needed answers, too. Sam was more than my best friend. He was like a big brother to me. I learned a lot about being a decent human being from him, so I had a big stake in getting to the truth about his death, too."

"I understand, and I apologize to you, too."

"Thank you. Here's my card. I'm going to write Mrs. Sanders' phone number on the back of it." I turned the card over and began to write the phone number I had dialed hundreds of times as I was growing up with Sam. The simple act of doing so brought with it a flood of memories and a piercing pain. "I must have dialed this number a thousand times over the years I was growing up. God, it hurts to write it now."

"I'm sorry, Mr. Cooper. I'm truly sorry."

"I believe you, Steve. Here." I handed the card to him. "Don't disappoint me, or Mrs. Sanders."

"I won't. I promise."

I rose to leave. "I'll call you soon. Goodbye, Steve."

"Goodbye, sir." He walked me to the door. We shook hands, and I walked back down the block to my car. It was now nearly six in the evening. I was exhausted but didn't want to spend another night in a cheap motel so I began the long drive home, arriving around midnight.

36.

RECKONING

FORTUNATELY, PAULA HAD cleared my calendar for the entire week, so I felt no obligation to go to the office that Thursday morning. Instead, I drove to Angel's Diner for a late breakfast washed down with lots of coffee. Over the previous three days I had driven nearly fifteen hundred miles and carried out the most emotionally exhausting interviews of my legal career. That morning, as I sat in the booth at Angel's, politely nodding to others who came and went, I reviewed the events of those days and the facts that had come to light. Sipping cup after cup, I mulled, again, the vast measure of pain that had been dredged to the surface—the unrelenting sorrow of parents who have lost children, the necrotizing effects that guilt and long-buried truth have on the soul. After breakfast, I returned to my apartment, showered and shaved, then phoned Mrs. Sanders. I did not want to talk over the phone, but merely wanted to see if she was free early that afternoon. She was, and insisted I come for lunch.

Over lunch I told her, in detail, everything I had learned on my trip, beginning with my visit with Chaplain Adamson and ending with the confessions of Steve Reynolds. She sat quietly, never interrupting my narrative. When at last I concluded, she sat in silence for what seemed like years, then drew a long breath and spoke.

"Well, Clint, nothing you learned comes as a shock to me. For a long time I'd been fairly certain James Boatwright had something to do with Sam's death. You've convinced me that he never intended to kill Sam, that it was a bad stunt gone terribly wrong. Strange as it sounds, I feel sorry for James and for his parents—especially his parents. I know how their loss feels. I guess I'm angrier at Steve Reynolds. Not really angry, but terribly disappointed. He could have come forward with the truth years ago. It hurts to know he knew and did nothing with what he knew. I know he was still just a boy in a lot of ways, but he's an adult now, and unless you had confronted him, I guess he would have carried this to his grave. So, what happens now?'

"Well, I'm going to call Commander Lightner and tell him what I found out, but I don't think the Navy will take any action at all. The only one who really could be prosecuted is James. Steve pulled a few juvenile pranks, but I believe he's telling the truth that he knew nothing about James' tinkering with the floor machine until after Sam had been killed. Like I said, I fully expect Steve will call you. If he doesn't, I'm going to be surprised and really disappointed in him. Honestly, the clock has run out on any civil action you might have been able to bring against him for conspiring and withholding facts. I don't know that justice can be served in all of this. I guess for me, personally, I feel like those guys got away with causing Sam's death."

"I'm not so sure about that, Clint. From what Steve told you, I think James was a tortured soul for what he did to Sam. It sounds to me like he went to Vietnam looking for death."

"I think you're right about that."

"And I think Steve has paid a price. If he's the man you seem to think he is, it seems like this had been gnawing at him for nearly fifteen years. That's a long sentence for making a stupid, juvenile mistake."

"I agree. He seemed genuinely remorseful. I guess we'll have a better idea of his sincerity when, and if, he calls you."

"I don't have a need to exact judgement on anybody in this, Clint. I came to you not because I needed vengeance, but because I needed answers, and you've gotten me those answers. I'm deeply grateful."

"Well, once I read through the letters, I needed answers, too. I don't know if I'm as much at peace with all this as you seem to be. James robbed me of a good bit of my youth and innocence. I really resent that. I don't know how I feel personally toward Steve. I don't know that it would have helped me as a kid to know the real circumstances of Sam's death. I guess I resent the fact that Steve could have come forward years ago and didn't. Not that it probably would have helped."

"Clint, if he calls, and if he's honest with me and seems sincere, I'm going to grant him absolution. I'm going to forgive him. I've already forgiven James. I just wish that he'd sent me a letter when he sent one to Steve, but that's water under the bridge. I have answers, now, and I can rest. And I believe that Sam can rest now that those of us who loved him know how and why he died."

"Yes ma'am. I suppose you're right. And I do feel sympathy for James' parents, and I don't see any reason that they need to know about any of this."

"Heavens no! It would just be hateful of me to call them up and tell them what their son had done to mine. That would only bring them more sorrow and wouldn't bring back either of our boys. No, they don't need to know all this, and I don't have a need to tell them."

"I think you might enjoy talking with Chaplain Adamson, though. He really thought highly of Sam. I just think it would mean a lot to you to talk with him."

"Yes. I'd like that."

"I'll leave you his number at the church. I promised him I'd call him with what I learned, so I'll tell him he can expect to hear from you, too."

"Thank you."

I left Mrs. Sanders shortly afterward and drove past my parents' home. They were both at work, so I'd find a time to share with them over the coming weekend the facts I'd uncovered surrounding Sam's death. I made my way down the long hill toward the river front and past the city dock. Glancing toward the river I recalled the times Sam and I had spent on that waterfront—crabbing, paddling the canoe in search of the Indian mound, visiting with the Hemingways aboard their yacht. Those memories brought a wave of joyful sadness—a contradiction of emotions. I debated within myself whether to go into the office, but quickly convinced my inner disciplinarian that I had earned a bit more time off. I spent the remains of the day reading Michener's *Chesapeake* on the tiny balcony off my bedroom.

Friday morning, I was at the office before Paula arrived. She gave me a raised eyebrow and a "surprised to see you so early'" in lieu of a cheery "good morning." I liked that in her. She was professional, highly competent, but decidedly unimpressed by me. We made a good team.

I wanted an early start because I knew I would spend the better part of the morning on the phone. I first called Chaplain Adamson at home. He answered on the first ring and was anxious to hear what I had learned. I provided him a summary of the facts I had uncovered on my trip, none of which seemed to surprise him. He then asked about Mrs. Sanders—how she had received the information. I told him she seemed unburdened and at peace, that she had already forgiven James and saw no value in torturing his parents with the knowledge that their son had caused the death of hers. I explained that she was hoping for a call from Steve Reynolds and, assuming he called and was remorseful, she intended to forgive him. Finally, I told the Chaplain that he should expect a call from her as she wanted to talk with him about the person he saw in Sam. He responded that he was anxious to talk with her and would welcome her call.

Before we ended our conversation, he pressed me for how I was doing personally with all this. I explained my thoughts and feelings as well as I was able. I described the conflicting emotions I had and continued to experience toward both James and Steve—anger bordering on rage, grief, and sympathy toward them at what they, too, had lost. As expected, he assured me that confusing mix of thoughts and feelings was not only normal but predictable, given what I had experienced as a boy and uncovered as an adult. He then asked if he could check in with me in a few weeks, and I readily agreed. He was easy to talk with, and I felt I could use a more objective listener. Sam found his counsel helpful. I was confident I would as well.

My next call was to Commander Lightner at the JAG office on base. He listened to my report, asking questions along the way. When I finished, he paused for a few moments before stating what I had already concluded: there was no remedy in law—military or otherwise—for Mrs. Sanders' loss. He stated that, had Steve Reynolds come forward immediately, things might well have been different. Now, with James long-dead and Steve long-discharged, there was nothing of substance to pursue against either of them. His conclusion, as he stated it, was to "leave the ghosts to haunt each other." I wasn't certain which ghosts were in his mind, but my hope was that the ghosts of Sam and James had long ago reconciled. I thanked him for his help in pointing me toward the truth, and we ended our conversation.

Although it was only mid-morning, I was already exhausted. I shuffled paperwork around on my desk for a short while, then tried to dictate a motion on a case that was soon to go to trial, but my thoughts kept chasing other things. Around 11:30, Paula buzzed me to say a Chris Fergusson was here to see me. I was not expecting anyone and didn't know a Chris Fergusson. Nonetheless, I asked Paula to show him in.

"Him" was not a him. "Him" was Crazy Christine Hawkins from my childhood and youth—my ten-year-old nemesis and my first real date. I had not seen her since we graduated high school. She swept into my office looking like a *Mademoiselle* fashion plate—a fitted skirt, double-breasted tuxedo jacket and ridiculously high heels. I was dumbstruck and suddenly that awkward thirteen-year-old trying to muster the courage to ask her to the Spring Dance.

"Christine! Holy shit!"

"And hello to you, too, Clint." We both laughed and the awkwardness fell away. I rounded the desk and we hugged.

"I haven't seen you since the night we graduated. Where are you now? What are you doing?"

"Funny you should ask."

"Here, have a seat." We took the chairs in front of my desk.

"Would it surprise you to know I joined the same sordid profession as you?"

"No, not really. You were always pretty litigious."

"Yes, I suppose you're right. No, I'm the newly appointed Assistant State's Attorney for the seventh district. I had heard you had moved back to Palatka, and thought I'd drop in to say 'Hi'."

"Congratulations! I guess we'll be sitting at opposing tables in the future. Do you live here in Palatka?"

"Oh, hell no! I live in St. Augustine. I've been in private practice over there since I finished law school and was just appointed last month to the dark side."

"So, 'Chris Fergusson'?"

"Yeah. The 'Chris' I've been using since law school. The 'Fergusson' I picked up through a very bad experiment with marriage. I really should have dropped it and gone back to 'Hawkins' but my practice was already established. So, what about you? Last I heard, you were with Williams and Blackwell in Jacksonville."

"Yeah. You have your sad story, that's mine."

"Honestly, I'm not surprised. That firm has a reputation for using fresh associates as cannon fodder. It doesn't seem like a good fit for you."

"By which you mean?"

"By which I mean you're a decent guy. I know you set the curve at UF and were highly recruited, but you also have a soul. Williams and Blackwell kind of specializes in soulless attorneys."

"So I discovered. So, are you free for lunch? We have a lot of catching up to do."

"Sure. As long as it's not Angel's."

"I love Angel's," I replied, defensively.

"So do I, but on Saturday afternoon on the way back from the beach."

"Gotcha. Hey, there's a nice place about two blocks up next to City Drug. Kind of a café-bistro place. How's that sound?"

"Sounds good. Plus, we can walk."

"That we can."

We exited my office, and as we passed Paula's desk I got my second raised eyebrow of the day. I introduced Chris as an old friend and a newly minted State's Attorney. Over lunch, she and I filled in most of the blanks from the intervening decade. I then shared with her my quest to find the truth behind Sam's death. When I finished that saga, she was visibly troubled.

"God, Clint, that's just awful. I never had a hint Sam was gay. For him to have to go through all that and to die that way. God, it's just unthinkable. Poor Mrs. Sanders. And you too. I mean, he was like a brother to you. I'm just so sorry."

"Thanks. Honestly, I'm still trying to make sense of all this. The day Mrs. Sanders came to see me and shared her belief that Sam's death wasn't an accident, well, it just flung me out of orbit. I thought I had boxed up all that pain, and her visit just turned that box upside down and dumped it right into my lap. It's like I've been obsessed with getting to the truth ever since. To think that one stupid stunt took him away from us forever! It's still more than I can process."

"You know, you might need to find someone to help you work through some of this."

"I know. Actually, I think the Chaplain's willing to help me with that. He's only about forty-five minutes away, and it would be good to work through this with someone who knew Sam. The fact that he's not here in little ole Palatka, where everybody knows your business, is a plus, too."

"You got that right. Hey, I hate to run, but I need to get down to Bunnell for a little motion hearing at three, so I'd better get going. Can we do this again?"

"Absolutely."

"Soon, OK?"

"I agree."

"Perfect. Oh, here's my card."

"And here's mine."

She snatched the check when it came. I protested to be polite but knew she would probably expense the lunch anyway.

"I parked over there behind the bank. It was great seeing you, Clint."

"You, too, Chris. I'm going to have to work on that Chris thing, you know?"

"I understand. I won't hold it against you if you slip up once in a while. At least you dropped the 'crazy.'"

I laughed. "You knew about that?"

"Oh, yes. Frankly, I rather liked it."

"I'm not the least surprised." We both shared a laugh.

"OK, then. And thanks for lunch. I'll call you soon."

"Please." We hugged again and left in opposite directions.

On Sunday afternoon, Mrs. Sanders phoned and asked me to come by if it was convenient. I had nothing going on, so I drove there immediately. When I arrived, she ushered me into the living room.

"Clint, Steve Reynolds called and we had a good conversation. Honestly, I felt sorry for the boy. He couldn't stop crying the whole time we talked. He was just beside himself with guilt. He apologized over and over to the point where I had to say, 'Steve, you don't need to apologize any more. I believe you're sincerely sorry, and I forgive you.' Then the flood gates really opened up. I know he's genuinely sorry for keeping this from me all these years, and I've fully forgiven him."

"I'm really glad he called. I was pretty certain he would, but you never know. Some folks are pretty good actors, but I thought he was being honest with me. Have you talked with Chaplain Adamson yet?"

"Yes, briefly. I'm actually going to drive up and see him. He offered, and I think I'd rather talk with him face-to-face."

"That sounds like a good idea. Actually, he and I are going to get together a few times, too. I need to work through some of my feelings about all of this, and he's willing to help me with that."

"Oh, Clint, that's so good. I'm so glad you're doing that. Frankly, I've felt a bit guilty for dumping all this on you like I did."

"Please don't ever feel that way. This has been hard, opening these old wounds, but there was infection there I needed to deal with."

"I completely understand. Listen, I've started going through Sam's stuff in his room. It's been a shrine long enough. I'm going to turn it into a sewing room. Anyway, there are a few things I thought you might like to have. Here, see if you want any of this." She handed me a cardboard box. Inside, were the sections of the model of the Mercury 7 launch vehicle Sam had built nearly twenty years ago and a cigar box containing carefully numbered shards of Indian pottery. My eyes began to tear.

"Yes, ma'am. I'd love to have this stuff. Thank you so much."

"You're more than welcome. And Clint."

"Yes ma'am."

"Don't forget him."

"Never, Mrs. Sanders." I rose to leave, and she walked me to the door. We hugged and I descended the steps I had so nervously ascended that chilly day in December so many years before. I carefully placed the box of Sam's things on the back seat of my car, waved, and opened the door to get in.

"Clint."

"Yes ma'am?"

"Don't be a stranger, OK?"

"No ma'am. I won't. I promise."

I waved, climbed into the driver's seat and pulled away from the Sanders' home. From there, I turned and drove up the hill, past the National Guard Armory, to and through the gates of the Ravine Gardens. The narrow road Sam and I so often biked is one-way, counter-clockwise, around the perimeter of the Ravines. I entered it and drove slowly. I chuckled as, here and there, I spied an errant golf ball lying in the sand beside the road. Finally, I came to the place near the end of the drive where Sam and I often rested before that last brutal climb. I pulled to the edge of the road, leaving barely enough room for another vehicle to pass, and walked down the steep embankment to the stream. Unchanged, it ran clear and cold—the grass verdant, the birds chittering overhead. I knelt and dipped my finger into the water, quickly withdrawing it. A few droplets fell from the tip of my finger leaving tiny concentric ringlets moving on the surface of the stream. These were quickly carried away by the flow. "I will never forget you, Sam. I promise. I will always remember."

EPILOGUE

APRIL 6, 1985

THE BANQUET ROOM at the Reitz Union on the campus of the University of Florida was aglow with candlelight, friends, academics, and community leaders. This evening had been long in the planning and Clint was nervous beyond anything he might have imagined. The nearly one hundred guests were dressed in formal attire, seated at beautifully decorated tables and conversing amiably. A string quartet provided quiet dinner music. The food had been impeccably prepared and expertly served. Everything had gone flawlessly, yet he was still fretful. Chris was seated beside him at the head table wearing a stunning black evening dress, her prominent baby bump making her all the more beautiful in his eyes. With them to either side were Sam's mother, Mrs. Sanders, Will, and their parents, Mr. and Mrs. Cooper, Jake Wilson, David Robinson, and the Dean of the College of Education.

Chris whispered to him, "Clint, it's time."

"I know. I don't know why I'm so nervous. This is a celebration."

"It is, but I know you want everything to go perfectly, and it has. Now relax, thank the guests and donors, let the dean give his spiel and let's wrap this up."

"Yes, sir, General Patton, sir. OK. Here goes."

He stood, tapped his water glass a few times with a teaspoon and stepped to the podium. "Good evening, friends, honored guests, and Dean Mixon. As most of you know, I'm Clint Hawkins-Cooper, and I'd like to take a moment to introduce those on the dais with me. First, to my right is my beautiful wife and co-chair of this event and of the scholarship committee, Assistant State's Attorney Chris Hawkins-Cooper, with little Samuel Hawkins-Cooper along for the ride." He paused for the generous laughter. "Beside her is Mrs. Edith Sanders, mother of Sam Sanders and a member of the scholarship committee, and to her right is Dr. Jacob Wilson, Professor of African American Studies at the University of North Florida and co-chair with Chris of the scholarship committee. To my left is my brother and the marketing brains behind this endeavor, Dr. Will Cooper. To his left are our parents, Mr. and Mrs. Alan Cooper, and to their left is Mr. David Robinson, Director of Community Action of North Florida and a member of the scholarship committee. Last, but far from least, on the end is Dr. Ronald Mixon, Dean of the College of Education here at the University of Florida.

"Friends, it is not my intention to cast a pall over this delightful evening, but this date was not chosen randomly. Twenty years ago this evening, my dear friend Sam Sanders, whose legacy we secure tonight, died at the young age of nineteen. But tonight is not intended to be an occasion to mourn his death, but rather, to honor his short life. Tonight is a celebration, a celebration of the culmination of nearly five years of work—I call it work, some of you would call it squeezing, cajoling, and thumb twisting." He paused again, joining the crowd in their laughter.

"I see you agree. Tonight, it is my great pleasure to announce to you that the Samuel A. Sanders Memorial Scholarship at the College of Education is fully funded in perpetuity." There was sincere applause across the room. "And that is, in part, due to the help of a familiar superhero. You might find it interesting to learn that, in addition to the heroes gathered here this evening, this endeavor was given an initial assist by none other than Spider-Man himself. You see, Sam had a remarkable collection of comic books, including every Spider-Man comic Marvel released between 1962 and the summer of 1965, and all in pristine condition. Following our very first conversation about this scholarship fund, Mrs. Sanders donated those comics, the sale of which began the fundraising effort that culminates tonight. So, my heroes, you are in good company, since, through your generous gifts, we have created an endowment that will fund this scholarship in Sam's name for years to come." More applause.

"Through your selfless generosity, beginning next fall and every year thereafter, an African American student of exceptional talent but limited financial means will receive a full four-year scholarship to study toward a career in education here at the University of Florida." Another pause for applause. "Sam Sanders was my friend and mentor, and, with the exception of my parents, perhaps the best teacher I had during my early years. One of the most important lessons Sam taught me was the reality of the great barrier to educational opportunity faced by Black students. Sadly, Sam never had the opportunity to pursue what he thought he might be good at—teaching our youth. Now, through what you have done, his memory will be sustained, and his vision realized—not through his one life, but through dozens, even hundreds of lives. So, let me again say thank you, and to Sam, who may well be looking down on this room tonight, I say 'We remember you, my friend.'"

The audience stood and applauded enthusiastically. As the applause subsided and the guests returned to their seats, Clint addressed the gathering again. "And now, it is my distinct honor to introduce Dr. Ronald Mixon, Dean of the College of Education, and one who has provided tremendous support to this endeavor, to share a few words with us."

Dr. Mixon moved to the podium, expressed his appreciation to Clint and Chris and spoke to the gathering regarding both the need for, and good use to which the university would put the Samuel A. Adams Memorial Scholarship. Following his brief remarks Clint again thanked all in attendance and brought the evening to a close.

When all the glad-handing had concluded and the room was empty, Clint and Chris walked hand-in-hand to their car. As they walked, she leaned her head on his shoulder and spoke quietly to him alone. "Whatever he wants to do with his life, I hope this little guy here lives up to his namesake."

"Me too. Me too."

The End

ACKNOWLEDGEMENTS

* First, and always, I thank my wife, Marsha, for honoring the sanctity of my writing cave, for tolerating my obsessed determination to write this book, and for reading the first draft.

* Thanks to my brilliant daughter, G. Beth Sherouse, PhD, for discounted (i.e., gratis) editing and for dragging me along in her quest for justice.

* I'm grateful to my friend Marlon Lynn for encouragement and for flexibility with respect to other obligations.

* Thanks, also, to those others who read the rough draft of this novel and contributed constructive ideas. You know who you are.

* Thanks to Jack Copley and the staff of Coliseum of Comics in Lakeland, Florida, for their expert knowledge of all things comic book.

* I offer humble apologies to the real town of Palatka, Florida, if anything in this novel appears to disparage a really wonderful place to have grown up.

CONNECT WITH THE author at *Neil@jnsherouse.com*

* For discussion materials for use by book clubs or classrooms

* To schedule a virtual Author Meet-Up for book clubs or classrooms

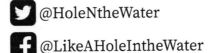 @HoleNtheWater

@LikeAHoleIntheWater

Made in the USA
Middletown, DE
15 July 2021